BLINDSIGHT
How far will people go to obtain donors for eye operations?
Murder is beyond comprehension. But seeing is believing . . .

"GRABS THE READER . . . MAINTAINS SUSPENSE
WITH SURPRISING STORY TWISTS."
—*Pittsburgh Press*

"RIVETING."   —*Nashville Banner*

VITAL SIGNS
Dr. Cook explores the frightening possibilities of experi-
mental fertilization—the passion to create life, and the
power to destroy it . . .

"CONSTANT SUSPENSE . . . BELIEVABLE AND CHILL-
ING."   —*Houston Chronicle*

"VINTAGE COOK . . . NONSTOP ACTION."
—*Kirkus Reviews*

HARMFUL INTENT
The explosive story of a doctor accused of malpractice—a
fugitive on the run who pierces the heart of a shocking
medical conspiracy . . .

"A REAL GRABBER!"   —*Los Angeles Times*

"TRULY EXCITING."   —*Associated Press*

continued . . .

MUTATION

On the forefront of genetic research, a brilliant doctor tries to create the son of his dreams—and invents a living nightmare . . .

"HOLDS YOU PAGE AFTER PAGE."
—Larry King, *USA Today*

"*REALLY* FRIGHTENING." —*Booklist*

MORTAL FEAR

A major scientific breakthrough becomes the ultimate experiment in terror when middle-aged patients begin to die— of old age . . .

"A CHILLING ODYSSEY INTO THE ORIGINS OF LIFE—AND DEATH." —*New York Times*

"COOK'S BEST BOOK SINCE *COMA*." —*People*

OUTBREAK

Murder and mystery reach epidemic proportions when a devastating plague sweeps the country . . .

"HIS MOST HARROWING MEDICAL HORROR STORY." —*New York Times*

"THE ULTIMATE NIGHTMARE . . . SPINE-TINGLING INTRIGUE AND FEVER-PITCHED ACTION."
—Associated Press

VECTOR

ROBIN COOK

BERKLEY BOOKS, NEW YORK

VECTOR

A Berkley Book / published by arrangement with
the author

PRINTING HISTORY
G. P. Putnam's Sons edition / March 1999
Berkley edition / January 2000

The Penguin Putnam Inc. World Wide Web site address is
http://www.penguinputnam.com

ISBN: 0-425-17299-6

BERKLEY®
Berkley Books are published by The Berkley Publishing Group,
a division of Penguin Putnam Inc.,
375 Hudson Street, New York, New York 10014.
BERKLEY and the "B" logo
are trademarks belonging to Penguin Putnam Inc.

PRINTED IN THE UNITED STATES OF AMERICA

10 9 8 7 6 5 4 3 2 1

continued...

ACCEPTABLE RISK

His most shocking thriller—a timely and terrifying glimpse into the dangers of antidepressant drugs . . .

"STERN AND BRACING . . . [A] SUSPENSEFUL THRILLER."
—*San Francisco Chronicle*

FATAL CURE

One of the most controversial books Robin Cook has ever written—a terrifying look at the darker implications of managed health care in America . . .

"A RIVETING PLOT, FILLED WITH ACTION."
—*San Diego Union-Tribune*

"A HAIR-RAISING, CAUTIONARY TALE ABOUT THE POSSIBLE PITFALLS OF IMPENDING HEALTH-CARE REFORM IN AMERICA."
—*Detroit News*

TERMINAL

Brain cancer patients are miraculously "cured"—when the rising cost of research sparks a medical conspiracy that lowers the price on human life . . .

"A SPELLBINDER . . . UNBEARABLE TENSION."
—*Houston Chronicle*

"STRAIGHT OUT OF TODAY'S HEADLINES."
—*UPI*

Also by Robin Cook

To Jean
with love, appreciation, and thanks

ACKNOWLEDGMENTS

Dr. Ken Alibek, Program Manager, Battelle Memorial Institute, Arlington, Virginia. Formerly Dr. Kanatjan Alibekov, First Deputy Chief of the Soviet Union's Biological Offensive Program.

Colonel Edward M. Eitzen, Jr., M.D., MC, U.S. Army, Chief Operational Medicine Division, U.S. Army Medical Research Institute of Infectious Disease (USAMRIID), Fort Detrick, Maryland.

Jerome M. Hauer, Director of the Mayor's Office of Emergency Management, New York City.

Jacki Lee, M.D., Deputy Chief Medical Examiner, Washington, D.C.

Raissa Rubenshteyn, M.D., Chief, Gynecological Medical Staff, Voronez City Hospital #8 in the former Soviet Union.

Charles Wetli, M.D., Chief Medical Examiner, Suffolk County, New York.

ne roy drugomu yamu, sam v neyo popadesh
(do not dig a hole for another,
you just might fall in it yourself)
RUSSIAN PROVERB

VECTOR: (medical) a carrier that transmits an
infectious agent from one host to another.

VECTOR

PROLOGUE

Jason Papparis had been in the rug business for almost thirty years. He started in the Plaka district of Athens in the late sixties, selling mostly goatskins, sheepskins, and fur rugs to American tourists. He did well and enjoyed himself, especially with the young, college-age female tourists to whom he invariably and graciously availed himself to show the night life of his beloved city.

Then fate intervened. On a sultry summer night, Helen Herman of Queens, New York, wandered into his shop and absently caressed some of Jason's higher-quality rugs. A romantic at heart, Helen found herself swept off her feet by an irresistible combination of Jason's soulful eyes and fervent attentions and the romantic mystique of Greece.

Jason's ardor had been no less. After Helen's departure for the States, Jason found himself inconsolably lonely. An impassioned correspondence began, followed by a visit. Jason's trip to New York only fanned the fires of desire. Ultimately he emigrated, married Helen, and took his business to Manhattan.

Jason's business thrived. The extensive contacts he had established over the years with rug producers in both Greece and Turkey stood him in good stead, and provided Jason with a monopoly of sorts. Instead of opening a retail shop in New York, Jason had wisely opted for a wholesale business. It was a lean operation. He had no employees. All he had was an office in Manhattan and a warehouse in Queens. He outsourced all his shipping and inventory control and occasionally he hired temps for clerical work.

The business operated by telephone and fax. Consequently Jason's office door was always locked.

On this particular Friday his mail was dropped through the mail slot as it always was, but due to a thick catalogue it landed with a louder than usual plop on the wooden floor. At his desk, Jason's attention was plucked from his bookkeeping. He balanced his omnipresent cigarette on the edge of his overflowing ashtray, then got up to retrieve the mail. He was counting on receiving a significant number of checks to alleviate his burgeoning accounts-receivable balance. Regaining his seat, he sorted through the mail, placing each piece in its appropriate pile and the junk mail directly into the wastebasket. Reaching the next-to-last envelope, he hesitated. It was thick and square instead of rectangular. Jason detected a small, irregular bulge in the center. Glancing at the postage, he noticed that it was a first-class letter, not bulk mail. In the lower left-hand corner the envelope was stamped with an admonition: *Hand Stamp.* The explanation was: *Fragile Contents!*

Jason turned the envelope over. It was made of rather thick, dense, high-quality paper. It was not the usual paper for an advertisement, yet the return address was for *ACME Cleaning Service: Leave Your Dust to Us.* The business was located on lower Broadway.

Flipping the envelope over once again, Jason noticed that it was addressed to him personally, not to the Corinthian Rug Company. Below the address were the words *personal and confidential.*

With his thumb and index finger, Jason tried to determine the source of the bulge. He had no idea. His curiosity getting the better of him, he picked up his letter opener and sliced through the envelope's top flap. Peeking inside he could see a folded card made with heavy paper of quality equal to that of the envelope.

"What the hell?" Jason said aloud. This was certainly not the usual advertisement. He pulled out the card, marveling that some advertising executive had been able to talk a cleaning service into sending out such an expensive gimmick. The card was sealed with a tab. In the center of the front of the card was the single word *Surprise!*

Jason worked the tab loose from its bed and as soon as he did the card leaped in his hands and snapped open. At the same time a coiled spring mechanism propelled a puff of dust along with a handful of tiny glittering stars into the air.

Jason was initially startled by the sudden, unexpected movement, and he sneezed several times from the dust. But then a smile quickly appeared. Inside the card was the caption *Call Us To Clean Up The Mess!*

Jason shook his head in amazement. He had to give credit to whoever was responsible for this advertisement for ACME Cleaners. It was certainly unique and clever—and effective. Jason found himself wishing that he could enlist ACME Cleaners, but he didn't need a cleaning service since his landlord provided one.

Jason tossed the card and envelope into his wastebasket, then leaned over to brush off the tiny glittering stars from the front of his shirt. As he did so he felt another tickle in his nose which caused him to sneeze several more times, hard enough to bring tears to his eyes.

As usual for a Friday, Jason finished work early. Enjoying the fall weather, he walked to Grand Central Station to board the five-fifteen commuter train. Forty-five minutes later, just as he was nearing his station, he felt the first twinges of discomfort in his chest. His first reflex was to swallow, but that had no effect. He then cleared his throat, which was equally ineffective. He then patted his chest and took several deep breaths.

The woman sitting next to Jason lowered the edge of her newspaper. "Are you okay?" she asked.

"Oh, yeah, no problem," Jason responded, feeling embarrassed. He wondered if he'd smoked more than usual that day.

That night, Jason tried to ignore the odd tickle in his chest, but it didn't subside. Helen became aware that something was wrong when he pushed his dinner around his plate instead of eating. They were at their usual Friday haunt, a local Greek restaurant. The couple had started going to the place at least once a week after their only daughter left home for college.

"My chest feels funny," Jason finally admitted when Helen asked.

"I hope you're not coming down with the flu again."

Although Jason was basically healthy, his heavy smoking made him susceptible to respiratory infections, particularly influenza. He'd also had a serious bout with pneumonia three years earlier.

"It can't be the flu," Jason said. "It's not flu season yet. Is it?"

"You're asking me?" Helen returned. "I don't know, but wasn't this about the time you got it last year?"

"That was November," Jason said.

When they got home, Helen insisted on taking Jason's temperature. It was ninety-nine point four, barely above normal. They discussed calling Dr. Goldstein, their primary care physician, but decided against it. They were reluctant to bother the doctor on a weekend.

"Why does something like this always happen on Friday night?" Helen complained.

Jason slept poorly. In the middle of the night he had a hot flash resulting in so much perspiration, he felt obliged to take a shower. While toweling off he had a chill.

"This settles it," Helen said after putting several blankets on her shivering husband. "We're calling the doctor first thing in the morning."

"What's he going to do?" Jason grumbled. "I got the flu. He's going to tell me to stay home, take aspirin, drink a lot of fluids, and rest."

"Maybe he'll give you some antibiotics," Helen said.

"There's some antibiotics left over from last year," Jason said. "They're in the medicine cabinet. Get them! I don't need a doctor."

Saturday was not a good day. By late afternoon Jason admitted that he was definitely worse despite the aspirin, fluids, and antibiotic. The discomfort in his chest had worsened to pain. His temperature had risen to one hundred and three, and he'd developed a cough. But what he complained about most was a splitting headache, along with generalized aching muscles.

Attempts to reach Dr. Goldstein were unsuccessful. The doctor had gone to Connecticut for the weekend. His answering service advised Helen to take her husband to the local emergency room.

After a long wait, Jason was finally seen by the emergency-room physician, who was impressed with his condition, especially after a chest X ray. To Helen's relief, the doctor advised Jason's immediate admission to the hospital and referred the case to Dr. Heitman, who was covering Dr. Goldstein's inpatients. The diagnosis was influenza with secondary pneumonia, and the emergency-room physician started Jason on intravenous antibiotics.

Jason had never felt worse in his life as he was taken to his hospital room just before midnight. He complained bitterly about his chest pain, which was excruciating when he coughed, and about his headache. When Dr. Heitman came by to see him, Jason pleaded for relief and was given Percodan.

It took almost a half hour for the pain medication to have an effect. By that time Dr. Heitman had departed. Jason lay on his bed, exhausted but unable to sleep. He sensed a mortal battle was raging inside his body. Allowing his head to loll to the side, he looked at Helen in the half light and gripped her hand. She was maintaining a silent vigil. A tear traced a path down the side of Jason's face. In his mind's eye Helen was still that young woman who'd wandered into his shop in the Plaka all those years ago.

Helen's image began to fade as welcome numbness suffused Jason's body. At twelve-thirty-five A.M. Jason Papparis fell asleep for the last time. Mercifully, he was unaware when he was later rushed to the intensive care unit by Dr. Kevin Fowler, who waged an unsuccessful battle for his life.

ONE

T he hum of the commuter plane's engines was ragged. One moment they were screaming as the plane headed inexorably earthward, the next they were eerily silent, as if they had been inadvertently switched off by the pilot.

Jack Stapleton watched in terror, knowing that his family was aboard and there was nothing he could do. The plane was going to crash! Helplessly he shouted NO! NO! NO!

Jack's shouting mercifully yanked him from the clutches of his recurrent nightmare, and he sat bolt upright in bed. He was breathing heavily as if he'd been playing full-court basketball, and perspiration dripped from the end of his nose. He was disoriented until his eyes swept about the interior of his bedroom. The intermittent sound wasn't coming from a commuter plane. It was his telephone. Its raucous jingle was relentlessly shattering the night.

Jack's eyes shot to the face of his radio alarm clock. The digital numbers glowed in the dark room. It was four-thirty in the morning! No one called Jack at four-thirty. As he reached for the phone, he remembered all too well the night eight years ago when he'd been awakened by a phone call informing him that his wife and two children had perished.

Snatching the receiver from its cradle Jack answered the phone with a rasping and panicky voice.

"Uh oh, I think I woke you up," a woman's voice said. There was a significant amount of static on the line.

"I don't know why you'd think that," Jack said, now conscious enough to be sarcastic. "Who is this?"

"It's Laurie. I'm sorry I've awakened you. It couldn't be helped." She giggled.

Jack closed his eyes, then looked back at the clock just to make sure he had not been mistaken. It indeed was four-thirty in the morning!

"Listen," Laurie continued. "I've got to make this fast. I want to have dinner with you tonight."

"This has got to be a joke," Jack said.

"No joke," Laurie said. "It's important. I have to talk with you, and I'd like to do it over dinner. It's my treat. Say *yes*!"

"I guess," Jack said, reluctant to commit.

"I'm going to take that as a *yes*," Laurie said. "I'll tell you where when I see you at the office later on this morning. Okay?"

"I suppose," Jack said. He wasn't as awake as he'd thought. His mind wasn't working up to speed.

"Perfect," Laurie said. "See you then."

Jack blinked when he realized Laurie had disconnected. He hung up the phone and stared at it in the darkness. He'd known Laurie Montgomery for more than four years as a fellow medical examiner in the Office of the Chief Medical Examiner for the City of New York. He'd also known her as a friend—in fact, more than a friend—and in all that time she'd never called him so early in the morning. And for good reason. He knew she was not a morning person. Laurie liked to read novels far into the night, which made getting up in the morning a daily ordeal for her.

Jack dropped back onto his pillow with the intent of sleeping for another hour and a half. In contrast to Laurie, he was a morning person, but four-thirty was a bit too early, even for him.

Unfortunately it was soon apparent to Jack that more sleep was not in the offing. Between the phone call and the nightmare, he couldn't get back to sleep. After half an hour of restless tossing and turning, he threw back the covers and padded into the bathroom in his sheepskin slippers.

With the light on, Jack regarded himself in the mirror while running a hand over his stubbled face. Absently he noted the chipped left incisor and the scar high on his forehead, both mementos of some extra-office investigating he'd done in relation to a series of infectious-disease cases. The unexpected fallout was that Jack had become the de facto guru of infectious diseases in the medical examiner's office.

Jack smiled at his image. Lately it had occurred to him that if he had been able to look into a crystal ball eight years previously to see himself now, he would never have recognized himself. Back then, he'd been a relatively portly, midwestern, suburban ophthalmologist, conservative in dress. Now he was a lean and mean medical examiner in the City of New York with closely cropped, gray-streaked hair, a chipped tooth, and a scarred face. As far as clothes were concerned, he now favored bomber jackets, faded jeans, and chambray shirts.

Avoiding thoughts of his family, Jack mulled over Laurie's surprising behavior. It was so out of character. She was always considerate and concerned about proper etiquette. She would never phone at such an hour without good reason. Jack wondered what that reason was.

Jack shaved and climbed into the shower while he tried to imagine why Laurie would have called in the middle of the night to arrange a dinner date. They had dinner together often, but it was usually decided on the spur of the moment. Why would Laurie need to line a date up at such an hour?

While Jack toweled himself dry, he decided to call Laurie back. It was ridiculous for him to guess what was going on in her mind. Since she had awakened him as she had, it was only reasonable that she explain herself. But when Jack made the call he got her answering machine. Thinking she might be in the shower, he left a message asking her to call him right back.

By the time Jack had eaten breakfast it was after six. Since Laurie still hadn't called, Jack tried her again. To his chagrin, the answering machine picked up for the second time. He hung up in the middle of her outgoing message.

Since it was now light outside, Jack entertained the idea of going to work early. That was when it occurred to him that perhaps Laurie had telephoned from the office. He was sure she wasn't on call, but there was the possibility that a case had come in that particularly interested her.

Jack called the medical examiner's office. Marjorie Zankowski, the night communications operator, answered. She told Jack that she was ninety percent sure that Dr. Laurie Montgomery was not there. She said that the only medical examiner there was the tour doctor.

With a sense of frustration bordering on anger, Jack gave up. He vowed not to spend any more mental energy trying to figure out what was on Laurie's mind. Instead he went into his living room and curled up on the couch with one of his many unread forensic journals.

At six-forty-five, Jack got up, tossed aside the reading, and hefted his Cannondale mountain bike from where it leaned against the living-room wall. With it balanced on his shoulder, he started down the four flights of his tenement. Early in the morning was the only time of the day that loud quarreling wasn't heard in apartment 2B. On the ground floor, Jack had to navigate around some trash that had been dropped down the stairwell during the night.

Emerging on West 106th Street, Jack took in a lungful of October air. For the first time that day he felt revived. Climbing onto his purple bike he headed for Central Park, passing the empty neighborhood basketball court on his left.

A few years ago, on the same day that he had been punched hard enough to chip his front tooth, Jack's first mountain bike had been stolen. Listening to warnings from his colleagues, particularly Laurie, about the dangers of bike riding in the city, Jack had resisted buying another. But after being mugged on the subway, Jack had gone ahead with the purchase.

Initially, Jack had been a relatively careful cyclist when riding his new bike. But over time that had changed. Now Jack was back to his old tricks. While commuting to and from the office, Jack indulged his self-destructive streak by taking a twice-daily, hair-raising walk on the wild side. Jack believed he had nothing more to lose. His reckless cycling, a habitual temptation of fate, was a way of saying that if his family had had to die, he should have been with them and maybe he'd join them sooner rather than later.

By the time Jack arrived at the medical examiner's office on the corner of First Avenue and Thirtieth Street, he'd had two protracted arguments with taxi drivers and a minor run-in with a city bus. Undaunted and not at all out of breath, Jack parked his bike on the ground floor next to the Hart Island coffins and made his way up to the ID room. Most people would have felt on edge after such a harrowing trip. But not Jack. The confrontations and physical exertion calmed him, preparing him for the day's invariable bureaucratic hurdles.

Jack flicked the edge of Vinnie Amendola's newspaper as he walked by the mortuary tech, who was sitting at his preferred location at the desk just inside the door. Jack also said hello, but Vinnie ignored him. As usual, Vinnie was committing to memory the previous day's sports stats.

Vinnie had been employed at the ME's office longer than Jack had. He was a good worker, although he'd come close to being fired a couple of years back for leaking information that had embarrassed the office and had put both Jack and Laurie in harm's way. The reason Vinnie was censured and put on probation rather than terminated was the extenuating circumstances of his behavior. An investigation had determined he'd been the victim of extortion by some unsavory underworld figures. Vinnie's father had had a loose association with the mob.

Jack said hello to Dr. George Fontworth, a corpulent medical examiner colleague who was Jack's senior in the office hierarchy by seven years. George was just starting his weekly stint as the person who reviewed the previous night's reported deaths, deciding which would be autopsied and by whom. That

was why he was at the office early. Normally, he was the last
to arrive.

"A fine welcome," Jack mumbled when George ignored him
as Vinnie had. Jack filled his mug with some of the coffee
that Vinnie had made on his arrival. Vinnie came in before
the other techs to assist the duty doctor if need arose. One of
his jobs was to brew the coffee in the communal pot.

With his coffee in hand Jack wandered over to George and
looked over his shoulder.

"Do you mind?" George said petulantly. He shielded the
papers in front of him. One of his pet peeves was people
reading over his shoulder.

Jack and George had never gotten along. Jack had little
tolerance for mediocrity and refused on principle to hide his
feelings. George might possess stellar credentials—he had
trained with one of the giants in the field of forensic pathology—but to Jack, his efforts on the job were merely perfunc-
tory. Jack had no respect for the man.

Jack smiled at George's reaction. He got perverse pleasure
out of goading him. "Anything particularly interesting?" Jack
asked. He walked around to the front of the desk. With his
index finger he began to shuffle through the folders so he
could read the presumed diagnoses.

"I have these in order!" George snapped. He pushed Jack's
hand away and restored the physical integrity of his stacks.
He was sorting them according to the cause and manner of
death.

"What do you have for me?" Jack asked. One of the things
that Jack loved about being a medical examiner was that he
never knew what each day would bring. Every day there was
something new. That had not been the case when he was an
ophthalmologist. Back then Jack knew what each day was going to be like three months in advance.

"I do have an infectious case," George said. "Although I
don't think it's particularly interesting. It's yours if you want
it."

"Why was it sent in?" Jack asked. "No diagnosis?"

"Only a presumed diagnosis," George said. "They listed it
as possible influenza with secondary pneumonia. But the pa-

tient died before any of the cultures came back. Complicating
the issue is that nothing was seen on gram stain. And on top
of that the man's doctor was away for the weekend."

Jack took the folder. The name was Jason Papparis. Jack
slipped out the information sheet filled out by Janice Jaeger,
the night-shift forensic investigator or physician's assistant,
called a PA for short. As Jack skimmed the sheet, he nodded
with admiration. Janice had proved herself a thorough re-
searcher. Ever since Jack had made the suggestion for her to
inquire about travel and contact with animals in infectious
cases, she never failed to do so.

"Mighty potent case of flu!" Jack commented. He noted that
the deceased had been in the hospital for less than twenty-four
hours. But he also noticed that the man had been a heavy
smoker and had a history of respiratory problems. That raised
the issue of whether the infectious agent was potent or the
patient unusually susceptible.

"Do you want it or not?" George asked. "We've got a lot
of cases this morning. I've already got you down for several
others, including a prisoner who died in custody."

"Groan," Jack mumbled. He knew that such cases frequently had complicated political and social fallout. "Are you
sure Calvin, our fearless deputy chief, won't want to do that
one himself?"

"He called earlier and told me to assign it to you," George
said. "He'd already heard from someone high up in the police
hierarchy and thought you'd be the best one to handle the job."

"Now that's ironic," Jack said. It didn't make sense. The
deputy chief as well as the chief himself were always complaining about Jack's lack of diplomacy and appreciation of
the political and social aspects of being a medical examiner.

"If you don't want the infectious case, I've got an overdose
you can do," George said.

"I'll take the infectious case," Jack said. He did not like
overdoses. They were repetitious and the office was inundated
with them. There was no intellectual challenge.

"Fine," George said. He made a notation on his master list.

Eager to get a jump on the day, Jack stepped over to Vinnie
and bent the edge of his paper down. Vinnie regarded him

morosely with his coal-black eyes. Vinnie was not pleased. He knew what was coming. It happened almost every day.

"Don't tell me you want to start already?" Vinnie whined.

"The early bird gets the worm," Jack said. The trite expression was Jack's stock response to Vinnie's invariable lack of early-morning enthusiasm. The comment never ceased to further provoke the mortuary tech even though he knew it was coming.

"I wish I knew why you couldn't come in when everyone else does," Vinnie grumbled.

Despite appearances Jack and Vinnie got along famously. Because of Jack's penchant for coming in early, they invariably worked together, and over the years they'd developed a well-oiled protocol. Jack preferred Vinnie over all the other techs, and Vinnie preferred Jack. In Vinnie's words, Jack did not "dick around."

"Have you seen Dr. Montgomery yet?" Jack asked as they headed for the elevator.

"She's too intelligent to come in here this early," Vinnie said. "She's normal, which you're not."

As they passed through communications Jack caught sight of a light on in Sergeant Murphy's cubbyhole office. The sergeant was a member of the NYPD Bureau of Missing Persons. He'd been assigned to the Office of the Chief Medical Examiner for years. He rarely arrived much before nine.

Curious whether the ebullient Irishman was already there, Jack detoured and glanced inside. Not only was Murphy there, he wasn't alone. Sitting across from him was Detective Lieutenant Lou Soldano of homicide, a frequent visitor to the morgue. Jack knew him reasonably well, particularly since he was a good friend of Laurie's. Next to him was another plainclothes gentleman whom Jack did not recognize.

"Jack!" Lou called out when he caught sight of him. "Come in here a minute. I want you to meet someone."

Jack stepped into the tiny room. Lou got to his feet. As usual, the detective appeared as if he'd been up all night. He hadn't shaved—the sides of his face looked as if they had been smeared with soot—and there were dark circles under his eyes. On top of that, his clothes were disheveled, the top button of his once white shirt was open, and his tie was loosened.

"This is Special Agent Gordon Tyrrell," Lou said, gesturing toward the man sitting next to him. The man got to his feet and stuck out his hand.

"Does that mean FBI?" Jack questioned as he shook the man's hand.

"It does indeed," Gordon said.

Jack had never shaken the hand of a member of the Federal Bureau of Investigation. It was not quite the experience he envisioned. Gordon's hand was slight, almost effeminate, and his grip loose and tentative. The agent was a small man with delicate features, certainly not the masculine stereotype Jack had grown up with. The agent's clothes were conservative but neat. All three buttons of his jacket were buttoned. In most respects he was the visual antithesis of Lou.

"What's going on here?" Jack questioned. "I can't remember the last time I saw the sergeant here this early."

Murphy laughed and started to protest, but Lou interrupted.

"There was a homicide last night that the FBI is particularly concerned about," Lou explained. "We're hoping the autopsy may shed some light."

"What kind of case?" Jack asked. "Gunshot or stabbing?"

"A little of everything," Lou said. "The body's a mess. Enough to turn even your stomach."

"Has there been an ID?" Jack asked. Sometimes with heavily damaged corpses identification was the most difficult part.

With raised eyebrows Lou glanced at Gordon. Lou didn't know how much was confidential about the case.

"It's okay," Gordon said.

"Yeah, there's been an ID," Lou said. "The name is Brad Cassidy. He's a twenty-two-year-old Caucasian skinhead."

"You mean one of those racist screwballs with Nazi tattoos, a black leather jacket, and black boots?" Jack asked. He'd seen such riffraff on occasion hanging around the city parks. He'd seen even more of them back home in the Midwest when he visited his mother.

"You got it," Lou said.

"Skinheads don't all have Nazi regalia," Gordon said.

"Now that's certainly true," Lou agreed. "In fact, some of them don't even have shaved heads anymore. The style has gone through some changes."

"The music hasn't," Gordon corrected. "That's probably been the most consistent part of the whole movement and certainly part of the style."

"That's something I don't know anything about," Lou said. "I've never been much into music."

"Well, it's important in regard to American skinheads," Gordon said. "The music has provided the movement with its ideology of hatred and violence."

"No kidding?" Lou said. "Just because of the music?"

"I'm not exaggerating," Gordon said. "Here in the U.S., in contrast to England, the skinhead movement started as just style, sorta like punks, posturing to be shockingly offensive in appearance and behavior. But the music of groups like Skrewdriver and Brutal Attack and a bunch of others created a change. The lyrics promoted a screwed-up philosophy of survival and rebellion. That's where the hatred and violence have come from."

"So you're kinda a skinhead expert?" Jack asked. He was impressed.

"Only by necessity," Gordon said. "My real area of interest is ultra-right-wing extremist militias. But I've had to expand my focus. Unfortunately, the White Aryan Resistance started a fad of recruiting skinheads as shock troops of sorts, tapping into that well of hatred and violence the music has engendered. Now a lot of the neo-fascist militia groups have followed suit, getting the kids to do a lot of their dirty work as well as getting the kids interested in neo-Nazi propaganda."

"Don't these kids usually beat up minorities?" Jack asked. "What happened in this guy's case? Did someone fight back?"

"Skinheads have a tendency to fight with each other as much as they attack others," Gordon said. "And this is a case of the former."

"Why so much interest in Brad Cassidy?" Jack asked. "I'd have thought that one less of these guys would just make your law enforcement lives that much easier."

Vinnie stuck his head in the room and informed Jack that

if Jack was going to continue jawboning, he was going back to his *New York Post*. Jack waved him away.

"Brad Cassidy had been recruited by us as a potential informant," Gordon said. "He'd plea-bargained a handful of felonies in return for cooperation. He was trying to find and penetrate an organization called the People's Aryan Army or PAA."

"I've never heard of them," Jack said.

"I hadn't, either," Lou admitted.

"It's a shadowy group," Gordon said. "All we know is what we've been able to intercept off the Internet, which, by the way, has become the major method of communication for these neo-fascist nuts. All we know about PAA is that it's located somewhere in the New York metropolitan area, and it's recruited some of the local skinheads. But the more disturbing part has been some vague references to an upcoming major event. We're worried they might be planning something violent."

"Something like the bombing of the Alfred P. Murrah building in Oklahoma City," Lou said. "Some major terrorist thing."

"Good God!" Jack said.

"We have no idea what, when, or where," Gordon said. "We're hoping they're just posturing and bragging, which these groups tend to do. But we're not taking any chances. Since counterintelligence is the only true defense against terrorism, we're doing the best we can. We've notified the emergency management people here in the city, but unfortunately there's little information we can give them."

"Right now our only positive lead is a dead skinhead," Lou said. "That's why we're so interested in the autopsy. We're hoping for a lead, any lead."

"You want me to do the post right now?" Jack said. "I was on my way to do an infectious case, but it can wait."

"I asked Laurie to do it," Lou said. He blushed as much as his dark, southern Italian skin would allow. "And she said she wanted to do it."

"When did you talk to Laurie?" Jack asked.

"This morning," Lou said.

"Really," Jack said. "Where did you get her? At home?"

"Actually she called me," Lou said. "She got me on my cell phone."

"What time was that?" Jack asked.

Lou hesitated.

"Was it around four-thirty in the morning?" Jack asked. The mystery about Laurie was deepening.

"Something like that," Lou admitted.

Jack took Lou by the elbow. "Excuse us," he said to Gordon and Sergeant Murphy. Jack took Lou out into the communications room. Marjorie Zankowski gave them a quick look before going back to her knitting. The switchboard was quiet.

"Laurie called me at four-thirty, too," Jack said in a whisper. "She woke me up. Not that I'm complaining. Actually it was good she woke me up. I was having a nightmare. But I know it was exactly four-thirty because I looked at the clock."

"Well, maybe it was four-forty-five when she called me," Lou said. "I don't remember exactly. It's been a busy night."

"What did she call for?" Jack asked. "That's a rather strange time to call, wouldn't you say?"

Lou fixed Jack with his dark eyes. It was apparent he was debating the appropriateness of revealing what Laurie had called him about.

"All right, maybe it's not a fair question," Jack said, raising his hands in mock defense. "Instead, why don't I tell you why she called me. She wanted to have dinner with me tonight. She said it was important that she talk with me. Does that make any sense given what she said to you?"

Lou blew out through pursed lips. "No," he said. "She said the same thing to me. She invited me to dinner, too."

"You're not pulling my leg, are you?" None of this was rational.

Lou shook his head.

"What did you say?" Jack asked.

"I said I'd go," Lou answered.

"What did you think she wants to talk to you about?" Jack asked.

Lou hesitated. It was again apparent he was uncomfortable.

"I guess I was hoping she wanted to tell me she missed me. You know, something like that."

Jack slapped a hand to his forehead. He was touched. It was obvious Lou was in love with Laurie. It was also a complication, because in many ways Jack felt the same way about her although he was reluctant to admit it to himself.

"You don't have to say anything," Lou said. "I know I'm a sap. It's just that I get lonely once in a while and I enjoy her company. Plus she likes my kids."

Jack took his hand away from his forehead and put it on Lou's shoulder. "I don't think you are a sap. Far from it. I was just hoping you could shed some light on what's up with her."

"We'll just have to ask her," Lou said. "She said she'd be a little late arriving this morning."

"Knowing Laurie she'll make us wait until tonight," Jack said. "Did she say how late she'd be?"

"No," Lou said.

"Even that's weird," Jack said. "If she was up and at 'em at four-thirty, how come she's late?"

Lou shrugged.

Jack went back into the ID room with his mind spinning about Laurie and terrorism. It was a strange combination. Realizing there was little he could do about either for the moment, he got Vinnie away from his paper for the second time and vowed to get his day under way. He looked forward to concentrating on a problem with an immediate resolution.

As Jack and Vinnie passed Janice Jaeger's office, Jack leaned inside.

"Hey, you did a good job on this Papparis case," Jack said.

Janice looked up from her desk. Her dark circles were as impressive as always. Jack couldn't help but wonder if the woman slept at all.

"Thanks," Janice said.

"You'd better get some rest," Jack said.

"I'll be leaving as soon as I wrap up this case."

"Anything extra we should know concerning Papparis?" Jack asked.

"I think it's all there," Janice said. "Except for the fact that the doctor I talked with was pretty upset. He told me he'd never seen a more aggressive infection. In fact, he'd like a call after you do the autopsy. His name and number are on the back of the information sheet."

"I'll call him as soon as we have something," Jack promised.

Once in the elevator Vinnie spoke up. "This case is starting to give me the creeps. It's reminding me of that plague case we had a few years ago. I hope this is not the start of some kind of epidemic."

"You and me both," Jack said. "It reminds me more of the influenza cases we saw after the plague. Let's be extra careful about contamination."

"That goes without saying," Vinnie said. "I'd put on two moon suits if it were possible."

Vinnie was already in his scrubs, so while Jack went into the locker room to get out of his street clothes, Vinnie went to don his moon suit. Then while Vinnie went into the autopsy room, or pit as it was called, Jack went through all the material in the folder, particularly Janice Jaeger's forensic investigator's report. On this more thorough reading Jack noticed something that he'd missed the first time through. The deceased had been in the rug business. Jack wondered what kind of rugs and where they were from. He made a mental note to bring the question up with the forensic investigators.

Next Jack snapped Papparis's morgue X-ray onto a view box. As a total-body film the X-ray was not much good diagnostically. In particular, the chest detail was indistinct. Regardless, two things caught Jack's attention. First, there was little evidence of pneumonia, which seemed surprising in view of the history of the patient's rapid respiratory deterioration; and second, the central part of the chest between the lungs, known anatomically as the mediastinum, seemed wider than usual.

By the time Jack got himself suited up in his biocontainment moon suit, with its hood, plastic face mask, and battery-powered HEPA filtered ventilation system, Vinnie had the body on the autopsy table and all the appropriate specimen jars lined up.

"What the hell have you been doing out there?" Vinnie complained when Jack appeared. "We could have been done by now."

Jack laughed.

"And look at this guy," Vinnie added, nodding to the corpse. "I don't think he's going to get to go to the prom."

"Good memory," Jack said. Jack had used that line when they'd started the plague case Vinnie had referred to earlier and it had become a staple of their black humor.

"And that's not all I remembered," Vinnie said. "While you were out there dicking around I looked for arthropod bites. There aren't any."

"Such recall!" Jack commented. "I'm impressed." During the plague case Jack had told Vinnie that arthropods, particularly insects and arachnids, played an important role as a vector in the spread of many infectious diseases. Searching for evidence of their involvement was an important part of the autopsy on such cases. "Soon you'll be taking over my job."

"What I'd like to do is take over your salary," Vinnie said. "The job you can have."

Jack did his own external exam. Vinnie was right: there were no signs of bites. There was also no purpura, or bleeding into the skin, although the skin did seem to have a slightly dusky tint.

The internal exam was another story. As soon as Jack removed the front wall of the chest the pathology was apparent. There was frank blood on the surface of the lungs, a finding called hemorrhagic pleural effusion. There was also a lot of bleeding and signs of inflammation in the structures located between the lungs, which included the esophagus, the trachea, the main bronchi, the great vessels, and a conglomeration of lymph nodes. This finding was called hemorrhagic mediastinitis, and it explained the wide shadow Jack had seen earlier on the X-ray.

"Whoa!" Jack commented. "With all this bleeding I don't think this could be the flu. Whatever it was, it was spreading like wildfire."

Vinnie nervously glanced up at Jack. He had difficulty seeing Jack's face because of the reflection from the overhead

fluorescent lights glinting off Jack's plastic face screen. Vinnie
didn't like the sound of Jack's voice. Jack was rarely impressed by what he saw in the autopsy room, but he seemed
to be now.

"What do you think it is?" Vinnie asked.

"I don't know," Jack admitted. "But the combination of
hemorrhagic mediastinitis and pleural effusion rings a bell in
the back of my mind. I've read about it someplace; I just can't
remember where. Whatever this bug is, it's got to be something mighty aggressive."

Vinnie instinctively took a step back from the body.

"Now don't go freaking out on me," Jack said. "Get back
over here and help me get out the abdominal organs."

"Yeah, well, promise me you'll be careful," Vinnie said.
"Sometimes you work too fast with the knife." He reluctantly
stepped back to the table.

"I'm always careful," Jack said.

"Sure!" Vinnie said sarcastically. "That's why you ride that
bike of yours around the city."

As the two men concentrated on the case, other bodies began arriving. They were placed on their respective tables by
the mortuary techs to await their autopsies. Eventually, the
other medical examiners began to drift in. It was promising to
be a busy day in the pit.

"Whatcha got?" a voice asked over Jack's shoulder.

Jack straightened up and turned to look at Dr. Chet Mc-
Govern, his officemate. Jack and Chet had joined the Office
of the Chief Medical Examiner within a month of each other.
They got along superbly, mainly because they shared a true
love and appreciation for their work. Both had tried other areas
of medicine before switching to forensic pathology.
Personality-wise they were quite different. Chet wasn't nearly
as sarcastic as Jack, and he didn't share Jack's problem with
authority.

Jack gave Chet a thumbnail sketch of the Papparis case and
showed him the pathology in the chest. He even showed him
the cut surface of the lung, which revealed minimal pneumonia.

"Interesting," Chet said. "The infection must have been airborne."

"No doubt," Jack said. "But why so little pneumonia?"

"Beats me," Chet said. "You're the infectious-disease expert."

"I wish that were true," Jack said. He carefully slipped the lung back into the pan. "I'm positive I've heard of this combination of findings. For the life of me I can't remember what it was."

"I'll wager you'll figure it out," Chet said. He started to move off, but Jack called after him, asking if he'd run into Laurie.

Chet shook his head. "Not yet."

Jack looked up at the wall clock. It was going on nine. She should have been there an hour ago. He shrugged and went back to work.

The next order of business was to remove the brain. Since Jack and Vinnie worked together so frequently, they had established a routine of cutting into the head that didn't require conversation. Although Vinnie did a significant amount of the work, it was always Jack who lifted off the skullcap.

"My, my," Jack commented as the brain came into view. As with the lungs, there was a significant amount of blood on its surface. When this was seen in an infectious case, it usually meant hemorrhagic meningitis, or inflammation of the meninges to the point of causing bleeding.

"This guy must have had one wicked headache," Vinnie said.

"That and crushing chest pain," Jack said. "The poor fellow probably felt like he'd gotten run over by a train."

"What do you have there, Doctor?" a deep, resonant voice asked. "A burst aneurysm or a trauma victim?"

"Neither," Jack said. "It's an infectious case." He turned and looked up at the imposing six-foot-seven silhouette of Dr. Calvin Washington, the deputy chief.

"How appropriate," Calvin said. "Contagion is right up your alley. Have you got a tentative diagnosis?"

Calvin leaned over the table to get a better look. His massive muscled bulk made Jack's stocky frame look tiny by comparison. As an athletically talented African-American giant, Calvin could have played professional football if he hadn't been so eager to get to medical school. His father had been a respected surgeon in Philadelphia and he was determined to follow a similar career pattern.

"I hadn't a clue until two seconds ago," Jack said. "But as soon as I saw the blood on the surface of the brain it hit me. I remembered reading about inhalational anthrax a couple of years ago when I was boning up about infectious disease."

"Anthrax?" Calvin gave a disbelieving chuckle. Jack had a penchant for coming up with outlandish diagnoses. Although he often turned out to be correct, anthrax seemed beyond the realm of possibility. In all Calvin's years as a pathologist he had seen only one case, and that had been in a cattleman in Oklahoma, and it wasn't inhalational. It had been the more common cutaneous form.

"At this point anthrax would be my guess," Jack said. "It will be interesting if the lab confirms it. Of course it might turn out that this patient had a compromised immune system that no one knew about. Then the bug could turn out to be a garden-variety pathogen."

"From sad experience I know better than to make a bet with you, but you've picked a mighty rare disease, at least here in the U.S."

"Well, I don't remember how rare it is," Jack said. "All I remember is that it's associated with hemorrhagic mediastinitis and meningitis."

"What about meningococcus?" Calvin asked. "Why not pick something a lot more common?"

"Meningococcus is possible," Jack said. "But it wouldn't be high on my list, not with the hemorrhagic mediastinitis. Besides, there was no purpura, and I'd expect more purulence on the brain surface with meningococcus."

"Well, if it turns out to be anthrax, let me know sooner rather than later," Calvin said. "I'm sure the Commissioner of Health would be interested. As for your next case, you've been informed that I want you to do it."

"Yes," Jack said. "But why me? You and the chief are always complaining about my lack of diplomacy. A police custody case usually stirs up a beehive of political turmoil. You sure you want me involved?"

"Your services were specifically requested by people outside the department," Calvin said. "Apparently your lack of diplomacy has been taken for a positive trait by the African-American community. You might be a headache to the chief and me, but you've managed to develop a reputation of professional integrity with certain community leaders."

"Probably from my exploits on the neighborhood basketball court," Jack said. "I rarely cheat."

"Why do you always have to denigrate a compliment?" Calvin questioned irritably.

"Maybe because they make me feel uncomfortable," Jack said. "I prefer criticism."

"Lord give me patience," Calvin commented. "Listen, by having you do the post we might be able to avoid any potential contention that this office is involved in any sort of cover-up."

"The victim is an African-American?" Jack asked.

"Obviously," Calvin said. "And the officer is white. Get the picture?"

"I get it," Jack said.

"Good," Calvin said. "Give a yell when you're ready to start. I'll lend a hand. In fact, we'll do it together."

Calvin left. Jack looked at Vinnie and groaned. "That post will take three hours! Calvin might be thorough, but he's slower than molasses."

"How communicable is anthrax?" Vinnie asked.

"Relax!" Jack said. "You're not going to come down with anything. As I recall, anthrax doesn't spread person to person."

"I never know when to believe you or not," Vinnie said.

"Sometimes I don't believe myself," Jack said self-mockingly. "But in this instance you can trust me."

With no more conversation Jack and Vinnie finished the Papparis case. As Jack was getting the lab specimens together to take upstairs, Laurie came into the pit. Jack recognized her by her characteristic laugh; her face was hidden by her bioprotective hood. She was apparently in a buoyant mood. She was accompanied by two others who Jack guessed were Lou and the FBI agent. All were dressed in moon suits.

As soon as he could, Jack stepped over to the table where the newcomers had grouped. By that time there was no more laughter.

"You're telling me this boy was crucified?" Laurie asked. She was holding up the corpse's right hand. Jack could see a large sixteen-penny spike protruding from the palm.

"That's what I'm telling you," Lou said. "And that was just the start. They'd nailed a cross to a telephone pole and then nailed the kid to it."

"Good grief," Laurie said.

"Then they tried to skin him," Lou said. "At least the front of him."

"How awful," Laurie said.

"Do you think he was alive when they were doing that?" Gordon asked.

"I'm afraid so," Laurie said. "You can see by the amount of bleeding involved. There's no doubt he was alive."

Jack stepped closer with the intention of getting Laurie's attention for a quick chat, but then he caught sight of the body. As jaded as he thought he'd become to the image of death, Brad Cassidy's corpse made Jack catch his breath. The young man had been crucified, partially skinned, his eyes gouged, and his genitals cut off. There were multiple superficial stab wounds all over his body. The skin of the thorax that had been removed was draped over his legs. On it was a large tattoo of a Viking. A small Nazi swastika was tattooed in the center of his forehead.

"Why a Viking?" Jack asked.

"Hello, Jack, dear," Laurie said brightly. "Have you finished your first case already? Have you met Agent Gordon Tyrrell? How was your ride in this morning?"

"Just fine," Jack said. Since the questions had come so quickly he only responded to the last.

"Jack insists on riding a bike around the city," Laurie explained. "He says it clears his mind."

"I wouldn't think that would be particularly safe," Gordon said.

"It's not," Lou agreed. "Yet with the crosstown traffic, there are times I wish I had a bike myself."

"Oh, come on, Lou!" Laurie exclaimed. "You can't be serious."

Jack experienced a distinct feeling of unreality as the conversation continued. It seemed absurd to be engaging in social banter dressed up in biocontainment moon suits in front of a mutilated corpse. Jack interrupted the discussion about bicycling by returning to his initial question about the Viking tattoo.

"It's from the Aryan myth," Gordon explained. "Like the style of the clothing and the boots, the Viking image is borrowed from the skinhead movement in England, where the whole thing started."

"But why specifically a Viking?" Jack repeated. "I thought they were into all the Nazi emblems."

"Their interest in the Vikings comes from a very revisionist view of history," Gordon said. "The skinheads think the marauding, murderous Vikings epitomized self-reliant masculine honor."

"That's why Gordon thinks he got skinned," Lou said. "Whoever killed him didn't think he deserved to die with an image of a Viking still attached."

"I thought this kind of torture went out with the Middle Ages," Jack said.

"I've seen a number of cases just as bad," Gordon said. "These are violent kids."

"And scary," Lou said. "They're true psychopaths."

"Pardon me, Laurie," Jack said. "Could I have a quick word with you? Alone."

"Of course," Laurie said. She excused herself from the others and stepped to the side of the room with Jack.

"Did you just get here?" Jack asked in a whisper.

"A few minutes ago," Laurie admitted. "What's up?"

"You're asking me what's up?" Jack questioned. "You're the one acting weird, and I'll tell you, the mystery is driving me crazy. What's going on? What is it that you want to talk to me and Lou about?"

Jack could see Laurie's smile despite her face mask.

"My goodness," she commented. "I don't think I've ever seen you this interested. I'm flattered."

"Come on, Laurie! Quit stalling. Out with it!"

"It would take too long," Laurie said.

"Just give me a quick synopsis," Jack said. "We can save the gory details for later."

"No! Jack," Laurie said forcibly. "You'll just have to wait until tonight, provided I'm still on my feet."

"What's that supposed to mean?"

"Jack! I can't talk now. I'll talk to you tonight like we decided."

"You decided," Jack said.

"I have to get to work," Laurie said. She turned away and went back to her table.

Jack felt frustrated and irritable. He could not believe Laurie was doing this to him. Grumbling under his breath, he pushed off the wall and went back to get Papparis's specimens. He wanted to get them up to Agnes Finn so that she could run a fluorescein antibody test for anthrax.

TWO

"*Chert! Chert! Chert!*" Yuri Davydov shouted. He beat the top edge of the steering wheel of his yellow Chevy Caprice taxi with the base of his right fist. Particularly when he was angry, Yuri reverted to his Russian mother tongue, and at the moment he was furious. He was stuck in bumper-to-bumper traffic and surrounded by a cacophony of automobile horns. Ahead of him was a stalled blur of yellow cabs with activated red brake lights. Worse yet, the next intersection was jammed with cars going perpendicular to his, so despite the green light, Yuri was stuck in hopeless gridlock.

The day had started badly during Yuri's first fare. As he was heading down Second Avenue, a bicyclist kicked a dent in the passenger-side door of Yuri's cab after complaining that Yuri had cut him off. Yuri had jumped out and lavished the jerk with a string of Russian expletives. Yuri had initially intended on being more physically aggressive but quickly changed his mind. The cyclist was his height, squarely built, as angry as Yuri, and obviously in far better physical shape.

At age forty-four, Yuri had let himself go. He was overweight and soft, and he knew it.

A slight thump coming from the rear of his car jolted Yuri. He leaned out his open window, shook his fist, and with his heavy accent, cursed the taxi driver behind him for bumping his car.

"Up yours," the driver called back. "Move!"

"Where do you want me to go?" Yuri yelled. "What's the matter with you?"

Yuri settled back into his beaded seat. He ran an anxious hand through his thick brown, almost black hair. Reaching up, he turned his rearview mirror to look at himself. His eyes were red and his face was flushed. He knew he had to calm down, otherwise he'd have a coronary. What he needed was a shot of vodka.

"What a joke!" Yuri muttered angrily in Russian. He wasn't referring to the current traffic situation but rather to his whole life. Metaphorically his life had a lot in common with the stalled traffic. It was dead in the water, and as a result, Yuri was completely disillusioned. By sad experience he now knew that the enticing American dream that had been his driving force was a sham, one foisted onto the world by the American Jewish-dominated media.

Ahead the cars began to move. Yuri lurched his car forward, hoping at least to get through the bottled-up intersection, but it was not to be. The car in front stopped short. Yuri was forced to do likewise. Then the taxi behind him hit him again. This second collision, like the first, was merely a bump, certainly not enough to do any damage, but for Yuri it added insult to injury.

Yuri stuck his head out the window again. "What the hell is the matter with you? Is this your first day driving?"

"Shut up, you goddamn foreigner," the driver behind yelled back. "Why don't you take your ass home to wherever the hell it was you came from."

Yuri started to respond but changed his mind. He settled back into his seat and exhaled noisily like a punctured tire deflating. The driver's comment had unwittingly awakened a sense of *toska* that descended over Yuri like a heavy wool blanket. *Toska* is a Russian word that connotes melancholy, depression, yearning, anguish, weariness, and nostalgia suffered all at once in the form of deep, psychic pain.

Yuri stared ahead with unseeing eyes. For the moment the disillusionment and anger about America was swept away by an evocative reminiscence. All at once an image popped into his mind of himself and his brother going to school on a crystalline, frosty morning in his home city of Sverdlovsk, USSR. In his mind's eye he could see the communal kitchen with its conviviality, and in his heart he could remember the pride of being part of the mighty Soviet Empire.

Of course there had been some deprivations under the Communist regime, like occasionally having the women wait in line for milk and other staples. But it hadn't been as bad as people had said or as bad as the fools here in America wanted to believe. In fact, the equality for everyone, excluding those high in the party, had been refreshing and conducive to friendship. There certainly had been less social conflict than here in America. At the time, Yuri didn't realize how good it had been. But now he remembered, and he was going home. Yuri was going back to *Rossiya-matoshka,* or little mother Russia. He'd made that decision months earlier.

But he wasn't leaving until he had had his revenge. He'd been deceived and denied. Now he would strike back in a way that would get everyone's attention in this smug, fraudulent country. And once home in Russia, he would offer his revenge as a gift to Vladimir Zhirinovsky, the true patriot of *rodina,* the motherland, who would surely return the glory of the USSR if given the chance.

Yuri's musings were rudely interrupted by one of the back doors of his cab being yanked open. A passenger tossed in an ostrich briefcase and then climbed in after it.

Irritably Yuri regarded his fare in the rearview mirror. He was a small, mustached man in an expensive Italian suit, white shirt, and silk tie. A matching pocket square ballooned out of his pocket. Yuri knew the man must be a businessman or a banker.

"Union Bank, 820 Fifth Avenue," the man said. He sat back and flipped open a cellular phone.

Yuri continued to stare at the man. He saw something he'd not seen at first. The man was wearing a yarmulke.

"What's the matter?" the man asked. "Are you off duty?"

"No, I'm on duty," Yuri said morosely. He rolled his eyes before turning the meter on and then gazing out at the stalled traffic. It was just what he needed: a Jewish banker, one of those creeps running the world into the ground.

While the man made a call, Yuri was able to inch ahead by one car length. At least now he was on the brink of the troublesome intersection. He drummed his fingers on the steering wheel. He toyed with the idea of telling the Jew to get the hell out of his cab. But he didn't. At least the creep was paying for him to sit there in traffic.

"Whoa, a lot of congestion," the man said after he'd finished his call. He leaned forward and poked his head through the gap in the Plexiglas divider. "I could walk faster than this."

"Be my guest," Yuri said.

"I got time," the man said. "It feels good to sit down for a moment. Luckily my next meeting isn't until after ten-thirty. Do you think you can get me to my destination by then?"

"I'll try," Yuri said indifferently.

"Is that a Russian accent?" the man asked.

"Yes," Yuri said. He sighed. This guy was going to drive him mad.

"I suppose I could have guessed by reading your name off the taxi license," the man said. "What part of Russia are you from, Mr. Yuri Davydov?"

"Central Russia," Yuri said.

"Very far from Moscow?"

"About eight hundred miles east. In the Ural Mountains."

"My name is Harvey Bloomburg."

Yuri glanced up at his fare in the rearview mirror and shook his head imperceptibly. He was mystified why people like Harvey wanted to tell him personal things. Yuri couldn't have cared less what Harvey's name was.

"I just got back from Moscow a week or so ago," Harvey said.

"Really?" Yuri questioned. He perked up. It had been a long time since Yuri had been there. He remembered the delight he'd felt the first time he'd visited Red Square, with the Cathedral of St. Basil sparkling like an architectural jewel. He'd never seen anything so beautiful or moving.

"I was there for almost five days," Harvey said.

"You're lucky," Yuri said. "Did you enjoy yourself?"

"Ha!" Harvey voiced with disdain and a wave of his hand. "I couldn't wait to get out. As soon as my meetings were over I fled to London. Moscow is out of control, what with the crime and the economic situation. The place is a disaster."

Yuri felt a renewed pang of anger from the knowledge that the current problems ravaging Russia had been created by the likes of Harvey Bloomburg and the rest of the worldwide Zionist conspiracy. Yuri could feel his face flush, but he held his tongue. Now he really needed a glass of vodka.

"How long have you been here in the States?" Harvey asked.

"Since 1994," Yuri grumbled. It had only been five years, but it felt like ten. At the same time Yuri could remember the first day he'd arrived as if it had been yesterday. He'd flown from Toronto, Canada, after a three-day problem with U.S. immigration, which resulted in his obtaining only a temporary visa.

Yuri's odyssey to get to America had been grueling and had taken over a year. It had started in Novosibirsk in Siberia, where he'd been working at a government company called Vector. He'd been there for eleven years but had lost his job when the institution was downsized. Luckily he'd saved a few rubles before being terminated, and by a combination of plane, train, and accommodating truck drivers, he'd made his way to Moscow.

In Moscow, disaster struck. Because of the sensitive nature of his previous job, the FSB (the successor to the KGB) was notified when he applied for an international passport. Yuri was arrested and thrown into Lefortovo Prison. After a number of months, he managed to get out of prison by agreeing to work at another government facility in Zagorsk. The problem was that they didn't pay him, at least not in money. He was given vodka and toilet paper in lieu of cash.

Fleeing in the dead of night on the evening prior to a midwinter holiday, he walked and hitchhiked the thousand miles to Tallinn, Estonia. It was a terrible trip, full of setbacks, illnesses, injury, near starvation, and unimaginable cold. It was the type of hardship that the armies of Napoleon and Hitler had experienced with disastrous results.

Although the Estonians were less than friendly to him as an ethnic Russian, and some Estonian youths had beaten him up one night, Yuri was able to earn enough money to buy fake papers that got him a job on a freighter plying the Baltic. In Sweden he jumped ship and applied for refugee status.

Sweden questioned the validity of his being a refugee but permitted him to stay temporarily. He was allowed to work at menial jobs to earn enough money to book a flight to Toronto and then to New York. When he finally arrived on U.S. soil, he bent down like the Pope and kissed the ground.

There were many times during the long, desperate quest to get to New York that Yuri was tempted to give up. But he didn't. Throughout the whole ordeal he was driven by the promise of America: freedom, riches, and the good life.

A sneer spread across Yuri's face. Some good life it turned out to be! It was more like a cruel joke. He was driving a cab twelve, sometimes fourteen hours a day just to survive. Taxes, rent, food, and health care for himself and the fat wife he'd had to marry for a green card were all killing him.

"You must thank Almighty God you got out of Russia when you did," Harvey said, unaware of Yuri's state of mind. "I don't know how the people are coping."

Yuri didn't respond. He just wanted Harvey to shut up. Suddenly the traffic opened up. Yuri stomped on the gas. The cab shot forward, throwing Harvey back against the rear seat. Yuri gripped the wheel and hunkered down. The tires screeched.

"Hey, my meeting's not important enough to risk death," Harvey shouted from the back seat.

Approaching the next intersection and a red light, Yuri hit the brakes. The car started to fishtail. Yuri expertly turned into a skid. The cab shot between a bus and a parked van, coming to an abrupt halt behind a garbage truck.

"My God!" Harvey called through the Plexiglas divider.

"What kind of work did you do back in Russia? Don't tell me you were a race car driver."

Yuri didn't answer.

Harvey moved forward. "I'm interested," he said. "What did you do? Last week I had a Russian cab driver who taught mathematics before coming over here. He said he was trained as an electrical engineer. Can you believe that?"

"I can believe it," Yuri said. "I was trained as an engineer myself." Yuri knew he was exaggerating, since he'd been a technician, not an engineer, but he didn't care.

"What kind of engineering?" Harvey asked.

"Biotechnological," Yuri said. The light changed and he pressed down on the accelerator. As soon as he could, he got out from behind the garbage truck and headed uptown, trying to get in sync with the lights.

"That's an impressive background indeed," Harvey said. "How come you're still driving a cab? I would think your skills would be in demand. Biotechnology is one of the fastest-growing fields in all of industry."

"There's a problem with getting credit for my education," Yuri said. "It's what you Americans call a Catch Twenty-two."

"Well, it's a shame," Harvey said. "My advice is for you to keep trying. It'll be worth it in the end."

Yuri didn't answer. He didn't have to put up with the indignity of trying any longer. He wasn't staying.

"Ah, it's a good thing that we won the Cold War," Harvey said. "At least the Russian people have a shot at prosperity and basic freedoms. I just hope they don't screw it up."

Yuri's irritation changed to rage. It drove him crazy to have to listen constantly to the falsehood that America won the Cold War and broke up the Soviet Empire. The Soviet Union had been betrayed from within: first by Gorbachev and his stupid Glasnost and Perestroika, and then by Yeltsin for no other reason than to indulge his ego.

Yuri gunned the engine of the taxi and roared uptown, weaving in among the traffic, running lights, and intimidating pedestrians.

"Hey!" Harvey shouted. "Slow the hell down! What's the matter with you?"

Yuri didn't respond. He hated Harvey's smug superiority, his expensive clothes, his ostrich briefcase, and most of all his stupid little hat he had pinned to his scraggly, thinning hair.

"Hey," Harvey yelled. He knocked on the plastic divider. "Slow down or I'm calling the police."

The warning about the police penetrated Yuri's fury. The last thing he wanted was a run-in with the authorities. Yuri eased up on the accelerator and took a deep breath to calm himself. "Sorry," he said. "I was just trying to get you to your meeting on time."

"I'd prefer to arrive alive," Harvey snapped.

Yuri kept his speed within the normal limits while he worked his way over to Fifth Avenue. Once there he headed south for less than two blocks. He pulled up in front of the Union Bank, stopped, and turned off the meter.

Harvey lost no time in getting out of the cab. While standing on the sidewalk he counted out the fare to the penny and plopped the cash into Yuri's waiting hand.

"No tip?" Yuri asked.

"You deserve a tip like I deserve a poke in the eye with a sharp stick," Harvey said. "You're lucky I'm paying you at all." He turned and headed for the revolving door of the fancy granite and glass bank building.

"I didn't expect a tip from a Zionist pig anyway," Yuri yelled after him.

Harvey flipped the cab driver the finger before disappearing from sight.

Yuri closed his eyes for a moment. He had to get control of himself before he did something stupid. He hoped to hell that Harvey Bloomburg lived on the Upper East Side because that was the part of the city that Yuri was going to devastate.

The next thing Yuri knew the back door to his cab was pulled open and someone climbed in. Yuri spun around.

"I'm off duty," he said. "Get out!"

"Your off-duty sign's not on," the woman said indignantly. She had a Louis Vuitton briefcase on one side and a leather laptop satchel on the other.

Yuri reached over to the proper switch and flicked it. "It's on now," he growled. "Out!"

"Oh, for crissake," the woman muttered. She grabbed her bags and got out of the cab. As a passive-aggressive gesture, she left the rear door ajar. She stepped out into the street, treated Yuri to a condescending look, then hailed another taxi.

Yuri stuck his hand out the driver's side window and gave the open door a push. It closed without a problem. He then pulled out into the traffic and headed downtown. For the moment he was in no mood to put up with any more haughty businesspeople, particularly Jewish bankers. Instead he wanted to revel in thinking about his revenge, and to do that he needed corroboration that his agent was as deadly as he imagined. That meant checking up on Jason Papparis.

The office for the Corinthian Rug Company was on Walker Street south of Canal. It was situated in a ground-level storefront with a couple of faded geometrically patterned Turkish rugs and goat hides in the window. Yuri slowed as he approached. The door had lettering stenciled in gold. It was closed, but Yuri knew that didn't mean anything. When Yuri had initially scouted the concern by making innumerable drive-bys, he'd always found the door closed.

Pulling into a loading area across the street from where he could watch the entrance, Yuri put his car in park. He'd decided to wait although he didn't know exactly what he was waiting for. Somehow he had to find out about Mr. Jason Papparis's state of health. Yuri was certain the man had gotten the ACME Cleaners envelope on Friday at the very latest.

The waiting calmed Yuri, and the thought of the next step in his grand scheme excited him. He'd be able to tell Curt Rogers that the anthrax was potent. That would mean that the only thing left to test would be the botulinum toxin. For the fateful day, Yuri had decided on two agents rather than one. He wanted to eliminate any possibility of technological screwups. The two agents killed in completely different ways, even though both were to be aerosolized.

Reaching under his seat and pushing his defensive tire iron out of the way, Yuri pulled out his flat pocket flask. He deserved a shot of vodka. After making sure no one was watching, he took a quick slug of the fiery fluid. He breathed out a sigh of relief as a sensation of warmth spread deliciously through his body. Now he felt even calmer. He was even capable of appreciating that there had been some recent bright spots in his life.

One of the luckiest things that had happened to Yuri since his arrival in the U.S. was meeting Curt Rogers and Curt's buddy Steve Henderson and striking up a relationship. It had been this relationship that had turned Yuri's fantasy of vengeance into a realistic possibility. The initial meeting had occurred purely by chance. After a very long day of hot summer driving Yuri had stopped at a hole-in-the-wall bar called White Pride in Bensonhurst, Brooklyn. His flask had long since been drained, and he needed a shot of vodka so bad he couldn't wait until he got home to Brighton Beach.

It was after eleven at night, and the local hangout was crowded, dark, and noisy with the heavy-metal beat of Skrewdriver reverberating off the walls. Most of the customers were tough working-class white youths with shaved heads, sleeveless T-shirts, and a profusion of tattoos. Yuri should have guessed the kind of clientele he'd encounter. Outside he'd seen a number of gleaming Harleys emblazoned with Nazi decals nosed in against the curb directly in front of the bar's open door.

Yuri could remember hesitating on the threshold while debating whether to go in. His intuition told him that danger hung in the air like a miasma above a swamp. People eyed him with hostility. After a moment's indecision Yuri had taken the risk to enter for two reasons. One was the fear that fleeing would have provoked a chase just like running from a vicious but indecisive dog. The other was that he really needed the vodka and that all the other bars in Bensonhurst would probably have been equally intimidating.

Yuri sat on an empty stool, hunched over the bar, and pulled in his elbows. He kept his eyes straight ahead. As soon as he ordered his drink, his accent caused a stir. A number of the youths with supercilious expressions closed around him. Just when Yuri feared trouble was about to occur, the punks parted and a clean-cut man in his late thirties or early forties appeared whom the youths seemed to respect.

The newcomer was dirty blond, tall, and lean. His hair was

short but his head was not shaved. The style was more like a military man's. He, too, was wearing a T-shirt, but it was clean, had short sleeves, and looked ironed. There was a small image of a red fireman's hat high on the left side of the shirt. Below that it said *Engine Company #7*. In sharp contrast to the skinheads, he appeared to have only the one tattoo. It was a small American flag on his right upper arm.

"I don't know whether you're brave or stupid for coming in here uninvited, friend," the blond-haired man said. "This is a private club."

"I'm sorry," Yuri mumbled. He started to get up. The blond man put a hand on his shoulder to keep him in his seat.

"You sound Russian," the man said.

"I am," Yuri admitted.

"Are you Jewish?"

"No!" Yuri blurted. "Not at all." The question surprised him.

"You live over in Brighton Beach?"

"That's right," Yuri said nervously. He didn't know where the conversation was going.

"I thought all you Russians over there were Jewish."

"Not me," Yuri said. The man knew what he was talking about. The majority of the Russian émigrés in Brighton Beach were Jewish. It was one of the reasons Yuri had so few friends. There were all sorts of Jewish organizations that welcomed their fellow religious refugees. The Jews had been the only people allowed out of Russia during the Communist regime, so there was already a sizable community there by the time of the fall of the USSR. Because of his lack of religious affiliation, Yuri had been ignored.

"Do I detect a negative attitude about the Jewish persuasion?" the blond man asked.

Yuri's eyes darted around at some of the slogans adorning the fronts of many of the skinheads' T-shirts. He saw things like *The Holocaust Is A Zionist Myth* and *Down With The Zionist Occupied U.S. Government.* Accordingly, Yuri wisely deemed it opportune to confess his current anti-Semitic bias.

Yuri had never thought much about Jews one way or the other until the most recent Russian presidential election. It was then that he'd been acculturated by neo-fascist Vladimir Zhirinovsky's and neo-Communist Gennedy Zyuganov's rhetoric. Because of Yuri's *toska* and his wounded nationalistic pride, he'd been an easy target for both demagogues' hackneyed scapegoat theories.

"You know, I think we've misjudged you, friend," the blond man said in response to Yuri's racist admission. The blond man patted Yuri on his back. "Not only are you welcome to drink here, you can have another one on me."

The blond man snapped his finger at the bartender, who'd moved away when he'd suspected a conflagration. The bartender brought the bottle of vodka over and filled Yuri's glass to the brim.

"My name's Curt Rogers," the blond man said. He eased himself onto the stool next to Yuri. "And this here is Steve Henderson." Curt gestured to a red-headed fellow who took the seat on the other side of Yuri. Although Steve was much more heavily muscled than Curt, he resembled Curt particularly in regard to his dress. His T-shirt had the exact same insignia.

The first meeting had led to several subsequent ones, since the three men found that they shared similar opinions on issues beside anti-Semitism. There was a particularly strong meeting of the minds concerning their respective views about the current U.S. government.

"The whole goddamn mess is illegal, oppressive, and unconstitutional," Curt had whispered when the issue first came up. "And there's only one solution. The U.S. government has to be overthrown by force of arms. There's no other way. And it's got to be soon, because the Zionists are getting stronger every day."

"Really?" Yuri had asked. He'd been shocked to hear that there were Americans who disliked the government. And according to Curt, who was an authority on all aspects of the U.S. government as well as U.S. history, the malcontents weren't just a tiny minority. The patriots, as Curt called them, were sprinkled all over the country. They were all heavily armed and waiting for the sign for them to rise up in revolt.

"Mark my word," Curt had whispered on another occasion.

"I've got it on unimpeachable authority that the government's training Gurkha troops in Montana with thousands upon thousands of black helicopters. Unless something's done to this renegade government they're going to swoop out of their base in the near future and take away every gun from every goddamn patriot in the country. Then we'll be defenseless against the worldwide Zionists."

Back then Yuri had not known what "unimpeachable" meant but he didn't bother to ask since he'd gotten the drift of Curt's message. The U.S. government was far more perverse and more dangerous than he'd imagined. It also became clear that both he and Curt wanted to do something about it, and indeed they could help each other since each could do something the other couldn't. Yuri had the technological experience and the know-how necessary to build a bioweapon of mass destruction, while Curt had the people who could get the necessary equipment and materials. Curt had started a skinhead militia he called the People's Aryan Army, and he claimed his shock troops would obey any order he gave them.

"An agricultural pest control sprayer? No problem!" Curt had said in response to one of Yuri's early inquiries. "We can steal one from out on Long Island when the need arises. They use them in the potato fields. Most of the time they're just sitting out there waiting for the taking."

Several weeks later over iced shots of vodka Curt, Yuri, and Steve had shaken hands on the commencement of what they called Operation Wolverine. Yuri hadn't known what a wolverine was, so Curt explained it was a small, extremely vicious, cunning animal. At the time Curt had winked at Steve, because Wolverine really referred to a group of youths in a survivalist movie classic called *Red Dawn*. It was Curt and Steve's favorite movie. In it the Wolverines had held off the entire invading Russian Army.

Yuri had wanted to call the plan Operation Revenge, but he gave in to Curt and Steve when they were adamant about the name Wolverine. Curt had explained that the name would have immediate significance to the far-right underground.

After they'd polished off their vodka, they were all excited.

Their relationship was, in Curt's words, a marriage made in Heaven.

"I have a feeling this is going to be the spark that ignites the conflagration," Curt had said. "Something huge like this happening here in New York is bound to start the general revolt. It's going to make what happened in Oklahoma City seem like a childish prank."

Whether Operation Revenge started a general uprising or not Yuri didn't care. He just wanted to severely slap the U.S. across its smug face. Any glory he might achieve he'd gladly donate to the Zhirinovsky movement and the return of the Soviet Empire.

A sudden knock on Yuri's fender shocked him from his reverie. He turned to see a meter maid.

"You got to move along, cabbie," the woman said. "This here's for loading."

"Sorry," Yuri said. He put his idling car in gear and drove off. But he didn't go far. He merely rounded the block and returned to the same spot. The meter maid was in the far distance heading away.

Yuri put his blinkers on to make it look as if he was waiting for a fare and climbed from his car. No one had gone in or out of the Corinthian Rug Company for the half hour he'd been watching. He ran across the street. With his hands around his face he leaned against the glass office door and looked inside. The place was empty. There were no lights on. He tried the door. It was locked.

Yuri walked a few steps to the west and went into a neighboring shop. He'd seen a number of people going in and out while he'd been sitting in his cab. It was a store for stamp collectors. Inside it was as quiet as a tomb after some bells attached to the door had ceased their tinkling. The proprietor appeared from an inner area with tiny reading glasses teetering on the end of a bulbous nose. On his bald head was a yarmulke that Yuri thought must have been stuck on with glue.

"I got a call to pick up a Mr. Papparis at the Corinthian Rug Company," Yuri explained. "That's my cab outside. Unfortunately the rug office is closed. Do you know Mr. Papparis?"

"Of course."

"Have you seen him?" Yuri asked. "Or heard anything about him?"

"I haven't seen him all day. But that's not surprising. Our paths rarely cross."

"Thanks," Yuri said.

"My pleasure."

Yuri went to the store on the east side of the Corinthian Rug office. He got the same response. He then got back into his cab and thought about what he should do next. He considered trying to call the neighborhood hospitals, but he gave up on the idea when he remembered he didn't know where Mr. Papparis lived. He pondered getting a phone book to see if he could find Mr. Papparis's number but quickly decided that calling his home would be foolhardy. Yuri had been extraordinarily careful so far and had no desire to take any unnecessary chances. For what he had in mind to do to New York, he didn't want there to be any warning.

Yuri drove off. When he came to the corner of Walker and Broadway it occurred to him that he was only a little more than six blocks away from Curt and Steve's fire station on Duane Street. Although Yuri had never visited his partners' workplace, he decided to drop by. He wouldn't yet be able to confirm that the anthrax was potent, a question Yuri thought was academic, but he could at least inform them that the trial was under way. That was exciting enough, because it meant that Operation Wolverine was truly imminent. All the planning and preliminaries were over. Now it was only a question of producing adequate amounts of the agents and dispersing them.

THREE

"Do you think we should be doing this?" Steve Henderson asked. "I can't imagine we're going to learn enough to justify the risk."

Curt grabbed his friend's sleeve and pulled him to a stop. They were standing in front of the Jacob Javits Federal Building at 26 Federal Plaza. Crowds of people were coming and going. It was a busy place. It housed nearly six thousand government employees and was visited daily by a thousand civilians.

Curt and Steve were dressed in their freshly pressed blue class B firefighter uniforms. Their black shoes glistened in the bright October sunlight. Curt's shirt was a lighter blue than Steve's, and Curt had a tiny gold bullhorn on his collar. Curt had made lieutenant four years previously.

"With an operation of this magnitude, reconnaissance is an absolute must," Curt hissed. He glanced furtively at the scurrying crowd to make sure no one was paying them any heed.

"What the hell did they teach you in the army? We're talking about basics here!"

Curt and Steve had been childhood friends. Both had grown up in the strongly blue-collar area of Bensonhurst, Brooklyn. Both had been quiet, polite, and neat loners who'd gravitated toward each other over the years as kindred spirits, particularly during high school. They had been indifferent students although they'd scored high on aptitude tests, Curt higher than Steve. Neither had played any sports despite Curt's older brother's being one of Bensonhurst's legendary football stars. They had mostly "hung out," as they explained in their own words. Both had ended up in the armed forces: Curt after an abortive six-month try at college and Steve after working for his plumber father for a year.

"The army taught me just as much as the Marines taught you," Steve shot back. "Don't give me any of your Marine Corps bullshit."

"Well, we're not going to carry the stuff in there on D day without having reconnoitered the place," Curt said. "It's got to go into the HVAC induction. We got to make sure we can get access."

Steve nervously glanced up at the huge building. "But we got the plans," he said. "We know it's on the third floor."

"Jesus Christ!" Curt exclaimed. He threw up his hands, including the one holding his clipboard. "No wonder you washed out of the Green Berets. Are you going to chicken out on me?"

In contrast to their desultory academic careers, both men had excelled in their respective branches of the service. Curt had gone to Camp Pendleton in California, while Steve had gone to Fort Bragg in North Carolina. Both had risen quickly to the ranks of non-commissioned officers. The regimentation and sense of purpose excited them, and they became model gung-ho, spit-and-polish soldiers. Of particular interest to each was any kind of ordnance, especially assault rifles and handguns. Both became decorated marksmen.

The two buddies corresponded infrequently over the years. Being in different branches of the service and stationed on different coasts was a barrier to their friendship. The only times they got together were on the rare occasions when their leaves happened to coincide, and they met up in Bensonhurst. Then it was like old times, and they traded "war stories." Both had participated in the Gulf War.

Although neither Curt nor Steve had said as much, they both assumed the military would be their careers. But it was not to be; ultimately both were disappointed by their respective branches.

Curt's experience was the more troubling. He'd risen to a position of leadership in the training of recruits for an elite Marine reconnaissance team. During a particularly grueling night maneuver and on specific orders from Curt to keep up, a recruit died. A subsequent inquiry implicated Curt as being responsible for a portion of the blame. Nothing was said about the fact that the man shouldn't have been in the program. He was a "mama's boy" who'd been accepted only because his father was a Washington bigwig.

Although Curt wasn't punished per se, the incident tarnished his record and precluded further advancement. He was devastated and ultimately furious over the episode. He felt the government had let him down after he had given his all for his country. When the time for his next reenlistment came up, Curt took an early out.

Steve's experience had been different. After a lengthy and frustrating application process, he'd finally been accepted into Green Beret training, only to have to drop out during the initial twenty-one-day assessment course. It was not his fault; he'd come down with the flu. When he learned he had to start the whole application process again despite everything he'd done for the army, he followed Curt's example, and with a sense of disgust and betrayal left the military.

After a series of odd jobs, mostly involving private security, Curt had been the first to join the New York City Fire Department. He liked it from the start, with its military-like hierarchy, uniforms, inspiring mission, pride, and interesting equipment. Without any sort of ordnance, it wasn't the Marine Corps, but it was close enough. Also on the positive side was the fact that he could live in Bensonhurst.

Soon Curt was encouraging Steve to follow suit and take

the civil service test. With some wrangling after Steve had gotten himself hired, they managed to get themselves assigned to the same firehouse and ultimately to the same engine company. Their story had come full circle. They were back living in Bensonhurst and were once again best friends.

"I'm not going to chicken out," Steve said morosely. "I just think we're asking for trouble. The building's not scheduled for a fire inspection. What if they call the firehouse?"

"Who's to know they're not scheduled?" Curt said. "And what difference does it make if someone calls? The captain's on vacation. Besides, we're out doing legitimate inspections, and I happened to have found out there'd been a violation on the fed building's last inspection. If a question arises, we're just checking to make sure the violation has been corrected."

"What kind of violation was it?"

"They'd installed a small grill in the ground-floor sandwich kiosk," Curt said. "Probably some food service manager just thought of it as an afterthought. I doubt they even pulled a permit. It got put in without a dry chemical Ansul unit. We're just making sure they rectified the oversight."

"Let me see," Steve said.

"What, you don't believe me?" Curt questioned. He slipped the copy of the violation from beneath the clasp on his clipboard and held it up in front of Steve's face.

"Well, I'll be a rat's ass," Steve said after glancing at the form. "That's perfect."

"Did you doubt a former Marine?" Curt quipped.

"Screw you," Steve said kiddingly.

The two men continued toward the entrance, moving like military men with their heads high and their shoulders squared.

"This is going to be a perfect operation," Curt said under his breath. "The largest FBI office outside of FBI Headquarters in D.C. is in here. Just thinking about it gives me goosebumps. It's going to be payback big time for Ruby Ridge."

"I just wish there were more ATF agents here," Steve said. "Then we'd be avenging Waco and the Branch Davidians at the same time."

"The government's going to get the message," Curt said. "Have no fear about that."

"Are you really sure Yuri is going to come through?" Steve asked.

Curt pulled his friend to a stop for the second time. People skirted them.

"What is it with you?" Curt asked, keeping his voice low. "How come all this negativity all of a sudden?"

"Hey, I'm just asking," Steve said. "After all, the guy's kind of a kook. You've admitted that yourself. And he was a Commie."

"He's no Commie now," Curt said.

"Do tigers change their stripes?" Steve asked. "He's been saying some weird things lately, like wanting the Soviet Union to get back together."

"That's just to be sure the nukes are safe," Curt said.

"I'm not so sure," Steve said. "What about that comment he made about Stalin not being as bad as people think? I mean, that's crazy. Stalin killed thirty million of his own people."

"That was weird," Curt admitted. He bit his lower lip. There were some loose screws in Yuri's brain, like Yuri not being content just to knock out the Jacob Javits Federal Building. He wanted to do a simultaneous laydown in Central Park so that the second agent would blow over the entire Upper East Side. His supposed rationale was to get as many Jewish bankers as possible. Curt thought that doing the fed building was more than enough, but Yuri had been adamant.

"We've made a lot of effort on his behalf," Steve continued. "We've had our boys steal those fermenters from the microbrewery over in New Jersey. We've been supplying him with all sorts of stuff. We got the Klan to send up those crazy boxes of dirt from Oklahoma which Yuri said would have the bacteria he needed in it. Those guys down in Dixie must think we've gone crazy asking for dirt from a cattleyard."

"Yuri said he could isolate the bacteria from it," Curt said. "I read the same thing on the Internet, so it's legitimate."

"Okay," Steve said. "So it's true that botulinum bacteria and anthrax bugs are in dirt, particularly in livestock areas in the South, but what do we have to show for it. Nothing! Yuri's not shown us anything. We've not seen any bacteria. We've not even seen this lab he's supposed to have built in his basement."

"You think he could be taking us for a ride?" Curt asked. The idea passed through his mind that Yuri might do his Central Park laydown and leave them high and dry.

"Anything's possible when you're dealing with a foreigner," Steve said. "Especially a Russian. They've hated our guts for seventy years."

"Ah, I think you're being paranoid," Curt said with a wave of his free hand. "Yuri is not mad at us. And I know he wants to hit this fed building. He's pissed at our government just like we are. They've refused to acknowledge his education. After all the years of schooling he's had, he's still driving a cab. Hell, I'd be pissed, too."

"But we don't know he's had all the schooling he says he's had," Steve said.

"That's true," Curt said. There had been no way to check.

"Maybe this isn't the time to be talking about all this," Steve said. "But now that we're on the brink of putting ourselves at risk going into this building when we are not supposed to, I wish we had more to go on to prove Yuri's doing his part."

"Do you think there's a chance Yuri didn't work in the Soviet bioweapons industry?" Curt asked.

"I think he did," Steve said. "He knows too much about it to be making it up, especially the personal stories like about his mother's death. But what I've been asking myself is why the CIA wasn't more interested in him when he got to the U.S. Maybe all he did was mop the floor instead of working on the production line like he's told us."

"It was because he got to the U.S. too late," Curt said. "Remember he told us about those two bioweapons big shots who'd defected a couple of years before he got here. Apparently they told the CIA all they wanted to know, including how much the Soviet Union had violated the 1972 bioweapons treaty."

"All I'm saying is I'd like to see some proof of what Yuri's doing," Steve said. "Anything."

"Last week he said he was close to testing the anthrax," Curt said.

"I'd settle for that," Steve said. "Provided the test works."

"You've got a good point," Curt admitted. "But I still think we should go ahead with this site visit. We're not risking anything, especially with the captain out."

"I guess you're right," Steve said. "Especially with that violation notice you found."

"So, you're game?"

"I'm game," Steve said.

The two men entered by way of the revolving door. They had to wait in line to go through the metal detector. Once through, they were directed to the maintenance office by the head of the security detail.

"So far so good," Steve whispered.

"Relax," Curt said. "This is going to be a breeze."

The maintenance door was ajar. Curt preceded Steve and presented himself in front of a secretary's desk. The office was busy with people answering phones and typing into word processors.

"Can I help you?" the secretary asked. She was a heavyset woman who was perspiring despite the air-conditioning.

Curt opened his wallet and showed his lieutenant's fire department badge. The only time he wore the badge was with a black ribbon at funerals when he dressed in his class A uniform.

"Fire inspection," Curt said.

"Of course," the secretary said. "Let me get the chief engineer."

She disappeared into an inner office.

Curt looked at Steve. "Piece of cake."

"Can you feel the amount of air movement in here?" Steve asked.

"I do," Curt said.

Steve gave him the thumbs-up. Curt nodded. He knew what Steve was thinking. The more the air moved around inside the building, the more efficiently the agent would be spread.

The chief engineer appeared a few moments later. He was a middle-aged African-American, dressed in a dark suit, white shirt, and tie. Curt was taken aback. He expected coveralls and grease stains. Curt glanced briefly at Steve to see if he was equally surprised. If he was, he didn't show it.

"My name is David Wilson. What can I do for you gentlemen? I'm surprised you are here. There was no fire inspection scheduled for today." David's tone was not confrontational, just questioning.

"That's correct, sir," Curt said. "This is a nonscheduled visit to check up on the violation noted on the last inspection involving the grill downstairs. But as long as we're here, we'd like to run down the normal list and check the stand pipes, extinguishers, sprinklers, hoses, smoke detectors . . . you know, the usual."

"The Ansul unit was installed immediately," David said. "We sent the paperwork to the fire department directly."

"We'd like to check the unit itself," Curt said. "Just to be on the safe side."

"Will it be all right if I send one of my maintenance workers with you?" David asked. "I'm in the middle of a meeting."

"That would be fine," Curt said agreeably.

Five minutes later Curt and Steve were accompanied by a tall, thin, taciturn individual who was dressed in the coveralls Curt had expected to see on David Wilson. The maintenance man's name was Reggy Sims. He was an electrician's assistant.

The first thing they checked was the grill in the sandwich kiosk on the ground floor. It was full of sizzling franks and burgers, since the noontime lunch rush was about to begin. It took about two seconds for Curt to declare that the Ansul unit was fine.

For the general inspection Curt and Steve just went through the motions, and they certainly didn't try to see everything. If the maintenance man was suspicious, he didn't show it in the slightest. Nor was he in any hurry to get back to his shop.

"What about the HVAC system?" Curt asked.

"What about it?" Reggy questioned.

"We should take a look at it," Curt said. "We've got to know how to turn it off or at least isolate areas if need be. If there was a fire, we wouldn't want to spread the smoke all over kingdom come. Where's the main control console?"

"It's in the machinery spaces on the third floor," Reggy said.

"How about the main air induction. Where's that?"

"Same place," Reggy said.

"Good," Curt said. "Let's take a look at it."

"How come?" Reggy asked.

"There's supposed to be smoke detectors both for the new air coming in and the recirculated air," Curt explained. "We've got to at least eyeball them. Actually, we're supposed to give them a test."

Reggy shrugged and led the way.

The noise level in the machinery spaces was horrendous. It was a huge room that was filled with all manner of equipment, including massive electrical panels, huge boilers, compressors, and pumps. A bewildering array of pipes, ducts, and conduits angled off in all directions. Few people ever paused to think of what it took to warm and cool a building the size of the Jacob Javits Federal Building or for the elevators to function or even for water to come out of a faucet on the thirty-second floor. It all required a lot of power and machinery, and it ran twenty-four hours a day.

The main air ducts were so large they didn't look like ducts. They ran along one wall of the oversized room before branching off like a large, felled tree. At intervals there were hatch-like doors that were dogged like those on a ship.

Reggy had to shout to be heard. He pounded the side of one of the ducts and yelled that it contained the fresh air being pulled in from outside. He showed where it mixed with recirculated air.

Reggy walked along the duct, then pounded it again. "Here's where the filters are located," he yelled. "What part of the duct do you want to see?"

"The part downstream from the filters," Curt yelled back.

Reggy nodded. He walked over to a huge circuit breaker switch and threw it. A portion of the cacophony of machinery noise in the room wound down.

"That's the switch to the main circulating fan," Reggy explained. Then he walked over to one of the hatch-like doors and undogged it. It opened into the room on creaky hinges.

"We're upstream of the main circulating fan," Reggy said.

"When it's running you can't open this door. There's too much suction."

Curt moved to the door and glanced into its dark interior. He slipped his flashlight from its holder on his belt and turned it on. First he directed the beam back at the filters. Steve tried to see over his shoulder, but the door was too narrow.

"Step inside if you'd like," Reggy suggested.

Curt ducked down and stepped over the lip. He shined the light back at the filter. Steve leaned in from the doorway. Reggy went over to the HVAC console to turn off the alarm announcing a fall in the system's pressure.

"See what I mean about the need to reconnoiter," Curt said. The insulated duct shielded most of the noise coming from the machinery room.

"I forgot about filters," Steve admitted.

Curt swept the light in the opposite direction. The huge blades of the main circulating fan were still slowly revolving. Angling the light up to the ceiling, Curt found the smoke detector. He'd need a ladder to test it.

"That's the one we'll want to go off," he said. "We'll have to find an accessible air return on this floor for one of the troops to set off a smoke bomb."

"You think there's a specific designator for this smoke detector on the fire control annunciator panel?" Steve asked.

"I'll be surprised if there isn't," Curt said. "And even if there isn't, the panel will tell us the activated smoke detector is in the HVAC system. One way or the other you and I will have a reason to come in here."

"Provided we beat Engine Company Number 6 from Beekman Street," Steve said.

"There's no way they could get here before us," Curt said. "Engine Number 6 has to come from the other side of City Hall. We'll be in this duct before they even reach the scene. If we have to worry about anybody, it's our own ladder company. We just have to be sure they keep themselves busy getting all the elevators down to the ground floor like they're supposed to."

"So what do we do when we get in here?" Steve asked. "Where do we put the stuff?" He glanced around at the floor of the duct. There was no place to hide anything.

"Yuri says it will be in the form of a fine powder in impervious plastic bags. We'll just place them in here and set the little timed detonators. When they go off, we'll be long gone."

"You don't think we have to hide the bags?"

"I don't see why," Curt said.

"What if someone comes in here after we leave?" Steve asked.

"Did you hear the hinges on the door when Reggy opened it?" Curt asked. "Nobody comes in here. Just to be sure we'll disarm the smoke detector as well as turn off the fire control system."

"That's a good idea," Steve said. He shrugged. "I guess it's going to work."

"Bet your ass it's going to work," Curt said. "Come on! Let's locate a good air return on this floor and then finish our sham fire inspection. We should be getting back to the station."

Finding an appropriate air return was easy. After leaving the machinery room, Curt had asked for the closest men's room. While Reggy waited outside, Curt and Steve found a convenient grate that would be easily removable. They imagined the duct was a straight shot back to the smoke detector they'd just seen.

"All one of our guys has to do is pop this grate off and toss in a smoke bomb," Curt said. "That will set off the alarm for sure."

A half hour later Curt and Steve recrossed the plaza in front of the federal building. The sun had gone in behind a bank of clouds, and gusts of wind were buffeting the local pigeons. Curt had to keep a tight grip on his clipboard to prevent the papers from blowing off. The two men climbed into their official car that they'd parked by the curb.

Curt started the engine and pulled out into the traffic. "Have you made any more progress on our route of retreat?" he asked. The way they'd divided up the planning was for Curt to concentrate on the event itself while Steve worked on their escape.

"It's done," Steve said. "I've been on the Internet every night for hours. I've got safe houses arranged for us all the way to Washington State and then up into Canada if need be. Every one of the militias I've contacted has been more than willing to help."

"Have they been curious about what's going down?" Curt asked.

"That's an understatement," Steve said. "But I haven't told them anything other than it's going to be big."

"It's going to be like *The Turner Diaries* coming true," Curt chortled. He was referring to his favorite novel, one widely circulated among the violent far right. In it the protagonist, Turner, started a general rebellion by bombing the FBI Headquarters in Washington, D.C.

Curt was feeling euphoric over his luck in having a weapon of mass destruction dropped into his lap. Now he finally had the power to strike back appropriately and dramatically at the government. Those Zionist bastards in Washington were going to learn the hard way that they shouldn't make war on their own citizens with the FBI and the ATF à la Ruby Ridge and Waco, nor should they conspire to take away people's cherished rights such as the right to bear arms, nor should they have backed abortion, gay rights, or affirmative action, or tolerated miscegenation. On top of all that was the illegality of the IRS and support for the United Nations. The list was almost endless.

Curt shook his head when he thought how far the government had wandered from its constitutional mandate. It deserved what was coming. Of course there were going to be civilian casualties. But that couldn't be avoided. After all, there had even been civilian casualties in the American Revolution. Like the "shot heard around the world," Operation Wolverine was going to be momentous, and if it succeeded in ushering in the new "Fifth Era" the way the Battle of Bunker Hill augered the birth of a new government, he realized he would probably be considered a kind of modern-day George Washington. It was all almost too heady to contemplate.

"A general revolt could start before we reach the West Coast," Steve said. "All the militias are waiting for some sign to start coordinated action. Even if only half the people Yuri expects die with Operation Wolverine, this could be it."

"I was just thinking along the same lines," Curt said. A self-satisfied smile spread across his face as he imagined how he'd be lionized on the far right's Internet bulletin boards.

"If there is a general uprising," Steve continued, "I think we should hole up in Michigan. From what I've learned the militias there are the most organized. It would be the safest place."

"How have you planned for us to get out of the city?" Curt asked.

"By a PATH train from the World Trade Center," Steve explained. "As soon as we get back to the station after we've planted the stuff we quit. We walk into the captain's office and say *sayonara*."

"He's going to blow his top," Curt said. He'd not heard about this part of the plan and hadn't given it much thought.

"It can't be helped," Steve said. "We have to get out of the city, particularly after Yuri does his laydown, which he says he's going to do at the same time we do ours. I don't feel as confident as he does that it's just going to blow over the Upper East Side."

"That's a good point," Curt said. "But why don't we just disappear? Why say anything to anybody?"

"Because that would cause too much attention," Steve explained. "They'd be looking for us right away, maybe even worried we'd been the victims of foul play. Yuri says that using a bioweapon gives a two- to five-day delay until all hell breaks loose. I want us to be far away by then."

"I guess you're right," Curt conceded.

"We'll tell the captain we've had it with the bureaucracy and the lack of discipline. That won't be a lie. We've both been complaining how the department has been deteriorating."

"What if the captain says he's not going to accept our resignations?"

"What is he going to do?" Steve asked. "Put us in leg irons?"

"I guess not," Curt said. He still felt uncomfortable about

having to face an irate captain. "But maybe we should give this part some more thought."

"Fine by me," Steve said. "As long as we're on a PATH train to New Jersey ASAP, I don't really care what we tell anybody. I'm confident of our getaway. I've got an old pickup truck over there in a garage near the first stop. That's going to take us to the first safe house, in Pennsylvania. There I've arranged for another vehicle. In fact, we'll be using a different vehicle after each stop."

"I like that," Curt said.

Curt turned into the Duane Street firehouse and pulled the car to the side so it didn't block any of the gleaming red fire trucks. He and Steve locked eyes for a moment and gave each other a thumbs-up.

"Operation Wolverine is on track," Curt said.

"Armageddon here we come," Steve said.

As the two men alighted from the vehicle, Bob King, one of the latest recruits, looked up from polishing engine #7. "Hey, Lieutenant!" he called.

Curt gazed over at the rookie and raised his eyebrows.

"There was a cabbie in here a little while ago asking for you," Bob yelled. "He was a short, squat guy with an accent that sounded Russian."

Curt glanced at Steve. Steve stared back, aghast. Obviously he didn't like this news any better than Curt did. There'd been an understanding that Yuri was never supposed to come to the fire station. Their contact had been limited to phone calls and meetings at the White Pride bar.

"What did he want?" Curt asked hoarsely. He had to clear his throat. With an operation of this magnitude, slipups were unacceptable.

"He wants you to call him," Bob said. "He seemed disappointed you weren't here."

"What did you do to him?" another firefighter called out from behind the truck. "Forget to tip him?"

Laughter erupted from a group of four firemen playing cards near the juncture of the firehouse and the sidewalk. The overhead doors were open to the October afternoon.

"Did he leave his name or phone number?" Curt asked.

"Nope," Bob said. "He just said to have you call him. I thought you'd know who he was."

"I haven't the slightest idea," Curt said.

"Well, maybe he'll be back," Bob said.

Curt motioned for Steve to follow him. They climbed the stairs to the living quarters. Curt pushed into the men's room. Once inside, he checked the stalls and the shower to make sure they were alone.

"I don't like this," Curt spat in a forced whisper. "What the hell did he come here for?"

"I told you the guy was a kook," Steve said.

Curt paced back and forth like a caged animal. He had his mildly prognathous jaw clamped shut. He couldn't believe Yuri could have been so stupid.

"I'm worried the guy is a kind of a loose cannon," Steve said. "I think we have to have a talk with him. At the same time, I'd like to see some proof that he hasn't been taking us for a ride."

Curt nodded as he paced, then stopped. "All right," he said. "After work we'll go by his house in Brighton Beach. We'll talk some sense into him about security. Then we'll demand to see his lab and demand some proof he's doing what he says he's doing."

"Do you know his address?" Steve asked.

"Fifteen Oceanview Lane," Curt said.

FOUR

"Knock, knock," a voice called.

Both Jack and Chet looked up from their desks to see Agnes Finn, the head of the microbiology lab, standing in the doorway.

"I feel like this is *déjà vu*," Agnes said. "Unfortunately it's a kind of *vu* I don't like." She had a tentative smile on her usually dour face. Her statement was the closest Jack had ever heard her come to humor. She was clutching a piece of paper in her hand.

Jack knew instantly what *déjà vu* she was referring to. Three years previously, when he'd made the shocking diagnosis of plague in a curious infectious case, she'd made it a point to bring the confirming results personally.

"Don't tell me it was anthrax," Jack said.

Agnes pushed her bottle-bottom glasses higher on her nose and handed the sheet of paper to Jack. It was the result of a direct fluorescent antibody test on one of the mediastinal lymph nodes. In bold capital letters it said: POSITIVE FOR ANTHRAX.

"This is unbelievable," Jack said. He handed the sheet to Chet, who read it with equal disbelief.

"I thought you'd like to know as soon as possible," Agnes said.

"Absolutely," Jack said vaguely. His eyes were glazed. His mind was churning.

"What's the reliability of this test?" Chet asked.

"About a hundred percent," Agnes said. "It's very specific and the reagents aren't old. After all the exotic diseases Jack diagnosed on that flurry of infectious-diseases a couple of years ago, I've made sure we've kept up to speed for most anything. Of course, for final confirmation we've planted cultures."

"This illness spreads by spores," Jack said as if waking from a trance. "Are there any tests for the spores or do you just have to grow them out and then test for the bacteria?"

"There's a polymerase chain reaction or PCR test for the spores," Agnes said. "We don't do that in micro, but I'm sure Ted Lynch in the DNA lab could help you. Do you have something you want to test for spores?"

"Not yet," Jack said.

"Uh oh," Chet moaned. "I don't like the sound of that. You're not planning on going out in the field, are you?"

"I don't know," Jack admitted. He was still in a daze. A case of inhalational anthrax in New York was as unexpected as plague.

"Have you forgotten what happened to you last time you got involved with infectious-disease field work?" Chet asked. "Let me remind you: you were almost killed."

"Thanks, Agnes," Jack said to the micro department head. He ignored Chet. He turned back to his desk and pushed away the files relating to the prisoner-in-custody death which Calvin wanted completed ASAP. Jack slipped the contents of Jason Papparis's file from the folder and thumbed through the papers until he came across Janice Jaeger's forensic investigator's report.

"Hey, I'm talking to you," Chet said. It always irked him the way Jack could tune him out.

"Here it is," Jack said. He held out Janice's report with his finger pointing to the sentence that said that Mr. Papparis was in the rug business. "Look!"

"I see it," Chet said with annoyance. "But did you hear me?"

"The problem is we don't know what kind of rugs," Jack said. "I think that could be important." Jack turned the report over. Just as Janice had said, there was the name and phone number of the house doctor who'd taken care of Mr. Papparis.

Jack spun around and picked up his phone. He dialed the number and got the central switchboard of the Bronx General Hospital.

"Fine," Chet said with a wave of dismissal. "You don't have to listen to me. Hell, I know that you'll just do whatever you want no matter what anybody else says." Disgusted, Chet turned back to his own work.

"Could you page Dr. Kevin Fowler for me?" Jack asked the hospital operator. While he waited he held the phone in the crook of his neck so he could lift down his copy of *Harrison's Principles of Internal Medicine*. The pages of the chapter on infectious diseases were dog-eared.

Jack turned to the section on anthrax. There were only two pages devoted to it. He was almost through reading when Dr. Kevin Fowler came on the line.

Jack explained who he was and why he was calling. Dr. Fowler was dumbfounded at the diagnosis.

"I've never seen a case of anthrax," Dr. Fowler admitted. "Of course, I'm only a resident, so I haven't had much experience."

"Now you're a member of a select group," Jack said. "I was just reading there's only been a handful of cases over the last decade here in the U.S., and all of those were the more common cutaneous form. The inhalational variety like Mr. Papparis had used to be called woolsorters' disease. The patients contracted it from contaminated animal hair and hides."

"I can tell you it was an extremely rapid downhill course," Dr. Fowler said. "I won't mind if I never have to take care of another case. I guess we get to see everything here in New York."

"Did you do a history on the patient?" Jack asked.

"No, not at all," Dr. Fowler said. "I was just called when the patient got into respiratory distress. All I knew about the history was what was in the chart."

"So you don't know what kind of rug business the patient was in?"

"I haven't the faintest idea," Dr. Fowler said. "Why don't you try the attending physician, Dr. Heitman."

"Have you got a telephone number for him?" Jack asked.

"Sure," Dr. Fowler said. "He's one of our staff attendings."

Jack placed a call to Dr. Heitman but learned that he had been merely covering for Dr. Bernard Goldstein and that Mr. Jason Papparis was actually Dr. Goldstein's patient. Jack then called Dr. Goldstein. It took a few minutes to get the doctor on the line, and he was less than friendly and rather impatient. Jack wasted no time in asking his question.

"What do you mean what kind of rug business?" Dr. Goldstein asked irritably. He obviously didn't like being interrupted in the middle of his day for what sounded to him like a frivolous inquiry. His secretary had been hesitant to bother the doctor even after Jack said that the call was an emergency.

"I want to know what kind of rugs he sold," Jack said. "Did he sell broadloom or something else?"

"He never said and I never asked," Dr. Goldstein said. Then he hung up.

"He's in the wrong profession," Jack said out loud. Jack found the identification sheet in Papparis's folder and saw that the body had been identified by the decedent's wife, Helen Papparis. There was a phone number on the sheet and Jack dialed it. He'd been hoping to avoid intruding on the family.

Helen Papparis turned out to be exquisitely polite and restrained. If she was in mourning, she hid it well, although Jack suspected her extreme politeness was her method of dealing with her loss. After Jack offered his sympathies and explained his official position as well as the nature of the exotic diagnosis, he asked his question about Mr. Papparis's business.

"The Corinthian Rug Company dealt exclusively in hand-made rugs," Helen said.

"From where?" Jack asked.

"Mostly from Turkey," Helen said. Jack detected a catch in her voice. "A few of the fur rugs came from Greece, but the vast majority came from Turkey."

"So he dealt with furs and hides as well as woven rugs," Jack said with academic satisfaction. The mystery was rapidly being resolved.

"That's correct," Helen said.

Jack's eyes dropped to the open textbook in front of him. Right in the middle of the anthrax section it described how the animal form of anthrax was a problem in a number of countries, including Turkey, and that animal products, particularly goat's hair, could be contaminated with the spores.

"Did he deal with goatskins?" Jack asked.

"Yes, of course," Helen said. "Sheepskins and goatskins were a large part of his business."

"Well, I think we've solved the mystery," Jack said. He explained the association to Helen.

"That's ironic," Helen said without a hint of rancor. "Those rugs have provided us with a comfortable life, including sending our only daughter to an Ivy League college."

"Did Mr. Papparis get any recent shipments?" Jack asked.

"About a month ago."

"Are any of those rugs in your home?"

"No," Helen said. "Jason felt it was enough to deal with them during the day. He refused to have any of them around the house."

"Under the circumstances that was a smart decision," Jack said. "Where are these rugs? Have many been sold?"

Helen explained that the rugs had gone into a warehouse in Queens, and she doubted many had been sold. She explained to Jack that Jason's business was wholesale and that shipments came in months before they were needed. She also said there no employees at the warehouse or at the office.

"Sounds like a one-man operation," Jack said.

"Very much so," Helen said.

Jack thanked her profusely and reiterated his sympathies.

Then he suggested that she contact her doctor about possible prophylactic antibiotics even though he explained that she was probably not at risk since person-to-person spread did not occur and she hadn't been exposed to the hides. Finally he told her she'd probably be hearing from other Department of Health professionals. She thanked him for the call, and they disconnected.

Jack swung around to face Chet, who couldn't have helped but overhear the conversation.

"Sounds like you solved that one pretty quickly," Chet said. "At least now you don't have to put your life at risk by going out there in the field."

"I'm disappointed," Jack said with a sigh.

"What can you possibly be disappointed about?" Chet asked with exasperated disbelief. "You've made a brilliant and rapid diagnosis and you've even solved what could have been a difficult epidemiological enigma."

"That's the problem," Jack said dispiritedly. "It was too easy, too pat. With my last exotic disease it was a real mystery. I like challenges."

"I don't know what you're complaining about," Chet said. "I wish some of my cases would have such nice tidy endings."

Jack grabbed his open textbook of medicine and stuck it under Chet's nose. He pointed to a specific paragraph and told his officemate to read it. Chet did as he was told. When he was finished, he looked up.

"Now *that* was an epidemiological challenge," Jack said. "Can you imagine? A slew of inhalation anthrax cases from spores leaking out of a bioweapons factory! What a disaster!"

"Where's Sverdlovsk?" Chet asked.

"How should I know?" Jack commented. "Obviously someplace in the former Soviet Union."

"I'd never heard about that 1979 incident," Chet said. He reread the paragraph. "What a joke! The Russians tried to pass it off as exposure to contaminated meat."

"From a forensic point of view, it would have been a fascinating case," Jack said. "Certainly a lot more provocative than picking up a case in a rug salesman."

Jack got to his feet. After appearing so animated earlier, he now looked depressed.

"Where are you going?" Chet asked.

"Down to see Calvin," Jack said. "He told me that if my case turned out to be anthrax he wanted to know right away."

"Cheer up!" Chet urged. "You look like death warmed over."

Jack tried to smile. He walked down to the elevator and pushed the button. What he didn't tell Chet was that his restless mood hadn't resulted only from the anthrax case's resolving itself so easily. It was also about the mystery with Laurie. Why had she called at 4:30 A.M. to make a dinner date? And why was Lou coming, too?

As the elevator descended, Jack tried to think how he could get back at her. The only idea that came to mind was to buy her a Christmas present over the next few days and then start giving her confusing hints. Laurie was always wildly curious about presents and the suspense ate at her. Two months of suspense would surely be adequate revenge.

Emerging on the first floor, Jack felt better. The Christmas present idea was sounding better and better, although now he'd have to think of something to buy.

Calvin was in his office working on the reams of paper that passed over his desk every day. His hand was so large that the way his fingers had to hold his pen looked comical. He glanced up when Jack approached the desk.

"Are you sure you don't want to bet on that anthrax diagnosis?" Jack asked.

"Don't tell me it was positive?" Calvin leaned back in his chair, and it protested loudly under his weight.

"According to Agnes it was anthrax," Jack said. "Cultures are pending."

"Holy crap!" Calvin exclaimed. "This is going to raise some hackles in the Department of Health."

"Actually I don't think that's the case," Jack said.

"Oh?" Calvin replied. Jack never failed to surprise him. "Why the hell not?"

"Because the disease does not spread person to person, and because it was an occupational exposure limited to the decedent. The source is apparently safely locked up in a warehouse in Queens."

"I'm all ears," Calvin said. "Talk to me!"

Jack explained the Corinthian Rug Company connection, and the recent shipment of rugs and goatskins from Turkey. Calvin nodded as Jack spoke.

"Thank the Lord for small favors," Calvin said. He tipped forward in his chair, and the workings again moaned in complaint. "I'll have Bingham call Patricia Markham, the Commissioner of Health. Why don't you phone the city epidemiologist: the one you worked with so closely concerning the plague case. What was his name?"

"Clint Abelard," Jack said.

"Yeah, that's the guy," Calvin said. "Give him a call. It will foster that cooperative interagency agenda the mayor's been harping on."

"Clint Abelard and I hardly worked closely," Jack said. "Back then when I tried to call him he wouldn't even talk to me on the phone."

"I'm sure he'll feel differently in light of what eventually transpired," Calvin said.

"Why not have someone else on our capable staff make the call?" Jack said. "Like one of the janitors."

"Hold the sarcasm," Calvin said. "Don't cause problems! Call the man! Case closed! Now, what about that prisoner death?"

"What do you mean, 'What about the prisoner death'?" Jack asked. "You saw the blood in the neck muscles and the broken hyoid bone. They had him in a deadly choke hold."

"What about his brain?" Calvin asked. "Did you find anything?"

"You mean like a temporal lobe tumor," Jack said. "So we could suggest he'd had a psychomotor seizure that turned him into a raving madman. Sorry! The brain was normal."

"Do me a favor and look at the histology carefully," Calvin said. "Find something!"

"This case is in the hands of our happy toxicologist," Jack said. "Maybe he'll come up with cocaine or something like that."

"I want the completed file including death certificate on my desk by Thursday," Calvin said. "I've already got a call from the attorney general's office."

"In that case it would help if you gave John DeVries a call," Jack said. "A request to the lab for a rapid result coming from the front office would have far more import than from a grunt like me."

"I'll call John," Calvin said. "But irrespective of what John comes up with, it's going to be your job to make sure there's something in the file that leaves the door open, even if only by a crack."

Jack rolled his eyes and headed for the door. He knew what Calvin was implying, namely that the police commissioner had impressed Bingham that the involved officers needed some justification for the deadly restraining force they'd used. Jack knew prisoners could be violent. Dealing with them was a job he did not envy. At the same time there had been episodes of abuse on the part of the police. Making judgments beyond the forensic facts was a slippery slope Jack refused to descend.

"Hold up!" Calvin called out before Jack was beyond earshot.

Jack leaned back in the deputy chief's office.

"There's someone else I want you to call about the anthrax case," Calvin said. "Stan Thornton. Do you know him?"

"Sure," Jack said.

Stan Thornton was the director of the Mayor's Office of Emergency Management. He'd been the featured speaker at one of the Thursday afternoon medical examiners' conferences organized in the spirit of interagency cooperation. The topic had been mortuary challenges in the event of a disaster associated with a weapon of mass destruction.

Jack had found the talk disturbing. Prior to the lecture he'd never seriously contemplated the logistics of dealing with a massive number of casualties. Just the problem of identification of thousands upon thousands of dead people was mindnumbing. On top of that was the dilemma of what to do with them.

"What would you like me to tell him?" Jack questioned.

"Tell him exactly what you told me," Calvin said. "Considering the case is a limited occupational exposure, it's more a courtesy call than anything else. But since anthrax came up in his discussion of bioterrorism, I'm sure he'd at least like to know about the incident."

"Why me?" Jack complained. "I'm not good at this professional courtesy stuff."

"You've got to learn," Calvin said. "Besides, it's your case. Now get out of here so I can get some work done."

Jack left the administration area, stopped on the second floor to get a sandwich out of a vending machine, then headed up to the fifth floor. Although he intended to return directly to his office, he couldn't resist sticking his head into Laurie's. His idea was to press her once more about the nature of the "big secret." Unfortunately she wasn't there. Dr. Riva Mehta, her officemate, told Jack that Laurie was closeted with the law enforcement officers in Bingham's office.

Grumbling under his breath about how his day was going, Jack plopped himself down in his desk chair.

"You look as bad as when you left," Chet said. "I hope you didn't provoke the deputy chief into some sort of argument."

Jack and Calvin were frequently at odds. Calvin believed in strict rules and set protocols. Jack viewed all regulations as guidelines. He believed that intelligence and native instincts were far more practical than bureaucratic edicts.

"It's a bad hair day," Jack said evasively. He scratched the top of his head and then cracked his knuckles while deciding which one of the unpleasant tasks he'd been assigned he should attack first. As he opened up his phone directory to look for Clint Abelard's number, an unpleasant idea occurred to him. Maybe Laurie had gotten a job offer someplace like Detroit, or worse yet, someplace on the West Coast. It made sense; if she were relocating, she'd certainly want to tell him and Lou, and since such a move would undoubtedly represent a promotion, she'd probably be excited about it. For a moment Jack stared into space while he tried to imagine what life in the Big Apple would be like without Laurie. It was difficult to contemplate; it was also depressing.

"Hey, I forgot to tell you about the show at the Met," Chet

said. "There's a Claude Monet exhibition that Colleen is dying to see. We got tickets for Thursday."

Chet had been dating Colleen Anderson on and off for three years. She was an art director for Willow and Heath, a Madison Avenue advertising firm. Jack was acquainted with both Colleen and Willow and Heath, having come into contact with them through the course of tracking the infectious-isease case that spawned his reputation.

"How about you and Laurie coming along to see the show?" Chet continued. "Then we could all go out to dinner afterward."

Jack cringed at the thought of not having Laurie around to join him for trips to the museum. And that would be nothing compared to how much he would miss seeing her every day. Not that Chet could have known the feelings that his invitation had provoked.

"I'll ask her," Jack said. He picked up the phone and dialed Clint Abelard's number.

"Let me know what she says," Chet added. "If it's a go, I'll have Colleen get extra tickets. As a member of the museum, she won't have any trouble."

"I'll be seeing Laurie tonight," Jack said as his call went through. "I have a number of things to talk to her about. I'll ask her then."

"Did you see that skinhead case she was doing this morning?" Chet questioned. "Talk about gruesome; that one deserves a prize. It's sickening what one human can do to another."

Jack asked for the city epidemiologist and was put on hold.

"Unfortunately I did see it," Jack said. He covered the phone's mouthpiece with his hand. "The FBI agent thought that the perpetrators were fellow skinheads."

"Those kids are nuts," Chet said.

"Do you know if Laurie found anything that was helpful for the police?" Jack asked.

"I've no idea," Chet said.

When Dr. Clint Abelard finally came on the line, Jack made an effort to be friendly and upbeat. Unfortunately, his overture was not reciprocated.

"Of course I remember you," Clint said dryly. "How could I forget? Thank God it's not every day a coroner makes my job harder."

Jack bit his tongue. In the past, when Jack had first met Clint, Jack had carefully explained the difference between a coroner and a medical examiner. As a medical examiner, Jack was a physician with training in pathology and training in a subspecialty, forensics. In contrast, a coroner could be merely a bureaucratic appointee with no medical training whatsoever.

"We medical examiners always aim to please," Jack said.

"Why are you calling me?" Clint asked.

"We had a case of inhalational anthrax this morning," Jack said. "We thought you'd like to know. The patient was brought in from the Bronx General Hospital."

"Just one case?"

"That's right," Jack said.

"Thank you," Clint said.

"Aren't you going to ask anything about its origins?" Jack asked.

"Finding out its origins is our job," Clint said flatly.

"That might be so," Jack said. "But just for the record, let me tell you what we've learned."

Jack went on to explain about the Corinthian Rug Company, about how a recent shipment of Turkish rugs and hides was locked up in the warehouse in Queens, that Jason Papparis was the only employee, and that he'd never taken any of the rugs home.

"Thank you," Clint said without emotion. "You're so very astute. If I have any epidemiological mysteries, I'll be sure to give you a call for your assistance."

"If you don't mind my asking," Jack said, ignoring Clint's sarcasm, "I'd like to know what you plan to do about this current anthrax episode?"

"I'll have one of my assistants go out to Queens and seal the warehouse," Clint said.

"Is that all?" Jack questioned.

"We've got a major cyclospora outbreak that's taxing our manpower at the moment," Clint said. "One case of a containable occupational illness doesn't constitute an epidemiological emergency. We'll get to it when we can, provided, of course, there are no more cases."

"I suppose you know your business," Jack said, "but it's my feeling . . ."

"Thank you for your vote of confidence," Clint interrupted. Then, without warning, he hung up.

Jack replaced the receiver. "Hell's bells," he said to Chet, who'd twisted around in his chair as the conversation progressed. "So much for intra-agency cooperation. That guy's more sarcastic than I am."

"You must have mortally wounded his ego when you dealt with him during that plague episode," Chet said.

"Well, let's see if I have any better luck with the director of the Mayor's Office of Emergency Management," Jack said.

"Why on earth are you calling him?" Chet asked.

"It's a courtesy call," Jack said. "Strict orders from our deputy chief."

A secretary answered, and Jack asked for Stan Thornton.

"Is that the guy who lectured to us on weapons of mass destruction?" Chet asked.

Jack nodded. To his surprise the director himself came on the line immediately. Jack explained who he was and why he was calling.

"Anthrax!" Stan exclaimed. It was obvious the man was impressed. In sharp contrast to Clint Abelard, he bombarded Jack with questions. Only after he learned that the probable cause was contained and that there was only one case did his voice lose its urgency.

"Just to be on the safe side," Stan said, "I'll use my contacts with the Department of Health to make sure there are no other inpatients in the city with suspicious symptoms."

"Good idea," Jack said.

"And I'll have that warehouse quarantined," Stan added.

"That's already in the works," Jack said. He related to Stan his conversation with Clint Abelard.

"Perfect!" Stan said. "Clint Abelard would have been high on my list to contact. I'll coordinate with him."

Good luck! Jack thought to himself.

"Thanks for your quick response," Stan continued. "As I

mentioned in my lecture, you medical people might be the first to see the effects of a bioterrorism event. The faster the response, the higher the possibility the event could be contained."

"We'll certainly keep that in mind," Jack said before winding up the conversation and hanging up.

"Congratulations," Chet said. "That was a very civilized conversation."

"My intra-agency diplomatic skills must be improving," Jack quipped. "I didn't irritate the guy in the slightest."

Jack gathered up the papers from Jason Papparis's file and stuffed them into the folder. He pushed it aside and redirected his attention to the prisoner-in-custody case.

For a few minutes, peace reigned in the cluttered office. The two medical examiners bent over their respective desks and went back to work. Chet glued his eyes to his microscope while he diligently scanned a section of liver from a case of fatal hepatitis. Jack began to outline the significant pathology on the prisoner case.

Unfortunately, the tranquillity didn't last long. A sound similar to a gunshot reverberated around the tiny room. Chet sat bolt upright. Jack uttered a string of expletives, making Chet even more anxious. But then Chet realized that they weren't in jeopardy of becoming their office's next two cases. The sudden noise had come from Jack's slamming his ballpoint pen down onto the desk's metal surface.

"Damn! You scared the hell out of me," Chet complained.

"I can't concentrate," Jack said.

"What's the matter now?"

"A lot of things," Jack said vaguely. He didn't want to get into a discussion about Laurie.

"That's not being very specific," Chet said.

Jack reached over and retrieved Jason Papparis's folder. "This case, for one."

"What could bother you now?" Chet questioned irritably. "You made the diagnosis, reported it to the deputy chief, called the city epidemiologist, and even the Director of Emergency Management. What the hell else can you do?"

Jack sighed. "Like I said before, it's too pat. It's like it was designed to go into a textbook, and it's bothering me."

"Bull!" Chet said. "Sounds to me like you're using it as an excuse. What else is on your mind?"

Jack blinked and eyed his officemate. Jack was impressed with Chet's clairvoyance. For a fleeting moment Jack considered telling Chet about Laurie's early-morning phone call, but then decided against it. Such a conversation might lead to questions about Jack's true feelings about Laurie, an issue Jack wasn't ready to probe, even on his own.

"There is something else," Jack said. His face fell into an exaggerated expression of emotional anguish. "I'm upset that *Seinfeld* is off the air."

"Oh, for crissake," Chet said disgustedly. "It's impossible to have a discussion with you. Fine! Stew by yourself, but at least do me the favor of doing it quietly or, if that's impossible, go someplace else!"

Chet swung around once again and replaced the slide on his microscope stage with another. He leaned over the eyepieces while mumbling under his breath how trying Jack could be.

"Clint Abelard said he'd see that the Corinthian Rug Company's warehouse was quarantined," Jack said. He poked Chet's shoulder with the corner of Jason Papparis's folder to make sure Chet was listening. "What about the office here in Manhattan? What if the rug merchant brought some of the hides to the office? And what about the advisability of going through the company's records to see if any of the recent shipment had been sold and shipped elsewhere?"

Chet swung back around. He examined his officemate's broad face and saw that he was being serious.

"What do you want me to say?" Chet asked.

"I want you to confirm my concerns," Jack said.

"Fine," Chet said. "You're right! So do something about it! Call back the epidemiologist and make sure he's thought of these issues! Get it off your chest. Then you and I can get some work done."

Jack eyed his phone, then looked back at Chet. "You really think so? He's not a fan of mine and he's not what you'd call receptive to suggestions, especially my suggestions."

"So what if the guy is a nerd?" Chet said. "At least you'll

have the satisfaction of having done everything you could possibly do. What do you care what he thinks of you?"

"I suppose you're right," Jack said as he reached for the
phone. "I can't expect everybody to love me like I do."

Jack called back the city epidemiologist. The secretary
asked for Jack's name, then put him on hold. Jack waited for
several minutes. He looked up at Chet.

"So the guy's being a little passive-aggressive," Chet said.
"Hang in there."

Jack nodded. He drew interlocking circles on his scratch
pad, then drummed his fingers on the desktop. Finally the secretary came back on the line.

"I'm sorry but the doctor is busy," she said. "You'll have
to call back."

Jack hung up. "I suppose I shouldn't be surprised. I just
love this intra-agency cooperation crap."

"Send him a fax," Chet suggested. "It will accomplish the
same thing without the aggravation of having to talk with
him."

"I've got a better idea," Jack said. He got out the identification sheet and retrieved Helen Papparis's phone number. He
then put in a second call to the rug dealer's bereaved wife.

"I'm sorry to bother you again," Jack said after identifying
himself.

"It's no bother," Helen said. She was as gracious as she'd
been on the first call.

"I wanted to ask if you'd heard from any of the city public
health people," Jack said.

"Yes, I have," Helen answered. "A Dr. Abelard called soon
after I spoke with you."

"I'm glad," Jack said. "Could I ask what he said?"

"He was very businesslike," Helen said. "He wanted the
address and the keys for the warehouse. Then he made arrangements for the local police to come by and get them."

"Excellent," Jack said. "What about the office in Manhattan? Did Dr. Abelard ask you about that?"

"Nothing was said about the office."

"I see," Jack said. He glanced at Chet, who shrugged. Jack
thought for a moment and then added: "I'd like to take a look

inside the office myself. Would you have a problem with that?"

Chet started waving his hands and silently but emphatically mouthing the word *no* over and over again. Jack ignored him.

"If you think it would help in any way," Helen said. "It's certainly all right by me."

Jack explained to the woman what he'd said to Chet, particularly about checking to see if any of the recent shipment had been sold and sent out. Helen understood immediately.

"Perhaps I can come up and get the keys," Jack suggested.

"That won't be necessary," Helen said. "The address is Twenty-seven Walker Street, and there is a stamp collecting firm right next door. The proprietor's name is Hyman Feingold. He was a friend of my husband. They had keys for each other's shops in case of an emergency. I can give him a call so that he is expecting you."

"That's perfect," Jack said. "Meanwhile, have you spoken with your physician?"

"I did," Helen said. "He's sending over some antibiotics. He's also recommended I get vaccinated."

"I think that is a good idea," Jack said.

After disconnecting, Jack stood up and got his bomber jacket from behind the door.

"Aren't you going to ask my opinion about this proposed field trip?" Chet asked.

"Nope," Jack said. "I already know your opinion. But I'm going just the same. I can't concentrate, so I might as well do something useful. Besides, now you'll be able to get some work done. Hold the fort, sport!"

Chet waved with an expression of irritated resignation. He thought it was crazy for Jack to go running out on a site visit, but from past experience he knew better than to try to change Jack's mind once it had been made up.

Whistling a merry tune, Jack took the stairs down to the third floor and ducked into the microbiology lab. Anticipating his bike ride downtown, he began to feel better than he had all day.

Agnes Finn wasn't available, so Jack spoke with the shift

supervisor. She was more than happy to supply him with a bag of culture tubes, latex gloves, micropore masks, an isolation gown, and a hood. Jack knew that a biological isolation suit would have been safer, but he felt it wasn't necessary. It also wouldn't be immediately available, and Jack didn't want to wait. And besides, he was still convinced that in all likelihood Mr. Jason Papparis had gotten his illness at his warehouse, not at his office.

With his supplies in hand Jack went down to the basement area and unlocked his bike. But instead of heading directly downtown, he rode over to the University Hospital. As a firm believer in the old adage "an ounce of prevention is worth a pound of cure," he'd decided it would be wise to take some prophylactic antibiotics.

The ride downtown was exhilarating and transpired almost without incident. Jack went south on Second Avenue, then cut west on Houston. He then used Broadway to get to Walker. On Broadway he had a minor run-in with the driver of a delivery van. But only a few heated words were exchanged before the van sped off.

Jack locked his bike to a "No Parking" sign just west of the Corinthian Rug Company office. He walked to the store's front window and gazed at the rugs and hides on display. There were only a handful, and all were bleached from sunlight and covered with a fine layer of dust, suggesting they'd not been moved in years. Jack was certain they'd not come from the new shipment.

Cupping his hands around his face, Jack peered into the office. It was sparsely furnished. There were two desks. One was functional as a desk with the usual accoutrements; the other supported a copy machine and a fax. There were several upright file cabinets. In the rear were two interior doors. Both were closed.

Jack walked to the door. The gold stenciling glittered against the darkened interior. Jack tried the door. It was locked, as he expected.

The stamp shop was just west of the rug shop, and Jack went there directly. The bells on the entrance door surprised him with their harsh jangle and made him realize he was tense.

A customer was seated, poring over a collection of stamps in glassine envelopes.

A man whom Jack took to be the proprietor stood behind the counter. As soon as he looked up, Jack introduced himself.

"Ah, Dr. Stapleton," Hyman said softly, as if the spoken word were somehow irreverent in the philatelic peacefulness. He motioned for Jack to step to the side.

"It's a terrible tragedy what happened to Mr. Papparis," Hyman whispered. He handed Jack a set of keys on a ring. "Do you think there is any reason for me to be alarmed?"

"No," Jack whispered. "Unless Mr. Papparis made it a habit to show you his merchandise."

Hyman shook his head.

"Did Mr. Papparis ever bring any of his rugs and hides to his office? I mean, other than the ones in his window."

"Not lately," Hyman said. "He used to bring in samples years ago when he'd go out on the road. But he didn't have to do that anymore."

Jack held up the keys. "Thanks for your help. I'll have these back to you in short order."

"Take your time," Hyman said. "I'm glad you're checking things out."

Jack went back out to his bike and got his supplies out of his basket. He then went to the door of the rug office and unlocked it. Before he opened it he put on the gown, the hood, the gloves, and the mask. A few of the passersby altered their pace ever so slightly when they caught a glimpse of Jack's preparations. Jack considered their indifference a tribute to the equanimity of New Yorkers.

Jack pushed open the door and stepped over the threshold. He felt the hackles on the back of his neck rise. There was something unnervingly sinister about the possibility that some of the motes dancing in the ray of light spilling in from the street could be lethal. For a second he considered backing out and leaving the job to others. Then he chided himself for what he called medieval superstition. He was, after all, reasonably protected.

The office was as spartan as it had appeared through the window. The only decoration was a series of travel posters of the Greek Islands put out by Olympic Airlines. A large wall calendar also had scenes of Greece. Although the hides and rugs in the window were dusty, the rest of the office was spotless and smelled slightly of cleanser. At Jack's feet were a few letters and magazines that had evidently been shoved through the mail slot. Jack picked them up and moved over to the desk.

The surface of the desk had a blotter, a metal in-and-out basket, and several small imitation ancient Greek vases. The office was neat and devoid of clutter. Jack dutifully put the mail in the "in" basket.

Jack turned on the overhead lights. He took out his collection of culture tubes and swabbed various surfaces. As he swabbed the desk he noticed something glittering in the center of the blotter. Bending down he could see that it was a tiny, cerulean blue, iridescent star. It seemed strangely out of place in the austere environment.

Jack peered into the wastebasket. It was empty. He walked back to the closed doors. One led to a lavatory, where he swabbed the sink and the back of the toilet. The other door led to a corridor that communicated with the central stairhall of the building. Except for the few in the window, there were no other rugs or hides.

When Jack finished with the culture tubes, he took them into the bathroom and washed their exteriors before putting them back into the bag he'd brought them in. Finally, he approached the file cabinets. Now he wanted to find out all he could about the last incoming shipment of rugs and hides and whether any had been sent out.

FIVE

Yuri looked up into the face of the smug businessman as he carefully counted out single greenbacks into Yuri's waiting palm. Yuri had brought the individual all the way from La Guardia Airport to a posh East Side manse. During the entire trip, Yuri had had to endure yet another long lecture on America's virtues and its inevitable Cold War victory. This time the emphasis was on Ronald Reagan, and how he had singlehandedly vanquished the "Evil Empire." The man had correctly guessed Yuri's ethnic origins from a glance at Yuri's name on his taxi license. This had provoked his monologue on U.S. superiority on all fronts: moral, economic, political.

Yuri had not said a word throughout the interminable harangue although he'd been sorely tempted at several junctures. Some of the fare's statements had made his blood boil, particularly when he condescendingly voiced pity for the Russian people who he thought were burdened with feelings of insecurity from having to endure continual inept leadership.

"And here's a couple of extra dollars for your trouble," the

man said with a wink as he added to the pile in Yuri's hand.
Yuri was holding twenty-nine ragged, single dollar bills. The
fare on the meter plus the Triboro Bridge toll was twenty-
seven dollars and fifty cents.

"Is that supposed to be the tip?" Yuri asked with obvious
disdain.

"Is something the matter with it?" the man asked. He
straightened up. His eyebrows arched indignantly. He slipped
his briefcase out from under his arm and held it as if he might
be tempted to use it defensively.

Yuri took his right hand off the steering wheel and lifted
the final two bills from the pile. He then let them go so that
they wafted in short, intersecting arcs toward the pavement.

The man's expression changed from one of indignation to
one of anger. His cheeks empurpled.

"That's a donation to the American economy," Yuri said.
He then pressed on the accelerator and sped away. In his rearview mirror he saw the businessman bending down and re-
trieving the money from the gutter. The image gave Yuri a
modicum of satisfaction. It was heartening to see the man
stoop for such a paltry sum. He couldn't believe how cheap
some Americans were despite their ostentatious wealth.

Yuri's day had improved dramatically following the vain
attempt to see Curt Rogers and Steve Henderson at the firehouse on Duane Street. As a treat and mini-celebration of his
imminent return to *rodina,* he'd gone to a small Russian restaurant for a sit-down lunch with hot borscht and a glass of
vodka. A conversation in Russian with the owner added to the
experience even though speaking in his native tongue also
made him feel a touch melancholy.

After lunch the fares had been okay and steady. They'd
generally kept to themselves except for the last guy on the run
in from La Guardia Airport.

Yuri stopped at a light on Park Avenue. He was intending
to head over to Fifth in hopes of getting some of the upscale
hotel work. Instead, an older woman in a babushka stepped
between parked cars and raised her hand. When the light
changed Yuri pulled alongside and the woman climbed in.

"Where to?" Yuri asked while eyeing his new fare in the

rearview mirror. Her clothes were functional and, although not threadbare, at least well worn. She looked like someone who should have been using the subway.

"One-oh-seven West Tenth Street," the woman said with an accent heavier than Yuri's. He recognized it immediately. It was Estonian, which brought mixed memories.

They drove in silence for a while. For the first time all day Yuri was the one tempted to speak. He glanced frequently at his passenger. There was something about her that was familiar. She had settled herself comfortably with her large hands folded in her lap. Her relaxed, peasantlike features coupled with tiny, twinkling eyes and faintly smiling lips radiated an inner tranquillity.

"Are you Estonian?" Yuri finally asked.

"I am," the woman said. "Are you Russian?"

Yuri nodded and watched the woman's reaction. After years of occupation, there was a strong anti-Russian sentiment in Estonia. Yuri's feelings about Estonia weren't as negative as he feared this woman's might be about Russia. Although he'd had difficulties there during his odyssey to America, he'd also met some friendly, generous, and helpful people.

"How long have you been here?" the woman asked. Her voice was devoid of malice.

"Since 1994," Yuri said.

"Did you leave your motherland with your whole family?"

"No," Yuri managed. His throat had gone dry. "I came by myself."

"That must have been very difficult," the woman said empathetically. "And very lonely."

The woman's simple question and her reaction to Yuri's answer unleashed a flood of emotion in Yuri, including a strong sense of shame at having abandoned his family, although there'd been very little to leave behind. The *toska* he'd struggled with earlier returned with a vengeance. At the same time he realized why the woman looked familiar. She reminded Yuri of his own mother, even though their features were not at all similar. It was less the woman's appearance than her bearing, particularly her powerful serenity, that made Yuri think of his mother.

Yuri did not think often about her. It was much too painful.
Nadya Davydov had loved Yuri and his younger brother Yegor and, to the best of her abilities, had protected her sons
from the brutal beatings their father, Anatoly, gave them at
the slightest provocation. Yuri still had scars on the back of
his legs from a beating he got when he was eleven. He was
in the fourth grade at the time and had been recently inducted
into the Young Pioneers. Part of the uniform was a red scout-
like tie worn with a red flag pin containing a tiny portrait of
Lenin. Somehow Yuri had lost the pin on the way home from
school, and when Anatoly found out about it that night, he
went berserk. In a drunken stupor induced by his consumption
of nearly a liter of vodka, he'd beaten Yuri until Yuri's pants
were clotted with blood.

For the most part Nadya had been able to divert Anatoly's
nightly drunken bursts of violence onto herself. The usual scenario was for Nadya stoically to withstand a few blows along
with Anatoly's barbed ranting. Then she would stand defiantly
between her husband and her children, sometimes with blood
streaming down her face. Anatoly would continue to swear at
her and threaten more blows. When she wouldn't move or
even speak, he'd shake his fists at his kids and shout that if
they ever committed the same transgression that had stimu-
lated his outburst, he'd kill them. He'd then stagger off to pass
out on the only couch in the apartment. It was a scene that
repeated itself almost nightly until Yuri had reached the eighth
grade.

In 1970, on the eve of May 1st, the major Soviet holiday,
Anatoly drank more than double his usual quota of vodka. In
a particularly foul mood, he chased the rest of his family from
the apartment, locked the door, and then passed out. During
the night, while Nadya, Yuri, and Yegor slept as best as they
could on the benches in the communal kitchen, Anatoly as-
pirated his own vomit. In the morning he was found cold and
stiff with rigor mortis.

It was difficult for the family after Anatoly's death. They
were forced to move from their two-room second-floor apartment to a single room on the top floor of their tenement that
was freezing cold in the winter and boiling hot in the summer.

More problematic was the loss of Anatoly's income, although that difficulty was partially offset by significantly less expense for vodka.

Luckily, the following year Nadya received a promotion at the ceramics factory where she'd been employed since her graduation from vocational school. That meant that Yuri could stay in school through the tenth grade.

Unfortunately, Yuri developed into a withdrawn and belligerent teenager who got into frequent fights in response to teasing by fellow classmates. As a consequence, his studies suffered. His final grades and test scores were not sufficient for the university where his mother had hoped he'd go. Instead, he enrolled in the local vocational college and studied to become a microbiological technician. He'd been advised there was a burgeoning demand for the field, especially in Sverdlovsk. Conveniently for Yuri, the government had built a large pharmaceutical factory to produce vaccines for human and animal use.

"Have you been home to Russia since coming to America?" the Estonian woman asked after they'd ridden for several blocks in silence.

"Not yet," Yuri said. He perked up at the thought of his imminent return. In fact he already had an open ticket to Moscow via Frankfurt and departing from Newark Airport. He'd chosen Newark since it was located to the west and south of Manhattan. He was planning on leaving the moment he finished the laydown of the bioweapon in Central Park, and he didn't want to risk going east to JFK Airport. The wind invariably blew west to east. The last thing he wanted was to be victimized by his own terrorism.

Obtaining the airline ticket had not been without difficulty. Yuri had never been able to obtain a Russian international passport, and although he had an American green card from the Immigration and Naturalization Service, he still didn't have an American passport. At least not an authentic one. Yuri had had to pay to have a fake passport made. But it didn't have to be a particularly good one, since all he intended to use it for was to buy the airline ticket. As a patriot, he was confident he'd have no trouble getting into Russia without proper documents, and he certainly didn't intend to return to the United States.

"My husband and I went back to Estonia last year," the woman said. "It was wonderful. Good things are happening in the Baltics. We might even eventually return to live in our hometown."

"America is not the heaven it wants the world to believe it is," Yuri said.

"People must work very hard here," the woman concurred. "And you must be careful. There are many thieves who want to take your money, like investment people and people wanting to sell you swampland in Florida."

Yuri nodded in agreement, although to him the real thief was what Curt Rogers called the Zionist Occupied Government. It wasn't only in a metaphorical sense relating to the American Dream hoax; it was also quite literal. Government agents always had their hands out to steal most of every dollar Yuri made. If it wasn't the criminals in Washington, it was the thieves in the state government in Albany or the bandits in the city government in Manhattan. According to Curt all this taxation was unconstitutional and therefore blatantly illegal.

"I hope you send some money home to your family," the woman continued, unaware of the effect her conversation was having on her driver. "My husband and I do as often as we can."

"I don't have any family in the old country," Yuri said, a bit too quickly. "I'm very much alone." He knew he wasn't being entirely honest. He had a maternal grandmother, a few aunts and uncles, and a collection of cousins in Ekaterinburg, as Sverdlovsk was now called. He also had an overweight wife in Brighton Beach.

"I'm sorry," the woman said. Her face clouded in sympathy. "I cannot imagine having no family. Perhaps over the holidays you'd like to come to us."

"Thank you," Yuri said. "It's very kind but I'm okay . . ." He intended to elaborate but found himself surprisingly choked up. Reluctantly his mind pulled him back to 1979, the fateful year he lost both his mother and his brother. In particular, he thought about April 2nd.

The day started like every other workday with the raucous alarm pulling Yuri from the depths of sleep. At five A.M. it was as black as midnight, since Sverdlovsk was at about the same latitude as Sitka, Alaska. Winter had loosened its grip on the city, but spring had yet to arrive. The apartment wasn't below freezing as it had been on February mornings and even into March, but it was cold just the same. Yuri dressed in the darkness without waking Nadya or Yegor, both of whom did not need to get up until seven. Nadya still worked at the ceramics factory. Yegor was in his last year of school and scheduled to finish that June.

After a quick, cold breakfast of stale bread and cheese in the deserted communal kitchen, Yuri set off in the darkness for the pharmaceutical plant. He'd been working there for only two years following the completion of his college training. Yet it had been a long enough period for him to know that the factory was not what it seemed. Yuri was not doing microbiological cultures for vaccine production as he'd been hired to do. Although some vaccines were being produced in the outer ring of the factory, Yuri worked in the larger, inner part. The vaccine work was a KGB cover for the real mission. The Sverdlovsk pharmaceutical facility was actually part of Biopreparat, the massive Soviet bioweapons program. Yuri was a single cog in a work force of fifty-five thousand spread among institutions throughout the Soviet Union.

The factory was benignly called Compound 19. At the gate Yuri had to stop and present his identification card. Yuri knew the man in the gatehouse was KGB. Yuri stamped his feet against the predawn cold as he waited. There were no words. None were needed. The man nodded, handed back the card, and Yuri entered.

Yuri was one of the first members of the day shift to arrive. The facility ran twenty-four hours a day, seven days a week. It fell to Yuri, a junior employee, and a few of his equivalent-level colleagues to do the required menial cleaning of the inner biocontainment core. The regular janitorial staff were not allowed into the area.

In the changing room Yuri nodded to his lockermate, Alexis. It was too early for conversation, especially since no one had had their morning tea or coffee. Silently they and two other peers donned their red biocontainment suits and switched on their ventilators. They didn't even bother to look at each other through their clear plastic face masks as they checked themselves.

Fully encapsulated the group waited outside the pressure door until it automatically opened. No one tried to communicate as the pressure dropped in the entrance chamber. When the inner door opened, they went silently to their assigned stations. They moved slowly in the cumbersome suits, walking rather stiff-legged and appearing more like futuristic robots than people.

The monotonous commencement of shifts was a carefully choreographed routine that did not change from week to week or month to month. And that particular morning of April 2, 1979, seemed like any other morning. But it wasn't. A potential problem existed unknown to the four young men trudging off to their work stations. No one had the slightest premonition of the disaster that was about to occur.

The Sverdlovsk facility dealt primarily with two types of microbes: *Bacillus anthracis* and *Clostridium botulinum*. The weaponized forms of these bacteria were spores of the former and crystallized toxin from the latter. The mission of the factory was to produce as much of both as possible.

When Yuri had first started working at Compound 19, he'd been rotated through various work stations to familiarize him with the operation of the entire plant. After the first month's rotation he'd been assigned to the anthrax department. For the two years he'd worked at the factory, he'd been in the processing section of the plant. It was here that the liquid cultures coming from the giant fermenters were dried into cakes, and the cakes were then ground into a powder that was almost pure anthrax spores. Yuri's specific job was monitoring the pulverizers.

The pulverizers were rotating steel drums containing steel balls. Careful testing with live animals in another part of the facility had determined that the deadliest and most efficacious size of the powder's particles was five microns. To achieve this size the pulverizers were rotated at a specific speed with specific-sized steel balls and for a predetermined period of time.

Normal operating procedure had the pulverizers inactivated during the night for routine maintenance. The shutdown was done by the supervisor of the evening shift. There was no equivalent shutdown of the dryers, which continued to function in order to produce a large supply of the light tan-colored cakes for the day shift to process. It took longer to dry the cakes than to grind them.

As he always did, Yuri began the day by hosing down the area around the pulverizers with high-pressure, heavily chlorinated water. Although the crushers were sealed units, tiny bits of the powder invariably escaped, especially if the unit had been opened for maintenance. Since a microscopic amount could kill a man, daily cleaning was mandatory even though no one approached the machinery without biocontainment suits.

Initially, Yuri had been terrified at the concept of working in an environment of such a deadly agent. But over the months he'd gradually adapted. On that particular morning of April 2nd it didn't even occur to him to be concerned. Yuri was like Ivan Denisovich in Solzhenitsyn's novel, demonstrating once again that humans have an inordinate ability to adapt.

After his cleaning duties were complete, Yuri turned a large hand crank to pull in the hose. The effort brought beads of perspiration to his forehead. Any degree of exertion turned the impervious biocontainment suit into a mobile sauna bath.

Once the cleaning apparatus was stored, Yuri went into the control room and closed the door. Insulated glass separated the control room from the pulverizer. When the unit went on-line, the noise was deafening, jarring, and generally annoying.

Yuri sat in front of the main control panel, and scanned the settings and the dials. All was in order for the start-up. He then turned to the logbook while his mind began eagerly to anticipate the nine A.M. morning break. It was one of Yuri's favorite times of day, even though it was only a half hour. He could almost taste the fresh coffee and bread.

With his gloved finger Yuri traced across the columns of figures to make sure that the pulverizers had worked smoothly during the last shift they'd operated. All seemed to be in order until he came to the column containing the readings for the negative air pressure inside the unit. As his eye traced across the page he noticed that the pressure had slowly risen as the shift progressed. He wasn't concerned, because the rise was small and the readings had stayed within acceptable limits.

Yuri glanced down to the bottom of the page where the shift supervisor summarized the shift's events. The slight rise in pressure was duly noted with the notation that maintenance had been informed. Below that entry was another by maintenance. The time was listed as two A.M. It said simply that the unit had been checked and the cause of the slight rise in pressure had been discovered and had been rectified.

Yuri shook his head. The maintenance entry was strange because there was no explanation of what the cause had been. Yet it didn't seem to matter. The readings had never been abnormal. Yuri shrugged. He didn't think maintenance's incomplete entry was his concern, especially since the problem, whatever it was, had been rectified.

When Yuri felt all was in order, he picked up the telephone that connected him to the day shift supervisor, Vladimir Gergiyev. He looked at his watch. It was just before seven A.M. and soon his mother and brother would be getting up.

"The pulverizers are standby, Comrade Gergiyev," Yuri said.

"Commence operation," Vladimir said tersely before ringing off.

Yuri had intended to mention the strange log entry, but his supervisor's abruptness prevented it. Yuri hung up the phone and for a brief moment debated calling back. Unfortunately, Vladimir's truculent personality did not encourage such spontaneity. Yuri decided to let it go.

Without the slightest idea of the horrific consequences, Yuri depressed the start button on the pulverizers. Almost instantaneously the jarring sound of the machinery penetrated the insulated control room. The day's production of deadly weaponized anthrax had begun.

The system was automatic. The cakes of dried spores were carried on an internal conveyer and dropped into the rotating steel pulverizer drums. After being ground by the cascading steel balls, the fine powder dropped out the base of the drums and was packed into sealed containers. The outsides of the containers were then disinfected. The completed containers could then be loaded into ordnance or into missile warheads.

Yuri's eyes went immediately to the interior pressure dial. The pressure dropped instantly with the commencement of the unit. Even the slight misgiving he felt due to the strange log entry evaporated when the pressure continued to fall past the slightly elevated level it had been when the unit had been shut down. It was obvious that maintenance had indeed rectified the problem as had been suggested.

Yuri scanned the other dials and readout devices. All were safely in their respective green zones. Picking up a pen he laboriously began the entry for the April 2nd day shift, copying each reading into its appropriate column. When he came to the interior pressure gauge he noted something surprising. It had continued to fall and now was as low as Yuri had ever seen it. In fact it was pegged at the lower edge of the scale.

Reaching over Yuri gave the dial a knock with the knuckle of his right index finger. He wanted to make sure the old-fashioned needle gauge was not stuck. It didn't move.

Yuri didn't know what to do, if anything. There was no lower limit to the green zone on the interior pressure, only an upper. The idea was to keep the powder inside with a constant flow of air from the room into the machine at any point there was a communication. Therefore it didn't make any difference if the pressure was lower than usual. In fact, it meant the system would function more efficiently.

Yuri eyed the phone again and thought about calling his shift supervisor, but again he decided against it. Yuri had been harangued by Vladimir for what the supervisor thought were stupid concerns, and Yuri didn't want to suffer a dressing-down again. Vladimir did not like to be bothered by insignificant details. He was far too busy.

At eight o'clock Yuri thought about his mother making her

way to the ceramics factory. The factory was located just south and east from Compound 19. Nadya frequently told Yuri she thought about him as she passed. Yuri had never told her exactly what kind of work he was doing. It would have been dangerous for both if he had.

Time dragged. Yuri yearned for the nine o'clock break. When there was only fifteen minutes to go, he recommenced recording in the log. When his eyes got to the dial for the internal pressure, he again hesitated. The needle had not moved from its position at the very lower end of the scale.

As Yuri stared at the dial he felt a sinking feeling in his chest. All at once a horrific thought had occurred to him.

"Please! Don't let it be so!" Yuri prayed. By reflex he reached out and hit the red stop button. The cacophony of the steel balls in the steel cylinders that had been penetrating the control room stopped. In its wake Yuri had a ringing in his ears.

Trembling with fear at what he would find, Yuri opened the door of the control room. Behind him he heard the phone ring. Instead of answering it, he walked over to the very end of the pulverizer. He was breathing hard enough to cause his plastic face shield to fog. He slowed as he approached a series of vertical doors in the system's cowling. Each was eight inches wide and three feet tall.

Yuri's hand trembled as he reached out and unlatched one of the doors. He hesitated for a moment before pulling it open. *"Blyad!"* Yuri blurted. He was horrified. The compartment was empty! Quickly he yanked open all the doors. All the compartments were empty. There were no HEPA filters in place! For two hours the system had been venting to the outside with no protection!

Yuri staggered back. It was a catastrophe. Only then did he become conscious that the phone was still incessantly ringing in the background. He knew who it was. It was the shift supervisor wondering why he'd stopped the pulverizer.

Yuri dashed into the control room while he mentally tried to estimate how many grams of weaponized anthrax had been spewed out over the unsuspecting city. From his walk to the factory he knew there was a moderate northwesterly wind.

That meant the spores would have been vectored to the southeast toward the main military compound. But more important, it meant that the spores would be heading toward the ceramics factory!

"It's the fourth house on the right," the Estonian woman said, yanking Yuri from the grip of his nightmare-like reverie. The woman's finger jutted through the Plexiglas divider and pointed at a set of white steps.

Yuri was instantly conscious he was perspiring profusely and his face felt hot. He'd been forced to remember an event that he actively avoided thinking about. After twenty years, the memory of that terrible day still had as powerful an effect on him as it did when it happened.

The Estonian woman paid the fare before climbing from the cab. She tried to give Yuri a tip, but he refused. He thanked her for her generosity and for the offer to share her holiday. Self-consciously he avoided looking at her. He was afraid she'd see his perspiration and flushed face. He was worried she might have thought he was having a heart attack.

As the Estonian woman mounted her steps, Yuri switched on his off-duty sign. He drove ahead to a fire hydrant and pulled to the curb. He needed a moment to get his breath. He reached under his seat and pulled out his flask of vodka. After making sure he was not being observed, he took a quick, healthy swig. He allowed the liquor to slide down his throat. The sensation was delicious and calming. The overwhelming anxiety he'd experienced just moments before abated. He wiped his mouth with the back of his hand.

The aftermath of the pulverizers being run without the HEPA filters turned out to be worse than Yuri could have imagined. As he'd feared, an invisible cloud of anthrax spores had drifted out over the southern part of the city, an area that included the major military installation as well as the ceramics factory. Hundreds of people became sick with inhalational anthrax and most of them died. One of the victims was Nadya.

Her first symptoms were fever and chest pain. Yuri knew immediately what she had but hoped he was wrong. Sworn to secrecy on the pain of death, he did not tell her his suspicions. She was taken to a special hospital and housed in a separate ward with other patients complaining of similar symptoms. The group included a number of military personnel. Her course was relentlessly downhill and extremely rapid. She was dead within twenty-four hours.

The KGB immediately began an elaborate campaign of misinformation, claiming the problem came from contaminated cattle carcasses processed at the Aramil meatpacking factory. The families of the dead were denied their loved ones' bodies. By decree all the dead were buried in deep graves in a separate part of the main city cemetery.

Yuri suffered terribly. It was more than the emotional trauma of losing his mother and the enormous personal guilt of knowing that he was involved in causing her death. As the most junior employee involved in the disaster, he was the designated scapegoat. Although the subsequent official investigation suggested that most of the responsibility lay with the night maintenance worker and the shift supervisor who did not replace the clogged filters with new ones nor adequately record that they had removed the old filters, it was Yuri who took most of the blame. Theoretically, he was supposed to check the presence of the filters before start-up, but since the filters lasted for months and were rarely changed, no one checked them on a daily basis, and Yuri had not been taught to do so by his shift supervisor during his orientation.

Because of national security issues and the required secrecy, Yuri was held for a time in a military stockade instead of a normal prison before being sent to Siberia. In Siberia he eventually ended up at another Biopreparat facility called Vector located in a city called Novosibirsk. Although Vector was known mostly for work with weaponized viruses, including smallpox, Yuri was assigned to a small team trying to improve the efficacy of weaponized anthrax and botulinum toxin.

As for his brother Yegor, Yuri had never seen him again. He'd not been infected by the released anthrax, but he was not allowed to visit Yuri during Yuri's confinement in the military stockade or in Siberia. Then, after graduating in June, Yegor was drafted into the army. In December 1979, he was sent into Afghanistan in the initial invasion and was one of the first casualties.

Yuri sighed. He did not like to think about his past miseries. It made him feel anxious and out of control. Furtively his eyes again scanned the neighborhood through the taxi's windshield and with the help of his side mirrors and rearview mirror. There were a few pedestrians, but no one paid him any heed. Yuri took another quick swig from his flask before replacing the now empty container under his seat. Once again he'd run out of vodka before the day was finished.

Still feeling agitated, Yuri opened the door and got out. He didn't step away from his cab. He merely stretched and twisted from side to side to relieve a chronic discomfort he felt in his lower back from sitting all day. He took several deep breaths. Somewhat soothed, he climbed back into the cab. He was about to switch off his off-duty light when he realized that his present location wasn't that far away from Walker Street and the Corinthian Rug Company. Needing a diversion, he decided to head down to the neighborhood. It would make him feel a lot better if he had some positive news about the rug merchant.

At three-thirty the city traffic was starting to coagulate as it always did as rush hour approached. It took Yuri more time than he expected to drive down Broadway, especially in and around Canal Street. Fighting to maintain his patience, Yuri finally was able to turn onto the relatively quiet Walker Street.

As he approached the Corinthian Rug Company office he fully expected to see it shut up tight as it had been earlier. He was prepared to accept the situation as further corroboration that Jason Papparis had been infected and was either dead or at death's door. The question in Yuri's mind was whether he should risk inquiring again in the stamp store. But to Yuri's surprise and consternation the front door of the rug company office was wide open and the lights were on!

Dismayed, Yuri put on the brakes and slowed his cab to give himself a glimpse inside the shop as he glided by. What he saw was Jason Papparis standing in front of one of his file cabinets!

"O Godspodi!" Yuri mumbled despite his atheistic beliefs. He pulled into a loading zone. Twisting around in his seat he looked back at the open door of the rug store office. What could have gone wrong? The powder had to be effective. He'd

used all the tricks that he and his team had devised at Vector. In the ten-plus years he'd worked at the Siberian facility he and his coworkers had increased the efficacy of weaponized anthrax by a factor approaching ten. Most of the increase had come from simple additives to the powder to maximize the suspension and the diffusion of the particles in the air, although some of the increase had come from the way the cultures were grown. With his current weapon, Yuri had used all the stratagems.

Yuri ran a hand through his hair. Maybe the letter had gotten lost or delivered to the wrong person? Or maybe even someone in the post office had decided to open it out of curiosity? Yuri wondered if he should have thought of a different way of infecting Mr. Papparis. At the time he'd come up with the letter idea, it had seemed so perfect.

Yuri got out of the cab. With the taxi's blinkers on he ran across the street, skirted a mountain bike locked to a "No Parking" sign, and passed the stamp store. As he came abreast of the window of the rug office he peered inside. Jason was nowhere to be seen. The two doors that he could see in the rear of the office were closed.

After making sure no meter maid or policeman was in sight, Yuri walked to the open door. He hesitated for a moment, unsure of what to do. Confused curiosity propelled him over the threshold. He had to talk to the rug merchant.

"Did someone call a taxi?" Yuri called. His voice was weak and uncertain.

A figure loomed up from behind the desk supporting the copy and fax machines clutching papers in his hand. To Yuri's shock the man was wearing a surgical mask, a hood, and a gown. The image was so unexpected that Yuri stepped back out the door.

"Wait!" Jack called. He tossed the papers he was holding onto the desk and ran after the taxi driver. He caught up to him on the sidewalk.

"Did you call a taxi, Mr. Papparis?" Yuri asked. He glanced over at his waiting cab. He wanted to get the hell out of there.

"I'm not Mr. Papparis," Jack said. He pulled off his latex gloves and struggled to get out his medical examiner badge.

He showed it to Yuri, who backed up another step. Yuri thought it was a police badge.

"The name's Jack Stapleton; I'm a medical examiner," Jack said. He put away his wallet, then undid his face mask. "How well did you know Mr. Papparis? Did you drive him often?"

"I'm just a cab driver," Yuri said meekly. He wasn't sure what a medical examiner was, although with an official badge he obviously worked for the government.

"How well did you know Mr. Papparis?" Jack repeated.

"I didn't know him," Yuri said. "I never drove him."

"How did you know his name?"

"I just got a call to pick him up."

"That's interesting," Jack said.

Yuri felt distinctly uncomfortable. He did not like dealing with state officials of any kind. Besides, the individual standing in front of him looked vaguely familiar, a fact that added to his unease. And on top of that the stranger was looking at him curiously, even suspiciously.

"Are you sure you got a call from a Mr. Papparis on Walker Street?" Jack said. "Mr. Papparis of the Corinthian Rug Company?"

"I think that's what dispatch said," Yuri said.

"I find that hard to believe," Jack said. "Mr. Papparis died over the weekend."

"Oh!" Yuri said. He coughed nervously while he struggled to come up with some plausible explanation. Nothing came to mind.

"Maybe he called last week?" Jack suggested.

"That could be," Yuri said.

"Maybe we should call your cab company," Jack suggested. "It would be helpful to know if Mr. Papparis was a regular customer. You see, he died of a rare infectious disease which I'm eager to investigate. Any information I could find out about his activities last week such as whether he visited his warehouse could be important. I'm also interested in contacts. Especially last week and particularly Friday."

"I can give you the dispatch phone number," Yuri said.

"Fair enough," Jack said. "Let me get a pencil and a piece of paper."

While Jack ducked back into the rug company office, Yuri breathed a sigh of relief. For a moment he thought that he'd made a terrible blunder coming to the rug company's office. Now he was confident there wouldn't be a problem. Dispatch wouldn't offer any information. They never did, especially not about yellow cabs.

Jack returned in a moment and wrote down the name and number.

"What kind of disease did Mr. Papparis die of?" Yuri asked. He was curious what the authorities knew or suspected.

"A disease called anthrax," Jack said.

"I know something about that," Yuri said. "It's a disease mostly of cattle."

"I'm impressed," Jack said. "How did you happen to know that?"

"I saw it as a boy," Yuri explained. "I grew up in the Soviet Union in a city called Sverdlovsk. In the rural areas outside the city cows and sheep occasionally were infected."

"I've heard of Sverdlovsk," Jack said. "In fact, it was just today. I read that there was a leak there of anthrax from a secret bioweapons plant."

Yuri practically gulped. He was staggered by Jack's offhand comment. It was so totally unexpected, especially after Yuri had just been torturing himself with its recollection.

"Did you ever hear anything about that episode?" Jack asked. "Apparently there were a lot of cases and a lot of deaths."

"I didn't hear about anything like that," Yuri said. He had to clear his throat.

"I'm not surprised," Jack said. "I don't think the Soviet government wanted anybody to know. For years they tried to say that it came from contaminated meat."

"There were episodes of contaminated meat," Yuri managed.

"The problem I'm talking about occurred in 1979," Jack said. "Did you live in Sverdlovsk then?"

"I guess," Yuri said vaguely. He was aware he was trembling. As soon as he could, Yuri broke away from Jack and hurried back to his cab. While he started the engine he looked back. Jack was putting his mask and gloves back on. At least he wasn't out in the street trying to write down Yuri's license number.

Putting the car in gear, Yuri drove off. His euphoria had been short-lived. Now he felt panic again. Although Jason Papparis's death confirmed the potency of his anthrax, Yuri was concerned that a state official who related anthrax to its use as a weapon was out on site investigating the case. He had taken pains to infect someone who could have gotten the disease through occupational exposure. That fact was supposed to preclude any investigation.

Despite his distress, Yuri snapped off his off-duty light. Rush hour was a prime time for taxi work, provided the traffic didn't bog down. Yuri needed the money. He had to work, and he picked up a fare almost immediately.

For the next hour, Yuri did short hops up and down Manhattan and back and forth across town. None of the customers bothered him too much, but the traffic did. Preoccupied and agitated, he found his patience stretched to the breaking point. After several near accidents, particularly one at Third Avenue and Fifty-fifth Street, Yuri decided to give up. When the fare climbed from the taxi at his destination, Yuri called it quits for the day. He put on his off-duty sign and headed for home in Brighton Beach. It was only a little after five P.M., his shortest day since he'd had the flu six months previously. But Yuri didn't care. What he needed was a shot of vodka and, unfortunately, his flask was dry.

During the trip across the Brooklyn Bridge, which seemed to take forever with the bumper-to-bumper traffic, Yuri agonized over the meeting with Jack Stapleton. He couldn't understand what was motivating the man. What worried him particularly was that Jack might find some residue from the ACME Cleaning Service letter if not the letter itself. Yuri had no idea what had become of it. His original assumption was that the letter would be thrown away like all junk mail. But now that Jack was on the scene, Yuri wasn't so confident.

South of Prospect Park Yuri stopped in a liquor store for a pint of vodka. Later, on Ocean Parkway, with the pint hidden in a brown paper bag, he took a couple of slugs when he was stopped for lights. That calmed him down considerably.

As he entered Brighton Beach and all the signs switched to the familiar Cyrillic alphabet, Yuri's agitation ratcheted down a notch. The familiar letters provided a sense of nostalgia. Yuri felt like he was already home in Mother Russia. With the calmness came an ability to think. The first thought that came to him was that it might be wise to consider pushing up the date for Operation Wolverine.

Yuri nodded to himself as he turned onto his street. There was no doubt that advancing the date would help in regard to security concerns. It wasn't that he was worried about being discovered. He just didn't want his plans to be suspected. To be truly effective, a bioweapon should be launched with no warning. Yet pushing up the date was not without problems, particularly two big ones.

The first was that Yuri had yet to test the botulinum toxin, although he was more confident of its toxicity than he'd been about the pathogenicity of the anthrax powder. The other stumbling block was production. He wanted at least four or five pounds of the anthrax and about a quarter pound of the crystallized botulinum toxin. He didn't care which agent he used for Central Park or which agent Curt used for the Jacob Javits Federal Building, since he was confident both would be equivalently effective. Meeting the production quota for the anthrax was not a problem, since he was already close to the amount needed, but the same was not true for the botulinum toxin. He was having difficulty with the *Clostridium botulinum* cultures. They just weren't growing as he'd hoped or expected.

Yuri slowed as he approached his house. It was located in a warren of small structures that had been built as summer cottages in the 1920s. They all had wooden frames and small yards with postage-stamp-sized areas of fenced-in grass. Yuri's house was one of the largest, and in contrast to most of the others, it had a freestanding two-car garage. Yuri rented the house from a man who'd moved to Florida but who was reluctant to give up his toehold in Brooklyn.

The garage door squeaked loudly as Yuri raised it. The interior was mostly empty, in contrast to the other garages in the area, which were crammed to the rafters with everything but cars. The floor of Yuri's garage was stained from more than a half century's worth of drippings from leaky vehicles. The stale smell of gas and oil fumes hung in the air. There was a small collection of yard tools, including an old push lawn mower against one wall. A wheelbarrow, some spare cinderblocks, and a collection of lumber leaned up against the other wall.

With his cab safely stored for the night, Yuri carried his empty flask and the half-empty pint of vodka to the house. With his house key he tried to open the back door. To his surprise the door was unlocked. He pushed it open and suspiciously looked inside.

Yuri had been robbed once. It had happened only months after renting the house. He'd come home around nine o'clock in the evening to find the place trashed. The burglars, apparently irritated at not finding anything of value, vented their frustration on Yuri's meager furniture.

Pausing to listen, Yuri could hear the television in Connie's bedroom. It was then that he noticed his wife's purse sitting in the middle of the Formica kitchen table along with the telltale wrappings from one of the neighborhood's fast-food joints.

Yuri had been married for almost four years. He'd met his wife, Connie, when he'd first started working for the taxi company as a radio car driver and before he had his own vehicle. At the time he'd been rather desperate. His visa was about to run out. Marriage to a U.S. citizen seemed his only option.

Connie was an African-American woman in her twenties who'd seemed bored with her life and had been happy to flirt with the newly arrived Russian. She went out of her way to be nice to him and, using her position as a dispatcher, made sure he got choice runs.

Yuri had initially been attracted to Connie separately from his necessity to obtain a green card. As a youth in the Soviet Union, he'd loved jazz, which he associated with American blacks. Becoming acquainted with one socially was exciting. He'd known no Negroes as he'd grown up in Sverdlovsk but had seen them on television, particularly in sporting events, and was duly impressed.

Connie's attentions were even more welcome in light of Yuri's loneliness. The mostly Russian Jewish community in Brighton Beach where he'd been advised to move ignored him. The couple began to date and frequented jazz clubs both in Manhattan, where Connie lived, and in Brooklyn near Yuri's apartment. At the same time Yuri began to learn about American racism, which initially confused him, since he'd assumed African-Americans would be held in high esteem for their cultural contributions. He'd never heard the term "nigger" until he and Connie were accosted on the street on several occasions. He was also surprised to learn that Connie's family, particularly her brother Flash and his friends, did not think highly of him. They called him a "honky," which he learned was as derogatory a term as "nigger."

For Yuri marriage solved both the green card and the loneliness issues, at least initially. Unfortunately, Yuri soon learned that Connie had no intention of being the wife that Yuri expected from his Russian heritage. She had no interest in domestic duties and anticipated eating out every night as they'd done during their brief courtship. As Yuri's climb up the economic ladder reached an impasse with the realization that he would not be able to use his microbiological background without expensive retraining and that he could not afford to stop driving a cab, his tolerance for Connie's lifestyle dwindled. If it wasn't for the fear of losing his green card, he would have kicked her out.

Connie's ardor ebbed equivalently. Initially she'd seen Yuri as a romantic figure who'd come from a distant land to rescue her from a boring life. But soon after their marriage Yuri refused to do anything except drive his cab and drink vodka in front of the television. And then there was the violence. Connie had never been beaten before. After the first incident she would have left if she'd had someplace to go. The problem was that she'd burned her bridges when she married Yuri against her family's wishes. Pride kept her rooted where she was.

Connie's method of dealing with her unhappiness was to eat. She could find solace in a quart of ice cream, french fried potatoes, and a Big Mac, and she sought that solace frequently.

Between that and a routine devoid of exercise, it wasn't long before Connie's weight ballooned. The more Yuri drank, the more Connie ate.

As they became more entrenched in their respective bad habits, their mutual hostility grew. Yuri and Connie lived in the same house but ignored each other until mere proximity would ignite a conflagration. Invariably, the quarrels escalated from stereotypic epithets to physical violence, and when they did, Connie suffered more.

A break in this pattern occurred when Yuri befriended Curt Rogers and Steve Henderson. He did not tell Connie about his new friends but spent much of his time away from home as a result of their acquaintance. Curt and Steve never came to Brighton Beach. Yuri always traveled to Bensonhurst to see them. Connie was convinced he was having an affair, a belief that caused several knock-down, drag-out fights.

Then, all at once, Yuri began spending inordinate amounts of time in the basement. First he did construction, and the hammering and sawing drove Connie crazy. When she asked him what was going on, he told her it was none of her business. Then he started bringing in equipment, including powerful fans. Connie even caught sight of large stainless steel drums being carried in by white-trash "honky" skinhead youths. Such people terrified Connie, and she made sure they didn't see her.

On more than one occasion, Connie demanded to know what was going on in her basement, but Yuri refused to discuss it. She began to think that Yuri was setting up a distillery to manufacture his own vodka. When she suggested this to him one evening, he responded by leaping at her and grabbing her throat.

"Yes, it's a still," Yuri snarled. "And if you tell anyone, I'll kill you! I swear! And if you ever mess with it, I'll beat you to a pulp. You stay the hell out of my basement!"

Connie had vainly tried to break Yuri's hold on her neck by pulling his arms away, but she couldn't. Usually when he was mad he just smacked her a few times, and that was it. But this was different. His black eyes drilled into her like he'd gone crazy.

In utter terror, Connie started to feel faint, her image of
Yuri's empurpled face began to blur, and her knees buckled.
Only then did Yuri let go of her. Connie staggered to regain
her balance and choked from the pressure he'd kept on her
throat. With a burst of tears she ran from the room and threw
herself onto her bed. From then on, Connie refrained from
bringing up the issue of what was going on in the basement.
Whatever it was, it wasn't worth risking her life.

Yuri was irritated that Connie was home. On Monday nights
she was supposed to work until at least nine. Her unexpected
presence only added to the stress of a day that had already
taken him on a roller coaster of emotions. With a trembling
hand he poured himself a glass of ice-cold vodka from the
freezer.

Leaning back against the countertop he took a sip of the
glacial fluid and eyed the greasy remains of the fast food. In
the background he heard the canned laughter of a television
sitcom. He took more of the vodka in an attempt to stem his
rising resentment. As he swallowed, his eyes wandered to the
basement door. He was surprised to see that it was partially
ajar.

"What the hell?" Yuri questioned. He usually swore in Russian, but through his friendship with Curt and Steve he'd become equally capable in English. Confused and progressively
dismayed, he put down his drink and stepped over to the door.
He was certain that he'd closed it that morning before heading
out in his cab. It was Yuri's routine to work in his basement
lab for at least an hour in the morning and another hour in the
evening to make sure his miniature bioweapons production
facility was working smoothly. On Wednesday, his usual day
off, he spent the whole day in the basement. That was when
he activated his makeshift pulverizer, since most of the neighbors were at work. Like the pulverizer in Sverdlovsk, it made
a racket even though it was a fraction of the size.

The door creaked as Yuri opened it wide. Snapping on the
light, he started down the stairs. He stopped dead when he had
a view of the stout combination steel and plywood door he'd

made for the lab. Someone had taken a crowbar to the padlock, snapping off the hasp.

Yuri stumbled down the rest of the stairs in haste. Outrage clouded his vision. His breath came in angry and worried snorts between clenched teeth. The lab and the revenge it promised was the current focus of his life. He was terrified it had been violated.

Beyond the plywood door was the entry chamber with a showerhead and plastic bottles of bleach. Hanging on a wooden peg was a SCBA hazardous materials suit Curt had managed to get out of the firehouse. The face mask was supplied by a steel cylinder filled with compressed air. When Yuri was in the lab he wore the suit with the cylinder on his back like a scuba diver.

The entry chamber had two other doors, both constructed similarly to that at the entrance. Both also had been secured by padlocks for safekeeping and both padlocks had been similarly broken off. Yuri yanked open the door to his left. It was his storage compartment and was surrounded on two sides with the concrete foundation walls of the house. The third wall contained floor-to-ceiling shelving, which was filled with microbiological supplies such as petri dishes, spare HEPA filters, agar, and jars of nutrients. The room's interior was undisturbed, despite the broken lock.

Steeling himself against what he might find, Yuri moved over to the door to the lab itself. He switched on the interior lights before cracking the door. He could tell the main circulating fans were functioning normally by the breeze flowing into the room. It rustled his hair and caressed his face. To be on the safe side, Yuri held his breath while he scanned the lab's interior.

The gleaming fermenters were arrayed directly in front of him along the back wall of the lab. His makeshift hood was to the right. It functioned as his incubator, with a heat lamp and a thermostat, and also as his repository for the bioweaponized anthrax and botulinum toxin he'd already produced.

Yuri's lab bench was to the immediate left. On the bench stood the glassware he used for crystallizing the botulinum toxin. Beyond the lab bench was the pulverizer and the dryer for the anthrax spores.

Yuri's pounding heart began to slow. The lab seemed normal with nothing out of place. It appeared exactly as it had when he left it that morning, including the way the glassware was positioned on the bench. With a sense of relief, Yuri pulled the door closed. It whistled from the inrushing air just before sealing on its weather stripping.

He looked down at the broken hasp. Although his anxiety had abated, his anger hadn't. Then his eye caught something on the floor. Next to his foot was a carelessly discarded French fried potato along with a small smear of ketchup. Connie!

A muffled titter of laughter filtered down from above. Yuri was consumed by fury. With a string of expletives, he rushed from the room and took the stairs two at a time. When he got to the partially open bedroom door he pounded it open with the flat of his palm.

Connie glanced up from her TV show. She was supine on her bed.

"Why did you go downstairs?" Yuri snarled.

"I wanted to know what was going on in my basement," Connie said. "I have a right, considering all the time you spend down there."

"Did you touch anything?" Yuri demanded.

"No, I didn't touch nothing! But I can tell you, that ain't no still, not with all that stuff that looks like it came from a hospital."

"I'll teach you to disobey me!" Yuri snarled as he hurled himself at his wife.

Connie screamed and rolled to the side. The combination of Yuri's impact and Connie's weight was too much for the slats under the box spring, and the bed collapsed to the floor.

SIX

Curt was driving his Dodge Ram pickup with Steve riding shotgun. They'd turned off Ocean Parkway onto Oceanview Avenue and were searching for Oceanview Lane.

"My God!" Steve commented as he surveyed the neighborhood. "I've lived in Brooklyn my whole life and I've never seen this cluster of little houses. It looks like someplace in the Carolinas."

"Seems they would have been knocked down by now and some high-rises put up," Curt said. "Keep your eye out for Oceanview Lane. It's one of these little alleyways."

"There it is," Steve said. He pointed through the windshield at a small hand-painted sign tacked to a telephone pole.

Curt turned into the lane and slowed appreciably. It was narrow and cluttered with trash cans and dead leaves.

The two firemen were still in their uniforms. They'd driven to Brighton Beach as soon as they got off work at five P.M. The trip had taken just over an hour. Night was falling rapidly with the overcast sky, and the lane was dark except where it was illuminated with Curt's headlights. There were no street-lamps.

"Do you see any house numbers?" Curt asked.

Steve laughed. "This place is a slum. I don't see any signs."

"There's thirteen," Curt said. He pointed to a trash can with the address painted on the rim. "Fifteen should be the next one."

Curt pulled up to a closed garage door and killed the engine, and the two men climbed out of the truck. For a moment they studied the house. Crammed in among the others, it was mildly dilapidated and sorely in need of paint.

"It doesn't look too stable," Steve said. "One little nudge and the whole thing might tip over."

"Can you imagine how fast this would go up in flames," Curt said.

Steve turned to glance at his friend. "Is that some kind of suggestion?"

Curt shrugged. "Just something to keep in mind. Come on, let's pay our Russky friend a visit."

They opened a gate in the chain-link fence that ran along the front of the house. The walkway beyond was cracked concrete just visible through a blanket of dead leaves. The tiny patch of lawn was overgrown with weeds.

Curt searched for a doorbell, but there wasn't one. He opened the torn screen door and was about to knock when a large crash sounded from within. The two firefighters looked at each other.

"What the hell was that?" Steve asked.

"Beats me," Curt answered. He was again about to knock when there was another crash. This time it was followed by the sound of broken glass. They also heard Yuri curse loudly in Russian.

"Sounds like our Commie friend is wrecking his house," Steve said.

"It better not have anything to do with the lab," Curt said. He rapped loudly on the door. He wanted to make sure Yuri heard him.

After waiting several minutes and hearing nothing from in-

side the house, Curt knocked again. This time there were foot-
falls, and the door was snatched open.

"Company," Curt said. He tried to look past Yuri to see if
he could tell what had broken.

Yuri's expression went from anger to surprise and obvious
delight as he recognized his friends. Although his face remained flushed, he smiled broadly. "Hey, guys!" His voice
was hoarse.

"We were in the neighborhood," Curt said. "We thought
we'd just drop by to say hello."

"I'm glad you did," Yuri said.

"We heard you'd been by the firehouse," Steve said.

Yuri nodded enthusiastically. "I was looking for you
guys . . ."

"So we heard," Curt said stiffly.

"You're not supposed to come to the firehouse," Steve said.

"Why not?" Yuri asked.

"If we have to tell you, then we've got a problem," Steve
said.

"Security is a big concern in an operation like we're planning," Curt said. "The fewer people who associate us publicly,
the better off we all are, especially with you being a foreigner
and all. We don't have too many friends with Russian accents.
You show up looking for us, the other firefighters are going
to start to wonder."

"I'm sorry," Yuri said. "I didn't think there was a problem
at the firehouse, especially when you mentioned that many of
your comrades think the same way you guys do."

"We've our share of patriots," Curt admitted. "But none
quite as patriotic as we are. Maybe we should have spelled it
out more clearly. Anyway, now you know you don't come to
the firehouse."

"Okay," Yuri said. "I don't come anymore."

"Aren't you going to invite us in?" Curt asked.

Yuri glanced over his shoulder in the direction of Connie's
bedroom. The door was ajar. "Yeah, okay, sure." He stepped
out of the way and gestured for Curt and Steve to enter. After
closing the door he guided his visitors toward the living area,
where there was a low, threadbare couch and two straight-back

chairs. He gathered up a collection of newspapers from the sofa cushion and deposited them on the floor.

Curt sat on the couch, with his knees jutting up into the air. Steve balanced his muscled bulk on one of the chairs.

"Can I offer you guys some iced vodka?" Yuri asked.

"I'll have a beer," Curt said.

"Same," Steve said.

"Sorry," Yuri said. "I only have vodka."

Steve rolled his eyes.

"Vodka it is," Curt said.

While Yuri went to the refrigerator for the drinks Steve leaned over and whispered: "Now you see why I'm concerned. The guy's a dimwit. It never dawned on him not to come to the firehouse. It didn't even enter his mind."

"Take it easy," Curt said. "He doesn't have a military background. We should've known to be more explicit with a non-professional. We've got to cut him a little slack. Besides, let's not forget, he's doing us one hell of a favor getting us a bio-weapon."

"If he comes through," Steve said.

A sound of a toilet flushing in the background drifted into the living room from Connie's open bedroom door. Curt's brow furrowed. "Did I just hear a goddamned toilet?"

"It's a toilet all right," Steve said. "But I'm not sure where it's coming from. These houses are so damn close, maybe it's coming from next door."

Yuri returned to the living room clutching a triangle of three tumblers each half-filled with ice-cold vodka. "I got good news for you guys," he said as he deposited the glasses on the coffee table then handed them out.

"We just heard a toilet," Curt said. He took the drink. "It sounded like it might have come from this house."

"Probably," Yuri said with a disgusted shrug. "My wife, Connie, is in the other room."

Curt and Steve exchanged an anxious glance.

"The reason I stopped by the firehouse . . ." Yuri began.

"Wait a second!" Curt interrupted. "You never said you were married."

"Why should I have?" Yuri said. He looked from Steve to

Curt. He could tell they were as uneasy about his marital status as they were about his visiting the firehouse.

"You told us you were alone," Curt said irritably. "You said you didn't have any friends."

"That's true," Yuri said. "I am alone, without friends."

"Yet you have a wife in the other room," Curt said. He looked at Steve, who rolled his eyes in disbelief.

"There's an expression in English," Yuri said, "about ships passing in the night. We have the same expression in Russian. That's me and Connie: two ships in the night. We never talk. Hell, we rarely even see each other."

Curt rested his elbows on his knees and rubbed his temples. He couldn't believe he was learning all this now, not after all their planning. It gave him a headache.

"Do you think your wife can hear what we're saying out here?" Steve questioned.

"I doubt it," Yuri said. "Besides, she couldn't care less what we're saying. She just eats and watches television."

"I don't hear a television," Steve said.

"Yeah, because I just broke it," Yuri said. "It was driving me crazy. All that fake laughter suggesting life here in America is so funny and wonderful."

"Maybe you should at least close the door," Curt said through clenched teeth.

"All right, sure," Yuri said. He went to the door.

"Now maybe you understand what I've been talking about," Steve whispered. "I'm telling you, this guy is a kook!"

"Shut up," Curt responded.

Yuri returned to his chair and took a slug from his vodka.

"Does your wife know what you did for a living in the Soviet Union?" Curt demanded in a lowered voice. He was afraid to hear the answer and winced when Yuri responded in the affirmative.

"What about your lab?" Steve questioned. "Does she know about the lab you've supposedly built in the basement?"

"What do you mean, supposedly?" Yuri asked. He was offended by the implication.

"We've never seen it," Steve said. "We've never seen anything, after all the effort we've expended getting all the stuff you say you've needed."

"You could have seen it any time you wanted," Yuri said indignantly.

"All right, settle down," Curt said. "Let's not argue. But maybe we should take a look at the lab, just for reassurance. We all have a lot riding on this operation."

"Fine by me," Yuri said. He stood up, put his drink down, and led the way over to the basement door.

The group trooped down in single file. Yuri pulled the outer door open by its sprung hasp.

"What happened to the lock?" Curt asked.

"My wife pried it off this afternoon," Yuri admitted. "I'd warned her not to come down here, and she didn't, until today. She came down here a couple of hours ago and used a crowbar to break in. But she didn't touch anything. I'm sure of that."

"Why today?" Curt asked while trying to maintain his composure. He didn't like the sound of any of this, and it kept getting worse.

"She said she just got curious," Yuri said. "Which doesn't make sense, since I told her I'd kill her if she came down here and messed with anything."

"We might have to do just that," Curt said.

"You mean actually kill her?" Yuri asked.

For a moment no one spoke. Curt finally nodded. "It's possible. As I said, this is an important operation for all of us. Maybe the most important thing all of us are going to do in our lifetime. To give you an idea of how strongly I feel, over the weekend it came to my attention that the People's Aryan Army had an infiltrator. His name was Brad Cassidy. Today Brad Cassidy is no longer with us, and his body is missing some of his favorite parts."

"Your wife is a monumental security risk," Steve explained. "Does she know what you're doing down here?"

"She thought it was a distillery until today," Yuri said.

"Which means she no longer thinks it's a still," Curt said.

"That's right," Yuri admitted.

"That's too bad," Curt said. "Since she knows you were

involved in the Soviet bioweapons industry, it wouldn't be hard for her to figure it out."

"Let's see the lab," Steve said.

Yuri stepped into the entry room followed closely by Curt and then Steve.

"Do you use that class A hazmat suit we got for you?" Curt asked. He nodded at the protective gear hanging on its peg.

"Absolutely," Yuri said. "Every second I'm in the lab I'm in the suit. I don't take any chances. When I open this inner door, don't go in! I'd also advise you to hold your breath just to be on the safe side. You'll feel the breeze of the air flow into the room."

Both Curt and Steve nodded. Now that they were so close, both wondered if it was really necessary to look inside. The mere idea of the possible presence of an invisible, fatal biological agent gave them gooseflesh, and with what they had seen already, they were more than willing to believe that Yuri was holding up his side of the bargain. But before either could say as much, Yuri cracked the inner door and stepped to the side. Warily, the two firefighters leaned forward and caught a glimpse of the fermenters and other equipment.

"Looks good," Curt said. He stepped back and motioned for Yuri to close the door.

"Would you like to see some of the finished product?" Yuri asked.

"I don't think that's necessary," Curt said quickly.

"I've seen enough," Steve added.

"What I think we should do," Curt said, "is go up and talk with your wife. She's the new problem. We have to know what she knows."

Yuri closed the door. "I'll get these locks back in order tonight," he said. He then led the way back upstairs. While Yuri went to Connie's bedroom door, Curt and Steve returned to the sitting area but stayed on their feet. Each fireman took a healthy swallow from his drink while they watched Yuri lean into the room beyond. They could hear him talking, but not clearly enough to make out what he was saying, although judging by his tone, he was apparently getting angry. Finally,

Yuri turned back to them. "She's coming," he said. "It just takes her a year and a day."

Curt and Steve exchanged a disgusted look. The situation was going from bad to worse.

"Come on, woman!" Yuri yelled impatiently.

Finally, Connie's silhouette filled the doorway. She was dressed in a monstrous pink bathrobe trimmed in sea-foam green. Her feet were stuffed into backless slippers. Her left eye was dark red and swollen shut. A dried trickle of blood came from the corner of her mouth.

Curt's jaw dropped. Steve mumbled an expletive. Both were dumbfounded, and their expressions reflected their stunned bewilderment.

"These men want to ask you a few questions," Yuri snapped. He then looked expectantly at Curt.

Curt had to clear his throat as well as organize his thoughts. "Mrs. Davydov, do you have any idea of what's going on downstairs? What your husband is doing?"

Connie eyed the two strangers defiantly. "No!" she spat. "Nor do I care."

"Do you have an inkling?"

Connie looked at Yuri.

"Answer!" Yuri yelled.

"I thought he was making vodka," Connie said.

"But you don't think that any longer?" Curt asked. "Even though those big silver tanks were borrowed from a brewery."

"I don't know about that," Connie said. "But those other little glass dishes. The flat ones! I've seen them at the hospital clinic. They're used for bacteria."

Curt nodded imperceptibly to Steve, who returned the gesture.

"That's enough," Curt called over to Yuri.

Yuri tried to shoo his wife back into her bedroom, but she stood her ground. "I ain't going back until you bring me your TV."

Yuri hesitated. Then he ducked into his room. He reappeared moments later carrying a small television with an old-fashioned rabbit-ear antenna. Only then did Connie back out of sight.

"Can you believe this?" Curt mumbled.

"Yeah, I can," Steve said. "And you wondered why I was voicing some concern this morning before we went into the federal building. This guy's worse than I thought."

"At least he did build a lab," Curt said. "Obviously he knows what he's doing scientifically."

"That I'll grant," Steve said. "And the lab setup is more impressive than I'd imagined."

Curt exhaled loudly in frustration. In the background the sudden sound of a TV sitcom burst from Connie's bedroom. The volume was turned down immediately to be barely audible. The next minute Yuri reappeared. He closed the door behind him and came over to the living area. He sat down, took a drink, and eyed his guests self-consciously.

Curt didn't know what to say. It had been one thing to learn Yuri was married, but quite another to find out he was married to a black woman. It went against everything Curt believed in, and here he was doing business with the man.

Curt had grown up in a tough, blue-collar, white neighborhood with a physically abusive construction-worker father who continually reminded Curt that he wasn't as good as his popular, football-star brother, Pete. Curt found solace in hatred. He embraced the bigotry so prevalent in his neighborhood. It was comforting and handy to have a readily identifiable group to blame rather than examine his own inadequacies. But it wasn't until he'd joined the Marines and moved to San Diego that his rather parochial bigotry was transformed into racial hatred with a particular abhorrence of miscegenation.

The transition had not happened overnight. It stemmed from an attitude that had its origins in a chance meeting with a man almost twice Curt's age. It was 1979. Curt was nineteen. He'd recently finished boot camp, which had provided a dramatic boost to his self-esteem. He and several of his newfound colleagues, which included several African-Americans, had left the base to visit a bar on Point Loma. It was a bar frequented by armed forces personnel, particularly navy divers and Marines.

The bar was dark and smoky. The only light emanated from low-wattage bulbs inside old-fashioned, hard-hat diving helmets. The music was mostly from a band Curt later learned was Skrewdriver, and the man who was feeding quarters into the jukebox was sitting next to it, at a small table by himself.

Curt and his buddies crowded in at the bar and ordered beers. They swapped war stories about their recent boot camp experiences and laughed heartily. Curt was content. It was the first time he had felt at all like part of a group. He'd even excelled during training and had been selected as a squadron leader.

Eventually tiring of the thudding, monotonous music, Curt drifted over to the jukebox. He'd had several beers and was euphorically mellow. He looked over the selections and fingered a handful of quarters.

"You don't like the music?" the man at the small table asked.

Curt looked down at the stranger. He was of moderate size with close-cropped hair. His features were sharp with narrow lips and straight, white teeth. He was clean-shaven and dressed in a T-shirt and ironed jeans. There was a small American flag tattooed on his right upper arm. But his most striking attribute was his eyes. Even in the semi-darkness, they had a piercing quality that Curt found almost hypnotic.

"The music's all right," Curt said. He squared his shoulders. It appeared as if the stranger was sizing him up.

"You should listen to the words, friend," the man said. He took a pull on his beer.

"Yeah, what would I hear?" Curt asked.

"A message that might save the goddamn country," the man said.

A wry smile crept onto Curt's face. He glanced over at his buddies, thinking they should hear this guy.

"My name's Tim Melcher," the man said. He pushed an empty chair out from his table with his foot. "Sit down. I'll buy you a beer."

Curt looked at the beer in his hand. It was down to the dregs.

"Come on, soldier," Tim said. "Take a load off your feet and do yourself a favor."

"I'm a Marine," Curt said.

"It's all the same," Tim said. "I was army myself. First Cavalry Division. I did two tours in Vietnam."

Curt nodded. The word *Vietnam* made his legs feel rubbery. It meant real war instead of the playacting Curt and his friends had been doing. It also reminded Curt of his older brother Pete, the Bensonhurst football star. Eight years older than Curt, he'd had the bad luck of being drafted. He'd been killed in Vietnam the year before the war was over.

Curt turned the chair around, threw a leg over it, and sat down. He leaned on the back of the chair and drained his beer.

"What'll it be?" Tim asked. "The same?"

Curt nodded.

"Harry!" Tim called to the bartender. "Send us over a couple of Buds."

"What's your name, soldier?"

"Curt Rogers."

"I like that," Tim said. "Nice Christian name. It fits you, too."

Curt shrugged. He didn't quite know what to make of the stranger, especially with his intense eyes.

With a fresh beer, Curt began to relax again.

"You know, I'm glad I met you," Tim said. "And you know why?"

Curt shook his head.

"Because I'm forming a group that I think you and a couple of your buddies ought to join."

"What kind of a group?" Curt asked skeptically.

"A border brigade," Tim said. "An armed border brigade. You see, the regular Border Patrol who are supposed to be protecting this country from illegal aliens are not doing their job. Hell, the Mexican border just ten freaking miles away is like a giant sieve."

"Really," Curt said. He'd not thought much about the border. He'd been much too preoccupied with the rigors of boot camp.

"Yes, really," Tim said, mocking Curt's response. "I'm telling you, this is a serious situation. You and I and the rest of our Aryan brothers and sisters are soon going to be the minority around here."

"I'd never thought about that," Curt said. It was the first time he'd even heard the word *Aryan* and had little idea of what it meant.

"Hey, you'd better wake up," Tim said. "It's happening. This country is on the brink of being taken over by niggers, spics, slanty-eyes, and queers. It's going to be up to people like you and me if our God-fearing, self-reliant culture is to survive where people work for a living and queers stay in the closet. I tell you, not only are these other races seeping in here like water through a sponge, but they're reproducing like flies. This is one hell of a problem. We just can't sit around on our asses anymore. If we do, we only have ourselves to blame."

"How are you going to arm the border brigade?" Curt asked. "If you got some crazy idea that people like me could help, think again. We can't take our ordnance off the base."

"Weapons are not a problem," Tim said. "I've got a goddamn arsenal in my basement, including fully automatic M1s, machine pistols, scoped sniper rifles, and Glocks. I even have uniforms for us 'cause I already got about ten navy guys involved. We've already been on patrol."

"Have you come across any aliens?" Curt asked. Awed by the firearms Tim described, Curt's estimation of the stranger soared.

"Bet your sweet ass," Tim said. "We've interdicted almost a dozen."

"What do you do with them once you catch them, turn them over to the Border Patrol?"

Tim laughed scornfully. "If we did that, they'd be back the next night. The Border Patrol's idea of interdiction is to slap their wrists, scold them, and then turn them loose."

"Well, then what do you do with them?" Curt asked although he sensed the answer.

Tim leaned over and whispered. "We shoot 'em and bury 'em." He wiped his hands rapidly as if brushing off dirt. "That way, it's over and done. There's no second chance."

Curt swallowed. His throat had gone dry. The idea of shooting illegal aliens was both arousing and scary at the same time.

"I got some copies of a magazine here in my briefcase," Tim said. "I'll be happy to give them to you if you hand them out to people like you and me. You understand what I'm saying when I say people like you and me?"

"Yeah, I suppose," Curt said. "What kind of magazines are they?"

"The one that I happen to have today is called *Blood and Honor*," Tim said. "I've got others, but this one is particularly good. It's from England, but it talks about the stuff we're discussing. Western Europe has the same problems we do. I also have a novel you can read. Do you like to read?"

"No, not much," Curt admitted. "Except gun manuals and stuff like that."

"Maybe this book will turn you into a reader," Tim said. "Reading is important." He bent over, unsnapped his briefcase, and lifted out a sizable paperback. "It's called *The Turner Diaries*." He handed it to Curt.

Curt took the book. He was skeptical. He'd only read one novel since high school: a pornographic story about a college call girl from Dallas named Barbara. He cracked open *The Turner Diaries* and read a few lines. He couldn't know then that it would become his favorite book.

Curt ended up taking six copies of the magazine *Blood and Honor* in addition to *The Turner Diaries*. After reading both he became progressively excited and concerned about the issues Tim had brought up. Curt made it a point to get the reading material to people Tim thought were appropriate. Soon he had amassed a cadre of like-minded Marines that began to share meals.

Curt's relationship with Tim Melcher blossomed. He spent a good deal of his free time with the man, helping to organize the border brigade, which he himself joined. Several Marines Curt had recruited joined as well. When Curt eventually got to see Tim's arsenal in his basement, it aroused him erotically. He'd never seen such a collection of guns and ammo outside of live-ammo Marine maneuvers. Tim even had a stash of Kalashnikov AK-47s. They weren't as technically good as the fully automatic M1s, but they had a romantic appeal.

Curt's first operational border brigade excursion had been disturbing. It had started auspiciously with lots of laughter. Everyone was drinking beer from ice chests in the back of the SUVs as they drove south in a convoy of three vehicles, hop-skipping down Interstate 5. Each vehicle was playing Skrewdriver cassettes, which Tim had gotten from England, at high volume. It was a festive atmosphere.

North of the border they'd turned east into the desert. At a site preselected by Tim, they stopped and bivouacked. They put up tents and started a fire. As night fell, they cleaned up their dishes, doused the fire, and set out toward the border. Dressed as they were in desert camouflage, they blended in except for their drunken hilarity.

Curt was having the time of his life. Finally he was truly a part of a group that was, according to Tim, racially pure and of like mind. He also felt they were doing something important, although he doubted they could sneak up on anyone. If nothing else they'd scare any aliens back the way they'd come.

Tim divided the group up into twos. He positioned the pairs at set intervals spread out about a quarter mile back from the border. He chose Curt as his partner, a fact that made Curt proud. It was also good because Tim had made sure he and Curt had the best location. They were on top of a mesa-like rise that was the highest point of the whole area.

They hunkered down on a patch of sand with the sandstone conveniently jutting up behind them. Leaning back against the rock, they broke out fresh beers from their portable thermos pack. The metallic snap of the tabs as they broke in unison was a delicious sound in the dark, arid wilderness.

The night was gorgeous and mild as the rock radiated its stored warmth. Above, the Milky Way appeared as if strewn with a million diamonds. A soft wind blew in from the Pacific, just strong enough to be felt on open skin.

"Beautiful, isn't it?" Tim commented. He unhooked his communicator from his belt and placed it on a flat rock. He used the radio to keep in touch with the other teams.

"It's unbelievable," Curt said. "When I grew up in Brooklyn, I never knew something like this existed."

"It's a great country," Tim said. "Too bad it's going to the dogs because of the freaking government."

Curt nodded but didn't say anything. As mesmerized as he was by the surroundings and numbed by beer, he didn't want to get into another discussion about the Zionist Occupied Government.

A few minutes passed in silence. Curt took another sip of his beer. "Have you ever been to this location on previous sorties?" Curt asked. At Tim's insistence they used military terms whenever possible.

"Several times," Tim said.

"Did you see any action?"

"Oh, yeah," Tim said. "The enemy was very cooperative." He laughed. "It was like a turkey shoot."

"Where did you see them?"

Tim pointed. "Coming along that gully that looks like a notch on the horizon."

Curt strained his eyes in the darkness. He needed a bit of imagination to believe he was looking at a ravine end on. There was no way he could see anyone approaching until they were practically on top of them. Curt wondered what it would be like if a group of men did suddenly spill out of the darkness. By reflex, his hand dropped down to his holstered Glock automatic. He unsnapped the cover. He didn't want to be fumbling with it if a need for the gun arose.

"I know what you're thinking," Tim said. "Let me show you something."

Tim unzipped his canvas gun bag that he'd put on the ground next to him and pulled out a weapon. Even in the darkness Curt could tell it was one of Tim's that he'd never seen.

"This here's my favorite," Tim said proudly. "I don't take it out except for real ops, like tonight."

He extended the weapon toward Curt. Curt took it and held it up close to his face. He recognized it immediately although he'd never held one. It was a Marine-modified Remington .308 sniper rifle.

"Where the hell did you get this?" Curt asked with awe.

"You can buy pretty much whatever you want from the

survivalist mags like *Mercenary*. All you have to do is look in the ads in the back."

"But this is Marine issue," Curt said. "How could someone get one in the first place?"

"How should I know?" Tim said. "I suppose someone probably stole it at some point or maybe somebody traded it for something else. You'll learn that there's a lot of bartering going on in the military."

"They modify these things at Quantico," Curt said. He ran his hand affectionately along the stock.

"Yeah, I know," Tim said. "It's got a floating barrel and fiberglass bedding. And the trigger pull has been adjusted to one pound."

"God, it's fantastic," Curt said. He could only dream of owning one. He'd come to love guns of any sort but especially high-tech ones.

"The best thing is the scope," Tim said. "Notice its size. It's a night-vision scope. Give it a try."

Curt lovingly lifted the weapon to his shoulder and sighted through the telescopic sight. The black night was miraculously transformed into a hazy green transparency. Even at a distance of several hundred yards Curt could make out details of the arid environment.

All of a sudden Curt's eyes caught movement and he turned the rifle slightly to his left. In the center of his field of vision were two men picking their way through the darkness, heading toward Curt on the diagonal.

"Holy crap!" Curt exclaimed. "I got two wetbacks in my sights. I can't believe it."

"No shit!" Tim said excitedly. "Don't take your eyes off them. You might not be able to find them again. Tell me: what are they wearing? They're not uniforms, are they?"

"Hell, no!" Curt said. "Looks like plaid shirts, jeans, cowboy hats, and they're carrying what look like old vinyl suitcases."

"Congratulations, soldier!" Tim said. "You got yourself a couple of turkeys. Pull off at least two rounds quick-like to make sure you get both. Of course if you can line them up maybe you can get away with one shot." Tim giggled.

"You want me to shoot them?" Curt asked nervously. He'd purposefully avoided thinking about this moment, especially since he was aware the men in his sights presented no immediate danger to himself. It wasn't like a battle situation where he was confident he'd react by reflex. This was more like bushwhacking two unarmed people he didn't even know. Curt could sense he was trembling since his field of vision had begun to jump around.

"No, I want you to walk out there and have an argument with them," Tim said sarcastically. "Of course I want you to shoot them. Hell, it's your right. You're the one who spotted them."

Curt felt perspiration appear on his forehead. He swallowed. An anxiety of indecision spread through him. He'd never done anything like this before.

"Come on, man," Tim said. "Don't let me or your country down."

Curt had no intention of letting Tim down. The past month or so had been the first time in his life that he was a member of a tight-knit assemblage whose ideology he truly believed. He'd found a home emotionally and intellectually, and he knew he owed it all to Tim. Taking in a breath and holding it, Curt squeezed the trigger.

The rifle recoiled but not enough for Curt to lose sight of his targets. The lead man went down like he'd been tripped. He didn't spin around or stagger as Curt had seen in the movies when people were shot. One minute the man was walking, the next he was gone. The second man had stopped, frozen in his tracks as the sound of the rifle echoed around the dark, harsh landscape.

Curt felt an orgasmic rush of adrenaline and a tremendous sense of power. Without another thought, he drew a bead on the second man and smoothly pulled the trigger. The gun again jumped and the second man disappeared. Curt lowered the rifle. For a brief moment there was a refreshing smell of cordite in the air before the breeze dispersed it.

"Well?" Tim asked expectantly.

"Both are down," Curt said.

"Fantastic!" Tim said. He gave Curt a pat on the shoulder

before reaching for the radio. He told the other teams that he and Curt were going out to dispose of a couple of targets. He told them not to fire on anything until they heard from him again.

"I don't want those crazy guys shooting at us," Tim said. He took the sniper rifle away from Curt, who gave it up without comment. Tim then got out a folding shovel and pick. "Come on," he said to Curt. "But keep your Glock handy in case you just winged the bastards. We might have to give them a 'coop de grass' or whatever the saying is."

Curt stumbled after Tim without saying a word. After the initial euphoria, he was flooded by self-doubt. Now that he'd actually shot someone, he didn't know how to deal with the idea that he might have killed another human being. The mental fog created by the many beers he'd consumed didn't help. The fact that Tim was acting as if he'd merely swatted two pesky flies didn't help, either.

"Come on, soldier!" Tim called over his shoulder when he became aware Curt was lagging behind. Tim had gone ahead with the flashlight, moving over rocky terrain in a slow jog.

Curt pushed himself forward and squared his shoulders. He was embarrassed that Tim might suspect his "candy ass" state of mind.

It took them almost half an hour to find the Mexicans since they had to crisscross the general area a number of times. As Tim's flashlight beam played over their bodies, he whistled in admiration. "I'm impressed," he said. "You drilled both of them through the head."

Curt looked down at the corpses. He'd never seen a dead person before outside of a funeral home. Both bodies had small entrance holes on their foreheads but were missing large chunks of scalp in the back. The ground in the area was sprinkled with bits and pieces of brain. The man in the front still had his hand wrapped around the handle of his suitcase.

"Oh my God!" Curt murmured.

Tim's head snapped up and he glared at his recruit. "What's the matter?" he demanded.

"What did I do?"

"You killed a couple of wetback illegal aliens," Tim snapped. "You did your country a favor."

"Jesus," Curt mumbled as he shook his head. The Mexicans' eyes were still open, and they were staring at him. Curt swayed a little on rubbery legs.

Tim reacted swiftly. He stepped over to his partner for the evening and slapped him hard. Tim then swore at the pain and shook his hand as if it were wet.

Curt recoiled and for a moment he saw red. He touched his stinging face, then glanced at his fingers as if he expected to see blood. He glared at Tim.

"I'm right here, tough guy," Tim jeered. He gestured with his tingling hand for Curt to come and try to hit him back.

Curt stared off into the black night. He didn't want to fight with Tim because now that he'd had a moment to think, he knew why Tim had hit him.

"You were going soft on me," Tim explained.

Curt nodded. It was true.

"Listen," Tim said. "Let me tell you something you don't know about me. I was ordained just this year as a minister in the True Believers Christian Church, which happens to be a local branch of the much bigger Christian Identity Church. You ever hear of that?"

Curt shook his head.

"It's a church that has used the Bible to prove that we white Anglo-Saxons are the true descendants of the lost tribe of Israel. All the other races are spawns of Satan or mud people, like these spics here." Tim nudged one of the Mexicans with his black boot. "That's why we have white skin and they have black, brown, yellow or whatever you want to call it."

"You're a minister?" Curt asked incredulously. The man had so many different sides it made Curt's head spin.

"Full-fledged," Tim said. "So I know what I'm talking about. The key thing is that God's word in the Bible says that the means to bring about divine judgment is not limited to actions of the body politic. It means that violence is not only okay, but it's necessary. The fact of the matter is that you've done God's work tonight, soldier."

"I've never heard anything about all this," Curt admitted.

"That's not surprising," Tim said. "Nor is it your fault. The Zionist Occupied Government doesn't want you to know about it. They keep it out of the schools, out of the newspapers, and off the TV, all of which they control. The reason is that they want to neutralize us by diluting us genetically. It's just like in *The Turner Diaries*. Remember?"

"I'm not sure," Curt said. He was impressed with Tim's vehemence as much as his erudition.

"It was part of the Cohen Act," Tim said. "It stipulated that the human relations councils it set up were to force Aryan whites to marry mud people. That kind of marriage is called miscegenation. Have you ever heard of that term?"

"No," Curt said.

"Then you get my point," Tim said. "It's a ZOG conspiracy. They don't even want kids to learn the term because encouraging miscegenation is the most insidious sin of all that ZOG is guilty of. And to God it's an abomination. It's Satan's attempt to do away with God's chosen people. It's the Holocaust in reverse."

"All right!" Curt spat, returning from his brief reverie. "It's time we put the cards on the table." He looked at Steve. Steve nodded in agreement. Curt looked at Yuri.

"What cards are you talking about?" Yuri questioned. He could tell that his guests were livid, particularly Curt.

Curt rolled his eyes in frustration. "It's an expression, for crissake. It means explaining everything to everybody so there are no surprises."

"Okay," Yuri said agreeably.

"I mean like you've shocked us tonight," Curt snapped. "Not only are you married, but you're married to a nigger woman. Calling that a surprise is putting it mildly."

"I needed a green card," Yuri explained.

"But you should not have married a black woman!" Steve barked.

"What difference does it make?" Yuri asked, although he thought he knew the answer. Over the four years he'd lived

in the United States he'd become well aware of social preju-
dices.

Curt held his tongue despite the foolishness of Yuri's question. He thought for a moment of explaining the whole issue
to Yuri the way Tim Melcher had explained it to him some
twenty years earlier. But he decided against it, because looking
at Yuri with a more critical eye, Curt couldn't decide if he
was Aryan or not.

"Marrying between the races, particularly when one member is white, is against God's word," Steve said.

"I'd never heard that," Yuri said.

"What's done is done," Curt said with a wave of his hand.
"More important at the moment is the question of what we are
going to do now. Your wife knows you are screwing around
with bacteria downstairs and she knows that you worked in
the Soviet bioweapons industry. Chances are she knows you're
making a bioweapon."

"She doesn't concern herself with what I'm doing," Yuri
said. "Trust me."

"But she could suddenly change her mind," Curt said. "And
that would be very bad."

"She could say something to her family," Steve suggested.

"She doesn't talk with her family," Yuri said. "Except for
her brother. He's the only one who cares about her."

"So, suppose she says something revealing to her brother,"
Curt said. "One way or the other, we can't take the risk. Like
we mentioned earlier she might have to go. Do you have a
problem with that?"

Yuri shook his head and took a healthy swallow from his
tumbler of vodka.

"Okay," Curt said. "At least we agree on that. The problem
is how do we do it without calling attention. I assume she'd
be missed if she were just to disappear."

"She'd be missed at work," Yuri agreed. "She's a taxi dispatcher."

"The key point is that we have to do it so that the police
are not involved," Curt said. "Does she have any medical
problems?"

"Something besides obesity," Steve added.

Yuri shook his head. "She's pretty healthy."

"Hey, maybe we could use her obesity," Steve offered. "As fat as she is, no one would question it if she had a heart attack."

"That's not a bad idea," Curt said. "But how do we make her have a heart attack?"

The three men looked at each other. No one had a clue how to simulate a heart attack.

"I could make her die of respiratory failure," Yuri suggested.

Both Curt and Steve raised their eyebrows.

"A lot of overweight people die of respiratory failure," Yuri said. "I could say she had asthma when we got to the hospital."

"How would you do it?" Curt asked.

"I'd use a large dose of my botulinum toxin," Yuri said. "Hell, I need to test it anyway. Why not on Connie? This way I can be sure of the dose."

"But wouldn't the doctors figure it out?" Curt asked.

"No," Yuri said. "Once someone is dead and you don't know the initial symptoms, there's no way to suspect it. And you have to suspect it, otherwise it's not thought of. There are too many other things that cause respiratory failure."

"Are you sure?" Curt asked.

"Of course I'm sure," Yuri said. "I was involved with a lot of the testing of the toxin back in the Soviet Union. With a big dose the person just stops breathing and turns blue. The KGB was very interested in it for covert assassinations because what constitutes a big dose is actually a very, very small amount."

"I like it," Curt said. "There's a certain poetic justice to it. After all, Connie is threatening the security of Operation Wolverine. When could you do it?"

"Tonight," Yuri said with a shrug. "One thing I never have trouble getting her to do is eat. Later on, after she calms down, I'll just call in some pizza and that will be that."

"Well," Curt declared while allowing his first smile of the evening. "With that bit of unpleasantness out of the way, let's go on to greener pastures. What's the good news you have for us?"

"I tested the anthrax," Yuri said eagerly. He moved forward in his chair. "It's as potent as I expected."

"Who did you test it on?" Curt asked. In light of current events involving Connie, security was Curt's first concern.

Yuri described how he'd picked Jason Papparis, a rug merchant, who was at risk for contracting anthrax from the merchandise he imported. Yuri explained that by doing so he'd certainly avoided any possible suspicions by the authorities for what they were planning.

"Very clever," Curt said. "On behalf of the People's Aryan Army, I commend your shrewdness."

Yuri allowed himself a self-satisfied smile.

"We've got some news for you as well," Curt said. He went on to describe the visit he and Steve had made to the Jacob Javits Federal Building that morning. He told Yuri that it was set up perfectly to put the bioweapon in the HVAC induction duct.

"Will you need an aerosolizer?" Yuri asked.

"No, not if the weapon comes in a fine powder," Curt said. "We'll use timed detonators to burst the packaging. The circulating fans will do the rest."

"That means you'll have to use the anthrax," Yuri said.

"That's all right by us," Curt said. "Is that a problem? You told us both agents would be equally potent."

"No, it's not a problem," Yuri said. "It's just that I'm having trouble getting the bacteria that makes the botulinum toxin to grow fast enough. I'm less than a week away from having plenty of anthrax, but more than three weeks away from having enough botulinum toxin."

"I don't think we want to wait three weeks," Curt said. "Not with the security problems we've been having."

"Why not just go with the anthrax for both targets?" Steve said. "Forget the toxin if the bacteria aren't cooperating."

"Because with the amount of anthrax we'll only have enough for one laydown, not two," Yuri said.

"Maybe Providence is telling us we should only hit the federal building," Curt said. "How about forgetting Central Park?"

"No!" Yuri said with emphasis. "I want to do the park."

"But why?" Curt asked. "The federal building is going to make a much bigger statement against the government, and it's going to get at least six or seven thousand people."

"But it's only government people," Yuri said. "I want to strike just as much against the fake American culture, particularly all those Jewish businessmen and bankers who've caused all the economic turmoil in Russia today."

Curt and Steve exchanged a disgruntled glance.

"This is a rootless culture," Yuri continued. "People are supposed to be free, but they're not. They're all scrambling for status and identity. We Slavs may have had some trouble down through history but at least we know who we are."

"I don't believe I'm hearing this," Curt said. "Why haven't you voiced this before?"

"You never asked me," Yuri said.

"America has some problems," Curt agreed. "But it's because of ZOG supporting gun control, miscegenation, nigger drug dealers, welfare cheats, and queers, all of who are eroding our original roots. That's what we're fighting against. We know we'll have some civilian casualties in the struggle. It's to be expected. But it's the government we're targeting."

"There are no civilians in my war," Yuri said. "That's why I want the laydown in Central Park. With a proper wind vector it will take out a large swath of the city. I'm talking about hundreds of thousands of casualties or even millions, not thousands. That's what a weapon of mass destruction is supposed to do. Hell, for your narrow objective you could use a regular old bomb."

"We wouldn't be able to get a bomb big enough into the building," Curt said. "That's the whole point. We'll have no trouble with four or five pounds of flour-like powder. I mean, that's how you described the weaponized anthrax."

"That's right," Yuri said. "A very, very fine flour that's so light it stays suspended."

For a few moments the three men stared at each other. All were aware of the tension.

"All right," Curt said, waving his hands in the air. "We're back to square one. We'll do both laydowns. The problem boils down to getting enough stuff."

"Where's my pest control truck you guys promised?" Yuri asked.

"The troops have located one," Curt said. "Don't worry."

"Where is it?"

"It's parked behind a pest control company out on Long Island," Curt said. "It's used for the potato crop in season. There's no security. It's there for the taking."

"I want it in my garage," Yuri said.

"What's this new belligerency?" Curt questioned. "With the surprises you've had for us tonight, we are the ones who should be mad."

"I just want the truck in the garage," Yuri demanded. "That was the deal. It was supposed to be there already."

"I think you'd better watch your tone," Steve said. "Otherwise we'll be sending the shock troops to pay you a visit."

"Don't threaten me," Yuri said. "Otherwise you won't get anything. I'll sabotage the whole program."

"Hey, hold up, you guys," Curt said. "This is getting out of hand. Let's not argue among ourselves. There's no problem here. We'll see that the truck is procured, brought into town, and put into your garage. Will that make you happy?"

"That was our agreement," Yuri said.

"Consider it done," Curt said. "Meanwhile on your end you've got to take care of Connie. Fair enough?"

"It will be done tonight," Yuri said. He visibly relaxed and polished off the last of his drink.

"Good," Curt said. He rubbed his hands in a show of eagerness. "Then let's talk about scheduling. What if you gave up on the toxin and converted the second fermenter to anthrax? Wouldn't that mean we'd have enough product sooner?"

"Probably," Yuri said.

"What's the time frame realistically?" Curt asked.

"By the end of the week or the beginning of the next if all goes well," Yuri said.

"That's music to my ears," Curt said, forcing himself to smile. He stood up. Steve followed suit.

"I have a question," Yuri said. "What's a medical examiner?"

"It's a guy that looks at dead people and figures out why they died," Steve said.

"I thought so," Yuri said. He got to his feet.

"That's a curious question," Curt remarked. "Why do you ask?"

"When I went back to the rug dealer's today to find out if he'd died, there was a man there taking cultures who said he was investigating the case."

"Wait a sec," Curt commented. "I thought you said that your ruse of infecting a rug dealer would preclude any investigation by the authorities."

"I didn't say that," Yuri responded. "I said that the authorities wouldn't suspect the release of a bioweapon."

"But the authorities know anthrax is used as a weapon," Curt said. "What will keep them from getting suspicious?"

"Because they'll have a logical explanation for the episode," Yuri said. "They'll be congratulating themselves for figuring it out. That's the way those people think."

"What if they don't find any source?" Curt asked. "Or did you leave something for them to find on one of the rugs?"

"No, I didn't do that," Yuri admitted.

"Could that be a problem?" Curt asked.

"Possibly," Yuri said. "But I doubt it."

"But you can't be a hundred percent certain," Curt said.

"Not a hundred percent but very close to it."

Curt let out an exasperated sigh. "Suddenly there seems to be so many loose ends."

"It's not going to be a problem," Yuri said. "And we had to test the product. There'd be no sense in releasing it if it wasn't pathogenic."

"Let's hope you're right," Curt said in a tired voice. He stood up and started for the door. "We'll be in touch. Some of the boys will come by late tonight to deliver the pest control truck."

"What if I'm not here?" Yuri asked.

"You'd better be here," Curt said. "You're the one making all the ruckus about this goddamn truck."

"But I have to take care of Connie," Yuri said. "I'll have

to call emergency after she's had her fit. I might be at the hospital."

"Oh, yeah," Curt said.

"I know what I'll do," Yuri said. "When I go out with Connie I'll leave the garage door unlocked."

"Perfect," Curt said. He waved and went out the door. Steve followed closely behind.

The two firemen trooped out of Yuri's house and climbed into the Dodge Ram without talking. Once the doors were closed Curt pounded the steering wheel with a closed fist. "We got ourselves involved with a goddamned fruitcake," he snarled.

"I'm not going to say I told you so," Steve said.

"Jesus Christ, he's out to kill civilians, not government people," Curt complained. "Here we are, patriots, trying to save the country, and we're forced to deal with a terrorist. What's this world coming to?"

"I think his wish for the Soviet Union to get back together involves a lot more than wanting to protect the nukes. I think he's a Commie."

Curt started his truck and pulled out into the lane. It was like a slalom course trying to avoid all the trash cans. "Maybe he is a Commie. But whatever he is, he has no concept of security. It's too bad, because if the authorities get even a hint of what's coming, we've got to reevaluate the whole operation. When we first started planning this, it seemed like it would be so easy."

"What are we going to do about him?" Steve asked.

"I don't know. The trouble is we've got to play along in order to get our hands on the bioweapon. He made that pretty clear with his threat to sabotage the whole setup, which I suppose means he'd trash the lab."

"So we're going to get him the pest control truck?"

"I don't see where we have much choice," Curt said as he pulled out onto Oceanview Avenue. "We'll get him the truck, but we'll also keep the pressure on him to come up with the eight or so pounds of anthrax powder as soon as possible. The sooner we can launch Operation Wolverine the better."

SEVEN

Jack scooted across First Avenue at Thirtieth Street just before the light turned green for the traffic heading uptown. He coasted to the medical examiner's office loading dock and nodded to security as he carried his bike into the building. He waved to Marvin Fletcher, the evening mortuary tech, who was busy in the mortuary office getting ready for the evening's body pickups.

After locking his bike in its usual spot, Jack got on the elevator and headed up to the second-floor toxicology lab. It was later than he'd planned on getting back to the office. Going through all the Corinthian Rug Company's records had taken much more time than he'd expected.

John DeVries, the chief toxicologist, had already left for the day. Jack was reduced to asking a night tech if the deputy chief had called about putting a rush on David Jefferson's specimens. David Jefferson was the prisoner-in-custody death Calvin was pressuring Jack about. Unfortunately, the night tech had no idea about the case.

Back in the elevator, Jack went up to the DNA lab on the sixth floor. Ted Lynch, the director, wasn't available, so Jack left his collection of culture tubes from the Corinthian Rug office with a technician. In the morning he wanted Ted to search for anthrax spores with the PCR.

Taking the stairs to the fifth floor, Jack ducked into the histology lab in hopes of encouraging Maureen O'Conner, the supervisor, to speed up processing Jefferson's microscopic sections. Jack had a good working relationship with Maureen, one he didn't share with John DeVries, but it made no difference. Maureen had also left for the day.

En route to his own office, Jack looked into Laurie's, expecting at the very least to find out the "when and where" for the evening's long-awaited dinner party. But Laurie's office was dark and deserted. To make matters worse, her door was locked. Jack knew that was incontrovertible evidence that she, too, had gone home.

"For crissake!" Jack said out loud. Feeling thwarted in all directions, he grumbled under his breath as he walked the rest of the way down the corridor. For a brief moment he entertained the idea of being unavailable for the rest of the evening so that Laurie would not be able to get ahold of him. But he quickly gave up the idea. It wasn't his style, and besides, he was genuinely curious.

Jack turned into his own office. At least Chet was still there, busily writing on a yellow legal tablet.

"Ah, the adventurer has returned," Chet commented as he caught sight of Jack. He put down his pencil. "I guess I can cancel the missing persons report I filed."

"Very funny," Jack commented as he hung up his bomber jacket.

"At least you arrived back in one piece," Chet said. "How was it out there in the field? Any attempts on your life? How many fellow civil service workers did you manage to enrage?"

"I'm in no mood to be teased," Jack stated. He plopped himself down heavily in his desk chair as if his legs had suddenly given out from under him.

"It doesn't sound like you enjoyed yourself," Chet remarked.

"It was a bust," Jack admitted. "Except for the bike ride."

"I'm not surprised," Chet said. "It was a doomed mission from the start. Did you learn anything at all?"

"I learned that it takes a long time to go through a company's records," Jack said. "Even a small company. And after all the effort, there was no payoff. In a perverted way I was hoping to find that some of the rug company's latest shipment of Turkish hides had been sent out so I could rub the information in flinty old Clint Abelard's face. But no soap. The whole shipment is locked up tight in the Queens warehouse."

"At least you meant well," Chet said with a self-satisfied chuckle.

"If you so much as whisper 'I told you so.' I'm taking you out of my will," Jack warned.

"I wouldn't stoop so low as to say I told you so." Chet laughed.

"Yeah, but I could hear you thinking it," Jack said.

"I do have to say you were missed. But not to worry. I covered for you. I used your old quip about that group of nuns you've been expecting. I said they'd come to town for a bowling convention, and you'd stepped out to welcome them."

"Who was asking for me?"

"Laurie for one," Chet said. "In fact, I was just writing you a note." Chet tore off the top page of his tablet and balled up the paper. Holding the ball between thumb and index finger, he arced it cleanly into the communal wastebasket.

"What was the message?" Jack demanded.

"I was to tell you that tonight's dinner is at Elio's on Second Avenue at eight-thirty."

"Eight-thirty!" Jack commented irritably. "Why so late?"

"She didn't say. But eight-thirty doesn't sound late to me."

"It's later than she likes to eat," Jack commented. He shook his head. The mystery kept deepening. He remembered her making the comment that morning about whether she'd be still on her feet that evening, suggesting she anticipated being tired. Why then would she make plans to meet late?

"Well, she didn't seem at all concerned," Chet said. "In fact, she was in a rare, spunky mood if you ask me."

"Really?" Jack asked.

"I'd even have to say ebullient."

"She was the same way this morning."

"She was so 'up' I mentioned the possible plan for Thursday evening," Chet said.

"You mean about the four of us going to the Monet exhibit?"

Chet nodded. "I hope you don't mind."

"What was her response?"

"She said she was very appreciative of our thinking of her, but she said she already had plans."

"She actually used the word 'appreciative'?"

"A direct quote," Chet said. "I questioned it, too. It seemed so uncharacteristically formal."

"Who else was looking for me?" Jack asked. He wanted to get away from talking about Laurie. It was making him even more curious—and anxious.

"Calvin stopped in," Chet said. "I think he'd been to histology and just stopped in because he was on the floor."

"What did he say?"

"He wanted to remind you that Jefferson's case has to be signed out by Thursday."

Jack made a gesture of dismissal with his hand. "That's going to be up to the lab, not me."

"Well, I'm on my way," Chet said. He stood up, stretched, and then retrieved his coat from behind the door.

"Let me ask you a question," Jack said. "You've lived in New York longer than I. What's the story with yellow cabs vis-à-vis radio calls?"

"Yellow cabs thrive on people hailing them," Chet explained. "They generally don't do radio calls. Among the drivers the expression is, you cruise or you lose. They don't want to sit around and wait or drive someplace empty. They have to hustle or they lose money."

"Why do a lot of them have radios?" Jack asked.

"They can do radio calls if they want," Chet said. "But it doesn't pay. Generally the radios just keep them informed of where there's the greatest need, like uptown or downtown or out at the airport. And what areas to stay out of because of traffic congestion, that sort of thing."

Jack nodded. "That's what I thought."

"Why do you ask?" Chet questioned.

"A cab driver came by the Corinthian Rug Company to pick up Jason Papparis while I was there," Jack said with a wry smile.

Chet laughed. "That's the first time I've heard of a dead man calling for a cab. It makes you wonder from where he placed the call."

"Or where he wanted the cab to take him."

Chet laughed again in an equally hollow manner.

"The driver gave me the number of the dispatcher," Jack said. "I called them to see if Jason was a frequent customer. I thought that if he was, then maybe the cab company might be a source of information about the last time the man went to his Queens warehouse."

"What did they say?"

"They were not helpful," Jack said. "They wouldn't even tell me when Jason Papparis had called to set up the pickup. They just said they don't give out any information on their drivers or their clients."

"That's being nice and helpful," Chet said. "It could be subpoenaed, I suppose."

"I can't imagine it would be worth it," Jack said.

"It's still curious," Chet said. "If someone calls for a cab in New York City, it's generally not a yellow cab that responds."

"I'll tell you something even more curious," Jack said. "The taxi driver was Russian and he'd grown up in Sverdlovsk."

"Sverdlovsk!" Chet exclaimed. "That's the Soviet town that had the anthrax bioweapons accident you pointed out to me in Harrison's textbook of medicine!"

"Can you believe it?" Jack asked. "I mean that's a coincidence."

"Only in New York," Chet said. "I suppose we shouldn't be surprised, because anything and everything happens here."

"This guy even knew about anthrax," Jack said.

"No kidding?"

"Well, he didn't know much," Jack added. "He just knew it was a disease mainly of cattle. He mentioned cows and sheep."

"I'd venture to guess that's more than the average New Yorker knows," Chet said.

After a bit more small talk about activities over the immediately preceding weekend, Chet said his goodbyes and left. Jack turned to his desk. Without enthusiasm he eyed his ever-burgeoning pile of uncompleted cases lying next to a stack of waiting histology slides. He thought briefly about getting out his microscope until he glanced at his watch. It was after seven. Knowing he had to pedal home, shower and dress, and then pedal back across town all before eight-thirty, Jack decided he didn't have time for more work.

The traffic on First Avenue had abated somewhat from a half hour earlier, and Jack ran with it beyond the United Nations building. Taking Forty-ninth Street, he crossed to Madison Avenue and then again turned north. He rarely used the same route home until he got to the Grand Army Plaza at the southeastern corner of Central Park. It was there that he took his nightly turn around the Pulitzer fountain to admire the gilded nude statue of Abundance atop it. Then he entered the park and his favorite part of the trip. Over the years he'd figured out the best and most scenic route and used it most nights.

With an eye peeled for other cyclists, joggers, and in-line skaters, Jack cranked up his pace. Although the trees still had most of their leaves, a lot had already fallen, and they swirled in his wake and filled him with the unmistakable scent of fall.

Although Jack immensely enjoyed his rapid transit through the park, it also made him feel edgy. Finding himself paradoxically isolated in the lonely expanse within the confines of the otherwise teeming city never failed to remind him of the night he'd almost been shot and killed here by a hired gang member. There was no doubt danger lurked in the park's silent shadows.

Jack burst out of the tranquil darkness onto the bustling avenue, Central Park West. It was like returning to civilization. Slowing his speed considerably, he wound his way north among the darting, honking clutch of yellow cabs. At 106th Street he turned west.

Knowing he didn't have a lot of time to spare, Jack had

fully intended on heading directly to his tenement. Instead, he couldn't resist the siren song of the basketball court. Even though he was unable to play that evening, he couldn't pass by without at least stopping to check out the action.

The court was part of a larger, mostly cement park featuring swings, monkey bars, and sandboxes for the younger children, as well as benches for the doting mothers. Jack loved to play B-ball. He'd played at Amherst, which had never had a very competitive team. Years later, when he'd first moved to New York City, he'd ventured one day onto the court merely to shoot baskets by himself as a diversion, but by chance the locals had had only nine players. So they'd lowered their standards and asked Jack to play. He'd been immediately hooked by the lively and often rough urban games. Now, weather permitting, it was almost a nightly ritual.

For almost a year, Jack had been the only Caucasian player among the horde of local and considerably younger African-American players. But over the next few years two other white players had ventured into the fray, as well as a number of African-Americans closer to Jack's age of forty-four.

As a regular and a fanatic, Jack financed new backboards, new outdoor balls, and mercury vapor lighting. He accomplished this combination philanthropic and self-serving gesture through negotiations with the local community leadership. The final deal stipulated that Jack had to pay to refurbish the other park amenities as well. Jack had not minded in the slightest and considered it a small price to pay to be welcomed into the neighborhood.

Jack pedaled his bike up to the massive chain-link fence that separated the B-ball court from the sidewalk. Without taking his feet from his toe clips, he grabbed onto the fence to support himself. As he'd expected, there was a game in progress, with the players sweeping up and down the court.

"Hey, Doc!" a voice called out. "Doc" was Jack's neighborhood sobriquet. "Where you been? Get your ass out here. You going to run or what?"

Jack glanced to the sidelines to see the heavily muscled Warren Wilson dribbling a ball in and out between his legs. His shaved head gleamed in the glare of the overhead lights.

He was standing with a pack of other fellows waiting to get into the game.

"I don't have time," Jack called back.

Warren detached himself from the others and started toward Jack. He was joined by Flash, one of the taller players whose level of ability was about on a par with Jack's. Warren was a quantum leap above both of them.

Jack nodded a greeting to Flash, who returned the gesture. Since their B-ball talent was roughly equivalent, they frequently covered each other when they were on opposing teams. Flash had the irritating knack of scoring on Jack when games were close, often winning the game. The situation had spawned a friendly rivalry.

"What do you mean you ain't got time?" Warren questioned as he leaned up against the fence. "You weren't out here much last week. Seems to me you're getting your priorities screwed up. What are you doing, letting work interfere?" He loved to tease Jack about their differing philosophies as to what was important in life.

"I have to meet Laurie across town at eight-thirty," Jack said.

"We've got winners," Flash said. He had a particularly deep, rich baritone voice. "It's going to be me, Warren, Spit, and Ron. We got room for one more if you could get your ass down here in record time. It'd be a killer matchup."

"You're tempting me," Jack admitted.

"We're going to sweep this team that's winning at the moment," Warren said. "It's going to be a new dynasty. But, hey, we shouldn't keep you from your shortie."

Jack glanced at his watch and then over at the game in progress. He was tempted, but there was no way he could do it without arriving late at Elio's, even if he played only one game. Ultimately he had to shake his head. "Sorry, not tonight."

"Natalie's been ragging me about getting together with you and Laurie," Warren said. "You guys have been making yourselves scarce."

"I'll say something to Laurie," Jack promised, although he couldn't be optimistic, not without knowing her current secret,

especially if she was moving to someplace like the West
Coast. The thought of Laurie leaving made him wince.

"Hey, man, you okay?" Warren asked. He leaned forward
and regarded Jack through the fence.

"Yeah, sure," Jack said, yanking himself out of his momentary worry.

"Are you and Laurie cool?" Warren questioned. "I mean,
you people aren't having words, are you?"

"No, we're cool," Jack fibbed. The truth of the matter was
that he and Laurie had not spent much time together over the
last month or so.

"I think you'd better get yourself out here for a run as soon
as you can," Warren said. "You look all wound up to me."

"You're right! I need a run," Jack agreed. "Tomorrow night
for sure."

Jack said his goodbyes and then rode diagonally across the
street to his building. Knowing he would be going right back
out, he locked his bike to the railing on the building's front
steps. Then he went up to his apartment and climbed into the
shower.

After the shower Jack scanned his limited wardrobe for
something to wear, only to get mad at himself for such stupid
indecision. He couldn't remember the last time he had trouble
deciding about clothes. Ultimately he donned his usual jeans,
blue chambray shirt, darker blue knitted tie, and tweed jacket
with leather patches on the elbows. After a quick brush of his
short hair to encourage it all to go in the direction it preferred,
Jack went back down to the street and retrieved his bicycle.

The ride across the park was uneventful. He went south on
Fifth Avenue until Eighty-fourth Street, which he took over to
Second. The restaurant was just a few doors up from the corner. With slightly tremulous fingers Jack secured his bike with
the requisite number of locks. As he entered the restaurant, he
wondered why he was as anxious as he was.

Elio's was crowded. To Jack's left the small bar was five
people deep. To his right were a group of tables with the usual
complement of TV personalities having their dinners. Pushing
his way deeper into the restaurant, Jack scanned the other din-

ers for Laurie's familiar face and burnished auburn hair. He
didn't see her.

"Can I help you?" a voice asked over the din. There was
the slightest guttural hint of a German accent.

Jack turned to face the smiling maître d'.

"We've a reservation, I assume," Jack said.

"And the name?"

"Montgomery, I suppose," Jack said.

The host consulted his list. "Ah, yes, of course. Miss Montgomery is not here yet, but one of the other members of your
party is. He's at the bar. I'll have your table in a moment."

Jack worked his way among the standing clientele, heading
in the general direction of the bar. He saw Lou sitting on one
of the tall stools, clutching a beer and intermittently pulling
on a cigarette. Jack touched him on the arm. Lou glanced up
at him with a hangdog expression.

"You don't look happy," Jack said.

Lou guiltily stubbed out his cigarette. "I'm not. I'm concerned. You got me worried about Laurie when you talked to
me this morning. Since I was with her a good part of the day,
I couldn't help but notice that she was acting weird, like she
was all gassed up about something. When I finally got up the
courage to ask her what was up, she just laughed and said I'd
find out tonight. I'm afraid she might be leaving town. I'm
thinking she got a job someplace else. You medical examiners
are in demand. I know that for a fact."

Jack couldn't suppress a smile. Looking at Lou was like
looking in a mirror, and the image was pathetic. Obviously,
Lou had been torturing himself with the same possibility.

"Go ahead and laugh at me," Lou said. "I deserve it."

"Hey, I'm not laughing at you. I'm laughing at us. I had
the exact same thought. In fact I even picked a place: the West
Coast."

"Seriously?"

Jack nodded.

"I don't know whether that makes me feel better or worse,"
Lou said. "It's nice to have company, but it probably means
we're right."

Jack leaned back so he could get a better look at Lou. He

was impressed. The detective had shaved to remove his usual five o'clock shadow and had even pomaded his hair so that it still looked wet from the shower along the edges of his knife-sharp part. Gone was the rumpled sport jacket and baggy pants. In their place was a crisply pressed suit, a freshly laundered shirt, and a newly knotted tie. Most astounding of all, he'd polished his shoes.

"I've never seen you in a suit before," Jack commented. "You look like you belong in a magazine, and I'm not talking about *True Detective*."

"I usually only wear it to funerals," Lou said.

"That's a happy thought," Jack responded.

"Excuse me," the maître d' said at Jack's elbow. "Your table is ready. Would you men like to sit down or do you want to stay here at the bar?"

"We'll sit down," Jack said without hesitation. He was eager to get away from the second-hand cigarette smoke.

The table was in the far back corner and to get there required some deft maneuvers, since as many tables as possible were crowded into the room. No sooner had Jack and Lou wedged themselves into their seats than a waiter appeared with an iced bottle of champagne plus two pricey bottles of Brunello. He immediately proceeded to open the champagne.

"Whoa!" Jack said to the man. "You got the wrong table. We haven't ordered anything yet."

"Isn't this the Montgomery party?" the waiter asked. He had a Spanish accent and an old-fashioned handlebar mustache. Even though Elio's was an Italian restaurant, it had a decidedly cosmopolitan staff.

"Yeah, but . . ." Jack said.

"Then it's been ordered," the waiter said. He popped the cork and nestled the bottle back into its ice bucket. He then uncorked the two bottles of wine.

"This looks like a good wine," Jack commented as he picked up one of the wine bottles and glanced at the label.

"Oh, very good!" the waiter agreed. "I'll be back with the glasses."

Jack looked over at Lou. "This isn't the jug wine I usually drink."

"I'm getting more nervous," Lou said. "Laurie's the thrifty sort."

"You got a point," Jack agreed. Whenever they went out, Laurie always insisted on paying her own way.

As soon as the waiter came back with the glasses, he proceeded to pour some champagne for Jack and Lou. Jack tried to say that they'd wait for Miss Montgomery, but the waiter insisted he was following the lady's orders.

After the waiter departed Jack picked up his flute. Lou did the same. They touched glasses although neither spoke. Jack tried to think of a toast but nothing appropriate or witty came to mind. Silently they tasted the sparkling wine.

"I suppose it's good," Lou said. "But I've never been a big fan of champagne. I think of it more as something to squirt around at athletic victories."

"My feeling exactly," Jack said. He took another sip and as he did, he caught sight of Laurie over the rim of his long-stemmed glass. She was dressed in a snug black velvet pants suit that outlined her undeniably shapely female form. A triple-stranded pearl necklace was clasped around her neck. To Jack she looked absolutely radiant. So much so that he momentarily choked on his champagne.

Both Jack and Lou struggled to their feet. The quarters were so tight that Lou nudged the table enough to spill his glass of champagne. Luckily Jack was still holding his.

"Oh, what a klutz!" Lou complained.

Laurie laughed, grabbed a napkin, and wiped up the spilled wine. The waiter appeared instantly to lend a hand.

"Thank you both for coming," Laurie said. She gave each a peck on the cheek.

It was at that point that Jack realized Laurie was not alone. Coming up behind her was a darkly tanned, olive-complected man with thick, wavy hair and a mouth full of startlingly white teeth. He wasn't too much taller than Laurie's five feet five inches, but he projected a confident and powerful air. Jack guessed he was close to his own age. He was dressed in a dark silk suit that made Lou's look as if it had come off a rack in a bargain basement. A bright foulard pocket square ballooned from his breast pocket.

"I want you to meet Paul Sutherland," Laurie said. Her voice quavered as if she was nervous.

Jack shook hands with the man after Lou. As their eyes met, Jack had trouble telling where the man's irises stopped and his pupils began. It was like looking into the depths of black marbles. His handshake was firm and resolute.

"Why are we standing?" Laurie asked.

Paul responded by instantly pulling Laurie's chair out from the table. Once Laurie was sitting the others followed suit. The waiter quickly filled the champagne glasses.

"I'd like to propose a toast," Laurie said. "To friends."

"Hear, hear!" Paul echoed.

They all touched glasses and drank.

There was a brief uncomfortable silence. Jack and Lou had no idea why Laurie had brought a stranger to their dinner party and were afraid to ask.

"Well," Laurie said finally. "What a day this has been, wouldn't you say, Lou?"

"Absolutely," Lou agreed.

"I hope you don't mind a little shop talk, Paul," Laurie said. "That skinhead case I mentioned to you earlier had Lou and me tied up for most of the day."

"Not at all," Paul said. "I'm sure I'll be fascinated. That old TV show about a medical examiner was one of my favorites."

"Paul is a businessman," Laurie explained.

Both Jack and Lou nodded in unison. Jack expected more of an explanation of what type of businessman, but Laurie changed the subject: "I learned more today about the violent far right than I wanted to know," she said. "Particularly about right-wing militias and skinheads."

"I didn't know anything about the role of music in the skinhead movement," Lou said.

"What amazes me and scares me is that this militia movement is nationwide," Laurie said. "Special Agent Gordon Tyrrell estimates there are some forty thousand armed survivalists spread across the country waiting for God knows what."

"I think they're waiting for the government to implode from the weight of its huge bureaucracy," Paul said. "Sort of like a neutron star. Then the survivalists will be in a position not only to survive but also to take over."

"They're not above helping it along," Laurie said. "Agent Tyrrell said that undermining the government has become the rationale for violence now that the Soviet Union is no longer the archetypal enemy."

"Revenge is also a rationale," Lou said. "Consider Timothy McVeigh. He was apparently trying to get back at the government for the raid on the Branch Davidians in Waco, Texas."

"Back then I was under the delusion that Timothy McVeigh was an anomaly," Laurie said. "But it's not true, and that's the terrifying part. There are forty thousand potential Timothy McVeighs out there. No one knows where one will strike next and on what pretense."

"Or with what," Jack said. "Remember the lecture we got from Stan Thornton and the Office of Emergency Management? It's not inconceivable for one of those nuts to get his hands on a weapon of mass destruction."

"God help us if that were ever to happen," Laurie said.

"Gordon Tyrrell doesn't think it's a question of *if*," Lou said. "His anti-terrorism department thinks the question is *when*. Just think of all the nuclear weapons that are not entirely accounted for in what used to be the Soviet Union."

"Let's order our dinners," Laurie said with a dejected shake of her head. "If we talk about this much longer, I'm going to lose my appetite."

The waiter came over to the table the moment he was summoned. He rattled off an impressive list of specials while divvying up the rest of the champagne. Once everyone had ordered, he disappeared into the kitchen.

"I've one last question about your skinhead case," Jack said to Laurie. "Did you find anything at autopsy that was helpful for the FBI?"

Laurie sighed and glanced at Lou. "Not really. What do you say, Lou?"

"Your impression that the stab wounds were made with a knife with a serrated upper edge might help," Lou said. "Provided the knife turns up. Also the bullet you took out of the brain might be useful, but it's hard to say at this point until ballistics looks at it. The fact that the crucifying nails were of Polish manufacture is not going to be any help because I've already found out they're widely distributed."

"So this PAA or People's Aryan Army is still a metropolitan unknown?" Jack asked.

"I'm afraid so," Lou said. "The only reassuring part is that Internet traffic concerning them has suddenly dropped off. We're hoping that means whatever they'd been planning has been canceled."

"Let's hope so," Jack said.

The appetizers began to arrive and the red wine was poured. The four concentrated on their food and for a time, conversation was minimal. Jack surreptitiously eyed Laurie but was unable to make any eye contact.

"Tell us about your case today," Laurie said to Jack. "I heard it was another interesting one."

Jack had to clear his throat. "Surprising yes, interesting . . . somewhat. It was a case of inhalation anthrax."

"Anthrax?" Lou questioned with obvious interest. "That's a potential bioweapon."

"It is indeed," Jack agreed. "But fortunately or unfortunately, depending on your point of view, this case has a more prosaic origin. The victim had just imported a bunch of rugs from Turkey, where the disease is endemic. He's apparently the only victim and the rugs are safely locked up in a warehouse in Queens. End of story. I couldn't even get a rise out of the city epidemiologist."

"Thank the Lord for small favors," Laurie said.

"Amen," Lou added.

The entrées arrived, and while the foursome ate their dinners the conversation stayed on neutral ground. The delay in addressing the real issue, whatever it was, only made Jack's curiosity and anxiety mount. Adding to his anxiety was the subtle and, he couldn't help but feel, inappropriate familiarity between Laurie and Paul. He noticed it in the way she touched his arm or the way he dabbed at the corner of her mouth with his napkin. In Jack's mind these small intimacies were inappropriate because he knew she couldn't have known the man long.

Finally, over coffee, Laurie cleared her throat and tapped her waterglass gently with her fork. Paul assumed a self-satisfied smile and leaned back. It was obvious that from his point of view this was Laurie's party.

"I guess you guys must wonder why I invited you here tonight," Laurie began.

No, the thought has never entered my mind, Jack said to himself while his pulse quickened.

"I don't quite know how to tell you this but . . ." Laurie looked at Paul, who shrugged his shoulders as if to say he didn't know either.

Out with it before I barf, Jack said silently.

"First of all, I owe you both an apology," Laurie said. She looked alternately at Jack and Lou. "I'm sorry I had to call you so early in the morning. At least early for your time."

Jack blinked. Laurie had lost him. Why was their time different from her time?

"The explanation is that I was calling from Paris, France," Laurie said. "Paul and I had gone there for the weekend, and we were waiting to board the Concorde to come back to New York."

Paul nodded, confirming this startling story.

"Paul had business in Paris," Laurie continued. "He was nice enough to invite me to go along. It was quite a weekend." She looked over at Paul and extended her right hand. He took it lovingly.

Jack smiled over gritted teeth. He suddenly saw Paul as a snake in the grass who'd managed to win Laurie with this grand, gallant gesture: a weekend in Paris.

"One of the things that happened was quite unexpected," Laurie continued. "At least for me."

Laurie took her left hand out from under the table, where she'd kept it discreetly for the entire dinner. It was balled in a fist as she extended it out over the tablecloth. When her arm was fully extended she dramatically opened her hand and spread her fingers.

Both Jack and Lou blinked. They found themselves looking down at a diamond that seemed to be the size of a golf ball on Laurie's ring finger. It caught all the light from the room and threw it back with blinding intensity.

"You guys are getting married," Lou said as if he were describing an upcoming cataclysm.

The couple interpreted his tone as one of awe, not dread.

"It seems that way," Laurie said with a smile. "I haven't unconditionally agreed yet, but as you can see Paul has convinced me to take the ring. We haven't even told our parents. You two are the first to know."

"We're flattered," Jack managed to say while his mind churned for an explanation for this unexpected turn of events. He'd thought of Laurie as being much too mature for what he considered adolescent behavior.

"It's been a whirlwind," Laurie said. She looked at Paul for confirmation.

"I'd describe it more as a tempest," Paul said with a lascivious wink.

Laurie and Paul then launched into an animated description of all the romantic things they'd been able to squeeze into the previous month. Jack and Lou found themselves reduced to nodding at appropriate moments while maintaining forced smiles.

When the stories drew to a close, Paul stood and excused himself. Laurie looked after him as he headed toward the rest rooms. Turning back to her two old friends, she sighed.

"He's really wonderful, isn't he?" she asked.

Jack and Lou looked at each other, hoping the other would respond.

"Well?" Laurie questioned.

Both Jack and Lou started speaking at the same time then hastily deferred to the other.

"What is this, a comedy routine?" Laurie demanded. Her beatific smile faded. "What's the matter with you two?"

"This situation has caught us off guard," Jack finally admitted. "We'd both guessed you'd gotten a job offer and were going to move out on us. We never thought you'd be getting married."

"And why not!" Laurie demanded. "That's almost insulting. What am I, too old?"

"I don't mean it that way," Jack said meekly.

"How long have you known this man?" Lou asked.

"A couple of months," Laurie said defensively. "I know that's not a lot of time, but I don't think that's so important. He's intelligent, warm, generous, confident, and willing and able to make a commitment. And all those are important characteristics as far as I'm concerned. Particularly the confidence and the ability to make a commitment."

Both Jack and Lou couldn't help but feel indicted.

"I don't believe this," Laurie said. "You two, of all people I know, I thought would be happy for me."

"What kind of business is he in?" Jack asked.

"What kind of a question is that?" Laurie demanded.

"Just a simple question," Jack said timidly.

"To tell you the truth, I don't know," Laurie said. "And I don't really care. It's him I'm interested in, not what he does for a living. You men are impossible."

"Have your parents met him?" Lou asked.

"Of course," Laurie said. "I met him through my parents."

"That's nice," Lou said.

Laurie let out a mirthless laugh. "This is not how I expected this evening to go."

Neither Jack nor Lou knew quite what to say. Luckily they were rescued by Paul's return. He was in an ebullient mood, totally unaware of what had transpired during his brief absence. He started to reclaim his seat, but Laurie stood up.

"I think it's time we go," Laurie said.

"No after-dinner drinks at the bar?" Paul asked.

"I think we've all had enough," Laurie said. "And as Jack is wont to say, it is a school night."

Jack smiled weakly. Sensing that he'd let Laurie down only made him feel worse. He got to his feet. "Congratulations, you guys," he said with manufactured enthusiasm. "In the spirit of the occasion, Lou and I will take care of the tab."

"It's all taken care of already," Paul said with an air of superiority. "It's our treat."

"I'd prefer to pay," Jack said. "It's only fair."

"Hogwash," Paul said. He reached over and shook Jack's and Lou's hand. "I've really enjoyed meeting Laurie's two closest friends. I can't tell you how highly she talks of you two and how often. It's enough to make a guy jealous." He laughed.

"See you tomorrow at the office," Laurie said. She turned and started across the crowded dining room. Paul gave a final wave and hurried after her.

Jack looked at Lou. "What do you want to do?"

"Go home and shoot myself," Lou said.

"You want company?" Jack asked.

The two men sank into their chairs. Jack felt shell-shocked. Laurie's getting married was worse than her going away. Instead of moving to the West Coast, it was more like her going to Venus. The episode startled him into realizing how much he'd been avoiding thoughts about the future. Guilt about his family still made it difficult for him to justify future happiness. That's why he found making a commitment so difficult.

Lou cradled his head in his hands. He was the picture of dejection. "I've worried about Laurie getting married," he said. "Especially to you."

"To me?" Jack questioned with surprise. "I actually worried she'd get married to you. I know you two dated before I came on the scene."

"You shouldn't have worried," Lou said. "It wasn't to be. It never would have worked. During the brief time we went out on a regular basis, I screwed it up. Every time there was the slightest blip, I thought she was breaking up with me, and I acted like an ass. It drove both of us batty, and we ended up having a long talk about it. Tonight when she mentioned about 'confidence' being an important personality characteristic for her, she was referring to me."

"The part about the ability to make a commitment was directed at me," Jack said.

"Was that the problem between you two?" Lou asked. "I never could figure out what happened. You guys seemed natural for each other. You know, similar backgrounds, fancy schools, and all the rest of that bullshit."

"It was part of it," Jack said. "But I'm so screwed up I don't even know all the reasons."

"It's a tragedy!" Lou complained. "For you and for me. At

least if she tied the knot with you, I could stay friends with both of you. When she marries this twerp, I'm out the door. I mean, I fantasized about Laurie and me staying friends even when she married. But tonight when I saw that rock on her finger, I instantly knew staying the kind of friends I envisioned was out of the question."

"I guess I was unrealistically hoping the present would never change," Jack said.

Lou nodded and thought for a moment before asking, "What did you think of this guy?"

"A snake in the grass," Jack said without hesitation. "But I don't know how objective I can be. I'm obviously jealous. It bugged me how they kept touching each other."

"It rubbed me the wrong way as well," Lou said with another nod. "Like puppy love. It was disgusting. But I question my objectivity, too. Yet it all seems too quick to me, like the guy's after her money even though she doesn't have any. Of course that can be the cynical detective talking."

Jack shook his head dejectedly. "We can sit here and say nasty things about him, but the fact is, he's a lot more spontaneous than we are, and he's got a lot more bucks. I mean, going to Paris for the weekend! There's no way I could do that. Worrying about how much it was costing would drive me bananas, and I'd be miserable to be with."

"It makes me mad to think that there are people that can do that sort of thing," Lou said. "What with my alimony payments and raising two kids, I'm lucky to have two nickels to scrape together."

"Envious might be a better word than mad," Jack said.

Lou scraped back his chair and stood up. "I got to get home to bed before I get too depressed. I've been up for two straight days."

"I'm with you," Jack said.

The two men wormed their way out of the restaurant feeling all the more depressed in light of the festive atmosphere.

EIGHT

After Curt and Steve left, Yuri had gone down to his beloved lab. The first thing he did was repair the damage Connie had caused when she'd pried off the padlocks. To be on the safe side he bolted the hasps to the door rather than replace the screws. With that setup, an intruder would most likely need something more powerful than a crowbar to pull them loose.

While he worked, he thought about Curt and Steve's disturbing visit. He was taken aback by their anger, particularly their anger about his stopping by the firehouse. The explanation that he was a security risk because he was a foreigner with a Russian accent didn't ring true. New York was much too cosmopolitan a city. Every other person had an accent.

Yuri thought there had to be another reason why they didn't want him seen there. Although he couldn't think of what it might have been, it made him feel uncomfortable. For the first time Yuri began to question where he stood with Curt and Steve. He knew they were strong on prejudice, so the thought passed through his mind they might be prejudiced against him, and if that was the case they certainly weren't the friends he imagined.

The other source of their anger—that Connie was black—was equally mysterious. It wasn't so much the prejudice itself that surprised Yuri. He was well aware of Curt and Steve's racial bigotry. What got him was the amount of anger involved. It was so out of proportion, and the pseudo-religious explanation Steve had given seemed contrived. Neither Curt nor Steve had ever said anything to suggest they were at all religious.

And finally, there was the issue of the pest control truck and aerosolizer. Yuri couldn't understand why they'd not obtained it yet. That was an important part of the agreement. Without it, Yuri would not be able to carry out his part of the operation. He needed a sprayer, and he needed it to be mobile. A point source was not anywhere near as effective.

In order to fix the inner door, Yuri suited up in the hazmat suit and opened the valve on the compressed air cylinder. The regulator wasn't the demand variety used for scuba diving. Instead it kept a constant flow of air into the suit as a means of keeping any particles from the environment from gaining entry.

It was much harder to work in the suit and it was very hot, but Yuri didn't mind. He knew the risk he'd be taking if he didn't wear it. But it did slow him down.

After the door was fixed, Yuri turned his attention to the fermenter with the *Clostridium botulinum*. He tested the bacterial concentration and was again disappointed. He could not figure out why the culture continued to grow so slowly. As far as he knew he'd followed the culture conditions carefully that had been used so successfully in the Soviet Union when he'd worked with the organism a decade previously. The conditions had been determined to produce maximum culture growth and maximum toxin production.

The only thing Yuri could imagine was that air was getting into the fermenter. *Clostridium botulinum* was a bacteria that grew without oxygen. Consequently, Yuri had used carbon dioxide gas instead of air over the culture. Perhaps there was something wrong with the cylinder of carbon dioxide Curt's troops had obtained for him. Unfortunately, Yuri didn't have any way to analyze it, and requesting a new cylinder would take too long.

Yuri stood up from where he'd been bending down to check the internal fermenter temperature. It was a few degrees cooler than optimum, so he adjusted his jury-rigged waterbath thermostat. Having the temperature off certainly didn't help, but it was not an adequate explanation for the slow growth.

He thought about Curt's suggestion to switch production in the *Clostridium* fermenter to anthrax so that both units would be producing the anthrax spores. There was a lot to be said for that idea. It was the only way he'd be able to produce enough material for both laydowns within the time frame they'd discussed. The trouble was that breaking down the fermenter was a big job and at the moment he had another worry: Connie.

Yuri went over to his hood and turned on the fan. Putting his already gloved hands into another pair of heavy rubber gloves secured to the edges of two holes in the hood's glass front, Yuri carefully picked up the beaker containing his most recently produced botulinum toxin. He poured some of it into a small glass vial.

Yuri had been using the acid precipitation technique in concentrating and purifying his toxin. After resuspending the toxin in an aqueous buffer, he'd reprecipitated it with ammonium sulfate to form a crystalline amalgam of pure toxin combined with a stabilizing protein. This form he'd dried into a powder.

Yuri wasn't as concerned about his safety when he worked with the botulinum toxin as he was with the anthrax powder. Although he'd been vaccinated against both agents back in the Soviet Union, he was more confident of his immunity to the toxin than he was to anthrax spores.

After sealing the small vial, Yuri washed its exterior before bringing it out from inside the hood. Then he went through the first phase of disinfecting and decontaminating himself with an overhead shower and a plastic container of bleach.

Leaving the lab, Yuri went through a second decon phase with more bleach and another shower. Only then did he slip out of his hazmat suit, turn off the compressed-air tank, and hang them up on their respective pegs. Then he carefully carried the vial up to the kitchen and hid it behind the overcounter dish cabinet.

Steeling himself against the inevitable abuse, Yuri went to Connie's door and opened it. As usual, his wife was propped up on the bed watching the television even though the mattress and box spring were now sitting on the floor.

"What do you want?" Connie grumbled. She was holding an ice pack to her swollen left eye.

"I'm going to get some pizza," Yuri said. "I thought maybe you might be hungry."

Connie lifted the ice pack away from her face and regarded her husband curiously. "What's the matter with you?" she questioned sarcastically. "You've never cared if I was hungry before."

"I was feeling guilty about hitting you," Yuri said, trying to sound sincere. "I'm sorry."

"Sorry, my ass," Connie shot back. "If you're saying this to get your TV back, it's not going to work."

"I don't want my TV back," Yuri said. "And I'm sorry I broke yours. I was out of my mind."

"So what else is new?"

"You don't understand," Yuri said, trying to sound contrite as well as sincere. "That lab downstairs is important to me."

"As if I couldn't guess with the amount of time you spend down there."

"It's my ticket out of this mess," Yuri said. "I mean our ticket."

Connie turned the sound down on the television and pushed herself up on one elbow. "What are you saying to me?"

"I'm trying to get back into microbiology," Yuri explained. "I need to practice and to prove I know what I'm doing. Then maybe I can get a decent job. I don't want to drive a cab the rest of my life."

"What kind of job are you talking about?"

"Anything in microbiology," Yuri said. "Those men who were here tonight have been helping me, but they're worried. It's against the law to have a lab like that in a private house, and if I get into trouble, they'll get into trouble."

"I thought you had to go back to school if you wanted to work with bacteria."

"Not if I can do something that proves I'm qualified," Yuri said. "And if I do, and I get a good job, then we can start a new life. You know, go out like we used to do."

"Yeah sure, when hell freezes over."

"It'll happen," Yuri promised. "But for now, you want some pizza?"

"Okay, why not," Connie said. "Pepperoni and anchovy. And have them bring over a pint of butter pecan ice cream."

"Right," Yuri said. He forced a smile and then closed the door. One thing was certain: nothing seemed to spoil that woman's appetite. But he wasn't complaining about the addition of the ice cream. As far as he was concerned, he thought it would be a better medium for the botulinum toxin, especially since he'd be sure she'd eat the whole tub.

Yuri used the wall phone in the kitchen to call the local pizza place. He ordered for Connie, then, for himself, he ordered a regular pizza with mozzarella, tomatoes, and basil. Just before he hung up he added a small tossed salad and a coffee to the order. He realized it might be a long night.

Yuri paced the apartment. As time passed he became progressively more nervous. Although he'd acted sure of himself when he'd been talking with Curt, he didn't know for certain what was going to happen after Connie ingested the toxin. One of the problems was that Yuri had no way of intelligently guessing how much to use. He would just have to sprinkle some into the ice cream and hope for the best. All he knew was that he had to err on the side of using too much. If Connie just got sick, and botulism was suspected, he'd be caught redhanded with the lab in his basement.

The sound of knocking on the door made Yuri jump. Half expecting trouble, he glanced out through the venetian blinds and was relieved to see the pizza delivery boy. Yuri opened the door, paid the kid, and took the packages. The two pizzas had been in an insulated carrier and were still hot to the touch.

Yuri pushed away the fast-food wrappings Connie had left earlier on the table, and put down the pizza boxes and the bag with the salad, coffee, and ice cream. He was most interested in the ice cream. He took it out of the bag and put it on the counter. The container was slightly soft. Unlike the pizzas, it hadn't been put in an insulated bag.

Quietly stepping out of the kitchen, Yuri moved over to Connie's door. He pressed his ear against it. He could hear the television clearly. He assumed Connie was still lying on the bed.

Returning to the kitchen, he struggled to open the ice cream container without ripping it. Once he had it open, he debated how to add the toxin. He was afraid to add it in one bolus, thinking Connie might taste it and then spit it out. After considering his options, he took out a bowl and emptied most of the ice cream into it. Then he took out the vial from the dish cabinet. Holding his breath, he sprinkled some of the material onto the ice cream.

"Oh what the hell," he whispered. He poured the rest into the ice cream. In total, it was no more than a pinch. But if the toxin was as lethal as he expected, it was a huge dose. Probably enough to knock off everybody in Brighton Beach.

Yuri rinsed out the vial in the sink and let the water run. With a fork, he mixed the ice cream as well as he could. Then with a spoon he ladled it back into the pint container. That turned out to be more difficult than he expected, since it seemed that he had more ice cream than he'd started with. It took a bit of force to get it all in. When he was finished he resealed the container as best as he could.

Yuri washed out the bowl. Even so, he vowed never to use it again. In fact after the evening was over he intended to throw it and the fork away.

After washing his hands carefully, Yuri got out a spoon. Then he picked up both the ice cream container and the pepperoni pizza box and headed for Connie's room.

"It took long enough," Connie commented when Yuri opened her door.

"Where do you want it?" Yuri asked.

"Over here on the floor," Connie said without taking her eyes off the TV.

Yuri bent down and put the food on the rug. He placed the spoon on top of the ice cream container and straightened up.

That was when Connie glanced over to see what he'd done.

"Hey, I don't want the ice cream," she said.

"What do you mean?" Yuri said with consternation.

"I mean I want you to put it in the goddamn refrigerator," Connie said. "I'll eat it after my pizza. I don't want it to melt."

"Fine," Yuri said with some relief. He picked up the ice cream and the spoon and backed to the door. "Give a yell when you want it, okay?"

Connie's head flopped to the side, and she regarded Yuri beneath knotted brows. "What's wrong with you, boy? You've never been this nice."

"I told you," Yuri said. "I feel guilty."

"I wish you'd feel guilty more often," Connie said.

Yuri went back out to the kitchen. Mumbling a few choice epithets about Connie, he put the ice cream in the freezer. His pulse was hammering in his temples. He needed a vodka. As he'd suspected, it was going to be a long night.

"Okay, everybody shut the hell up!" Curt yelled out over the unruly group. He'd called a meeting of the People's Aryan Army, and they'd gathered in the back pool room of the White Pride bar. The owner of the bar was Jeff Connolly, an old acquaintance of Curt's. Jeff wasn't an official member of the group, although he was entirely sympathetic to the PAA's positions: namely anti-government, anti-black, anti-Semitic, anti-Hispanic, anti-immigration, anti-feminist, anti-NAFTA, anti-abortion, and anti-gay. He was more than happy to clear out the pool room whenever the PAA needed to assemble.

On Curt's insistence the organization of his group was entirely clandestine. There were no membership cards or even membership memorabilia. He urged people never to use the name, although he and Steve did when they communicated to other militias via the Internet. Otherwise, all communication was by word of mouth, person to person. To call the meeting that night, there'd been no phone calls and no written messages. People had to seek each other out. What made it easy was that most members came to the White Pride at some time during each and every night.

Curt had recruited eight skinheads using methods he'd learned from Tim Melcher. He'd isolate a teenager at one of the many local skinhead bars and strike up a conversation. The conversation was more like an interview. Whenever Curt thought the kid was fertile ground for his views, he then started in on ideology. It was easy, because the skinheads were eager for some organization and to have a focus for their violent dispositions. Besides, from personal experience Curt knew their struggles and resentments and could therefore fan their fledgling bigotries and hatreds.

But keeping such a group under a semblance of control was not easy. For one thing, many of those involved were stupid, like Yuri, and lacked a proper sense for security. Offering Brad Cassidy an opportunity to join the group when he'd approached a couple of the troops directly was a case in point. They'd bought his original story. But Curt hadn't. First of all, Curt was suspicious of anyone who wasn't from the immediate area. Second, no one was considered for membership without being interviewed by Curt first. When Curt got to talk with him, Brad contradicted himself several times. Then, with a little prodding with a knife and the judicious use of a length of piano wire, the true story came out. He was a government spy.

The other problem was the group's appetite for violence, a trait Curt wanted to channel. At first he thought that in between legitimate missions just talk about violent acts would satisfy their urges. But it turned out that talking was not enough. Occasionally, Curt had to risk confrontation with the authorities, letting them cruise around to other parts of Brooklyn or even Manhattan to find someone to beat up.

The clothes and the tattoos bothered Curt, too. He tried to get them to tame their style of dress, arguing that they should let their actions speak for themselves. They could be more effective, he argued, if they could blend in. But it was like talking to a wall. There was something about their shaved heads, T-shirts, Nazi regalia, and black boots that appealed to them on a gut level. No amount of persuasion could alter their opinion.

"Come on, you guys," Steve called out. "You heard Curt. Listen up!"

Kevin Smith and Luke Benn straightened up by the pool table. Thumping the heels of their pool cues on the floor they stood in a ragged form of attention. Stew Manson, who was having an argument with Clark Ebersol and Nat Jenkins, turned to Curt and swayed. He'd been drinking beer since eight and was feeling no pain. Mike Compisano, Matt Sylvester, and Carl Ryerson looked up from their rambunctious card game. Even among this crowd, Carl stood out, with a crudely drawn swastika tattooed in the middle of his forehead.

"We've got a mission tonight," Curt said. "It's going to require finesse, which I'm not sure any of you understand."

A titter sounded from a few of the troops.

"We've got to go out on the Island," Curt continued. "Out to the Hamptons, to be exact, and steal a truck."

"No need to go way the hell out there for a truck," Stew said. He slurred his words. "There's plenty of trucks right here in Brooklyn."

"We're talking about a special type of truck," Curt said. "Who's good at getting into a vehicle quickly and hotwiring it?"

Most of the troops turned to Clark Ebersol. "I guess that's me," Clark said. He was a slight fellow with a bumpy scalp that made shaving it a chore. "I've been joyriding since I was twelve." He now worked at a local garage.

"Compisano is good if there's an electronic alarm," Kevin said. Kevin was a redhead like Steve, but with his hair shaved it was hard to tell save for his freckled complexion. He was also the youngest of the group at sixteen although he was a big, husky kid. The others ranged up to twenty-two. The oldest was Luke Benn.

"I'm mostly used to house alarms, not car alarms," Mike Compisano said. In spite of his Italian name, Mike had been a towhead since birth. His blond eyebrows were almost transparent, giving him an expression of perpetual surprise.

"At least you know something about alarms," Curt said. "That could come in handy. So you and Clark will ride with me and Steve. The rest of you go in Nat's truck." Of all the troops, Nat was the best off financially. His brother was in the garbage business. He had a king cab pickup like Curt's with two rows of seats.

"Stew, you stay here," Curt said.

"The hell I will," Stew said. "I'm going with the action."

"That's an order!" Curt snapped. "You're tanked. I can tell you've had about five beers more than anyone else. I don't want this mission compromised."

"Shit, man!" Stew complained.

"No argument!" Curt ordered. "Let's move out."

While Stew Manson sulked, the others eagerly hustled out of the pool room. At the bar most bought beers for the road. Outside they tumbled into the respective vehicles.

"Stay behind me at a reasonable distance," Curt called to Nat before he started his truck. Nat gave him a thumbs-up sign. The next moment Nat's truck erupted with the throbbing base of the group Brutal Attack. Nat had a special speaker system with a woofer capable of loosening his lug bolts.

They moved in a convoy of two vehicles. Nat followed orders and stayed comfortably behind Curt. Halfway out on Long Island they stopped at a service center so everyone could relieve themselves.

"We're almost out of beer," Nat said to Curt as he leaned into a urinal. "Can we make a detour at the next town to stock up?"

"No more beer until the mission is over," Curt shot back.

The second part of the trip went considerably faster than the first as the traffic dropped off dramatically. The congestion of the city and the surrounding metropolitan area had been replaced by the tranquillity of small towns, farms, and palatial, seasonal estates.

It was well past midnight when they drove into Sagamaunatuck, a thriving summertime town that served as a commercial hub for that section of the island. Slowing deliberately to less than the posted speed limit, Curt advanced down Main Street. Most of the shops had been long since shut for the night. The only activity emanated from two local bars that sat opposite each other across the main drag. Their doors were ajar to the mild mid-October night. Each had a handful of patrons. A bit of competing, low-volume music spilled out into the street.

"A nice quiet town," Steve commented.

"Let's hope it stays that way," Curt said.

"Hey, there's a kosher Jewish delicatessen!" Carl said excitedly from the back seat. He pointed to the dark store. "Look at all that stupid foreign writing on the window."

"Don't get any ideas," Curt said. "We're here for one reason only."

Curt and Steve had reconnoitered the place a month earlier and knew where they were going. The pest control company was on the next street over running parallel with Main Street.

Curt turned left at the next corner onto Banks Street and then left again onto Hancock. Wouton's Pest Control was on the right in a one-story cinderblock building. A large sign advertised that their expertise ranged from residential to agricultural and other commercial applications. To the right of the building was a parking lot surrounded by a chain-link fence with a gate secured by a padlock. Three vehicles featuring the Wouton logo of a cartoon wasp were nosed in at the side of the building. Two were vans. The other was a pickup with a load in its bed covered by a mounded vinyl tarp.

Curt pulled to the curb. He cut his engine, turned out his lights, and motioned for Nat to come alongside. Windows were lowered.

"How many communicators do you have?" Curt asked. In order to coordinate on missions, Curt had purchased an inexpensive radio system that worked within a radius of several city blocks.

"Two," Kevin said. He was sitting in the front passenger seat of Nat's truck.

"Here's another," Curt said. He handed over an additional communicator. "Now here's what I want to do. I want two guys up at the next corner of Hancock and Willow with a radio. I want two guys back behind us at the corner of Hancock and Banks with another radio. Nat, I want you to position yourself so that you can pick up either group if the need arises."

"What are we supposed to do?" Kevin questioned. "Just stand out there in the dark?"

"You're going to be point men, you big lunkhead," Curt snapped. "Lookouts."

"What are we to look for?" Kevin questioned. "This town's deader than a doornail."

"The local fuzz," Curt said. "Last time Steve and I were out here, they cruised around a lot. Let's hope they don't show up, but if they do, you're to create some kind of diversion: whatever it takes to keep the cops busy while we get the truck out of the enclosure, and on its way."

"I don't know what you mean," Kevin persisted.

"Just make a fuss," Curt said with exasperation. "Argue or yell at each other. Once the cops get a load of your appearance, it'll be like flies to flypaper. If they want to take you to the stationhouse, let them. As usual, tell them nothing. The worst-case scenario is that they might keep you overnight, but that would be it. Trust me."

"I got it," Nat called from the driver's seat.

Kevin started to argue that he had no intention of being in jail overnight, but Nat cuffed him on top of the head and told him to shut up.

"Nat, you give me a call when everybody is in position," Curt said.

"No problem," Nat said, and he drove forward.

Nat had advanced no more than fifty feet when a police cruiser rounded the corner ahead and started toward the two trucks.

"Shit!" Curt cried. "Everybody down!"

Curt and the others hunkered down in their seats as the police cruiser's headlights penetrated the cab.

"This is just what I was afraid of," Curt whispered. The sudden appearance of the police reminded him of the experience they'd had when they'd stolen the fermenters from the microbrewery in New Jersey. They'd been startled by a security guard who'd walked into their midst while the crew was busy unhooking the plumbing. Curt had not thought about positioning lookouts, so they'd been caught completely unawares.

Unfortunately the security guard happened to be African-American, and Stew Manson, who'd had his usual Olympian quota of beer, went berserk. He shouted "nigger" at the guard, who was unarmed, and smashed him over the head as hard as he could with a heavy-duty plumber's wrench. The man's head squashed like an uncooked egg, skyrocketing the risk of the mission. Instead of participating in a robbery, they were all suddenly accessories to a murder. Curt was determined to avoid comparable surprises on this mission.

"What did Nat do?" Steve asked.

"I don't know," Curt said. "I didn't see."

The police cruiser rolled past. Curt craned his neck to watch the car's progress in his rearview mirror. Luckily, it didn't stop. Rather, it turned right on Banks Street. Glancing ahead, Curt saw that Nat had stopped at the intersection and two figures had gotten out. The passenger door closed and the truck disappeared around the corner. The men stepped into the shadows.

Curt let out a breath of air. He'd not been aware he'd been holding his breath.

"Let's hope that means they won't be back for a while," Clark said from the back seat.

"I have a bad feeling about this," Steve said.

"I'm with you," Curt agreed. "But we've got to get the truck."

"How about coming back tomorrow night?" Steve suggested.

"It would be no different," Curt said. "And we promised Yuri we'd get it tonight."

The four men sat in silence for a few minutes as the tension rose. Eventually Mike spoke up: "Anybody got any beer left?"

"No drinking until the mission is over!" Curt snapped. He couldn't believe how juvenile his troops could be. There were times he thought they had no common sense whatsoever.

Just when Curt was becoming concerned that too much time had elapsed, the communicator in his hand vibrated. He pressed the "listen" button and, through static, heard Nat say that everybody was in place. That meant Kevin and Luke on Willow Street, and Matt and Carl on Banks.

"Ten-four," Curt said. He pocketed the small radio. "That's it, everybody, let's go!"

They piled out of the vehicle. Clark had a Slim Jim and a flashlight. Mike had a couple of small screwdrivers, a pair of wire cutters, and several lengths of insulated electrical wire. Curt reached into the bed of his truck and extracted a pair of heavy bolt cutters that he'd borrowed from the firehouse. He slipped them under his jacket. The steel jaws felt cold through his thin T-shirt.

"Act as if we belong here and we're just checking things out," Curt said as they approached the padlocked gate. He knew that if anybody happened to be looking out the windows of the apartments across the street, they'd be seen. Although there were no streetlights, it wasn't particularly dark. The night was crystal clear with a bright, gibbous moon poking in and out amid scudding clouds.

"Which truck are we taking?" Clark asked.

"I hope the pickup," Curt said. "Depends on what's in it."

Clark's question took Curt back to his and Steve's reconnaissance to Sagamaunatuck the previous month. At that time they'd seen the same truck. When they'd checked it out parked on Main Street, there'd been pest control equipment attached in the bed, along with cylinders of compressed air. The driver was a friendly, ruddy-faced bearded man wearing a baseball hat with the Wouton wasp logo emblazoned above the visor. He'd just been into the local diner for lunch and was in an expansive mood.

"Yup, this here equipment is a sprayer," the man had said in response to Curt's question. Neither Curt nor Steve knew anything about pest control machinery. "Well, that's not quite true," the man corrected himself. "It's really a duster, not a sprayer. It's designed for powder, not liquids."

"Looks impressive," Curt commented while he winked at Steve. It was exactly what they were looking for, ending a weeklong search.

"You bet," the man said. He gave the machinery a proud pat. "It's the best on the market. It's called a Power Row Crop Duster."

"How does it work?" Curt asked.

"The pest control powder goes into this hopper." The man pointed to a dark green metal box. Most of the apparatus was green, except for the nozzles, which were orange. "It's got an agitator in there to fluff up the powder with the help of compressed air. After going through a metering device, the centrifugal fan powers the material along with air out the nozzles."

"So it's pretty effective?" Curt asked.

"It's unbelievable," the man said. "The fan can go up to twenty-two thousand RPMs, which can push out up to a thousand cubic feet of air a minute. At that speed the air leaving the nozzles is moving at close to a hundred miles an hour."

Curt and Steve whistled in admiration and began plotting how to get the truck back to the city. The plan they'd conceived they were now executing.

"Let's just make sure that cop car's not in the area," Curt said. He took out his radio and checked with each of the other groups. When he got an all clear, he slipped the bolt cutters out from his jacket and made short work of the padlock. He gave the cutters to Steve before yanking off the broken lock. The gate squeaked as he pushed it open.

"Let's make this fast," Curt said as the three jogged to the pickup truck.

Steve raised the edge of the tarpaulin. Even in the moonlight, Curt and Steve recognized the dark green of the Power Row Crop Duster.

"All right, go to work," Curt said to Mike and Clark.

Clark deftly wielded the Slim Jim between the driver's side window and the truck's side panel. Instantly the door unlocked. He looked over at Mike.

"Open the door," Mike said from where he was standing in front of the pickup. "If an alarm goes off, pop the hood."

"Wait a second!" Curt said. "You mean to tell me an alarm might sound?"

"There's no way to keep it from going off if there's an alarm," Mike said. "But it won't go long provided I get under the hood."

Curt scanned the neighborhood. As late as it was, there were still a few lights in the apartments across the street. Recognizing he had little choice, he nodded to Clark to go ahead. But he wasn't happy.

The instant Clark opened the door, the truck's horn began beeping and the headlights began flashing.

Clark popped the hood open. Mike put the flashlight on the engine. In seconds, though not soon enough for Curt, the horn stopped and the lights went out. Mike closed the hood as quietly as possible and came around to the driver's side of the vehicle. Clark was already leaning into the cab, expertly working under the steering column.

"I need the light," Clark said. He stuck his hand out behind his back. Mike passed him the flashlight like a relay racer handing off a baton.

With his ears still ringing from the truck horn, Curt looked up and down the street. He half expected to see lights go on in windows all over the apartment building opposite. Instead his radio vibrated.

While Curt brought the communicator to his ear, the pickup truck engine turned over weakly.

"Shit, it sounds like the battery is low," Clark said. He was now sitting behind the steering wheel. "This heap must have been parked here for a long time."

Curt pressed the "listen" button. Nat's voice came through, along with the usual static, saying that there was a problem.

"What kind of problem?" Curt demanded nervously.

"Kevin and Luke have taken off after a couple of fags," Nat said.

"Oh, for God's sake," Curt spat. "Go get them and get them back in your truck! And get the others, too."

"Ten-four," Nat said.

Curt threw up his hands in exasperation.

"What's the matter?" Steve questioned.

"Don't ask," Curt said. "I'm going to kill them all!"

"Do you have any cables in your truck?" Carl called. "We may have to jump-start this sucker."

"What else can go wrong?" Curt didn't like the idea of driving his own truck into the fenced-in parking area, but there was no other way. He sprinted back to his vehicle. As he climbed into the cab, Nat went by in his truck heading for

Willow Street and beeped in greeting. Matt and Carl waved and grinned. Curt swore under his breath. How had he teamed up with such a bunch of lunatics?

As quickly as he could, Curt pulled into the parking area and nosed in next to the Wouton pickup. With his engine still running, he opened his hood, then leaped out. He grabbed his jumper cables from under the seat. Mike took the other ends as Curt attached his to his battery.

As soon as the leads were connected, the pest control truck engine leaped to life. Curt disconnected the leads from his own truck while Mike did the same with the Wouton vehicle.

"All right," Curt blurted anxiously. "Steve, you and Clark drive this freaking pest control contraption back to the White Pride, but don't drive back through town and go left here on Hancock! And drive the speed limit, no faster! If you're stopped by the fuzz, the mission is a failure. Mike, you come with me!"

"But the White Pride will be closed," Steve complained.

"So ring Jeff's goddamn buzzer," Curt retorted. "Jeez, do I have to think of everything?"

Curt swung into his cab and quickly backed out onto the street. Then he climbed back out of the truck as Clark steered the Wouton pickup through the gate.

"Where're you going?" Mike questioned.

"I want to close the gate," Curt said. "I don't want to advertise that the truck's gone."

As the gate's hinges squeaked closed, Curt heard distant shouts and cries for help coming from the direction of Willow Street. It made his hackles rise.

Back in the truck, Curt gunned the engine and took off toward Willow Street. He left his lights off.

"Did you hear those yells?" Mike questioned.

"Of course I heard them," Curt snapped.

"It pisses me off," Mike said. "I miss all the fun."

Curt shot his minion a dirty look but resisted telling him off.

Curt screeched to a stop in the middle of the intersection so he could look both ways on Willow. He saw Nat's truck about half a block down the street in the direction away from the commercial part of town. Turning the steering wheel hard, he headed in its direction. Off to the right on a lawn he could just make out figures in the darkness pummeling others who were sprawled on the ground. Lights in the surrounding houses were coming on in response to the commotion. That's when he heard the police siren.

"Shit!" Curt yelled. As he pulled to a sudden stop behind Nat's truck, he glanced in the rearview mirror. The blinking lights of a police cruiser were racing toward them.

"Get their asses into Nat's truck," Curt barked to Mike, who leaped out of the cab. Mike didn't protest; the urgency of the situation was obvious.

Curt watched the police car approaching in the mirror. At first he thought he'd merely hunker down and stay out of sight until the cop exited his car and joined the melee. That would give him a chance to speed away and leave the troops to the fate they deserved. But then he got another idea. Having been to a half-dozen demolition derbies, he knew the best way to incapacitate another vehicle with your own was to back into the other's front.

The critical question was whether the cop would pull up behind Curt as he expected. Fortunately he did.

The moment the lone policeman began to exit his vehicle, Curt put his truck into reverse and stomped on his accelerator, pressing it firmly against the floor. The truck tires spun with an ear-splitting screech before suddenly catching. The heavy king cab pickup lurched backward and gained considerable speed in the short distance between the two vehicles before smashing into the police cruiser.

Despite tensing for the collision, Curt's head snapped back on impact. The sound was like beer cans being crushed and the siren, which until that moment had been piercing the night, went silent. The police cruiser's hood popped open and a geyser erupted.

More important from Curt's point of view was that the opened driver's side door had been ripped off its hinges by its own momentum. It went skidding out across the road. The policeman, whose hand was still on the door, ended up face down on the pavement.

"Glory be," Curt remarked. He put his truck into drive and stepped on the gas. At first the cop car remained attached to his rear bumper. By backing up a little and then going forward again, Curt succeeded in detaching the vehicles. Glancing into the street, he noticed the policeman had not moved.

Ahead, amid laughter and loud banter, the troops were piling into Nat's truck, except for Mike. He sprinted back and got in next to Curt. In the middle of the lawn were two still, supine figures.

"Hey, cool move with the fuzzmobile!" Mike shouted while looking back through the rear window at the crushed front of the cop car. The geyser had abated. Now the engine just steamed in the glare of the car's still functioning revolving lights.

Curt didn't say anything. He pulled forward, then braked alongside Nat's vehicle. "Listen, you clowns," he snapped after the windows had come down. "No stops, drive the speed limit, and go directly to the White Pride for a debriefing! Got it?"

"Got it," Nat answered amid more laughter.

Curt accelerated, shaking his head in frustration. The whole operation was like a comedy movie that wasn't funny.

"The cop car looks like it's going to catch on fire," said Mike. Curt glanced at the vehicle and was going to explain that the smoke was merely steam from the coolant coming in contact with the hot manifold when he caught his troops' final stupid move of the night. Instead of pulling forward, Nat backed up so that he ran over the prone policeman. Curt winced. He didn't regard local sheriffs as the enemy the way he did federal agents or city police.

Mike faced forward when Curt turned west at the next intersection, heading back toward the city. "I know why Kevin and Luke took after those two fags," he said.

"Sure you do," Curt mumbled irritably and without particular interest. No matter what the explanation, Curt was planning on giving Kevin and Luke one hell of a dressing-down when they got back to base. Disobeying orders, even implied orders, was not to be tolerated.

"They were a mixed couple," Mike said. "One of them was

a paleface, the other was a nigger, and the bastards were holding hands."

"No wonder!" Curt's change of heart was genuine. Queer
miscegenators. He immediately understood how provocative
such a situation would have been.

Yuri's eyes blinked open. He sat up from where he'd fallen
asleep on the couch. He wasn't sure what had awakened him.
He looked at his watch. It was a little after one in the morning.
The sound of the TV drifted through Connie's closed door.

With a few choice Russian expletives, Yuri lifted his feet
from the couch and slipped them into his slippers. Since driving the cab required early-morning rising, Yuri always went
to bed early. Consequently, he had no idea of Connie's bed-
time habits other than knowing she stayed up later than he did.
Yet after one was later than he'd imagined she stayed up.
There was a good chance she'd fallen asleep without having
enjoyed her butter pecan ice cream.

Standing up, Yuri winced against a momentary pulsating
pain in his temples. He shivered through a fleeting wave of
nausea that made him quickly close the cover of the cold, half-
eaten pizza on the coffee table. Its congealed surface looked
disgusting.

Yuri was exhausted and felt miserable. He drained off the
residue of vodka in his tumbler and collected his thoughts. He
had to do something. He couldn't wait any longer for Connie
to request her dessert.

Outside her door he paused for a moment. He debated
whether to knock or just open it as he usually did on the rare
occasions he went into her room. In the end, he just opened
the door.

Connie looked away from the classic movie she was watching and glanced briefly at Yuri. Her left eye was even more
swollen than before. At the side of her bed was the open and
empty pizza box.

"What about your ice cream?" Yuri said in a gravelly voice.

"Are you still up?" Connie questioned. "What's the matter?
Are you sick?"

"Just tired."

"I thought you'd gone to bed."

"I fell asleep on the couch," Yuri said. "How about that ice cream?"

"You're like a dog with a bone about this ice cream," Connie said. "Besides, it's pretty late. I was about to fall asleep myself."

"Come on," Yuri urged. "You made me buy it from the take-out place."

"Are you sure you're not sick?" Connie asked again. "You're making me worried the way you're acting."

"God damn it!" Yuri yelled, losing patience. "I told you, I felt guilty after hitting you and smashing your TV. I'm trying to do something nice, but you won't even let me do that."

"Now you're sounding more like yourself," Connie said. "Fine! Bring the ice cream if it'll make you feel better! And you can take this pizza box while you're at it."

Relieved but still exasperated, Yuri snatched up the empty box and carried it back to the kitchen. He took the ice cream out of the freezer. From a drawer he got a spoon. He carried both back into Connie's room and handed them to her.

Straining under her own weight, Connie worked her way up to a semi-sitting position and took the ice cream and spoon.

"This container has been opened," she said. She looked up at Yuri for an explanation.

"I tried a taste earlier," Yuri lied.

Connie let out a huff. "You didn't ask me," she complained.

Yuri didn't respond. He was eyeing the phone next to Connie's bed. He hadn't thought of the possibility of her calling someone to describe her soon-to-arrive initial symptoms, provided she ate the ice cream. Anxious that she not reach a doctor, Yuri had to do something about the phone.

"I'm talking to you," Connie persisted. "You know I don't like people eating my food."

"It was just one taste," Yuri said.

"Just one?" Connie questioned. "You didn't put the spoon in and out a bunch of times?"

"Just once," Yuri said. "Open it up and look."

Connie grumbled as she pushed the flaps open. The ice

cream bulged from the container with a smooth, unblemished surface.

Yuri couldn't think of any excuse to take the phone out of the room without raising Connie's suspicions.

"I don't see where you ate any," Connie said.

"Because I took such a small amount," Yuri said. "For crissake, forget it! Just enjoy it!"

"All right," Connie said. "Leave me in peace."

"Gladly," Yuri said. "Just give a yell when you want me to come in here and take the container."

Connie raised her unswollen eyebrow in disbelief, glared at Yuri suspiciously, then redirected her attention to her movie. "Maybe I'll call you and maybe I won't," she said.

Yuri backed out of the room. He saw Connie absently take her first spoonful and swallow before he pulled the door partway closed. Retreating back to the sitting area he found that by positioning himself at the very end of the sofa, he could see into Connie's room. It was only a narrow swath, but it included the foot of the bed and the tips of her toes.

Time dragged incredibly slowly for Yuri. He couldn't be sure that Connie was eating the ice cream, although he would have been shocked if she didn't once she'd started. The movie seemed to go on forever despite the numerous times the soundtrack seemed to come to a concluding crescendo. He was hoping that Connie would get up and go into the bathroom, giving him time to get the phone off her bedside table.

Finally, forty-five minutes later, Connie obliged him when the movie concluded.

Yuri moved quickly. He pushed open the door. The ice cream container was on the floor next to the bed with the spoon sticking out the top. Unfortunately, the door to the bathroom was not completely closed. A commercial was playing on the television. It was the only source of light in the room.

With his pulse racing, Yuri stepped over to the bedside table. From that angle he could see a portion of the bathroom but no Connie. He picked up the phone and pulled the connecting wire taut to lead him to the wall plug. The trail led behind the table laden with dirty dishes and glasses.

As Yuri slipped his hand down the wire, he nudged the

table. Several of the glasses toppled off and shattered on the floor. The noise was louder than the high-volume commercial on the TV.

Guessing that Connie would appear in an instant, Yuri yanked on the wire, tearing it out of the wall. The motion sent another glass smashing to the ground. Yuri bent down to retrieve the empty ice cream container. As he feared, the bathroom door swung fully open, and Connie's form filled the doorway. She was brushing her teeth.

"What was that crash?" she demanded, cupping her mouth for fear of drooling her toothpaste. The toothbrush was clenched in her large fist.

"I don't know," Yuri said, hoping for the best. "Maybe it was something on the television." He was holding the phone behind his back with his left hand. His right hand had the ice cream container. He raised it to show her and said, "I just came in to get this."

Connie was as bewildered at Yuri's behavior as she'd been earlier. But she didn't say anything. She stuck her toothbrush back into her mouth, recommenced brushing, and returned to the bathroom.

Relieved, Yuri stepped out of the room and hurried into the kitchen. The first thing he did was hide the phone under the sink. Then he washed out the ice cream container before throwing it away. He did the same with the spoon, the bowl he'd used earlier, and the fork.

With a trembling hand, Yuri got out a highball glass and poured himself another healthy dollop of iced vodka. He was in dire need of its calming effect. In truth, he was disappointed to realize how nervous he was.

Retreating to the couch, Yuri sat down to wait. Unfortunately, he had no idea how long he would have to sit there. He wondered what would happen if Connie were to fall asleep before any symptoms appeared. He worried that maybe she'd just never wake up.

Yuri looked at his watch. The other thing that was bothering him was that it was two o'clock in the morning and there was still no pest control truck. Curt had promised. Yuri wondered what it meant for the future of Operation Wolverine.

Despite his anxieties, Yuri fell asleep again. When he awoke a half hour later, he knew immediately what had disturbed him. Connie was calling his name repeatedly but in a peculiar manner. She couldn't seem to pronounce the letter "R." She sounded drunk.

Yuri stood up and swayed. He had to lean on the arm of the couch to steady himself before walking toward his wife's bedroom on rubbery legs. He pushed open the door. Connie was lying on the collapsed bed. But there was something different about the way she was looking at him. Instead of the usual angry defiance, Yuri could tell that she was afraid.

"What's the matter?" Yuri questioned.

"Something's wrong," Connie managed. She was having difficulty articulating her words.

"What now?" Yuri asked. He pretended to be irritated.

"I got stomach cramps," Connie said. "And I threw up. I don't think the ice cream agreed with me."

"If something made you sick it was probably the pizza," Yuri said. "Personally, anchovies always do a number on my stomach."

"But it's not my stomach that concerns me."

"What is it then?" Yuri questioned impatiently.

"I can't watch the TV," Connie said, having particular difficulty pronouncing the letter T. "I'm seeing double. There're two TV sets."

"Then turn it off," Yuri said. "Go to sleep. It's late."

"I can't sleep," Connie said. "I'm all jazzed up for some reason and it scares me to see double."

"Try covering your swollen eye," Yuri suggested.

Connie reached up with her hand.

"What's it like now?" Yuri asked.

"It's better," Connie agreed. "There's only one TV set."

"Call me if there are any more problems," Yuri said. He began to back out the door.

"There is another problem," Connie said, slurring her words. "I'm thirsty. My throat is as dry as a bone."

"Well, get yourself some water," Yuri said. He started to close the door.

"I'm afraid to get up!" Connie called. "When I got up earlier I was dizzy and weak. I almost fell over."

"With all that fat it's no wonder," Yuri said.

"Please, get me some water."

Yuri wondered if the thirst had anything to do with the toxin. He didn't know. But he was certain the double vision did, and the difficulty in speaking. What was worrying him was the vomiting. It would be tragically ironic if she threw up most of the poison because he'd used too much. But then again, the nausea could be coming from a bolus of the toxin having been absorbed. Yuri didn't know too much about botulism except with mice, rats, dogs, and monkeys.

"All right, I'll get you some water."

"Maybe I should go to the hospital," Connie said without pronouncing the "H" at all.

"What? For some stomach cramps? Don't be ridiculous!"

"I'm scared. I feel strange."

"I'll get the water," Yuri said. He closed the door and walked into the kitchen. The whole affair was more nerve-racking than he'd anticipated. If a doctor saw her now they might make the diagnosis. While he was filling a glass under the faucet at the sink, a sudden, loud knocking reverberated against the front door. The unexpected sound made him jump from a type of fear only someone who'd been forced to live under a despotic, totalitarian government would understand. His own throat went dry. He took a quick sip of water, steadying the glass with both hands.

Trembling, he went over to the venetian blinds to peek out to see who could be there. He'd been so focused on Connie, he'd forgotten about Curt until he saw the man's familiar features illuminated by the exterior light. Steve was standing behind in the semi-darkness with his hands thrust into his pockets.

At first Yuri was relieved. But as he unlocked the door, he cursed under his breath. This was the wrong time for them to be showing up.

"We got a present for you, partner," Curt said. He motioned over his shoulder.

Yuri glanced into the alleyway. Behind Curt's truck was a

dark vehicle with "Wouton's Pest Control" written in block letters on the driver's side door.

"Does it have a sprayer?" Yuri asked.

"Let's get the goddamn thing in the garage before we get into that," Curt said.

"Okay," Yuri said. "I'll be right out." He closed the door. Running into the kitchen, he picked up the water and dashed back into Connie's room. He extended the glass toward her. When she tried to take it, her arm flailed aimlessly, missing entirely.

"I'm too weak," she admitted. Her arm flopped helplessly back onto the bed. "It's even hard for me to breathe."

"Never mind," Yuri said. "I'll hold the glass for you." He lowered the tumbler and pressed it to her lips as she tried vainly to raise her head. She sputtered and the water dribbled down the side of her face. She coughed and her face turned red.

"I'll be right back to give you some more," Yuri said. He tried to put the glass on the bedside table. Since there was no room he put it on the floor in the midst of the broken shards. Connie tried to speak in the midst of her coughing but Yuri ignored her.

Dashing out of the room Yuri went to the kitchen to get his keys before returning to the front door. When he opened it, it was apparent Curt was none too happy.

"Thanks for leaving us out here in the goddamn dark," Curt snapped.

"Sorry," Yuri said. He pulled the door shut behind him. "Things are just coming to a head with Connie."

"What's that supposed to mean?" Curt demanded.

"She didn't get the toxin until late," Yuri explained. He started toward the garage. "She's just starting to have symptoms."

"But you're sure she's going to check out," Curt said. He followed Yuri while Steve went around to get into the Wouton truck.

"That's my guess," Yuri said. He opened the side door to the garage.

"Wait a second!" Curt said. He grabbed Yuri's arm and

pulled him to a stop. "At this point there's no room for guessing. Any screwup could undermine this whole operation. I'm only interested in sureties."

"I gave her enough stuff to kill everybody in Brooklyn," Yuri shot back. "Is that good enough for you? Give me a break!"

Yuri and Curt glared at each other for a moment in the dark shadows beneath the eaves of the garage.

"I want to make sure you truly understand the need for security," Curt spat. "This whole mess with your mystery wife has us as nervous as hell."

"I'm taking care of it like we agreed," Yuri retorted.

"I hope so," Curt said. "The fact of the matter is, we cannot take any chances from here on out. Earlier tonight I mentioned we'd had an infiltrator in the People's Aryan Army. Brad Cassidy. What I didn't say was that he was working for the FBI."

"Oh no!" Yuri moaned. "What tipped them off?"

"Nothing about Operation Wolverine," Curt said. "We believe they're concerned about our militia in general. Since none of the troops have even the slightest inkling about the big plan, we're not directly at risk. The bureau must have picked up something from Steve's contacting other militias on the Internet on behalf of the PAA. But the point is, we've got to be extremely careful. And the sooner we launch the operation the better."

"My feelings exactly," Yuri said.

"Have you thought any more about switching the second fermenter to anthrax?"

"I'm going to do it as soon as I have time," Yuri said. "Probably tomorrow. As soon as this Connie business is over and done."

"Good," Curt said. "Now let's get this pest control truck off the street before someone sees the damn thing. I'm sure your neighbors would begin to wonder what kind of pests we're dealing with in the middle of the night."

Yuri snapped on the light before entering the garage. He skirted around the back of his taxicab. As soon as he had the rollaway door up, Steve pulled the Wouton pickup inside. Yuri closed the door behind him and locked it.

Curt stepped around to the back of the vehicle. He unhooked the edge of the tarp and folded it back to reveal the
apparatus sitting in the truck's bed. "Do you recognize this
thing?" he asked Yuri.

"Not specifically," Yuri admitted. "But those orange things
look like spray nozzles."

"Bingo!" Curt said. He reached over and gave the piece of
machinery a pat. "It's a Power Row Crop Duster. Whatever
powder you're using goes into this hopper." Curt pointed out
the component just as the Wouton driver had done that summer.

"So the agent doesn't have to be mixed with fluid?" Yuri
questioned. His face had lit up like a young boy with a Christmas bike.

"Nope," Curt responded. "Powder in and powder out, and
I'll tell you, it's one wicked little engine. We were told the
fan in there is capable of putting out a thousand cubic feet of
air a minute. The amount of powder you want in that thousand
cubic feet can be varied by the dial on the metering device."

"It's perfect," Yuri said. He was impressed. It was better
than he'd hoped.

"I'm glad you approve," Curt said. "I don't mind telling
you it took a bit of work and a lot of aggravation getting this
thing. Now it's up to you to come through with your end of
the bargain."

"I'm working on it," Yuri promised. "Have no fear!"

"I hope so," Curt said.

They shook hands before stepping back out into the night.
The two Americans climbed into their truck. Yuri stood by
the side of the road.

"Let's talk again tomorrow," Curt said. "We'll be interested
in how the rest of the evening goes as far as your wife is
concerned."

"Okay," Yuri said. He waved as Curt started his engine and
drove off.

Yuri stood for a moment watching the Dodge Ram's tail-
lights until they disappeared where Oceanview Lane butted
into Oceanview Avenue. He was still tired, but he felt better
than he had all day. Uncertainties that had been plaguing him

earlier had vanished. He knew in his gut that Operation Wolverine was imminently to come to pass as planned. He even allowed himself a half smile as he realized that soon he would stand in the company of other great Soviet patriots, even some of the greatest from the Great Patriotic War.

A gust of wind rustled dead leaves in the alley and caused Yuri's torn screen door to bang repeatedly against its jamb. The noise yanked Yuri back to the present reality. There was still work to be done before the great event, and the immediate concern was Connie.

Hurrying back inside, Yuri went to his wife's door. He paused for a moment to listen. All he could hear was the TV. Slowly he opened the door, unsure of what he'd see.

Connie had not moved, but her color had changed drastically. Her skin had taken on a dark mauve tint, particularly her lips.

Yuri advanced to the bed.

"Connie?" Yuri called. He jiggled her shoulder. She didn't move. He picked up her arm. It was flaccid. He let it fall back to the bed. Leaning down, he put his ear next to her mouth. It was only in that way that he could tell she was breathing, although just barely. He grasped her wrist. He could feel a pulse, but it was rapid and weak.

He straightened up. He wondered if it was time to call emergency or if he should wait a little longer. It was a hard decision, because he didn't want her waking up when she was given oxygen in the emergency room. If that happened she might be able to tell the doctors and nurses the progression of her symptoms. At the same time, Yuri felt it would be best if she was still alive when she got to the hospital. He reasoned there would be fewer questions about why she hadn't been brought in sooner.

Yuri turned on the bedside light before pulling open her right eye. Her pupil was widely dilated and fixed. As far as he was concerned, that meant it was time to call emergency.

Returning to the kitchen, Yuri used the wall phone. He tried to sound as distraught as possible, claiming he'd found his wife passed out and hardly breathing. He described her color as dusky and said that she'd been wheezing earlier in the evening. He gave the address and was told an ambulance would be there as soon as possible.

Returning to the bedroom, Yuri looked down at his wife. It was then he started to worry about the swollen left eye. He didn't want anyone to suspect domestic abuse, since it might lead to suspicions of foul play. He reasoned that he could say that she'd fallen, but he was worried it would be unconvincing, since she was lying in bed. Glancing through the open bathroom door gave him an idea.

Going around to the opposite side of the bed, Yuri tried to get Connie into a sitting position. Unfortunately her sheer bulk and weight made it extremely difficult, especially since her body was completely limp. Instead he rolled her slightly onto her left side facing away from him and got his arms under her armpits. Putting one foot on the edge of the mattress, he succeeded in slowly dragging her toward him. But then disaster struck.

Just when Yuri had managed to get Connie's torso clear of the bed, the throw rug he was standing on slid out from under him. Yuri fell onto his back and Connie rolled over on top of him, knocking the wind out of him so that he was unable to breathe.

For almost a minute, Yuri struggled for air. Under Connie's weight, he couldn't inhale. The room began to blur; he was afraid he might pass out.

In a final, desperate movement, Yuri was able to twist to the side enough to let him get at least enough air to keep from asphyxiating. Then it became a matter of disengaging himself from Connie's flaccid, spread-eagle embrace.

Finally, after great effort, Yuri squeezed free from Connie's near mortal clasp. He struggled to his feet gasping for breath. He was tempted to flee but found himself rooted in place while staring down at his wife's now prone figure. He shuddered with a wave of unearthly fear. In her half-dead state, Connie had nearly exacted her revenge.

The distant sound of an approaching siren shocked Yuri into action. He had to do something. Explaining how his battered wife had ended up prone alongside a collapsed bed might be difficult. It would have been better to have left her in the bed where she'd been originally, but getting her back was an impossibility.

Knowing he had little time, Yuri squatted down. Pulling Connie's arms he managed to twist her around so that her head was pointing toward the bathroom. Then, after rolling her over onto her back, he again seized her by the armpits and dragged her into the bathroom. His idea was to make it look as if she'd collapsed in there, hitting her eye on any one of a number of likely fixtures.

As the sound of the ambulance got progressively louder, Yuri checked himself and Connie for any last-minute problems. All seemed to be in order. Then he rushed back into the bedroom, where he hastily straightened the sheets that had been dragged with Connie when he'd pulled her onto the floor.

Vigorous pounding on the front door sent Yuri running. Two uniformed EMTs burst into the room as soon as Yuri pulled the door open. One was a woman, the other a man. Both were carrying equipment.

"Where's the patient?" the woman barked.

Yuri pointed. "In the bathroom through that bedroom."

Yuri followed the technicians as they ran to the rescue. They squeezed into the bathroom and began to administer to Connie. The first thing they did was get oxygen on her face. Yuri crossed his fingers that there wasn't going to be a miraculous resurrection.

"She's breathing shallowly and she's got a heartbeat," the woman said to the man. "But her color's poor. We'd better bag her."

Yuri watched as the technicians forced oxygen into Connie's lungs. Her chest rose perceptibly higher than when she'd been breathing on her own.

"No obstruction," the man said who was compressing the breathing bag at a set interval.

"What happened here?" the woman asked Yuri, who was standing in the doorway trying to look tormented. She worked while she talked, putting EKG leads onto Connie.

"I don't know," Yuri said. "She'd been having a little trouble breathing this evening, but it wasn't bad. Then I heard her fall in here. That's how I found her."

The woman nodded. "Does she have a history of asthma?"

"Yeah," Yuri said. "Quite a bit."

"How about allergies?" the woman asked.

"Those, too," Yuri said.

"Did she complain of any chest pain?"

"No, not at all," Yuri said.

The woman nodded again. She ran a rhythm strip with her EKG. She showed it to her partner and commented that it was slow but regular. He nodded.

The woman looked up at Yuri. "How much does she weigh?"

"I don't know," Yuri admitted. "A lot."

"That I can see," the woman said. She pulled her radio from its belt holster and called into her base. She told the dispatcher they needed assistance to carry an unconscious, obese patient who seemed to be momentarily stable. She said they'd need at least three more guys.

It took considerable effort for the EMTs to get Connie out of the bathroom, onto a stretcher, and out into the ambulance. Yuri was generally ignored through this process, but he was allowed to ride with Connie to the hospital. She was intubated and given oxygen continuously during the ordeal.

At the hospital, Connie was taken into the treatment area while Yuri had to spend time giving the details of Connie's insurance. Then he was relegated to the waiting room. At one point a disheveled doctor with a ponytail came out and went over the history, particularly in regard to the asthma and allergy. Yuri said that Connie had not had much trouble with her breathing recently, at least since they'd been married. He told the doctor that his wife had described lots of hospital visits and trips to the emergency room before they'd met. In regard to specific allergies, Yuri said he wasn't sure what she was allergic to but thought it was things like nuts, cats, dust, and pollen.

"How's she doing?" Yuri asked hesitantly when the doctor got up to leave.

"To be truthful, she's not doing well," the doctor admitted. "We're afraid her brain was denied oxygen for too long. She has no peripheral reflexes whatsoever, which doesn't bode well for her brain function. I'm afraid it doesn't look good. I'm sorry."

Yuri nodded. He wished he could make himself cry, but he couldn't. Instead he hung his head. The doctor gave his shoulder a squeeze and then disappeared.

An hour later the same doctor reappeared. This time he had a white coat over his crumpled pajama-like outfit. His name tag said *Dr. Michael Cooper*. He came over to Yuri and sat down. Yuri looked into the man's gray-green eyes.

"I'm afraid I have bad news," Dr. Cooper said.

Yuri visibly stiffened. In his mind's eye he could see Connie suddenly sit up someplace within the depths of the emergency room and say it was something in the ice cream that had first made her see double.

"Your wife has passed away," Dr. Cooper said softly. "We did all we could, but we just couldn't help her. I'm terribly sorry."

Tears sprang into Yuri's eyes. That they were tears of joy made no difference. He was thrilled the tears had come to add to his theatrics. But mostly he was thrilled that he'd been right about how to get rid of Connie. Despite all his anxieties, it had worked. He was free, and Curt was going to be pleased.

"I know this must be a terrible shock to you," Dr. Cooper continued. "She is such a young person."

"Thank you," Yuri said. He wiped his tears away with the knuckle of his right index finger, making sure the doctor saw the maneuver. "I suppose I have to make some sort of arrangements for her body. Do you think someone could help me? It's something I don't know anything about."

"Absolutely," Dr. Cooper said. "I can have Social Service come and talk with you in a few minutes. But I can relieve your understandable anxiety by saying that you don't have to make any decisions tonight."

"No?" Yuri questioned. "Why not?"

"Because your wife is going to be what we call a medical examiner case," Dr. Cooper explained.

"Does that mean an autopsy?" Yuri asked with consternation.

"Yes, it does," Dr. Cooper said. "But I can assure you it's done with full respect for the deceased."

"But why an autopsy?" Yuri demanded. "You have the diagnosis."

"That's true," Dr. Cooper said. "We know she died of acute respiratory distress with a history of asthma. But she is a relatively young person who was, prior to this unfortunate attack, a healthy, albeit obese, individual. We all think it best to have the medical examiner take a look in case we're missing something. I don't want you to be concerned. It's purely routine in such cases."

"I'm sure you're not missing anything," Yuri sputtered.

"Thank you for your vote of confidence," Dr. Cooper said. "But I'm sure even you will have an easier time coming to terms with your loss when the cause for this tragedy is proved beyond the shadow of doubt. You understand what I'm saying, don't you?"

"Certainly," Yuri managed to reply as the anxieties he'd felt earlier came back like an avalanche.

NINE

Tuesday, October 19
6:43 A.M.

Laurie surprised herself by waking up before her alarm. She couldn't remember having done that for years. It was especially surprising considering her expected jet lag from having flown in from Paris the morning before. But then with a simple calculation she realized that at that moment it was already after noon in the French capital, and even though she'd only been in France for a couple of days, she must have made some adaption to the local time.

At Laurie's first stirring, her eight-month-old cat, Tom-2, stood up, stretched, and came up to the head of the bed for his customary dose of petting. Laurie was happy to comply. In contrast to the mongrel Tom, Laurie's first cat whom she'd rescued from Animal Control and who'd been brutally killed, Tom-2 was a pedigree Burmese she'd purchased from Fabulous Felines on Second Avenue. Tom-2's hair color was not too dissimilar from Laurie's, but lacked the reddish highlights.

Laurie bounded out of bed with more than the usual enthusiasm. Over the month since she'd met Paul, her spirits had been buoyant. In the kitchen she started her coffee machine, which she'd prepared the night before. Back in her tiny bathroom she climbed into the shower.

Laurie had lived in her small, one-bedroom apartment ever since she'd started working at the Office of the Chief Medical Examiner for the City of New York eight years ago. By now she could afford cushier digs, but she'd grown accustomed to her old fifth-floor flat. Also, being only eleven blocks from the office, she often walked both directions. That was a convenience that few of her colleagues enjoyed.

As Laurie washed her hair, she mulled over the previous evening's dinner party and couldn't help suppressing a smile. Initially she'd been disappointed at Jack and Lou's response to her news, but after she'd thought about their behavior, she changed her mind. Now she thought there was an element of humor in their obvious shock and inability to wish the best for her. And she had to admit to a sense of satisfaction. Neither had been willing to make even the most modest commitment. What had they expected her to do, let life pass her by?

Laurie had long suspected that both men were attracted to her romantically but were afraid to follow up on their feelings. Although she valued their friendship, the situation had been frustrating for Laurie, especially since she'd always known that she'd wanted children. She understood that Jack in particular needed plenty of time to recover from the painful loss of his family. So she'd been patient. But could she really put her future on hold indefinitely? In the years that Laurie had known him, Jack had shown no signs of getting over his grief. To Laurie, his whole life still seemed defined as a reaction to that tragic incident.

With Lou, it was different. His ingrained inferiority complex seemed to be immune to Laurie's efforts. Laurie had tried to dent his defensive shield with multiple ploys, but with no luck. In fact, the harder she had tried, the more defensive he'd become, to the point of argument. Ultimately, she'd given up and was content with his enduring friendship.

Laurie vigorously toweled her hair, then combed it out before using the electric hair dryer. As far as she was concerned, it was far better to concentrate on the positive, and that meant thinking about Paul Sutherland. Such thoughts brought an even bigger smile to her face.

Over the last few years Laurie had developed progressively greater insights into her personality. She realized that she'd made careful, rational decisions all her life, a trait that had obviously stood her in good stead career-wise but that at times might have been limiting. She'd taken few chances except for a minor teenage rebellion or two. Now with Paul there was an opportunity. It was like being offered the brass ring on the whirling carousel of life. All she had to do was reach out and seize it.

With her hair done to her satisfaction, Laurie turned to her makeup routine. She didn't wear a lot of makeup, so it didn't take long. While she was applying it, she mused about her whirlwind romance with Paul. Thanks to his generosity and spontaneity, they'd not only been to Paris, they'd spent weekends in Los Angeles and Caracas as well. In New York they'd eaten out almost every night at some of the best restaurants in the city. They'd been to the theater, dance recitals, and the symphony.

After dressing, Laurie went back into her kitchen for her breakfast of cereal, fruit, yogurt, and coffee. While she ate, she admitted to herself that she was a bit overwhelmed by the speed of the courtship. She was still somewhat stunned by Paul's proposal. He'd taken her totally by surprise. She was also immensely pleased and flattered to be with a man who seemed to appreciate her and was desperate not to let her get away.

The main reason she'd not officially accepted was her desire to have a last word with Jack and with Lou, but particularly with Jack. She knew they'd squirm, but they deserved to. And she felt she owed it to them and to herself to present her situation openly and honestly. They could act if they so chose, or forever hold their peace. And if they decided to hold their peace, Laurie intended to grab the brass ring and make her future with Paul, even if she and Paul didn't share that immediate animal attraction she'd had so abundantly with Jack.

Laurie's door buzzer pulled her from her thoughts. She glanced at the clock. She couldn't imagine who could be there

at seven-thirty in the morning. Laurie moved over to the ancient intercom device and put the earphone to her ear. She
pushed the speak button and said hello. Despite the static she
recognized the voice that came back. It was Paul.

Laurie buzzed him in. Then she raced around the apartment
snatching panties off the arm of the couch, a bra from a side
table, and stockings from the floor. When she'd arrived home
the night before, she'd been exhausted and had undressed en
route to her bed, dropping clothing in her wake.

When there was a knock on her door, Laurie checked
through the peephole by reflex. She found herself looking directly into one of Paul's dark eyes. He'd put his face up to
the tiny lens.

Laurie undid the extensive array of locks a former tenant
had installed on her front door and pulled it open. "You
clown," she commented teasingly at Paul's antics. He had a
playful side that was unpredictable but which could embarrass
her in public, like when he surprisingly joined her in the Lil-
liputian commode on the Concorde. Laurie had been mortified
when she'd emerged, but later she'd laughed at herself and
the stodgy businessmen who pretended not to have noticed.

"Surprise," Paul said as he pulled a bouquet of fall flowers
from behind his back.

"What's the occasion?" Laurie asked.

"No occasion," Paul said. "I just thought they looked at-
tractive at one of those all-night Korean convenience stores."

"Well, thank you," Laurie said. She gave him a light kiss
and took the flowers. While she went for a vase, Paul took off
his coat. He was dressed for business in a suit similar to the
one he had on the previous evening.

"Come on in here if you want any coffee," Laurie called
from the kitchen. Paul appeared a moment later. He was carrying Tom-2, who was purring loudly. "What'll it be?" Laurie
asked. "I'm having filtered coffee, but I could make you an
espresso." She finished with the flowers and put the vase on
the table.

"Nothing for me," Paul said energetically. "I've had enough
coffee to last me the whole day, maybe the week. The phone

woke me up early. If only Europe wasn't six hours ahead of us, my life would be ten times easier."

"Do you mind that I finish my breakfast?" Laurie said. "I don't have a lot of time."

"Of course not," Paul said. He sat down across from her at the tiny table. He continued to stroke the cat, who was content in his lap.

"You're certainly full of surprises," Laurie said between mouthfuls. "I never expected to see you this morning."

"I know," Paul said with a sly smile. "But I had a specific surprise I wanted to share with you. I thought it would be better in person."

"That sounds intriguing," Laurie said. "What kind of a surprise?"

"First, let me tell you how much I enjoyed meeting your friends last night," Paul said. "Certainly impressive guys."

"I'm glad," Laurie said. "Thank you. But what is this surprise you're talking about?"

Paul smiled. Knowing Laurie's curiosity, he was purposefully stringing her along. "I was particularly impressed by Jack riding his bike around the city," Paul continued.

"Paul!" Laurie intoned with frustration.

"And Lou," Paul said. "I can't remember the last time I met a more modest guy."

"I'm going to flip some of my yogurt onto your silk tie if you don't tell me what you're trying to say." Laurie held the bowl of her spoon back with her left index finger, turning the spoon into a potential miniature catapult.

"Okay, okay," Paul laughed. He raised his palms in surrender. Sensing trouble, Tom-2 bailed out from Paul's lap and disappeared into the living room.

"You have five seconds," Laurie teased.

"The surprise is that we're going back to Europe this weekend," Paul said. "We'll take the Concorde to Paris on Friday, then connect to Budapest. And let me tell you, Budapest has become one of the more interesting cities in Europe. You're going to love it. I even got us a suite at the Hilton overlooking the Danube."

Paul stared at Laurie with a self-satisfied smile. Laurie returned the gaze but didn't respond. Paul's smile faded. "What's the matter?" he asked.

"I can't go to Budapest this weekend," Laurie said.

"Why not?" Paul questioned.

"I've got to catch up with work," Laurie said with a half laugh. "I've never had so many uncompleted folders on my desk."

"You're not going to let work interfere with our weekends, are you?" Paul asked. He was astonished. "You can work all week."

"I've got too much to do," Laurie said. "I've had to let things slide as it is, especially after spending most of yesterday with the FBI over the skinhead case."

Paul rolled his eyes. "I'll tell you what: we'll cut back on what we have planned for the rest of the week. After all, today is only Tuesday. We'll even scrap the ballet Thursday night even though I had to beg, borrow, and steal for the tickets. It's not as important as a weekend in Budapest."

"I can't go to Budapest!" Laurie said with a tone that precluded debate.

There was a lull in the conversation. Laurie looked at her near-fiancé. He wasn't returning her stare but rather looking down at his hands while shaking his head in a way that was almost imperceptible. "This is a surprise for me," he admitted, breaking the silence. Now he was nodding ever so slightly but still looking down at his lap. "I was so sure you'd want to go."

"It's not that I don't want to go," Laurie said. She softened. "It's just that I have other obligations because of my work."

"I don't think it's healthy that you are letting your work control you," Paul said. Finally he raised his coal-black eyes to hers. "Life's too short for that."

"Now that's hardly a fair thing to say," Laurie responded. "The real reason we went to Paris last weekend was for your work, not that we didn't enjoy ourselves when you were free. I'm assuming the same situation holds for Budapest. I mean, the reason you're going there is for business. In other words, you're working on weekends, so why is it so different if I have to do the same?"

"It's different," Paul said.

"Really?" Laurie questioned. "I fail to see how it's different."

Paul stared back at Laurie. His face had reddened.

"As far as I can see the only way it's different is that I can't work in Budapest."

"There are other differences than that," Paul snapped.

"Give me some examples!" Laurie said.

Paul sighed and shook his head. "It's not important."

"But it must be, otherwise you wouldn't be upset."

"I'm upset because you're not willing to go."

"It's not that I wouldn't like to," Laurie explained. "You do understand that point, don't you?"

"I suppose," Paul said unconvincingly.

"What kind of work do you do anyway?" Laurie asked. She could remember Jack asking the same question the night before. She truly had no idea, and until then it had never occurred to her to ask. She'd always thought he'd just tell her when it was relevant. Having dated so many men who could talk only about their business, she'd found Paul a relief. Yet she was beginning to feel that it was strange that she had no idea what field he was in.

"Does it matter?" Paul questioned contentiously.

"No, it doesn't," Laurie said. She could tell she'd hurt his feelings by suggesting it did. "And I don't think this should be an argument."

"You're right," Paul said. "I'm sorry for reacting the way I have. The problem is, I don't have a choice about this trip. I have to go, and frankly it's lonely. With you along it would actually be a pleasure."

"Thank you for saying that," Laurie said. "And I'm grateful for your asking me. It's just that I can't go away every weekend. And we have gone away three weekends in a row."

"I understand," Paul said. He smiled weakly.

Laurie looked into his eyes. She wondered if he was being sincere.

Paul had a radio-dispatched Town Car waiting for him outside of Laurie's building. He was happy to give her a ride. He said he was going in the same direction. His first meeting for the day was at the United Nations. Laurie was impressed and even more curious about the nature of his business. She was tempted to ask who he was seeing, but was afraid her motive would be too transparent.

Outside of the Office of the Chief Medical Examiner Laurie waved as Paul's car accelerated north on First Avenue. Then she turned and mounted the steps of the blue-glazed brick building. As she entered, she felt vaguely out of sorts, which was not how she'd started the day. Although she and Paul had not had an argument, they'd come close. It had been the first such episode in their wildly romantic relationship. She hoped it wasn't a premonition of things to come, and that the hint of male chauvinism in his responses didn't mask outright sexist views.

Laurie crossed the empty waiting area and approached the main interior entrance that led to the first-floor corridor. "Excuse me!" she called out to Marlene Wilson, the African-American receptionist. Laurie needed Marlene to buzz her in.

"Dr. Montgomery! Hold on!" Marlene said when she caught sight of Laurie. "You've got some visitors who've been waiting for you."

A middle-aged couple whom Laurie had never seen stood up from one of the waiting room's vinyl couches. The burly man was in a heavy red-checked wool jacket and needed a shave. He was holding a hunting cap with earmuffs tied over the top. The woman seemed frail. There was a lace collar around her coat. The two looked as if they belonged in a small town in the Midwest. They were plainly intimidated, and exhausted, as if they'd been traveling all night.

"Can I help you?" Laurie asked.

"We hope so," the man said. "I'm Chester Cassidy and this here is my wife, Shirley."

Laurie recoiled at the surname, realizing that she was most likely facing the parents of Brad Cassidy. Instantly, the horrific image of the tortured young man she'd posted the day before sprang unbidden into her mind's eye. She remembered the gouged eye sockets, the huge nail that had been pounded through the boy's palm, and the naked part of his chest and abdomen where he'd been skinned alive. She shuddered.

"What can I do for you?" Laurie managed to say.

"We understand you are the doctor who took care of our son, Brad," Chester said. His large, gnarled hands were unconsciously worrying his hat.

Laurie nodded, although "taking care of Brad" was hardly an appropriate euphemism for what she'd had to do.

"We would like to talk to you for a few moments," Chester added. "Provided you have the time."

"Of course," Laurie said, although she wasn't looking forward to the conversation. Dealing with bereaved parents was not easy for her. "But I'm just arriving at this very moment. You'll have to give me about fifteen minutes."

"We understand," Chester said. With an arm around his wife, Chester retreated to the couch.

Laurie had herself buzzed into the building. Preoccupied with the upcoming meeting with the Cassidy family, she took the elevator up to the fifth floor and went into her office. She hung her coat behind the door. A quick glance at the mound of unfinished folders on her desk made her thankful she'd been steadfast in her decision not to go on the Budapest trip.

Laurie found Brad Cassidy's folder near the top of the stack. Using her index finger she went through the contents until she came to the identification sheet. She pulled it out. She was curious who had made the ID. The name was listed as Helen Trautman, the deceased's sister.

Back down on the first floor she took the circuitous route through communications to the ID room. She wanted a bolt of coffee before facing the Cassidys. As she entered, she ran into Jack and Vinnie on their way down to the autopsy room. As usual, they were getting a jump on the day.

"Could we talk for a moment?" Jack asked sheepishly the moment he saw Laurie.

"Can it wait?" Laurie asked. She looked at Jack curiously; sheepishness was hardly one of Jack's typical behavioral traits. "There's a couple waiting for me out in the waiting room. I have a feeling they've been here for a long time."

"It'll only take a second," Jack promised. "Vinnie, run down and get set up in the autopsy room! I'll be down in a couple of minutes."

"Why don't I just go back to my newspaper?" Vinnie suggested. "I don't want to be standing down there in the deserted pit twiddling my thumbs. Some of your spontaneous conversations go on for half an hour."

"Not this time," Jack said. "Get!"

Vinnie slunk off. Jack watched him go until he was out of earshot. Then he stepped over to Laurie, who was helping herself to the community coffee. Jack cast a quick glance at George Fontworth, but he was ignoring them while busily sorting the cases that had come in over the night.

"Where's the Hope diamond ring?" Jack asked.

Laurie glanced at her naked finger as if she expected the ring to be there. "It's hidden in the freezer compartment of my refrigerator."

"On ice, so to speak," Jack said.

Laurie couldn't help but smile. Such a comment was much more like the Jack she knew. "I'm not officially engaged," she said. "I mentioned that last night, in case you don't remember."

"I guess not until you tell your parents," Jack said.

"That and a few other things," Laurie said.

"Anyway," Jack stammered. "I wanted to apologize for last night."

"Apologize for what?" Laurie asked. Apology wasn't one of Jack's strong suits either.

"For not being more positive about Paul," Jack said. "He seems like a nice enough guy, and I'm impressed by you two going to Paris for the weekend. I could never do that in a million years."

"Is that all you want to say?"

"I guess," Jack said.

"Then your apology is accepted," Laurie said matter-of-factly. She tossed back the quarter cup of coffee she'd poured for herself, flashed Jack a quick, fake smile, then headed for the meeting with the Cassidys. She knew Jack was transfixed and probably baffled by her behavior, but she didn't care. She hadn't wanted an apology, especially not an insincere one. What she wanted to hear from him was how he felt about her possible plans to marry. But she now knew it wasn't going to happen, and it frustrated her.

Laurie first checked one of the small side rooms used for relatives during the emotional identification process. In the past, people had to go down to the morgue and view the body, but that was an unnecessarily cruel procedure for individuals still coping with the shock of loss of a loved one. Now Polaroid pictures were used, and it was a lot easier on everyone.

Once Laurie was certain the room was reasonably clean, she went to get the Cassidys. They filed in silently and sat in two of the straight-back chairs. Laurie leaned against the scarred wooden desk. The only other things in the room were a box of tissues, a wastebasket, and several chipped ashtrays.

"Could I get either of you some coffee?" Laurie questioned as a way of introduction.

"I don't reckon so," Chester said. He'd taken off his coat. His plaid flannel shirt was buttoned to the neck. "We don't want to take too much of your time."

"It's quite all right," Laurie said. "We're really here to serve the public, quite literally. And let me say that I'm very sorry about your son. I'm sure it was a big shock for you."

"In some ways yes and in some ways no," Chester said. "He'd been a kinda wayward kid. Nothing like his older sister or older brother. To tell you the truth, we were embarrassed by the way he dressed and looked, especially with that Nazi sign he tattooed on his forehead. My uncle died fighting those Nazis. Brad and I had a set-to about that tattoo, the good it did."

"Teenage rebellion is sometimes hard to understand," Laurie offered. She wanted to steer the conversation away from the boy's appearance. One of her worries was that the Cassidys would request to see the pictures of their son that had been taken on his arrival at the morgue. Such photographs were not fit for any layperson to see, much less a parent.

"Trouble was, he was no longer a teenager," Chester said. Shirley nodded in agreement. "But he'd gotten in with the wrong crowd. They all had that Nazi stuff. And then they started going around beating up on people who were different, like gays and Puerto Ricans."

"That's how he got in trouble the first time," Shirley said, speaking up for the first time. She had an unexpectedly high, strident voice.

"I understand he'd had difficulties with the police," Laurie said. She started to relax. It seemed as if the Cassidys merely wanted to talk. Laurie could appreciate that kind of urge, considering their grief and bafflement at their son's untimely death. The only problem was that there were things that Lou and Agent Tyrrell had told her about the victim that she wasn't in a position to disclose, such as the fact that he'd been co-operating with the authorities as part of a plea bargain.

"We heard that some awful things had happened to Brad from our daughter, Helen," Chester said. "Brad had come down here recently to stay with her in the city. But she couldn't tell us very much about the details of his death. That's why we came ourselves from where we live upstate."

"What would you like to know?" Laurie asked. She was hoping she could speak in generalities.

The husband and wife glanced at each other to see who should go first. Chester cleared his throat: "One of the things we wanted to know was whether he was shot."

"He was," Laurie said. "Most definitely."

"I told you so," Shirley said to Chester, as if the news validated her position in an argument. "For all they who taketh the sword shall perish with the sword: Matthew twenty-six."

"Do you know what kind of gun it was?" Chester asked.

"No," Laurie said. "And I'm not sure we'll ever know. The bullet, of course, will be examined, and if a particular gun was believed to be involved, it could be implicated."

"Was he shot only once?" Chester asked.

"We believe so," Laurie said with less emphasis. She was uncomfortable giving more than sketchy details, since Brad's homicide was under investigation.

"Then maybe it wasn't one of his guns," Chester said to Shirley. "If it had been, then he probably would have been hit many times."

"Did your son have a lot of guns?" Laurie asked.

"Too many guns," Shirley said. "That's how he got in trouble the second time. We thought he was going to go to prison.

I tell you: I don't know what men see in guns."

"Now, it's not all guns that are bad," Chester said.

"Most of them, if you ask me," Shirley snapped. "Particularly those automatic ones." Then turning to Laurie she added: "That's what Brad got involved in. He was selling assault rifles."

"Where did he get them?" Laurie asked. The idea of a skinhead youth selling assault rifles in upstate New York gave her a shiver.

"We don't rightly know," Chester said. "They came from Bulgaria originally. At least that's where they'd been made. I came across a bunch of them hidden in our barn."

"That's terrible," Laurie said. She knew it was a trite response, but she meant it. With her particular interest in the forensics of gunshot wounds, she'd seen a lot of cases, more than anyone else at the office. She couldn't help but wonder if she'd ever autopsied anyone victimized by one of Brad Cassidy's customers.

"There's one other thing we'd like to ask," Shirley said haltingly. "We'd like to know if our boy suffered."

Laurie looked away for a moment while her mind wrestled with the question. She hated to have to choose between truth and compassion. It was undeniable that Brad Cassidy had been mercilessly tortured, but what purpose would it serve to relate such horror to his grieving parents? On the other hand, she hated to lie.

"You can tell us straight," Chester said, as if sensing Laurie's quandary.

"He was shot in the head, and I believe he died instantly," Laurie said, suddenly realizing she had an out. By such a statement she wasn't being entirely honest, since she was not answering Shirley's question, yet she wasn't lying either. It was up to the Cassidys to ask the critical question about the order of events preceding Brad's murder.

"Thank the Lord!" Shirley said. "He was a troubled boy and certainly not a good boy, but the idea that he might have suffered bothered me deeply."

"I'm glad we could be of service," Laurie said. She pushed off the desk, eager to avoid more questions by breaking up the meeting. "If there's anything else I can do, please give me a call."

Chester and Shirley stood up. They were grateful to Laurie, and the father pumped her hand enthusiastically. Laurie gave him one of her cards as she escorted them out of the cubicle and across the ID room. She opened the door to the waiting room, and the Cassidys filed out.

After a final goodbye, Laurie let the door close and lock. Then she breathed a sigh of relief.

"Were you doing an ID in there of a case I don't know about?" George Fontworth asked. He was bent over the list of fatalities, trying to schedule the day's autopsies.

"No! They were the parents of one of yesterday's cases," Laurie said while staring off into the middle distance. With the Cassidys gone, she found herself preoccupied by the horror of their son selling assault rifles, probably to other skinheads. With what she'd learned the day before from Special Agent Gordon Tyrrell, putting such deadly weapons in the hands of such violent and bigoted people was an invitation to disaster, especially since the far-right neo-Nazi militias were busily recruiting the skinheads as shock troops.

What's this world coming to? Laurie voicelessly questioned to herself. Her strong support for gun control ratcheted up yet another notch.

TEN

With the cab's motor running, Yuri got out and opened his garage door. Despite his exhaustion, the sight of the pest control truck brought a smile to his face. The fact that it was sitting there waiting for the big day was a source of great satisfaction and gave meaning to the effort he was expending and the anxieties he was suffering. Yuri pulled his taxi inside and shut the overhead door. He didn't want anyone to see the truck.

At his back door Yuri hesitated for a moment and let his eyes roam his immediate neighborhood. He wanted to make sure no one was paying him any heed. It wasn't usual for him to be coming home in the middle of the morning. And certainly all the commotion of the ambulance in the wee hours of that morning must have gotten the neighbors' attention. Yet he saw no one. It was a peaceful Indian summer day with the temperature in the low seventies. For the moment, there weren't even any dogs barking.

Inside, Yuri went directly to his refrigerator and poured

himself a vodka. He leaned against the counter and took a calming sip. He was still nervous about Connie's body having been taken to the medical examiner's office at Kings County Hospital. He'd gone with it for purposes of identification, even though he'd been told it wasn't necessary since he'd made adequate identification at Coney Island Hospital. But he'd gone anyway in hopes of talking the doctors out of doing the autopsy. Yet it turned out he never even got to see a doctor. The person he'd met with described herself as a forensic investigator. At least Yuri made sure she got the story about the asthma and the allergies. She told him that the autopsy wouldn't take place until some time after eight, when the medical examiners arrived.

It had been five o'clock in the morning by the time Yuri had gotten home. Although exhausted, he'd sensed there was no chance that he'd sleep. He was too keyed up, so he'd taken his cab out for a jump on rush hour.

It had been a good decision. Not only had he been able to earn some decent money, but the work took his mind off his worries, at least while he'd been busy. As soon as there was a lull, it was a different story, and Yuri had started for home. Besides, he had other, more important things to do than spend the day driving. He was eager to get down into his lab.

Even though he wasn't hungry, Yuri forced himself to eat some cold cereal. His empty stomach was growling from the previous night's pizza and too much coffee, and now vodka. As he ate, he eyed the telephone. The forensic investigator had given him a number to call that afternoon to find out when Connie's body would be released to the funeral home Yuri had selected. Yuri wondered if she was already set to be moved. As far as he was concerned, the sooner Connie was out of the medical examiner's office the better.

Yuri dialed. To his surprise the phone was answered by a person rather than an answering machine. He identified himself and asked about his wife's body.

"What was that name again?" the operator asked.

"Davydov," Yuri reiterated. "Connie Davydov."

"Hold on a second, let me check."

Yuri felt his pulse quicken. He hated dealing with bureaucracy of any sort.

"I don't seem to find a Davydov," the operator said. "Are you sure your wife came to the Brooklyn office?"

"Of course!" Yuri said. "I was there myself."

"How do you spell Davydov?"

Yuri spelled out his surname. His anxiety mounted. Maybe they'd made the diagnosis and the police were called. Maybe the police were already on their way to his house that very minute. Maybe . . .

"Oh, here it is," the woman said. "No wonder I couldn't find it. Your wife wasn't autopsied."

"You mean they haven't done it yet?" Yuri questioned.

"No, I mean the doctors decided she didn't need to be posted," the operator said.

"Why not?" Yuri asked. It sounded too good to be true.

"They don't tell us operators anything like that. You'll have to speak to the duty doctor. Today it's Dr. Randolph Sanders. Just a moment!"

Yuri tried to get the operator's attention, since he wasn't sure he wanted to talk to the duty doctor, but she'd put him on hold. Elevator music flowed out of the receiver.

Yuri struggled to control his excitement as he waited. The fact that it had been decided not to autopsy Connie was unexpected good news, provided it was true. He drummed his fingers nervously on the countertop. He took another swig of vodka.

"This is Dr. Sanders," a voice said, cutting off the music. "Can I help you?"

Nervously Yuri explained who he was and what he'd been told.

"Ah, yes," Dr. Sanders said. "I know the case well. I was the one who decided the autopsy was not necessary."

"So the body can be released?" Yuri asked.

"Absolutely," Dr. Sanders said. "It can be picked up at any time by the funeral home you've chosen. I believe that's Strickland's."

"That's right," Yuri said. "Should I call them to let them know?"

"I'm sure our mortuary office has done that already," Dr. Sanders said. "Or at least they'll be doing it very soon."

"Thank you very much," Yuri said, purposefully toning down his excitement lest it be interpreted correctly. "Out of curiosity, why the change of plans? I mean, I'm relieved there was no autopsy because I was not happy about my wife's body being disturbed."

"It was not really a change in plans," Dr. Sanders explained. "Not every patient who's sent in is autopsied. There is a constant evaluation of the need. In your wife's case the attending physician certified the cause of death, which was certainly consistent with her history of asthma. Of course, her weight probably didn't help her situation either."

"I'm sure not," Yuri said. "Thank you for talking with me."

"My pleasure," Dr. Sanders said. "And my condolences for your loss."

"It is a difficult time for me," Yuri said. "Thank you for your concern."

Yuri replaced the receiver as a wonderful sense of self-satisfaction spread through him. It was as if the last barrier for Operation Wolverine had crumbled and the goal was in sight. He couldn't wait to tell Curt.

Yuri rinsed his cereal dish, polished off the rest of the vodka, then headed down into the basement. He whistled as he opened the lock on the entry chamber. In his euphoria he didn't even feel particularly tired.

He took off the padlock on the storeroom and stepped into the space. Facing the shelving he selected the culture nutrients and other supplies he needed. He brought it all out and placed it next to the door into the lab. Then he donned his breathing apparatus and finally the hazmat suit. When he was ready he opened the inner door and lifted in all the supplies.

The first thing he did was take out the anthrax cakes from the dryer and put them into the pulverizer. When he turned the pulverizer on he was thankful for the sound of the compressed air inside his hood. It helped compete with the racket of the steel ball bearings in the metal cylinder.

The next order of business was to harvest more anthrax spores from the fermenter and get the slurry into the dryer.

After that was completed, Yuri recharged the fermenter with fresh nutrients to let the bacteria continue their rapid reproduction and spore formation.

Finally, Yuri turned to the second fermenter. Once again he checked the level of growth of the *Clostridium botulinum* and once again it was less than it should have been. Yuri was still mystified, but no longer concerned now that he was going to convert the fermenter to *Bacillus anthracis*. With both fermenters producing the anthrax spores, he'd have the required eight to ten pounds in a matter of days.

Pausing in his labors, Yuri pondered what he should do with the existing culture of the *Clostridium botulinum*. Even though the growth had been far less than anticipated, the unit contained gargantuan numbers of the bacteria. He looked around for some kind of storage facility. The only thing that might have worked was using the empty nutrient containers, but he'd been discarding them as he'd gone along. What he currently had on hand wasn't enough to hold the fermenter's volume.

There was only one other solution: let the entire contents of the fermenter drain directly into the sewer. Yuri tried to think if there would be any consequences that might alert the authorities. He stood for a moment and pondered the consequences, but he couldn't think of any. He couldn't imagine that sewage treatment plants would worry about the bacterial content of the influx. They only worried about the outflow.

Confident of his decision, Yuri got out the plumbing tools he left in the lab and set to work. The job only required opening a few valves, since Yuri had originally plumbed the fermenters to a drain for flushing purposes.

With the appropriate valves open, Yuri watched the fermenter's level fall. A gurgle issued forth from a relief valve on top of the unit.

Once the fermenter was empty, Yuri flushed it out. Then he began loading it with fresh nutrient broth. Finally he seeded it with a fresh growth of anthrax from the original culture he'd isolated from the Oklahoma soil sample.

When Yuri was finished, he straightened up. He gave the fermenter a pat and told it to make him proud. Then he turned his attention back to the pulverizer to see how much time was left on the current run. As soon as that was over and he'd unloaded the powder, he planned on going upstairs and taking a long-needed and deserved nap.

ELEVEN

Jack tossed aside the textbook on infectious disease that he'd gotten from the library and cursed loudly. He was trying to read more about anthrax. The case of Jason Papparis was still bothering him, but he found concentrating difficult. He swung around and eyed Chet's empty chair, wondering where his officemate was. Jack was eager to relate his most recent experience confirming his suspicion that women were impossible.

During the night, Jack had awakened to agonize over letting Laurie down by not being more positive about her new boyfriend. Although Jack was well aware that jealousy played a role in his evaluation of the man, he still felt there was something about the individual that he legitimately didn't care for. As he'd implied to Lou, it involved the overly gallant gesture of sweeping Laurie off to Paris for the weekend. To Jack such behavior smacked of a kind of bribery. In Jack's experience such men invariably resorted to overt male chauvinism once a relationship was established and the woman was emotionally committed.

Around four o'clock in the morning, Jack decided he'd eat humble pie. Even though it irked him, he resolved to go the whole nine yards and apologize. Then he'd compliment Paul in some way that he'd figure out on the spur of the moment. The decision had taken a number of hours. What had tipped the balance was Jack's realization of how important Laurie's friendship was to him.

But things had hardly gone the way Jack envisioned. After doing what he'd resolved to do, Laurie barely accepted his apology before walking off. All morning she'd gone out of her way to avoid him, much less voice any kind of appreciation of his gesture. Jack felt damned either way. She'd been mad because he'd not been complimentary about Paul and now she was mad because he had been. Jack shook his head. He didn't know what more he could do.

Twisting around in his chair again, Jack reached for his phone. If he couldn't read about anthrax, at least he could work the phone. Over the previous hour he'd called a half dozen New York hospitals to talk with chief residents in infectious disease or, if the hospital didn't have one, the chief resident in internal medicine.

When he'd gotten the appropriate individual on the phone, he outlined the case of inhalational anthrax that had come from the Bronx General Hospital and asked if there were any cases in their hospital that might be anthrax. The responses had been uniformly negative, but at least Jack felt he was planting the seed of suspicion with the right people. In that way, if a case did come in or if they had a case undiagnosed, they'd at least think about it. Anthrax was never high on any New York hospital house staff's differential diagnosis list.

The chief resident in infectious disease at Columbia Presbyterian Medical Center picked up Jack's page, and Jack went through his spiel. Although shocked to hear about Mr. Papparis, the resident assured Jack that there was no one in his medical center who'd be considered a candidate for a diagnosis of anthrax.

Jack hung up and looked over to the open page in the yellow

telephone directory for the number of another hospital. Before he could dial, the phone rang. He picked it up eagerly. But it wasn't a resident calling him back with potentially interesting news. It was Mrs. Sanford, the chief's secretary, with a familiar request. The chief wanted to see Jack ASAP.

Hardly in the mood for bureaucratic nonsense, as Jack termed his frequent run-ins with the front office, he took the elevator down to the first floor. Like a schoolboy expecting to be chastised, he presented himself to Mrs. Cheryl Sanford, who smiled at him and winked. Over the years Jack and Cheryl had become well acquainted, since every time the chief demanded Jack come quickly, Jack invariably had to wait. The time provided an opportunity for friendly conversation.

Jack winked back. It was part of an established method of nonverbal communication the two had evolved. It meant that Jack could relax, since the upcoming confrontation with the chief was procedural only, meaning the chief felt obligated, not motivated, to bawl Jack out for whatever the transgression was.

"How's that boy of yours?" Jack asked as he sat down on the rock-hard vinyl sofa across from the secretary's desk. The door to the chief's office was to Cheryl's left and it was always ajar. The chief could be heard on the phone.

"Just fine," Cheryl said proudly. "He's still getting all A's in school."

"Fantastic," Jack said. By coincidence Jack knew Cheryl's son, Arnold. Occasionally he played basketball on the same court as Jack. He was a young, tentative player but with obvious natural skill. Cheryl, an African-American single mother, lived in a building on 105th Street that Jack could see from his bedroom window.

"He says he hopes to be able to play basketball as well as you some day," Cheryl said.

Jack let out a derisive laugh. "He's going to be ten times better than I ever was." Jack was not exaggerating; Arnold had only recently turned fifteen and yet was a player sought after even by Warren.

"I'd prefer to see him take after your doctoring skills," Cheryl said.

"He's expressed some interest," Jack said. "He and I had a chat last week when we were both waiting to get into the game."

"He told me," Cheryl said. "I appreciate you taking the time."

"Hey, he's a nice kid," Jack said. "It's a pleasure talking with him."

At that moment the chief, Dr. Harold Bingham, bellowed for Jack to get the hell into his office.

Jack stood up and headed for the door. As he passed Cheryl's desk she whispered, "Be nice now! Don't aggravate him! He'll be a bear all day."

The chief was ensconced behind his massive, cluttered desk. He'd just reached his sixty-fifth birthday and looked every bit of it. In the four years Jack had been working at the OCME, Bingham's bulbous nose had seemingly expanded along with the web of capillaries hugging his nasal alae. Light from the window behind him bounced off his perspiring bald pate to create a glare that made Jack squint.

"Sit down!" Dr. Bingham commanded.

Jack did as he was told and waited. He had no idea what he'd been called down for but knew there were lots of potential topics.

"Don't you get tired of this routine?" Bingham questioned. He narrowed his rheumy, steel-blue eyes that were unwaveringly studying Jack through wire-rimmed glasses. Although he looked as old as Methuselah, the chief was as sharp as ever and was a veritable walking encyclopedia of forensic data and experience. He was recognized the world over as one of the giants of the field.

"It's nice to see you once in a while, chief," Jack said. He winced; he knew by his flippancy he'd already ignored Cheryl's admonition.

Bingham took his glasses off and rubbed his eyes with his thick fingers. He shook his head. "Sometimes I wish you weren't quite as sharp as you are, because then I'd know exactly what to do with you."

"Thank you for the compliment, chief. I needed a little boost today."

"The problem is, you are one big pain in the ass."

Jack bit his tongue. A few witty quips came to his mind, but he resisted voicing them in deference to Cheryl. After all, she had to be around Bingham for the rest of the day. Bingham's temper was almost as legendary as his wealth of forensic knowledge.

"Do you have any idea why you're down here?" Bingham demanded.

"I refuse to answer on grounds of self-incrimination," Jack said.

Bingham smiled in spite of himself, but the grin vanished as quickly as it had appeared. "You are a trip, my boy. But listen! I got a call from Dr. Patricia Markham, the Commissioner of Health, a little while ago. Seems you've been aggravating the city epidemiologist again, Dr. . . ."

Bingham slipped on his glasses and rummaged through the papers in front of him looking for the name.

"Dr. Abelard," Jack offered.

"Yeah, that's the one," Bingham said.

"What was the charge?" Jack asked.

"He was angry that you were doing his job," Bingham said. "What's the matter? Don't we give you enough to do around here?"

"I called the man, as Dr. Washington suggested," Jack said. "I thought he'd want to know about the case of anthrax I diagnosed."

"So I heard from Calvin," Bingham said.

"But Dr. Abelard took the news in stride," Jack said. "He said he'd get to it when he had time, or something like that."

"But I understand the source is locked up tight in Queens," Bingham said.

"True," Jack admitted.

"Yet you took it on yourself to go out and rifle through the victim's business records," Bingham snapped. "What's the matter with you, are you crazy? What if some civil liberty lawyer got ahold of this? You didn't have a warrant or anything."

"I asked the man's wife," Jack said with a shrug.

"Oh, that would hold up well in court," Bingham said sarcastically.

"I was worried that some of the victim's recent shipment had been sold. If it had, then the anthrax could have spread. We could have had a mini-epidemic."

"Dr. Abelard is right," Bingham fumed. "What you're talking about is his job, not yours."

"We're supposed to be protecting the public," Jack said. "I felt there was a risk that Dr. Abelard was not addressing. He wasn't giving the situation the attention it deserved."

"When you feel that way about a fellow civil servant, then come to me!" Bingham roared. "Instead of you running around playing epidemiologist detective, I could have called Pat Markham. As Commissioner of Health she can surely get people up off their fat asses if need be. That's the way the system is supposed to work."

"Okay," Jack said with a shrug. In further deference to Cheryl he wasn't about to get into an argument about bureaucratic inefficiency and frequent civil servant incompetence. It had been Jack's experience as a city worker that all too often if he didn't do something himself it didn't get done.

"Fine, then get the hell out," Bingham said with a wave of his hand. His mind had already switched to the next problem on his agenda.

Jack got up and walked out of the chief's office. He paused at Cheryl's desk. "How'd I do?"

"Honestly, about a C," Cheryl said with a wry smile. "But since you generally get an F, meaning you aggravate him to a point just shy of apoplexy, I'd say you're showing progress."

Jack waved and started for the corridor. But he didn't get far. Calvin caught sight of him through his open office door.

"How's progress on the David Jefferson case?" Calvin yelled.

Jack leaned in through the door. "Nothing's back yet. Did you call John DeVries up in toxicology to speed things up from his lab?"

"Right after I said I would," Calvin said.

"Okay, then I'll head up there right now," Jack said.

"Remember, I want that case signed out by Thursday!" Calvin said.

Jack gave the deputy chief a thumbs-up sign even though he doubted it was going to happen, since all the lab work wouldn't be back. But there was no use arguing about it now. Instead, Jack took an elevator to the fourth floor. There was always the chance of a miracle.

Jack found John DeVries in his tiny, windowless cubicle and asked about the prisoner-in-custody case. In response, John launched into an impassioned lament about toxicology funding. By the time Jack left, he was even more sure he would not be able to finish the case by Thursday.

Using the stairs, Jack climbed up to the sixth floor and entered the DNA lab. Ted Lynch, the director, was in front of one of his many high-tech machines along with one of his technicians. The machine's instruction manual was open on the counter. It was apparent the unit was malfunctioning.

"Ah, just the man I want to see," Ted said when he caught sight of Jack. He straightened up and then stretched his back. Ted was a big man and a former Ivy League football star.

Jack's face brightened. "Does that mean you have some positive results for me?"

"Yup," Ted said. "One of all those samples you dropped off was positive for anthrax spores."

"No kidding," Jack said. He was surprised. Despite making the effort to take all the cultures, he'd not expected any positive results. "Which one of the samples? Can you remember?"

"Absolutely," Ted said. "It was the one with the tiny blue iridescent star in it."

"My word!" Jack commented. He could remember finding the star in the middle of the blotter on the desk. It seemed so out of place in the spartan surroundings. Jack had figured it was all that remained of some long-past celebration.

"Can you tell me anything else about it?" Jack asked.

"Yup," Ted said agreeably. "I had Agnes send up a sample of the culture she'd taken from the patient. We're running a DNA fingerprint now. We'll be able to tell if it's the same strain. I mean, one would assume it was, but it will be nice to have confirmation."

"Indeed," Jack said. "Anything else?"

"Like what?" Ted questioned peevishly. He thought Jack would have been more than satisfied with what he'd been told already.

"I don't know," Jack said. "You're the one with all this high-tech wizardry. I don't even know the right questions to ask."

"I'm no mind reader," Ted said. "I need to know what you want to know."

"Well, how about whether the star was heavily contaminated with spores or only lightly contaminated."

"That's an interesting question," Ted said. He stared off and chewed on the inside of his cheek for a moment while he pondered. "I'll have to give that some thought."

"And I'll have to give some thought to how it got contaminated," Jack said.

"Wasn't this from the victim's office?" Ted asked.

"It was," Jack said. "The star was on the desk in the office, but the source for the anthrax spores was his warehouse, not the office. Apparently the spores came in a shipment of goat skins and rugs from Turkey."

"I see," Ted said.

"I suppose the spores could have been on his person," Jack said. "So when he came back to his office and sat down, they dropped off."

"Seems reasonable to me," Ted said. "Or what about the possibility of his coughing out some of the spores. I understand it was an inhalational case."

"That's an idea, too," Jack said. "But either way, why the hell were they only on the star? I cultured several spots on the desk, and they were all negative."

"Maybe he coughed out the star," Ted said with a laugh.

"Now that's a helpful suggestion," Jack said sarcastically.

"Well, I'll leave the sleuthing to you," Ted said. "Meanwhile I've got to get back to my sick piece of equipment."

"Yeah, sure," Jack said absently. He continued to wrestle with the puzzle of the contaminated star as he wandered out of the DNA lab and descended the stairs to the fifth floor. He had the uncomfortable feeling the star was trying to tell him something that he couldn't understand. It was like a message in a code without a key.

Jack leaned into Laurie's office, but she wasn't there. Riva, Laurie's officemate, glanced up from her desk. In her soft, charming Indian-émigré-accented voice, she told Jack that Laurie was still in the autopsy room.

Still in a daze about the star, Jack headed for his own office. It occurred to him that the star might have had a slight electrostatic charge, since its sheen suggested it was made of either metallic or plastic material. That might have explained the reason the spores had stuck to it.

He turned into his office and sat at his desk, still obsessed by the mystery of the tiny, cerulean blue star. With his head cradled in his hands, he tried to think.

"What kind of blue star are you mumbling about?" a voice questioned.

Jack glanced up. He was surprised to see Lou. The detective's expression was as hangdog as it had been when they met at the bar the night before, but he was back to his crumpled, perpetually disheveled look. Gone were the pressed suit and the polished shoes.

"Was I talking out loud?" Jack questioned.

"No, I'm a mind reader," Lou said. "Can I come in?"

"Sure," Jack said. He reached over and pulled one of the straight-back chairs he and Chet shared closer to his desk. He patted the seat with his hand.

Lou sat down heavily. It didn't appear as if he'd shaved that morning.

"If you're looking for Laurie, she's down in the pit," Jack said.

"I was looking for you," Lou said.

Jack raised his eyebrows. "I'm flattered. What's up?"

"I've got a confession to make," Lou said.

"This sounds interesting," Jack said.

"I felt so bad about it, I couldn't sleep. I was up most of the night."

"Sounds familiar," Jack offered.

"I don't want you to think badly about me or anything."

"I'll try not to." Jack drummed his fingers impatiently.

"Because this is not something I usually do. I want you to know that."

"For crissake, Lou, confess! How else am I going to give you absolution?"

Lou looked down at his clasped hands and sighed.

"Okay, let me guess," Jack said. "You masturbated and had unclean thoughts."

"I'm not joking around!" Lou snapped.

"Then tell me so I don't have to guess."

"Okay," Lou said. "I ran Paul Sutherland's name through the system."

"Is that it?" Jack questioned with exaggerated disappointment. "I was hoping you'd done something significantly more salacious."

"But it's abusing my law enforcement prerogatives."

"Maybe so, but I would have done the same thing," Jack admitted.

"Honest?"

"Absolutely," Jack said. "So, what did you find?"

Lou leaned forward conspiratorially and lowered his voice. "He's got a sheet."

"Something serious?" Jack asked.

"Not really all that serious," Lou said. "I suppose it depends on your point of view. The charge was cocaine possession."

"Is that all?"

"It was a sizable amount of cocaine," Lou said. "Not enough to suggest he was dealing, but enough for quite a party. He pleaded no contest and got probation and community service."

"Are you going to tell Laurie?" Jack asked.

"I don't know," Lou admitted. "That's what I wanted to ask you."

"Oh, jeez," Jack said. He rubbed his forehead. It was a difficult question.

"I'd be asking myself why I was telling her," Lou said.

Jack nodded. "I understand what you mean. She might ask the same question and then take out any anger the news generates on the messenger."

"My thoughts exactly," Lou said. "Yet as a friend, I kinda

think she should know. Of course, he may have already told her."

"My intuition tells me he hasn't," Jack said. "He's too full of himself."

"I feel the same," Lou said.

Out of the corner of his eye, Jack saw a figure fill his entire doorway. It was Ted Lynch from the DNA lab.

"I'm sorry," Ted said. "I didn't think you'd be busy."

"It's okay," Jack said. He introduced Ted and Lou, but they said they'd already met.

"I couldn't get your question out of my mind," Ted said.

"You mean about the degree of contamination of the blue star?"

"Uh huh! And there is a way to do it!" Ted said excitedly. "It's called TaqMan technology. It's a new wrinkle on the PCR."

"What's PCR again?" Lou asked.

"Polymerase chain reaction," Jack said. "It's a way of augmenting a tiny piece of DNA so that it can be analyzed."

"Right!" Lou said, pretending he understood.

"Anyway this technique is fantastic," Ted said eagerly. "It involves putting a specific enzyme in the PCR reaction mix. What the enzyme does is gobble up single strands of DNA like that old video game PacMan. Remember that?"

Both Jack and Lou nodded.

"The slick thing is that when it hits an attached probe for whatever it is you're looking for, the enzyme signals. Isn't that sharp? So you can quantify what was in the sample originally by knowing the number of doublings the reaction has gone through, since that's time-related."

Both Jack and Lou looked blankly at the excited DNA expert.

"So you want me to do it?" Ted asked.

"Yeah, sure," Jack said. "That would be great."

"I'll get right on it," Ted said. He disappeared as quickly as he'd appeared.

"Did you understand that?" Lou asked.

"Not a word," Jack admitted. "Ted's in his own world up

there. That's why they put the DNA lab on the top floor. We all think the results are coming from heaven."

"I've got to learn more about that DNA stuff," Lou admitted. "It's becoming more and more important in law enforcement."

"The trouble is the technology is changing so rapidly," Jack said.

"What's this about a blue star?" Lou asked. "Is that the same blue star you were mumbling about when I came in?"

"One and the same," Jack said. He went on to tell Lou the story of the tiny, glittering star, including the fact that it was the only thing in the Corinthian Rug Company office that was contaminated with anthrax spores.

"I've seen little stars like you're describing," Lou said. "In fact, just this year the invitation I got to the Police Ball had them inside the envelope."

"You're right!" Jack said. "I once got an invitation with them in it as well. I'd been wondering where I'd seen them."

"It's a curious thing to find in a rug office," Lou said. "I wonder if they'd had a party."

"Let's get back to your question," Jack said. "How are you going to make this decision whether to tell Laurie or not about her new boyfriend's criminal record?"

"I don't know," Lou said. "I suppose I was hoping you'd offer to tell her."

"Oh, no, you don't," Jack said. "This is your ball game. You got this information, and it's up to you to decide what to do with it."

"Well, there is more," Lou said.

Jack's ears picked up. "I'm listening."

"I found out what kind of business he's in."

"That's in his police record?" Jack questioned.

Lou nodded. "He's an arms dealer."

Jack's jaw slowly dropped open. As far as he was concerned, Paul Sutherland's being an arms dealer was far more important vis-à-vis Laurie than his having been convicted of cocaine possession.

"He used to have a monopoly of sorts importing Bulgarian AK-47s, at least until 1994 when the Omnibus Crime Bill was passed and they were banned along with eighteen other semi-automatic assault weapons."

"This is serious," Jack said.

"Of course it's serious," Lou said. "These Bulgarian AK-47s are very popular with far-right militia groups and other screwy survivalists."

"I'm talking about in relation to Laurie," Jack said. "Do you have any idea of her stand on gun control?"

"Not exactly," Lou admitted.

"Well, let me tell you," Jack said. "She'd like to disarm the entire country, including patrolmen. She's made gunshot wounds her forensic specialty."

"She never mentioned that to me," Lou said. He sounded hurt.

"Well, I think the fact that her potential fiancé deals in guns is a hell of a lot more important to tell her about than the cocaine bust."

"Does that mean you'll do it?"

"Oh, hell," Jack said. "Won't you? You found out about it, and she'll surely ask me my source. I'll have to say it was you anyway."

"It doesn't matter," Lou said. "I think you could do it better than I. You've got so much more in common with her."

"Coward," Jack said.

"Well, you're hardly being courageous," Lou pointed out. "Come on! You see her much more than I do. I mean, you work in the same building."

"All right, I'll think about it," Jack said. "But I'm not making any promises."

Jack's phone rang. He snatched the handset from its cradle and his voice sounded almost angry. He quickly mellowed when he heard himself. Marlene Wilson, the receptionist, was on the other end of the line.

"I hope I'm not bothering you, Dr. Stapleton," Marlene said. She had a slight Southern accent.

"Not at all," Jack said. "What's up?"

"There are several gentlemen down here to see you," Marlene said. "Are you expecting anyone?"

"Not that I know of," Jack said. "What are their names?"

"Just a moment," Marlene said.

"Hey, I gotta go," Lou said. He stood up. "I better get out of here before I run into Laurie."

"Keep in touch," Jack said with a wave. "We're going to have to make a decision about this sensitive intelligence you've gathered."

Lou nodded and disappeared from view.

Marlene came back on the line. "It's Mr. Warren Wilson and a Mr. Flash Thomas. What would you like me to say to them?"

"My word," Jack said. "Tell them to come on up!"

Jack slowly hung up the phone. He couldn't believe that Warren had come to visit him. Jack had suggested it a few times when he thought Warren would find it interesting to see firsthand what Jack did for a living. It was part of Jack's attempt to get Warren to go back to school. But Warren had said that there was only one way he'd visit a morgue and that was dead!

Jack got the straight-back chair from next to Chet's desk and pulled it over next to the other one. Then he stepped out into the hall and walked down toward the elevators. He'd timed it just about right, because when he got there the doors opened and out stepped his two basketball buddies.

"This place sucks," Warren said, making an expression of disgust. Then he smiled. "How's it going, man?" He held up his hand.

Jack smacked it as if they were greeting each other on the basketball court. He did the same with Flash, who was clearly more intimidated at the surroundings than Warren was.

"It's going like most days," Jack said. "Except for your visit. I'm shocked to see you guys, but come on into my office."

Jack led the way down the hall.

"This place smells weird," Flash said.

"It reminds me of a hospital," Warren said.

"No hospital I'd ever want to be in," Flash said with a nervous laugh.

"You told me you did autopsies in a place called the pit," Warren said. "This whole place looks like a pit."

"It could use a bit of a renovation," Jack admitted. He gestured inside his office.

The three sat down.

Jack smiled. "Did you fellows come all the way down here just to make sure I was going to play tonight?"

"You should have played last night," Warren said. "You had your chance to run with us. We never lost."

"Maybe I'll luck out tonight," Jack said.

Warren looked at Flash. "You want to ask him or you want me to?"

"You do it," Flash said as he fidgeted in his seat. He was clearly agitated.

Warren turned to Jack. "Flash got some bad news this morning. His sister died."

"I'm sorry to hear that," Jack said. He glanced at Flash, but Flash avoided his eyes.

"She wasn't all that old," Warren said. "About your age. It was sudden-like. And Flash here thinks there had to be some negative stuff going on. You see, she and her old man didn't get on too well, you hear what I'm saying?"

"Am I to assume there was a little domestic violence involved in this relationship?" Jack asked.

"If that's what you call his smacking her around now and then," Warren said.

"That's the usual euphemism," Jack said.

"A lot of domestic violence," Flash interjected heatedly.

"Cool it," Warren said to Flash. He gave Flash's shoulder a reassuring pat. Turning back to Jack he added, "I had to talk Flash out of going out there and beating the pulp out of his sister's hubby."

"The son of a bitch killed her," Flash growled.

"Come on, man!" Warren pleaded. "You don't know that for sure."

"I know it," Flash said.

Warren turned to Jack. "You see what I'm up against. If Flash goes out there, there's going to be trouble. Somebody's going to be dead, and I don't think it's going to be Flash."

"What can I do to help?" Jack asked.

"See if you can find out what killed her," Warren said. "If

she died of something natural-like, then Flash here's going to have to take his irritation out on something else, like on you and me on the court." Warren gave Flash a friendly cuff on the top of the head. Flash parried the blow irritably.

"Where is her body at the moment?" Jack asked.

"At the morgue in Brooklyn," Warren said. "At least that's what Flash was told by the Coney Island Hospital where she'd been treated."

"Well, then it's going to be easy," Jack said. "I'll talk to whoever does her autopsy, and we'll have the answer."

"There ain't going to be no autopsy," Flash blurted. "That's part of what's bothering me. They took her to the morgue to have an autopsy, but now she's not going to. Something's wrong here, you know what I'm saying?"

"Not necessarily," Jack said. "Not every corpse brought into the medical examiner's office is autopsied. In fact, that she wasn't autopsied means that the chances of foul play are small. Since she died at a hospital, it means that the attending doctor certified the cause of death, and in that case an autopsy is not mandatory."

"Flash is thinking conspiracy here," Warren said.

"I can assure you there's no conspiracy," Jack said. "Incompetence, maybe, but conspiracy, no."

"But . . ." Flash began.

"Hold on!" Jack interrupted. "I'll still look into it for you. What was her name?"

"Connie Davydov," Flash said.

Jack wrote the name down and reached for the phone. He called the Brooklyn office, which administratively was part of the Office of the Chief Medical Examiner of New York. Technically Bingham was chief, but the Brooklyn office had its own acting head. His name was Jim Bennett.

"Who's the scheduling ME this week?" Jack asked the operator who answered after Jack had identified himself.

"Dr. Randolph Sanders," the operator said. "Would you like me to page him?"

"If you wouldn't mind," Jack said. He wasn't pleased. He was reasonably acquainted with Randolph, whom he put in the same category with perfunctories like George Fontworth. Jack tapped his pencil while he waited. He wished he'd be dealing with any one of the four other Brooklyn MEs.

When Randolph came on the line Jack wasted no time getting to the point. He asked why an autopsy wasn't done on Connie Davydov.

"I'll have to get the folder," Randolph said. "Why do you ask?"

"I've gotten a request to look into the case," Jack said. He left it vague who had asked him. If Randolph wanted to think it was Bingham or Calvin, that was fine with Jack.

"Hold on," Randolph said.

Jack turned to Flash with his palm over the mouthpiece of the phone. "Davydov doesn't sound like any African-American name I've ever heard."

"It's not," Flash said. "Connie's husband is a white boy."

Jack nodded, sensing there was more reason for possible hostility between Flash and Connie's spouse than the purported history of domestic violence. "Did he get along with the rest of your family?"

"Ha!" Flash voiced contemptuously. "The family wouldn't talk to either one of them. They didn't want her to marry him, no way."

"Okay, I have the folder," Randolph said into the phone, capturing Jack's attention. "And I've got the PA's report in front of me."

"What's the scoop?" Jack asked.

"The attending doctor, Michael Cooper, gave a diagnosis of status asthmaticus leading to death," Randolph said. "There was a long history of asthma with hospitalizations and multiple ER visits. She was also grossly obese, which I'm sure didn't help her breathing when she got into trouble. It also says she had lots of allergies."

"I see," Jack said. "Tell me, did you look at the body?"

"Of course I looked at the body!" Randolph was clearly offended by the query.

"In your professional opinion, were there any signs of domestic violence?" Jack asked.

"If there'd been signs of domestic violence I would have done the goddamned autopsy," Randolph said defensively.

"Any signs of suffocation?" Jack asked. "Like petechial hemorrhages in the sclera. Anything like that?"

"You're insulting me with such questions," Randolph shot back.

"How about toxicology?" Jack asked. "Were any samples taken?"

"An autopsy wasn't done!" Randolph snapped. "We don't do toxicology on cases we don't post. Neither do you."

Randolph disconnected without another word. Jack raised his eyebrows as he hung up the receiver. "Kinda sensitive guy although in his defense my lack of diplomatic skills is legendary. Anyhow, did you hear the other end of that conversation?"

Both Warren and Flash nodded.

"He said there was no sign of domestic violence," Jack said. "Now he's not the world's greatest medical examiner in my opinion, but recognizing domestic violence isn't that hard even though it can be subtle."

"Why did you ask about toxicology?" Warren questioned.

"Poisons, things like that are picked up in toxicology," Jack said. "That kind of stuff goes on."

Warren looked at Flash.

"Do you want me to continue looking into this?" Jack asked.

Flash nodded. "I'm sure he killed her."

"After what you just heard, why do you still feel that way?"

"Because she didn't have no strong history of asthma and allergies."

"Are you sure?" Jack asked with astonishment.

"Yeah, I'm sure," Flash said. "I'm her brother, ain't I? Hey, she had a little when she was young. But I'm talking about when she was ten. Over the last couple of years I've been talking to her at least once a week. She didn't have no allergies and no asthma."

"My word," Jack said. "That puts a new spin on all this."

"What else can you do?" Warren asked.

"I can call the attending doctor, for one thing," Jack said. "The doctor that took care of her at the Coney Island Hospital."

Since Jack had the Yellow Pages open to the hospital section, it was easy for him to get the number. He called and asked for Dr. Michael Cooper to be paged. When he got the man on the line, he went through his usual ME routine of explaining who he was and why he was calling. In contrast to Randolph, Michael was cooperative and not at all defensive.

"I do remember Connie Davydov," Michael said. "Tough case! She came in essentially moribund. The EMTs described her as very cyanotic when they arrived at her home and barely breathing if at all. She'd collapsed in the bathroom where her husband found her. They gave her oxygen immediately and ventilated her. When she got here to the ER she was acidotic with a CO_2 off the chart and low arterial oxygen saturation. The numbers improved with adequate ventilation but her clinical state didn't. She had no peripheral reflexes, dilated and fixed pupils, and an essentially flat EEG. There wasn't much we could do."

"How did her chest sound?" Jack asked.

"By the time she got here, it sounded clear," Michael said. "But that didn't surprise us with the low oxygen saturation and the degree of acidosis she had. All her muscles, including her smooth muscles, were essentially paralyzed. Considering her size, she was like a beached whale."

"Any suggestion of a heart attack?"

"Nope," Michael said. "The EKG was essentially normal, although the rate was very slow, and there were some changes consistent with her low arterial oxygen."

"What about stroke?"

"We ruled that out with a CAT scan that was normal," Michael said. "We also did an LP, and the fluid was clear."

"Any fever, skin lesions, or other signs of infection?" Jack asked.

"Nothing," Michael said. "In fact, her temperature was subnormal."

"And you did get a strong history of asthma and allergies," Jack said. "How did you get it? Was it through hospital records?"

"No, from the husband," Michael said. "He was pretty together despite his ordeal and was able to give us a good history."

Jack thanked the man and hung up. He turned to Warren and Flash. "This is getting more interesting. It doesn't sound as if the history was corroborated. I think maybe I ought to take a look at Connie."

"Can you do that?" Warren asked.

"Why not?" Jack said.

Jack went back to the phone to try to get Randolph on the line directly, but no one picked up. Next he tried paging him. When the operator came back to ask who was calling, Jack gave his name and waited again. When the operator returned the second time, she told him that the doctor was busy. Jack left a message that he was on his way over.

"Seems that Dr. Sanders is indulging in a bit of passive-aggressive behavior," Jack said as he stood up. He picked up his cellular phone and his small camera and pocketed both. "What do you guys want to do? You're welcome to come along."

"You want to go?" Warren asked Flash. "I got the time."

Flash nodded. "I want to see this to the end."

"How'd you get here to the ME's office?" Jack asked.

Warren held up an ignition key. "I got my wheels parked right outside on Thirtieth Street."

"Perfect," Jack said. "Let's go!"

They took the elevator down to the basement and were about to exit through the loading dock area when Jack paused.

"I've just been thinking," he said. "Who knows what my reception's going to be over in Brooklyn. It might be best to bring my own supplies."

"What kind of supplies you talking about?" Warren asked.

"It'll take too long to explain," Jack said. "You guys wait here or out by the car. I'll be right back."

Jack detoured into the depths of the morgue, passing the bank of refrigerated compartments where the bodies were stored prior to being autopsied. Conveniently, he ran into Vinnie coming out of the pit. Jack asked the mortuary tech to get him a bunch of sample containers for various body fluids, a mask, rubber gloves, a clutch of syringes, a couple of scalpels, and a nasogastric tube.

"What the hell are you going to do?" Vinnie asked. He eyed Jack suspiciously.

"Probably going to get myself in hot water," Jack said.

"Are you going out of house?"

"I'm afraid so."

"You want me to come along?" Vinnie asked.

"Thank you, but no," Jack said. "But I appreciate the offer."

It didn't take Vinnie long to get the material, and by the time he reappeared Jack had gotten a small satchel he used to carry an extra set of underclothes back and forth between work and his apartment. Especially during the summer, he sweated profusely on his morning bicycle commute and had to shower and change.

Jack threw all the supplies into the satchel, thanked Vinnie, and headed back to the loading dock. He found Warren and Flash on the sidewalk. They were again arguing about whether Flash should go out to confront his brother-in-law.

As they piled into the car the two lifelong friends behaved as if they were angry with each other. Jack got into the spacious back seat, while Warren and Flash climbed into the front. The car was a five-year-old Cadillac.

"Can't we make this a pleasant trip?" Jack asked, hoping to ease the tense atmosphere.

"He's crazy!" Warren complained throwing his hands in the air. "He's going to get himself in big trouble or killed, you know what I'm saying?"

"Yeah, but it was my sister who was murdered," Flash shot back. "If it were yours, you'd feel the same way I do."

"But you don't know she was murdered," Warren said. "That's the whole point. That's why we're here talking to the doc."

"Listen, Flash," Jack said. "I'm reasonably confident I'll be able to tell if there was foul play, but you might have to be patient. I might not be able to say definitively for a couple of days."

"How come a couple of days?" Flash asked. He swung

around in his seat to glare at Jack. "I thought you could tell if you just looked at her."

"That might be," Jack said. "But I kinda doubt it, since Randolph didn't see anything. He's not that bad an ME. What I'm concerned about is some kind of poison."

"Like what?" Warren asked. He looked at Jack in his rear-view mirror.

"Cyanide, for instance," Jack said. "Of course that doesn't fit, since the oxygen level in her blood was low. Still, it's something to think about."

"What else?" Warren asked.

"Carbon monoxide has to be considered," Jack said. "But the trouble with that is that she was described as being cyanotic, or blue, by the EMTs."

"Is that all?" Warren asked. "No other poisons?"

"What is this, a test?" Jack asked.

"No, I'm just interested," Warren said.

"Well, now you're pushing me," Jack said. "But I suppose I'll be thinking about barbiturates, benzodiazepines, like Valium, ethylene glycol, and stuff like that. What all these agents have in common is they cause respiratory depression, which apparently Connie had."

"How could her husband have killed her with carbon monoxide?" Flash asked.

"Did they have a car?"

"Yeah," Flash said. "They even had a garage."

"Well, he could have gotten her drunk or drugged enough to put her in the car while it was running in the garage," Jack said. "Or better still, with the exhaust piped directly into it. Then when she was nearly dead, he could have carried her into the bathroom and called nine-one-one."

"He couldn't have carried her anyplace," Flash said. "She was about three hundred fifty pounds."

"I'm just giving you a hypothetical situation," Jack said. "Jeez, you guys! Come on, let's go!"

"You gotta tell me where to," Warren said.

"Kings County Hospital," Jack said. "It's southeast of Prospect Park over in Brooklyn."

"Should I take the FDR Drive?" Warren asked.

"Yes," Jack said. "And go over the Brooklyn Bridge. Then get on Flatbush Ave."

Warren started his car and they set off.

"Flash," Jack called from the back seat as they were heading along the East River. "What are the chances that your sister could have committed suicide?"

"No way!" Flash said without hesitation. "She wasn't the type."

"Was she ever depressed?"

"Not in the usual sense," Flash said. "But maybe a little. It could have been why she ate so much. She knew she'd married a mental case."

"How so?" Jack asked.

"The dude did nothing," Flash said angrily. "He'd come home from work and drink in front of the television. That was it, at least until a few months ago, when he started spending all his time in the basement."

"Doing what?" Jack asked.

"Tinkering around, I guess," Flash said. "Connie didn't tell me what he did. I don't think she knew."

"Did she drink a lot herself?"

"Nope," Flash said. "Provided you're talking about booze. Milkshakes are another story."

"What about drugs?" Jack asked.

"She wasn't into drugs," Flash said. "Never was."

"Where in Brooklyn did she live?" Jack asked.

"Fifteen Oceanview Lane," Flash said.

"Where's that?"

"Brighton Beach," Flash said. "She lived in a kinda cute area with a bunch of small wooden cottages. In the summer she could walk to the beach and take a swim. It was pretty nice."

"Hmmm," Jack commented. He wondered what the place looked like. He couldn't imagine cottages within the New York City limits.

Parking around Kings County Hospital was a nightmare come true, but it didn't rattle Warren. In the trunk he had an old beat-up ash can with the bottom cut out. All he did was find a spot in front of a fire hydrant, park, and then cover the hydrant with the modified garbage can. Jack marveled at the adaptations that city living required.

Outside of the medical examiner's office both Warren and Flash paused.

"Maybe we should wait out here," Warren said. He looked at Flash. Flash nodded.

"Fine by me," Jack said. "I'll try to make it fast."

Jack entered the building. He flashed his badge to the receptionist, who'd never seen him before. Duly impressed, she buzzed him in.

Not wanting to waste time, Jack went directly to the mortuary office next to the autopsy room and walked through the open door. A mortuary tech was at the desk.

"Hi, I'm Dr. Jack Stapleton from the Manhattan office," Jack said with alacrity. He showed his badge as he'd done with the receptionist.

"Hello. I'm Doug Smithers. What can I do for you?" The man was plainly surprised. Exchange visits were not the norm.

"A couple of things," Jack said. "First, as a courtesy, would you page Dr. Randolph Sanders for me? Ask him if he wouldn't mind coming down here."

"Okay," Doug said with a tinge of uncertainty. It wasn't part of a mortuary tech's job description to dictate to the MEs. He picked up the phone. When he got the doctor on the line, he relayed Jack's request verbatim.

"Perfect!" Jack said. "Now I'd like you to find a body for me and wheel it someplace where I can take a look at it."

"Would you like it on a table in the autopsy room?"

"No," Jack said. "I'm not going to be suiting up. I merely want to take a peek at the corpse and take a few body fluid samples. So just find someplace with adequate lighting."

Doug Smithers got to his feet. "What's the accession number?"

"That I don't know," Jack said. "The name is Connie Davydov. She came in, I believe, early this morning."

"That body's not here," Doug said.

"You're joking."

"No, I'm not. It went out not that long ago: maybe a half hour."

"Damn!" Jack yelled with a shake of his head for emphasis. He tossed his satchel onto the desk with a clatter. His face reddened.

"I'm sorry," Doug said. He hunkered down as if he expected Jack to take a swing at him.

"It's not your fault," Jack snapped. He cracked his knuckles in frustration. "Where did the body go?"

Doug warily bent over the ledger book on the desk. He used his index finger to scan down the column. "It went to Strickland's Funeral Home."

"Where the hell is that?"

"I believe it's on Caton Avenue over near Greenwood Cemetery."

"Jesus H. Christ!" Jack muttered. He began to pace while he tried to think what to do next.

"Dr. Stapleton, I presume," a voice said with a distinctly condescending air. "Aren't you wandering a little far afield?"

Jack glanced up at the doorway. Framed between the jambs was Dr. Randolph Sanders. He was a bit older than Jack with mostly gray hair brushed back from his narrow face. He wore thick-rimmed black glasses that gave him an owlish appearance. In the hierarchy of the medical examiner's office, he was far above Jack, with almost twenty years of experience.

"I thought I'd dash over here and give you some very needed help," Jack shot back.

"Oh, please!" Randolph remarked contemptuously.

"Why in hell's name did you send the Davydov body out when you knew I was coming over here?"

"I got a mysterious message that you might pay us a visit, but there was no request to keep the body here."

"I suppose I shouldn't be surprised, since an IQ of fifty or more would have been necessary to have presumed as much."

"I don't have to listen to your juvenile slander," Randolph said. "Have a nice trip back to Manhattan." He spun on his heels and disappeared from view.

Jack stepped out into the hall. He called out to the retreating Randolph. "Well, let me tell you something. Connie Davydov did not have either asthma or allergies. She was an entirely healthy woman who suddenly experienced respiratory failure without having a heart attack or a stroke. If that's not the kind of case that deserves an autopsy, I don't know what is!"

Randolph stopped at the elevators and faced around.

"How do you know she didn't have asthma and allergies?" he demanded.

"From her brother," Jack said.

"Well, let me tell you something," Randolph said disdainfully. "My source of the woman's history happens to be this office's most experienced forensic investigator. You can believe whomever you wish. I'll rely on a professional."

Randolph turned and calmly pressed the elevator button. He glanced back briefly to give Jack a condescending smile.

Jack was about to counter angrily Randolph's last statement when it dawned on him how ludicrous it was for him to be arguing with such a blockhead. Besides, a confrontation with this ME would do nothing to advance his looking into Connie Davydov's case. Shaking his head, Jack went back into the mortuary office and grabbed his satchel from the desk. Doug looked at him curiously but didn't say anything.

Still fuming, Jack stalked out of the Brooklyn ME's office and strode down the sidewalk toward Warren's car. Warren and Flash were leaning up against the Caddy's fenders. They looked at Jack expectantly as he approached, but Jack didn't say a word. He just climbed into the back seat.

Warren and Flash glanced at each other and shrugged before climbing into the car themselves. Each twisted in his seat and regarded Jack, who had his mouth and lips clamped shut.

"You look pissed," Warren commented.

"I am," Jack admitted. He looked off for a moment, obviously thinking.

"What happened?" Flash asked.

"They sent the body to a local funeral home," Jack said.

"How come?" Warren asked. "They knew you were coming."

"It has something to do with how competitive doctors are with each other," Jack said. "It's hard to explain and you probably wouldn't believe it."

"I'll take your word," Warren said. "So what are we going to do?"

"I don't know," Jack said. "I'm thinking."

"I know what I'm going to do," Flash said. "I'm going to Brighton Beach."

"Shut up, man," Warren said. "This is just a wrinkle here."

"Some wrinkle," Flash said. "If she'd been white, none of this would have happened."

"Flash, that's not the problem," Jack said. "There's a lot of racism around this city, that I'll grant you, but it's not the problem here, believe me."

"Why can't you just have the funeral home send the body back?" Warren suggested.

"I wish it were that easy," Jack said. "The problem is it's a Brooklyn case, and I'm from the Manhattan office, which means there's a lot of politics involved. I'd have to get the super chief to do it, which would get the Brooklyn chief defensive, since he'd assume the affair was a reflection of how he's running the office. It would become a bureaucratic turf war of sorts. Plus it would take eons. By the time all the paperwork was done, the phone calls made, and the battles waged, the funeral home might have embalmed the body, or worse yet, cremated it."

"Shit," Warren said.

"That settles it," Flash said. "I'm going to Brighton Beach."

"No, let's all go to the funeral home," Jack said. "It might create some waves, but I don't see we have much choice to keep Flash from self-destructing. Maybe we'll be lucky. It's on Caton Avenue near the Greenwood Cemetery. You got a map?"

Warren nodded. He had Flash dig it out of the glove box. While the two of them bent over it, Jack tried to anticipate what they'd be up against in the funeral home. He imagined the funeral director would not be particularly cooperative.

"When we go into the funeral home we're going to have to kinda barge in and overwhelm them," Jack said.

Warren looked up. "What do you mean?"

"We've got to try to do what we have to do before they have much of a chance to think about it."

"But you're a medical examiner," Warren said. "You're a city official."

"Yeah, but this is irregular, to say the least," Jack said. "The funeral director is not going to like it. You see, the way the system works is that the body is technically released to the next of kin, in this case the husband, even though the funeral home picks the body up. Nothing is supposed to happen to the body unless the husband says so. Obviously we don't want them calling the husband, because if he's guilty of what Flash suspects, he'd scream bloody murder."

"Why not just say you're from the Brooklyn office and there was a couple things you forgot to do."

"The funeral director would be sure to call the Brooklyn office," Jack said. "They'd wonder why they hadn't gotten a call to bring the body back. Remember, they work with them all the time and know the MEs. For me to suddenly show up will be very irregular. Trust me!"

"So what do you propose?" Warren asked.

"I'm thinking," Jack said. "Did you find it on the map?"

"I think so," Flash said.

"Let's go before I chicken out," Jack said.

After driving a few blocks Jack got an idea. Taking out his cell phone, he placed a call to Bingham's office. As expected, Cheryl Sanford answered with her honeyed voice. Jack identified himself and asked if the chief was within earshot.

"Hardly," Cheryl said. "He's over at the Commissioner of Health's office for an impromptu meeting."

"That's even better," Jack said. "Listen, I have a problem, and I need your help."

"Is this going to get me into trouble?" Cheryl said warily. She knew Jack too well, given the number of times that he'd been on the carpet in Bingham's office.

"It's possible," Jack admitted. "If it does, I'll take full responsibility. But it's for a good cause."

Jack went on to explain about Flash's loss, the dilemma about Connie's body, and the discrepancy about the medical history suggesting foul play. Ultimately, Cheryl's generous nature and sense of fairness won out. She agreed to at least hear what Jack had in mind.

Jack cleared his throat: "If you get a call from Strickland's Funeral Home within the next half hour or so for the chief, tell them that he's with the commissioner, which is true. But then add that Dr. Jack Stapleton has been authorized to take some body fluid samples from Connie Davydov."

"Is that all?" Cheryl asked.

"That's it," Jack said. "If you want to get fancy, you can say that you'd meant to call earlier, but it had slipped your mind with the chief's sudden need to see the commissioner."

"You are devious," Cheryl commented. "But it is a good cause, especially if a homicide is involved. Anyway, I'll do it."

"I like to think of myself as resourceful, not devious," Jack joked. He thanked Cheryl on both his behalf and Flash's, then said goodbye and hung up.

"Sounds like you got it arranged," Warren said.

"We'll see," Jack said. He wasn't all that confident. In his experience, funeral directors tended to be both touchy and sticklers for detail. There were a lot of potential pitfalls. If there was a big staff, Jack could even envision them physically restraining him.

Strickland's Funeral Home was a two-story stucco building that in a previous life had been a grand home of some wealthy Brooklynite. It was painted white in an apparent attempt to make it look cheerful. Even so, it remained a ponderously bulky structure of indeterminate style. All its windows were blocked by heavy drapes. From its parking lot a wedge of Greenwood Cemetery could be seen bristling with headstones.

Warren put on his emergency brake and turned off the ignition.

"Kinda ominous-looking, isn't it?" Jack commented.

"What do they do in there?" Warren questioned. "I've always wondered."

"Don't ask! You don't want to know," Jack said. "Let's get this over with before I lose my nerve."

"We'll wait here," Warren said. He glanced at Flash. Flash nodded in agreement.

"Oh, no! Not this time," Jack said. "When I said 'we' earlier, I meant it. This is going to be like a mini-invasion, and

I need both you guys' powerful presence. Besides, Flash, you're kin, which lends us some legitimacy."

"Are you serious, man?" Warren said.

"Absolutely," Jack said. "Come on! This isn't up for discussion."

Jack resolutely headed for the front door carrying his satchel. He could hear Warren's and Flash's footsteps behind him. He knew they were coming reluctantly. He didn't blame them. He knew that they were emotionally unprepared for what they were going to see.

The interior of the funeral home was fairly standard. There was a lot of dark wood, velvet drapes, soft lighting, and low-volume hymns playing in the background, giving an overall impression of serenity. In the entrance hall a visitors' book was open on a console table. Next to it stood an austere-looking woman in a black dress. In the center of the room to the right was an open casket on a waist-high bier with a few rows of folding chairs set before it. The lid's interior was upholstered in white satin. Jack could just make out the profile of the casket's occupant.

"May I help you?" the woman asked in a voice barely above a whisper.

"Yes," Jack said. "Where's the director?"

"He's in the office," the woman said. "Should I get him?"

"Please," Jack said. "And quickly if you wouldn't mind. This is an emergency."

Jack looked over his shoulder at Warren and Flash who were close behind him.

"Shit, man!" Warren whispered. "Are you sure you need us?"

"Without a doubt," Jack whispered back. "Just stay cool."

It took only a few minutes for the worried director to emerge from a side door accompanied by a pair of brawny men in suits who could have moonlighted as bouncers. The funeral director could have been from central casting, with his immaculate black suit, crisp white shirt, and pomaded, painstakingly combed hair. The only thing out of place was his complexion. He was tanned as if he'd just come back from a Florida vacation.

"My name is Gordon Strickland," he said in a hushed tone. "I understand there is an emergency. How can we be of assistance?"

"My name is Dr. Jack Stapleton," Jack said with all the authority he could muster. He held up his medical examiner badge in front of Gordon's nose. "I'm a representative from the Office of the Chief Medical Examiner in Manhattan, Dr. Harold Bingham."

Gordon tilted his head so he could see Jack around the medical examiner's badge. "I've heard the name. How does this involve us here in Brooklyn?"

"I've been sent to view the body of Connie Davydov," Jack said. "As well as to obtain some needed body fluid samples. I assume you got a call to that effect."

"No, we didn't get a call," Gordon said. His upper lip began to twitch.

"Then I apologize for the surprise," Jack said. "But we do have to see the body." He took a step forward in the direction of a pair of double doors heading into the center of the building.

"Just a minute!" Gordon said, holding up his hand. "Who are these other gentlemen?"

"This is Warren Wilson," Jack said while nodding toward Warren. "He is my assistant. This other gentleman is Frank Thomas, the brother of the deceased." Jack couldn't help wonder how all this was going to play, since both his friends were clothed in a modified hip-hop style. Warren certainly didn't look professional by any stretch of the imagination.

"I don't understand," Gordon said. "The body was released to a Mr. Davydov. He's not contacted us about this situation either."

"We're investigating a potential homicide," Jack said. "New information has become available."

"Homicide?" Gordon repeated. The frequency of the twitch increased.

"Indeed," Jack said. He started forward again, forcing Gordon to back up. "Now if you'll just direct us to your cooler or wherever you keep your newly arrived bodies, we'll do our thing and be on our way."

"The body is in the embalming room," Gordon said. "We've been awaiting Mr. Davydov's instructions. He was supposed to call once it got here."

"Then we'll view the body in the embalming room," Jack said. "It's all the same to us."

Nonplussed, Gordon turned around and pushed through the double doors. Jack, Warren, and Flash followed. Gordon's silent minions brought up the rear.

"This is highly irregular," Gordon voiced to no one in particular as they walked down the hall. "We haven't heard anything from the Brooklyn ME's office either. Maybe I should give them a call."

"It would save time to call Dr. Harold Bingham directly," Jack said. "Of course, you know the Brooklyn ME's office is under the control of the Manhattan office."

"I didn't know that," Gordon said.

Jack pulled out his cellular phone, punched the number to speed-dial the chief, and handed the phone to Gordon. Gordon took the phone and pressed it to his ear. Jack could hear Cheryl Sanford answer with her usual preamble: "Dr. Harold Bingham's office, Chief Medical Examiner. How may I help you?"

The entire group slowed to a halt outside a second set of double doors as Gordon spoke to Cheryl. Jack could hear only bits of Cheryl's side of the conversation. Gordon was nodding and saying "I see," "yes," and "I understand" several times. Finally he said, "Thank you, Mrs. Sanford. I understand perfectly and there is no need for you to apologize. I'll do what I can to help Dr. Stapleton."

Gordon disconnected and handed the phone back to Jack. As Jack took the phone he noticed that Gordon's lip was twitching almost continuously. The man obviously wasn't entirely comfortable with the situation, but at least he was momentarily mollified.

"In here," Gordon said, pointing to the double doors.

The entire group entered the embalming room, which was redolent with the cloying smell of a sickly-sweet deodorant. The space was larger than Jack expected, about the size of the autopsy room where he worked most days. But in contrast to the autopsy room's eight tables, here there were only four, two of which were occupied. The farthest table held a male who was in the process of being embalmed. The nearest held an obese woman.

"Mrs. Davydov is right here," Gordon said, pointing to the nearest corpse.

"Right!" Jack said. He quickly put his satchel down on a nearby wheeled table and pulled it close. After snapping open the bag he looked up at his two friends. They were frozen in place near the door. Warren was transfixed by the embalming process going on in the end of the room; Flash was staring at his sister. Both their faces had gone slack. Jack could only imagine what they must be feeling.

Jack clapped his hands loudly to keep the situation from deteriorating. The sound was like a gunshot in the tiled room. Everyone was jolted. Even the two people doing the embalming looked up from their gruesome task. "Okay!" Jack said eagerly, as if he relished what he was about to do. "Let's get this show on the road so these gentlemen can get on with their business. Frank Thomas, can you identify this woman?"

Flash nodded his head. "It's my sister. Connie Thomas Davydov."

"Are you absolutely certain?" Jack asked while he looked down at the deceased's face for the first time. He was immediately surprised by the obvious evidence of trauma. The left eye was purplish and swollen almost shut. The skin over the cheekbone was bruised.

"Dead sure," said Flash. He took a step closer and pointed to the swollen eye. "And the bastard popped her just like he'd done in the past."

"Let's not jump to conclusions," Jack said quickly. "Remember! The EMTs found her in the bathroom, where she'd collapsed. A bathroom is a dangerous place to collapse between the sink, tub, and toilet, not to mention the towel racks and the faucets."

"About a month ago when I had lunch with her, her eye looked just like that," Flash said, ignoring Jack. "She told me he'd punched her. The only reason I didn't go flying out there to beat the shit out of him then was because she made me promise not to do it."

"Okay, calm down!" Jack said. Now that he was about to get his samples, he didn't want Flash to gum up the works. To that end he suggested to Flash that it might be best for him to wait outside. Flash offered no argument; he spun around, banged open both double doors, and left. With a nod from the director, the two funeral home heavies quickly followed.

"This is very difficult for him," Jack explained. "So, it's best we do what we have to do, and get him out of here."

Gordon stepped up to the table while Jack snapped on his latex gloves. "I hope you're not planning on marring the body in any visible way," Gordon warned. "We have no idea if Mr. Davydov is planning on an open casket or not."

"All we're going to do is take some body fluids," Jack said. He motioned for Warren to come closer and handed him several sample bottles. He had to make it look as if Warren really was his assistant to justify his intimidating presence. Jack wanted him there because Jack was planning on doing what Gordon had just warned him not to do, namely taking a sample of the bruised facial skin. Of course, he also would have liked samples of brain, liver, kidneys, lung, and fat, if he could have thought of some way to get away with it.

The first thing Jack did was take out his camera. Before Gordon could complain, he took a series of photographs of the body with particular attention to the facial trauma. Jack was careful to position the head for maximum exposure. In the process, he also looked for any subtle signs of strangulation or smothering. There weren't any.

After putting the camera away he completed his rapid but thorough external exam. While he worked, he kept up a verbal description for Warren's benefit. He mentioned that there were no signs of injections other than iatrogenic ones, no trauma other than to the eye and cheek, and no signs of infectious disease.

Next, Jack got out his collection of syringes and began taking body fluid samples. He got blood from the heart, urine from the bladder, vitreous from the eyeballs, and cerebrospinal fluid from the central nervous system. Then he got out the nasogastric tube and got some stomach contents. He worked quickly for fear of being interrupted before he was finished.

Warren tried to keep his eyes closed through it all.

The funeral director had moved back against the wall. He stood vigilantly with his arms folded across his chest. It was obvious by his expression and the fact that his lip continued to twitch that he was not enthralled by Jack's efforts, but he stayed silent. At least until Jack's scalpel flashed in the bright fluorescent light.

"Wait!" Gordon cried when he caught a fleeting view of the knife. Pushing off the wall he quickly came forward. "What are you going to do now?"

"It's done," Jack said. He straightened up and plopped a wedge of facial tissue and eyelid into a sample bottle. He'd taken the sample with blinding speed.

"But you promised," Gordon sputtered. With dismay he looked down at the gap in the skin of Connie's face.

"True," Jack said. "But I realized we're obligated to make sure this swollen eye isn't the result of an infectious process. And with my usual surgical precision I took only the tiniest sample. I've full confidence that you can all but make it disappear with your cosmetic wizardry."

"This is outrageous!" Gordon complained. He bent over to study the defect and was dismayed. In his estimation, it was hardly tiny. Connie's face looked horribly and irrevocably altered.

As rapidly as possible Jack threw all the sample containers, his used supplies, and even his inside-out rubber gloves into the satchel and snapped it closed. At this point he felt like a bank robber who'd just been given the cash and had to make his getaway. Grabbing Warren by the sleeve of his hooded sweatshirt, he pulled him toward the door.

"Let's make this fast but orderly," Jack whispered.

They went through the first set of double doors still hearing Gordon swearing in the background. After clearing the second set of doors, they began looking for Flash. He was nowhere to be seen. Exiting the building, they found him pacing on the front walk.

"Let's go!" Jack ordered.

The three men walked quickly to the car. Jack wasn't worried they'd be pursued, yet he wanted to get away as soon as possible. He knew he'd pushed Gordon over the edge with the skin sample maneuver. To a funeral director, disfiguring the face was the worst possible sin.

They piled into the car. Warren got it going, and they headed back toward Prospect Park, driving in silence. It was Flash who finally spoke: "Well, aren't you guys going to say anything? What did you find?"

"I found out that I'm never going back into a funeral home until I'm carried in," Warren said. "What in God's name were they doing to that guy on the other table, vacuuming out his insides? I almost lost it, I gotta tell you. Man, this has been the worst experience of my life."

"In other words," Flash said angrily, "you didn't learn crap about what happened to Connie."

"We got the samples we needed," Jack said. "Now you're going to have to be patient. Like I said earlier, we won't know anything definitive until these samples get processed."

"I could see that he smacked her in the face," Flash said. "That's enough for me."

Warren glanced up at Jack in the rearview mirror. "See what I'm up against with this guy? It's like talking to a wall, you know what I'm saying?"

"Listen, Flash," Jack said heatedly. "I've put myself out on a limb here for you. Do you understand?"

"I suppose," Flash admitted reluctantly.

"I could be in deep trouble if Strickland or the Brooklyn office makes a stink about this, especially if the samples turn out to be negative. Now the least I can expect from you in return is to promise you won't go out there to your brother-in-law's house."

"What about that black eye?" Flash demanded.

"For the last time, we don't know how she got it," Jack said. "I took a skin sample and we'll see what it shows. It might have been from a punch, but then again, it might not have been. I'm telling you, I've seen bathroom falls much worse. In fact, I've seen it where it was the fall itself that killed the victim, not whatever went on before."

"Promise the man," Warren said. "Or I'm going to be roy-ally pissed myself. I mean, there's a lot of things I'd rather be doing today than standing in that funeral home getting grossed out, you know what I'm saying?"

"All right, I promise," Flash said. "Are you guys happy now?"

"Relieved is a better word," Jack said. He looked out the window at the rush-hour traffic and wondered what kind of price he would have to pay for his shenanigans.

TWELVE

The snow stretched in an immaculately white blanket all the way down Fatherland Hill. Yuri and his brother, Yegor, had named the slope in celebration of its being the finest sledding hill in all of the Soviet Union. After crowding onto a sled that they had fashioned themselves out of discarded wood and metal, they pushed off down the steep slope. Yegor was in the front and Yuri in the back.

For Yuri, it was like being launched into a fairyland. The crystalline snow swirled about them as they hurtled down toward the farmhouses along Lake Niznije. It was like flying, and Yuri yelled with delight.

As they streaked toward the main road, they saw a sleigh coming from town pulled by two horses as white as the snow. As their paths drew closer, Yuri could hear the sleigh bells jangle in time with the horses' canter. It got louder and louder until Yuri was yanked from his favorite dream. The jangling wasn't sleigh bells, it was the phone.

Sitting up suddenly, Yuri nearly fainted. He steadied himself and leaned over so his head was between his knees. When he felt normal, he slowly sat up. The dizziness had disappeared, but the phone was still insistently ringing.

Yuri got up on slightly unsteady legs and headed for the kitchen. He'd fallen asleep on the sofa, and a quick glance at his watch suggested he'd slept soundly for more than four hours. Snatching the phone from its cradle, he found that his voice was hoarse and that he had to clear his throat.

"This is Gordon Strickland calling. I'm sorry to bother you, Mr. Davydov, but there's been a problem that you should know about."

Yuri rubbed his forehead while his sleepy mind wrestled with the name Strickland. He knew he'd heard it, but he couldn't remember in what context. Then, with a start, he remembered. It was the funeral home that he had arranged to take Connie.

"What kind of problem?" Yuri asked. His mind fought through the fog of sleep. He didn't like the sound of "problem."

"Something very irregular has happened," Gordon continued. "Not long after your poor deceased wife arrived here at our facility, three men appeared demanding to see her body and take samples."

"What kind of samples?" Yuri demanded.

"Body fluids for analysis," Gordon said. "I want to apologize for this whole affair and for not calling you immediately and asking your permission. Unfortunately, it all happened so quickly. They were authorized by the chief medical examiner, but now, after the fact, I'm confused as to the legality of it. You might consider retaining counsel. You could possibly have grounds for a big award from the city."

"But I don't understand," Yuri said. "My wife wasn't autopsied."

"Precisely," Gordon said. "That's why this is so irregular. I've been in this business for almost thirty years, and my father for a lifetime before that, and nothing like this has ever happened in either of our experience."

"Who were these men?" Yuri asked. He put the phone in the crook of his neck so he could get a glass. From the freezer he got the vodka and poured himself a slug. He needed it.

"One of them was a medical examiner," Gordon said. "Dr. Jack Stapleton. He had an assistant . . ."

"What was the doctor's name?" Yuri demanded, interrupting the funeral director mid-sentence. Even in Yuri's sleepy state the name rang a discordant bell in his mind.

When Gordon repeated the name, Yuri took another belt of his vodka. Jack Stapleton had been the man in the Corinthian Rug Company office!

"The medical examiner was also accompanied by a relative of your late wife," Gordon went on to say. "At least that was what we were told. He was introduced as Frank Thomas, although I heard Dr. Stapleton refer to him by the sobriquet 'Flash.' "

Yuri felt a chill down his spine. He grabbed one of the kitchen chairs and pulled it over to the phone so he could sit down. His legs had suddenly turned to rubber. Flash Thomas was the one person in the world who Yuri truly feared. Not only was he a big, muscled man, he'd threatened Yuri on several occasions. The last time had been on the telephone, when he'd said that if Yuri ever hit Connie again he'd come out there to Brighton Beach and kill him.

"Are you still there?" Gordon questioned. Yuri had not responded to his last statement.

"Yes, I'm still here," Yuri managed. His pulse was racing. What could it mean that Flash Thomas was with this mysterious Jack Stapleton? What kind of weird coincidence could this be?

"We're going to need some directions from you," Gordon repeated. "Were you intending to have an open casket?"

"No!" Yuri yelled. Then he calmed himself. "No. I just want to do this as simply as possible. That's what Connie would have preferred."

"But you will have to come and choose an appropriate casket."

"What is the least expensive?" Yuri asked.

"It would be far better if you were to come in," Gordon said in his unctuous business voice. "We could show you our whole line, with descriptions of the benefits and disadvantages of each."

"What about cremation?" Yuri asked.

"That can be arranged," Gordon said. "But there is still the issue of choosing an appropriate vessel."

"I want her cremated," Yuri said. "And I want it soon. Today, in fact!"

"There's to be no viewing or service?" Gordon questioned.

"No," Yuri said. "It is my religious belief it should be done as soon as possible."

"Very well," Gordon said.

"What kind of samples did Dr. Stapleton take?" Yuri demanded.

"Just a small piece of tissue and some fluids," Gordon said nervously.

"I didn't want her body violated," Yuri complained. He wondered what could have provoked this Dr. Stapleton to collect samples after the authorities had decided there was to be no autopsy.

"All I can do is apologize again," Gordon said. "But you have to understand, it was beyond our control."

"I'll come by in the next day or so to choose a container for her ashes and settle the account," Yuri said.

"That will be most appreciated," Gordon said.

"Meanwhile, make sure she's cremated before her body is violated again."

"We'll see to it forthwith," Gordon promised.

Yuri hung up the phone and then stared across the room with unseeing eyes. Could it be that the authorities suspected the botulinum toxin? Yuri could not see how. But Flash Thomas posed a more immediate threat. Yuri tried to imagine what he'd do if his brother-in-law suddenly appeared at the door. It was a terrifying thought. There was no way Yuri could defend himself, if Flash got to him. Yuri knew he had to do something to protect himself, because he couldn't abandon his lab, at least not until he'd done the final harvest.

Glancing at the clock above the refrigerator gave Yuri an idea. It was nearly five, which meant that Curt would soon be getting off work. Yuri picked up the phone. He got the number for the fire station on Duane Street and immediately put through a call. When the phone was answered by one of the firemen, Yuri asked for Lieutenant Curt Rogers.

"Hold on," the firefighter said.

Yuri glanced over at the kitchen door, which he'd used when he'd come home that morning. He wanted to see if it was properly locked. It wasn't. Yuri could see that he'd failed to secure the deadbolt. Standing up and stretching the phone cord to its absolute limit, Yuri pushed the bolt home with a reassuring thunk.

"Lieutenant Rogers," Curt said in a tone befitting his rank.

"Curt, this is Yuri. I need your help."

There was an extended pause.

"Curt, are you there?"

"What in God's name are you calling me for here at the station?" Curt growled in a hushed voice. "I thought I made it clear that this was off-limits."

"You said not to come," Yuri said. "But you didn't say not to call."

"What do I have to do, spell everything out for you?" Curt hissed. "Use your goddamn brain! You've got a Russian accent, and it's just as apparent on the phone as it is when you're in person. I don't want anybody here knowing I'm dealing with a Russian."

"But I had to call," Yuri explained. "Like I said, I've got a problem."

"What kind of a problem?" Curt demanded irritably.

"I need a gun," Yuri said. "You told me how many guns you and the PAA have. I just need one."

"What the hell for?"

"Because of Connie's brother," Yuri said. "I've just heard he'd been to see her body at the funeral home."

"So what!"

"So plenty," Yuri said. "You saw her eye last night. I'd swatted her, and her brother told me once that if I ever hit her, he'd kill me."

"Jesus Christ!" Curt snarled.

"I'm serious," Yuri said. "He's a big black guy, and I'm

not going to stay here and work in the lab without some protection."

"All right, we'll get you a freaking gun."

"I need it right away," Yuri said.

"We're getting off work at five," Curt said. "We'll bring it around."

"Thanks," Yuri said.

"Yeah, sure," Curt said and hung up.

Yuri shook his head dejectedly as he hung up the phone. He'd planned on telling Curt about Jack Stapleton after he'd mentioned Connie's brother but had changed his mind when he'd heard Curt's tone of voice. Again there'd been surprising anger and hostility like there'd been the night before. To Yuri, such an attitude was entirely inappropriate for people who were supposed to be working together. He was forced to consider again that Curt was no friend.

In one gulp, Yuri finished off the rest of the vodka and put the glass in the sink. Then he wondered if he'd have enough time to suit up and go into the lab to check the second fermenter before Curt got there. In the end, he decided that he'd feel safer around his anthrax powder.

THIRTEEN

Jack had Warren drop him off on the Thirtieth Street side of the ME's office so he could duck into the building via the loading dock. He wanted to avoid running into the chief or Calvin in case his Brooklyn exploits had already caused a stir. What he hoped to have prior to any confrontation were the results of the samples he'd taken from Connie Davydov. They were to serve as a justification for his actions.

Jack's intuition told him that Flash was probably right about his sister having been the victim of foul play. With a heart attack, a stroke, and generalized infectious disease ruled out, poisoning was quite probable considering the history of domestic strife. Lending considerable credence to the theory was the black eye. Even though Jack had been reluctant to admit it to Flash, Jack's professional judgment told him the black eye had come from trauma and not infection, and that the trauma was the result of a fist rather than an inanimate object in the woman's bathroom.

In hopes of generating his alibi sooner rather than later as well as providing evidence to prompt a homicide investigation, Jack went directly to the toxicology lab on the fourth floor. He purposefully avoided the supervisor, John DeVries, who'd most likely keep him waiting for a week or more. Instead, Jack sought out Peter Letterman, the thin, blond, androgynous technician who acted as if he were married to the lab. Jack had seen him there as late as ten P.M.

"I need your help desperately," Jack said even before saying hello when he found the tech at the gas chromatography unit.

Peter raised his eyebrows. He was accustomed to all sorts of creative pleas to cut through the typical toxicology log jam. There was no doubt the department was underfunded. But then, every department in the ME's office was underfunded.

"I might be out selling pencils if we don't get a positive out of this one," Jack said. He put his satchel down and began removing the sample bottles while giving Peter a thumbnail sketch of what he'd been up to that afternoon. The story about the funeral home brought a smile to Peter's usually serious, boyish face.

"You think I'm making this up, don't you?" Jack asked, noting Peter's expression.

"No, I don't," Peter said. "What you're telling me is too far out to be fiction."

"Good," Jack said. "Then you can appreciate that I might be in hot water about this?"

"Oh, yeah!" Peter said without hesitation.

"So you'll help?" Jack asked.

"What is it that you're looking for?"

"Something that has suppressed respiration. You know, the usual prescription drugs plus cyanide, carbon monoxide, ethylene glycol, and hell, anything else you can think of. It doesn't have to be quantitative on this go-round. Just find something."

"All right," Peter said. "I'll give it a whirl."

"How soon can you do it?" Jack asked.

"Why not right now?" Peter said agreeably. "I can assay the samples pretty quickly for what you have in mind."

Unable to contain himself, Jack threw his arms around Peter and gave him a hug.

Peter seemed embarrassed when Jack let him go. He blushed and avoided looking Jack in the eye.

"I'll be upstairs in my office," Jack said. "I've got plenty to keep me busy. Just give a shout when you're done."

Peter nodded.

"Dinner's on me in the near future," Jack said. He gave Peter a light pat on the back.

"Sure," Peter said. He began to pick up the bottles.

"Let me fill out some property receipts first," Jack said. "We've got to establish a chain of custody here if this turns out to be a homicide case."

After leaving the toxicology lab, Jack took the stairs to the fifth floor. He was feeling considerably better. With a spring to his step he ducked into histology. He found Maureen O'Conner, the supervisor, with her coat on in preparation for leaving.

"Just my luck!" Maureen said in her quaint Irish brogue. "I'm late for a pathology conference and Mr. Right walks in looking chipper and eager."

Laughter resonated around the room.

Jack and his officemate, Chet, were the only two unmarried male medical examiners on staff, and Maureen and her team of woman histology assistants got great enjoyment out of teasing both of them. They had plenty of opportunity, since their office was just down the hall.

"I don't have any conference to go to," one of the other women offered. "I'm available." More laughter erupted.

Jack opened his satchel and took out the bottle with the ellipse of Connie's skin.

"Oh, drat," Maureen moaned. "It doesn't look like a social call."

Jack smiled. "On this visit all I'm looking for are some slides from this skin sample, but tomorrow is another day."

"Hear that, girls?" Maureen called out.

A chorus of enthusiastic "yeses" rang out.

Maureen took Jack's sample bottle and handed it off to the nearest technician. "Consider it done," she said to Jack. "What kind of stains?"

"Just the usual," Jack said. "I want to make sure the pathology is trauma, not infection."

"When do you need it?"

"The sooner the better," Jack said.

"Why do I bother asking?" Maureen said while tilting her head back as if talking to God.

Jack left the histology lab and started down the corridor. As he approached Laurie's office, he could see that her light was on. Veering into her doorway, he stopped. Seated inside were Laurie and Lou. Neither was talking, but rather they were staring off in different directions. The atmosphere was tense.

"Is this a wake?" Jack asked.

Laurie and Lou looked up. Laurie was plainly irritated. Lou was obviously contrite.

"Partners in crime, I hear," Laurie snapped when she caught sight of Jack.

Jack raised his hands. "I surrender. What's the crime?"

"I told her about Paul Sutherland's sheet," Lou confessed. "And I told her that you knew."

"I see," Jack said. "And as we feared the messenger is getting blamed."

"Now don't you start supporting him," Laurie said. "He wasn't supposed to be snooping like that. I certainly didn't ask him to."

"I suppose that's true," Jack said. "But under the circumstances, I think you should know your future husband's line of work."

"What do you mean, 'line of work'?" Laurie questioned with renewed anger. "What on earth are you implying?"

"I only told her about the cocaine possession," Lou explained.

"Uh oh," Jack said. He swallowed uncomfortably.

"Paul does not deal in drugs," Laurie said indignantly. "If that's what you are implying."

"Can I come in?" Jack asked.

"You'd better," Laurie snapped. "And you'd better explain yourself."

Jack pulled over a chair and sat next to Lou. He looked Laurie in the eye. She stared back defiantly.

"Paul Sutherland is an arms dealer," Jack said. Laurie's blue-green eyes swept back and forth between Jack and Lou. "How do you know that?" she demanded in a voice that had lost a shade of its anger.

"Lou found that out at the same time he found out about the cocaine possession," Jack said.

Lou nodded guiltily. He looked down at his hands in his lap.

"What do I care if he's an arms dealer?" Laurie said airily, trying to make it sound as if it didn't matter.

Neither Jack nor Lou responded. Knowing Laurie as well as they did, they weren't fooled.

"What kind of arms?" Laurie asked.

"At the moment I'm not sure," Lou said. "But as recently as 1994 he specialized in AK-47 assault rifles of Bulgarian manufacture."

The color drained from Laurie's face.

"Lou and I argued about who should tell you this," Jack said. "But one way or the other, we thought you should know, given your feelings about gun control."

Laurie nodded, sighed, and looked off. Jack wasn't sure if she was angry or sad or both. For a full minute no one spoke. Finally, Laurie broke the silence: "Thank you, gentlemen, for discharging your civic duty. I've been informed. Now if you'll excuse me, I've got a lot of work to catch up on."

Jack exchanged a glance with Lou. They both got to their feet and put their chairs back where they thought they should go. They said their goodbyes, but Laurie didn't respond. She'd already pulled the contents of one of her uncompleted cases from its file folder and seemed to be absorbed in it.

The two men walked down the hall toward Jack's office. They didn't speak until they thought Laurie couldn't hear.

"I was going to congratulate you on your courage in talking to Laurie," Jack said, "until I realized you'd cleverly engineered it so that I had to spill the real beans."

"Thank God you arrived," Lou said. "She was making me feel like dirt, which wasn't hard, since I was already questioning my own motives."

"I still think it was the best thing for Laurie," Jack said, "even if there's a chance we did it for ourselves as well as for her."

"I suppose I can try to look at it like that," Lou said without enthusiasm.

"Listen, you got a moment? I want to tell you about a case."

Lou glanced at his watch. "As late as I am, I suppose another half hour doesn't matter."

"It won't take that long," Jack said.

Jack preceded Lou into his office and snapped on his light. "Where the hell is Chet? I haven't seen him since this morning. It's not like him to just disappear."

Lou sat down while Jack picked up a sheet of paper from the center of his desk.

"Hmmm," Jack voiced after reading the note. "This is from Ted Lynch, the DNA guru. It seems that the tiny blue star from the Corinthian Rug Company office was heavily contaminated with anthrax spores. Considering the surface area, he estimates that there wouldn't be room for one more spore. Now that's curious."

"What does it mean?" Lou asked.

"Beats me," Jack said. He tossed the paper onto his desk. "I suppose it's telling me something, but I haven't the foggiest notion what it is. It sounds almost as if the star had been dropped into a bowl of anthrax."

"Let's hear about this case you wanted to tell me about," Lou said.

Jack told the story of Connie Davydov. Lou listened intently and smiled about the part involving the funeral home. "Had Warren ever been in that kind of place before?" Lou questioned. Lou knew Warren through Jack.

Jack shook his head.

"He must have squirmed when he had to see the guy getting embalmed."

"He said it was the worst experience of his life."

"I can imagine," Lou said.

"But it couldn't be helped," Jack said. "I needed him there to intimidate the funeral director. Actually, I'm surprised I got away with doing what I did."

"Why are you telling me this story now?" Lou questioned. "Can I help somehow?"

"I'm wondering if you can do something about the body," Jack said. "I've no idea what the plans are concerning embalming or cremation, but I'd like it to stay intact. I'd really like to do a full postmortem. Is there a way you could intervene?"

"Not without some involvement of this office," Lou said.

"That's what I was afraid of," Jack said. "Well, no harm in asking. I'm going to wait around tonight for the results of the assay. If it's positive for some kind of poison or overdose, I'll give you a call."

"I'll be available via my cell phone," Lou said. He stood up and took a few steps into the hall. He looked down toward Laurie's office. "Do you think I should go back and say anything to our friend?"

"I think we've said about all we could," Jack said. "Now she's got to mull it over and decide its importance."

"I suppose you're right," Lou said. "See you around."

"Take care," Jack said.

Jack straightened some of the piles of uncompleted case folders that stood on his desk. He hung up his jacket behind the door, then sat down to work. Having been out of the office the last two afternoons, he was more behind than usual.

FOURTEEN

Curt turned onto Oceanview Lane. Although it wasn't quite dark yet, he switched on his headlights because of the deep shadows within the confines of the narrow roadway. Just like the night before, there were multiple trash cans littering the pavement's periphery. He pulled up alongside Yuri's garage and cut both the lights and the engine.

"I'm happy with everything we've decided except the idea of giving this Commie a gun," Steve said. "I have to tell you, I don't like it."

"What the hell choice do we have?" Curt complained. "I told you, he's terrified of his brother-in-law. The guy threatened to kill him."

"I know what you told me," Steve said. "But as weird as Yuri's been acting and the crazy stuff he's been saying, like all that bullshit about this being a rootless culture, I tell you, I don't like him having a gun. Especially not one of ours. What if he turns it on us?"

"He's not going to turn it on us," Curt said irritably. "For crissake, we're the only friends he's got. Besides, he probably couldn't hit a barn from inside. And you've got your gun, right?"

"Of course," Steve said.

"Well, I've got mine, too," Curt said. "There's no way you and I couldn't handle one tubby little Russian. Come on! Let's get this over with!"

The two men got out of the truck. They met at the front and started for Yuri's door. Curt was carrying a brown paper bag.

"The main thing is we have to keep him working in the lab," Curt said. "If it takes giving him a gun, so be it. We're so close. We can't let Operation Wolverine die on the vine because Yuri's scared of his nigger brother-in-law."

"But if he's got a gun, he might be harder for the troops to handle," Steve said.

Curt pulled his partner to a stop. "You think one Glock automatic is going to make a difference against a half-dozen Kalashnikovs? Come on! Be serious!"

"I guess not," Steve said.

"Of course not," Curt said. "Right after we take possession of our part of the anthrax powder and get it safely back to the White Pride, we'll send in the troops. Glock or no Glock, the mission will be over in five seconds. Hell, we'll tell 'em to burn this freaking place down in the process."

"Okay, you're right," Steve said. "I just want to be sure. The more I've thought about it, the more I don't want him spraying anthrax around Central Park."

"I feel the same," Curt said. "Clearly it's not a military objective like the Jacob Javits Federal Building."

"And it bugged me when he was carrying on about how many more casualties his plan would cause than ours. I don't buy it. Hell, the federal building's HVAC vents outside. Not only are we going to knock out the entire building, the anthrax will spread around that whole section of the city."

"Damn straight," Curt said. "It'll vector east toward the courthouses. I mean, is that not perfect or what?"

"It couldn't be any better," Steve agreed.

"Once we give the word to the troops, Yuri's a dead man," Curt said. "You know that. End of story."

Steve nodded. They recommenced walking.

"I don't see any lights on inside," Curt said as they reached the door. He had to squint in the glare of an exterior carriage lamp mounted to the left of the jamb. "He better the hell be here!"

Curt pulled open the torn screen door and rapped loudly against the inner door. It opened almost immediately. Yuri peered out from the inner gloom.

"Thank goodness," Yuri said with relief. "Come in!"

Curt and Steve filed past the Russian but found themselves in darkness, still momentarily blinded by the bright outdoor light.

"What the hell have you been doing in here?" Curt questioned. "I can't see my hand in front of my face."

"Sorry," Yuri said as he scurried to turn on a lamp next to the couch. "I was afraid Connie's brother might show up before you got here, and I wanted it to look like no one was home."

"That's better," Curt said when he could see.

"Can I get you men some iced vodka?" Yuri asked.

"I think I'll pass," Curt said.

"Same with me," Steve said.

"Did you bring the gun?" Yuri questioned.

"Sure, I got it," Curt said. He held up the bag. "But let's talk first."

"Okay," Yuri said. "Do you mind if I get some vodka for myself?"

"Not at all," Curt said.

While Yuri went to the kitchen, Curt and Steve sat down. Curt took the couch while Steve sat in one of two straight-back chairs. They left the other for Yuri so that he would be more or less between them.

"It's amazing to think of what's going to come out of this trashy hellhole's basement," Curt whispered. "Just the thought of it gives me a rush."

"I know what you mean," Steve whispered back. "Like Christ being born in a stable, extraordinary things can come from lowly surroundings. This bioweapon is probably going to change the world."

"Let's content ourselves with saving the country," Curt responded.

With glass in hand, Yuri joined the others. He sat down in the empty chair.

"What would you like to talk about?" Yuri asked. He took a sip of his drink and relished its taste. Despite some recent misgivings about his relationship with his guests, he was happy and relieved they were there.

"With all these unexpected problems that have been popping up, we've decided things have to be speeded up," Curt said. "Like we told you last night, we're worried about security. After talking about it all day, we've decided we want to schedule the event for Friday. So, we want our half of the anthrax powder Thursday night. That's two days from now."

"This is very sudden," Yuri said. He was visibly shocked. The plan had been to wait until he had enough of the bioweapon before they'd plan the actual day of release.

"Maybe so," Curt said. "But we feel strongly that this is the way it has to be."

"It's going to be difficult," Yuri said. His eyes darted nervously back and forth between Curt and Steve. "Both laydowns need at least four or five pounds for maximum effect."

"That means we want at least four and preferably five pounds Thursday night," Curt said. "This is not a discussion. Am I making myself clear?"

"I don't know what to say," Yuri stammered.

"Just say, 'Fine, Curt: just come by and I'll have it ready for you.' You originally told us it would be sealed in clear plastic and look like large sausages. Is that still the case?"

"Yes," Yuri said. He took a sip from his glass and his hand trembled.

"And it's safe to handle in that form," Curt said. "I mean without a hazmat suit."

"Unless the plastic breaks," Yuri said. "The sausages will be heat-sealed and their outsides will be decontaminated."

"How tough is this plastic?" Curt asked. "Like if we happened to drop one of the sausages, would that be a problem?"

"I haven't tested that," Yuri admitted. "But I wouldn't advise dropping it or sticking it with anything. Under ideal conditions each one of these sausages will be capable of killing up to a hundred thousand people."

"How many pounds do you have now?" Curt asked.

"I'm not sure," Yuri said.

"Last night you said you might have enough by the end of the week," Curt reminded him. "So you must have an idea. I mean, Thursday night is pretty close to the end of the week."

"I did another harvest this morning," Yuri said. "I didn't weigh it."

"So you're close," Curt said.

"Yes, I'm close," Yuri said. He nodded a few times as if agreeing with himself before taking a deep breath and exhaling through pursed lips. It was like he'd been under stress but was now able to relax. He gestured with his glass toward both Curt and Steve as if he was giving a toast and then took another, larger slug of his drink. He held the vodka in his mouth for a moment before swallowing as if it was fine wine.

"What about the second fermenter?" Steve asked. "Have you converted it to anthrax?"

"Yes, this morning," Yuri said.

"How is it going?" Curt asked.

"Extremely well," Yuri said. He managed a smile. "It's growing much better than the *Clostridium botulinum.* In fact I was amazed when I checked just a few minutes before you arrived. I'll be able to harvest an entire batch this evening."

"We could steal you another fermenter tonight," Steve suggested. "If that could help."

"There's no need," Yuri said with a wave of his free hand. "Not with the second one running. Now that I've had a chance to think, I'm sure I'll be able to make delivery Thursday night."

"Really?" Curt questioned.

"Absolutely," Yuri said.

"You weren't so sure just a few moments ago," Curt said.

"I wasn't," Yuri admitted. "Not until Steve reminded me of the second fermenter. With it running like it is, I'll be able to have at least ten pounds, maybe even a bit more if I work nonstop."

"Is there any reason you can't do that?" Curt asked.

"No," Yuri said. "I just won't drive the cab."

"There is one more thing we want you to do before tomorrow night," Curt said.

Yuri's face, which had recently assumed a smile, reverted to a troubled expression.

"Now, don't get upset," Curt said, noticing the change in Yuri's demeanor. "This is an easy request: at least easy for you. I'd like you to write down how you've created this anthrax powder. Since you'll be back in Russia, we're going to have to find someone else if we want to stage an encore."

Yuri's smile returned. He nodded. "Sure, I can do that. In fact I'll be happy to do it."

"Perfect!" Curt said. He smiled to himself before picking up the paper bag from the couch and handing it across to Yuri. As Yuri accepted the parcel, Curt's other hand slipped behind to grasp the butt of his own pistol nestled in its holster in the small of his back. Unbeknownst to Yuri, who was happily opening the package, Steve did the same with his gun.

Yuri lifted the automatic out by its barrel. Dropping the paper bag, he examined the gun closely. He hefted it. "It's lightweight," he said.

"It is," Curt said. "It's called a Glock. It's a very good weapon. It's the preferred handgun with the militias."

"Is there anything particular that I should know about it?" Yuri said. He released the magazine catch and slipped it out. He glanced at the bullets and counted them.

"You just point it at your brother-in-law and pull the trigger," Curt said. "The gun does the rest."

Yuri laughed. He slipped his finger within the trigger guard and pointed the gun at his refrigerator. "Bang!" he said and jerked the gun as if it had recoiled. He laughed again before placing the gun on the coffee table.

Curt and Steve relaxed and sat back in their seats.

"There's something else in the bag," Curt said.

"There is?" Yuri questioned. He reached down and retrieved the package. He pulled out a cellophane bag that seemed to be filled with black hair. The corners of Yuri's mouth drew up into a half smile. He thought it was some kind of joke. "What the hell is this?"

"It's something we picked up in a costume store on the way over here," Curt said. "It's a beard."

"What on earth for?" Yuri asked.

"It's to make a point," Curt said. "The gun is only for an absolute emergency. We don't want you using it. Stay away from your brother-in-law and take your phone off the hook. Don't talk to him. When you go out, make sure he's not around and wear the stupid beard. If he happens to come around, don't let him in. Just get rid of him. The problem is, that if you use the gun, it'll bring the police, and if the police come here and start snooping around, Operation Wolverine goes down the toilet. If that happens, Steve and I and the PAA troops are going to be very unhappy. Am I making myself clear?"

"Don't worry," Yuri said with a wave of dismissal. "I'll only use the gun to avoid being killed myself. It's more to just make me feel safe."

"That's what I was hoping," Curt said.

"After all," Yuri added as he tore open the cellophane package, "Operation Wolverine is just as important to me as it is to you. The last thing I'd want to do is something that would interfere with it."

Yuri pulled out the fake beard and held it up against his face. "How do I look?"

"Ridiculous," Curt said.

Yuri laughed and put the cellophane and the beard back into the paper bag.

Curt stood up, and Steve and Yuri followed suit. Curt stuck out his hand and Yuri shook it enthusiastically.

"So what time Thursday night?" Curt asked.

"As you wish," Yuri said. "It will be ready when you want."

"Excellent," Curt said. "We'll come by sometime after dark. I'll have a firefighter's rabbit tool bag. It's about twenty inches by ten and about ten high. It's like a small duffel bag. Will that be big enough for the plastic sausages?"

"More than enough," Yuri said. "The key thing is to make

sure there are no sharp edges on the inside. In fact, I'll give you a towel to roll them up in."

"Sounds good," Curt said. He gave a halfhearted military salute. Self-consciously, Yuri returned the gesture.

Curt preceded Steve out the door. They could hear Yuri bolt it as they descended the front walk. Reaching the truck they climbed in their respective sides.

"So what was your take?" Curt questioned as he started the engine.

"I was encouraged," Steve said. "At first when he acted so nervous I had my doubts. I thought he was going to try to give us a hard time about getting the anthrax or maybe argue we should do Central Park rather than the federal building."

"I did, too," Curt said. "But then it was like he suddenly saw the light and realized that Operation Wolverine had better be executed fast before something else goes wrong. Thank God we came out here and put pressure on him. I suppose we should have done it a week ago. But at the moment, it doesn't matter. What matters is that Operation Wolverine is going to happen, and come Friday all hell's going to break loose here in the Big Apple."

"I'm glad he's decided to be cooperative, but he's still one weird duck," Steve said. "Did it make you nervous when he took the gun out?"

"A little," Curt admitted. "But it was more because of what you'd said before we went in. I actually think the guy's pathetic. Pretending to shoot the gun like that was so juvenile. And when he put that beard on, I almost cracked up."

"I think it was a brilliant idea to ask him to write out how to make the anthrax powder," Steve said.

"It was a touch of genius," Curt said with a wry smile as he made the turn onto Ocean Avenue. "The idea just came to me like a bolt out of the heavens. If this all goes as well as I'm sure it will, we'll probably want to make future strikes."

FIFTEEN

Jack liked to work after hours. With few people in the building and no phone calls to distract him, he was able to get much more done than he could during the day. The only person he'd seen over the previous hour had been one of the janitors, who'd whisked by the door with a large dust mop.

For efficiency's sake, he'd spread himself all around the one office, bunching similar tasks for different cases in the same location. He'd even arrogated Chet's desk, where he'd set up his microscope for examining the histology slides. Taking advantage of the wheels on his desk chair, he moved from station to station.

"My God, I'm homeless," a voice said, breaking the silence.

Jack glanced up to see Chet looking forlornly at his commandeered desk.

"Ah, the missing ME!" Jack said. "Talk about me going out in the field! Where on earth have you been? I haven't seen you since early this morning."

"I told you I was going to the pathology conference," Chet said.

"You did?"

"Of course I did," Chet said. "In the ID room this morning over coffee."

"Sorry, I guess I forgot," Jack said. He remembered being preoccupied about his planned apology to Laurie. "I'm kinda in a fog. A lot's going on."

"It looks like a cyclone hit this office."

"I suppose it does," Jack said. "Here, let me get my stuff off your desk."

"Hey, not on my account," Chet said. "I've just stopped in to pick up my briefcase. It's got my exercise clothes. I'm heading over to the gym."

"Are you sure you don't want me to move my junk?"

"Absolutely," Chet said. He gingerly stepped over folders Jack had strategically placed around the floor. "You should have come to the conference. It was one of the best I've attended."

"Really?" Jack questioned without interest. He'd turned his attention back to the prisoner-in-custody case, whose slides had appeared in a miraculously short time from the histology lab.

"The last seminar was particularly fantastic," Chet continued. He pulled open the top drawer of his file cabinet and lifted out his briefcase. "It was on zoonoses. You know, diseases of animals that people can get."

"I know what zoonoses are," Jack said absently.

"What made it so good was that a number of city veterinarians were on the panel," Chet said. "I was bowled over by the number of animal diseases which they're constantly contending with. It's incredible."

"No kidding," Jack said vaguely. He was trying to find the slides of David Jefferson's brain, particularly the sections of the temporal lobe.

"And I'm not just talking about the ones you hear about in the media like rabies in raccoons. In fact, one of the guys said that just today there was a major die-off of sewer rats in Brooklyn way out in Brighton Beach."

Jack's head popped up. "What was that?"

"As usual, you're not listening to me," Chet complained.

"I just missed the last part."

Chet repeated what he'd said about the rats.

"And this was in Brighton Beach?" Jack asked. He stared off.

"Yes!" Chet said, mildly miffed. As usual it irritated him the way Jack could tune him out. "Why does Brighton Beach surprise you?"

Jack didn't answer. It was as if he was in a trance.

"Hello!" Chet called, waving his hand in front of Jack's face. "Earth to Jack! Come in please!" Chet shook his head. "God, I haven't used that phrase since the third grade."

"What did the rats die of?" Jack asked. "Was it plague or something like that?"

"No!" Chet said. "That's the big mystery. They haven't been able to come up with a cause yet. But they're very concerned. And just to add to the mystery, two out of the hundreds of dead rats they've collected had cutaneous ulcers that turned out to be anthrax."

"Now that is weird!" Jack said. "Do they think the others had anthrax?"

"No, not at all," Chet said. "They've pretty much ruled out bacteria as the culprit, including anthrax. Now they're focusing mostly on some kind of virus. The anthrax is just a curious corollary."

"This is the second time I've heard about Brighton Beach today," Jack said. "And before that, I never knew it existed."

"What amazed me was to learn that this kind of problem, maybe not quite as dramatic as with the rats, occurs all the time. We just don't hear about it. These veterinary epidemiologists are busy guys."

"Do they have any idea where the anthrax came from?" Jack asked.

"Nope," Chet said. "But it has them thinking that maybe some of the rats are hosts, which is not what the textbooks say. I tell you, it's fascinating stuff."

"Let me tell you about my Brighton Beach case," Jack said. "Do you have a minute?"

"Provided it doesn't take too long," Chet said while peeking at his watch. "I don't want to miss this particular aerobics class. There's this one girl with a figure to die for who only comes on Tuesday nights."

Jack gave a quick synopsis of Connie Davydov, focusing on the diagnostic mystery. Jack listed all the agents he'd been considering. Then he asked Chet if he had any ideas.

Chet screwed up his face and pondered for a few moments. He shook his head. "I think you've pretty well covered the landscape."

"It is kinda curious that Connie Davydov suddenly dies from what I think was a mysterious poisoning the day there's a major rat die-off in the same town."

"Whoa!" Chet said with a smile. "That's a giant leap of association, unless, of course, Ms. Davydov spent some quality time during the previous twenty-four hours in the sewer or a portion of the town's rat population hung out in her apartment."

Jack ran the fingers of both hands through his hair while laughing at Chet's absurd suggestions. "Of course you're right! But what a strange coincidence, especially when you add the anthrax to the picture, and the case of human anthrax I had yesterday here in Manhattan. What a couple of days!"

"Well, I'm going to leave you to ponder these mysteries," Chet said. "While I go ponder another more enjoyable one in aerobics class."

"Excuse me, Dr. Stapleton!"

Jack and Chet turned to see Peter Letterman standing in the doorway in his long white coat with its inevitable pattern of colorful stains. He was holding a computer printout.

"Peter!" Jack said eagerly. He searched the man's face for a hint of his news, but Peter's delicate features were unrevealing.

"I've run all the assays you suggested," Peter said.

"And?" Jack questioned expectantly. It was like waiting for the envelope to be opened at the Academy Awards.

Peter handed Jack the printout. Jack scanned it. He had no idea what he was looking at.

"Everything came out negative," Peter said guiltily. "I haven't found anything."

"Nothing?" Jack questioned. He looked up. He was dismayed.

Peter shook his head. "I'm sorry. I know you were counting on a positive, so I ran some of the assays several times. Everything came back negative."

"Oh, crap!" Jack said. He threw up his hands. "So much for my intuition. Maybe even my job."

"You checked for carbon monoxide?" Chet asked.

"Absolutely," Peter said.

"And cyanide?" Chet asked.

"Everything that Dr. Stapleton requested plus a few drugs he didn't mention."

"Thank you very much," Jack said. "At the moment I might not sound as appreciative as I should, but I am thankful for you staying late and doing this."

"If you can think of anything else you want me to test for, give me a call."

"Right," Jack said.

Peter left.

"Oh, well," Jack said. He threw his pen onto his desk. Then he started gathering together all the disparate papers from the various cases and jamming them into their folders.

Chet watched for a few minutes. "If I can think of anything else to test for, I'll give you a call."

Jack gave him a weak smile and continued straightening up.

"Are you heading home?" Chet asked.

"Yup," Jack said. "I think I need a little physical activity myself."

After saying goodbye, Chet left. As Jack moved his microscope over onto his own desk, he thought about all the strange events over the previous twenty-four hours. It was all a mystery, yet he had to smile. Such conundrums were, after all, what he liked about the job.

After locking his office door, Jack glanced down the hall toward Laurie's. It was closed. Obviously, Laurie had left without saying goodbye. Jack shrugged. He really didn't know what to do about her.

Downstairs, Jack unlocked his bike and rolled it out of the receiving dock. After getting it down to the pavement, he got on and cycled out onto First Avenue.

As usual, the ride home was an opportunity for Jack to break away literally and figuratively. Rush-hour traffic had already abated, and he flew. The sun had set an hour or so earlier and the sky was a silvery blue-violet that deepened to indigo with every passing moment. In the middle of the darkened park he even got to see stars twinkling in the firmament.

Entering his own street, Jack headed directly for the chain-link fence separating the basketball court from the sidewalk. As he pulled to a stop, he saw what he wanted to see: a game in progress. As the men swept down the court in his direction, he noticed that Warren and Flash were already playing, although on opposing teams.

With a sense of urgency, Jack carried his bike up to his apartment and tore off his clothes. Redressed in his basketball gear, he thundered down the stairs and out across the street. When he arrived at the game's sidelines, he was slightly out of breath.

Unfortunately, another game had started in the time Jack had taken to get on his togs, which meant he'd have to wait one or maybe two games to get into the friendly fray. As usual, Warren's team had won-so he was still on the court. Flash, on the other hand, was standing in the midst of those waiting to play. Jack walked over to him.

"Hey, man, how's it going?" Flash said when he caught sight of Jack. It was the typical B-ball-court, offhand manner of greeting, even though they'd spent a good part of the afternoon together.

"It's going fine," Jack said. "You doing okay?"

"So far," Flash said. He didn't look at Jack but rather kept his eyes glued to the game in progress. "I'd be better if we'd won the last game."

"Listen," Jack said. "I gave the laboratory all the samples I took from your sister today. So they're in the works. I want to make sure you're going to be patient and not do anything rash."

"I'm cool," Flash said.

"Glad to hear it," Jack said. He was reluctant to tell Flash about the lab results just yet. Despite the negative results on the assays Peter had run, Jack was still inclined to intuit that Connie had been poisoned in some way or another.

"I'm curious about where she lived," Jack said. "You mentioned it was in an area with small wooden cottages. Is it an historic area?"

"I don't think it's historic," Flash said. "But it's old."

"How old?"

"Man, I don't know," Flash said. "What are you asking me this for?"

Jack shrugged. "Like I said, I'm curious. There aren't too many parts of New York City that still have cottages. Could they be a hundred years old?"

"Something like that, I suppose," Flash said. "I think they must have been summer cottages at some point."

Jack nodded as he tried mentally to visualize a group of old wood-framed houses built as summer cottages a hundred years ago. What immediately came to mind was that their plumbing might be rudimentary at best. In fact, they might even have septic systems instead of being connected to the city sewer.

"What was the address again?" Jack asked. "Was it Fifteen Oceanview Lane?"

"Yeah, that was it," Flash said. "Why do you ask? Are you going to go out there?"

"I might," Jack said. "Sometimes medical examiners have to visit the site of the death in order to reconstruct the series of events preceding it. But, of course, that's usually when the body is still where it was found."

"But I was told she died at Coney Island Hospital," Flash said.

"That's very true," Jack said. He gave Flash a pat on the back. "But it was supposedly in her bathroom where she got into trouble. Anyway, I'll keep you informed about whatever I learn."

"Thanks, Doc," Flash said.

Jack picked up one of the loose basketballs and took it over to one of the side baskets. He thought he'd warm up by taking a few jump shots. While he did, he mulled over the coincidence of Connie Davydov's dying from some unknown poison, possibly in her bathroom in the same town where there was a die-off of sewer rats, also caused by some unknown agent.

Jack tossed the ball through the hoop and then watched it bounce in decreasing altitude until it was stationary. His mind was churning. As crazy as the notion sounded, he couldn't help but question if Connie and the rats might have succumbed to the same agent. What if it had been some kind of gas and the drains in Connie's bathroom didn't have functioning traps? The trouble was, sewer gas stank, and the EMTs would have noted it.

"Ah, it's impossible," Jack voiced out loud. He went over and picked up the ball. He tried to think of other things, but he couldn't. As he took practice shots his mind kept dredging up Connie and the rats and images of the Brighton Beach summer cottages.

Laurie put down the dessert menu and shook her head. "I'm stuffed," she said. "I can't possibly eat dessert."

"Do you mind if I order something that we could both nibble on?" Paul asked. "I know how much you like chocolate."

"Of course," Laurie said. "As long as you understand that you're going to have to eat nine-tenths of it. But I'll have a decaf cappuccino."

"Coming up!" Paul said. He raised his hand to get the waiter's attention.

The evening had gone well, and Laurie was feeling considerably better than she had earlier after talking with Lou and Jack. When Laurie had first gotten home she'd considered canceling the week-old plans she had made with Paul to go to the ballet at Lincoln Center followed by dinner. But after some time by herself she decided that the information she'd gotten from Lou and Jack didn't necessitate an angry confrontation. She wasn't entirely confident what they'd said was true, and even if it was, she was more than willing to hear an explanation. It was more the surprise of it all that had upset her.

"How about some dessert wine?" Paul asked.

Laurie smiled and shook her head. They'd had a wonderful red wine with dinner, and Laurie was luxuriating in its afterglow. She knew she'd had quite enough alcohol.

Paul had arrived for the evening with more flowers and an apology for his insensitivity that morning. He'd assured her that he understood her commitment to her work, and he even went so far as to say that he truly admired and valued that she had such a commitment.

As they'd talked, Laurie had been tempted to bring up the issue of the nature of his work in the context of the discussion of hers, but decided against it. In the face of his sincere apology, she didn't want to seem unappreciative or insensitive. She'd decided to wait for a more opportune time.

And then there'd been the other surprise. Paul had told her that he'd managed to change the Budapest trip until the following weekend in hopes that her schedule would permit her to go. He'd even said she had all week to decide.

The dessert arrived, and it was a piece of vertical chocolate art. At its core was a moist, dark, flourless chocolate cake that Laurie could not resist. After a taste she smacked her lips with delight.

Paul had ordered a brandy. When it arrived, he swirled it, smelled it, and then took a taste. Satisfied, he leaned back and smiled. He was the picture of contentment.

"There's something I want to ask you, Paul," Laurie said, sensing there could not be a better time to bring up the work issue. "I know when I asked you this question this morning, it seemed confrontational. I didn't mean it to be, and I certainly don't mean it to be now, but I'd like to know what kind of business you are in."

Paul stopped swirling his brandy and regarded Laurie with his coal-black eyes. "Why do you want to know?" he asked with a calm, even voice.

"As your future wife, I'd think you'd want me to know," Laurie said with some surprise. She didn't expect his response to be a question. "If you didn't know what I did, I'd certainly want to tell you."

"My response this morning was to ask if it mattered," Paul said. "Does it?"

"It could," Laurie said. "Take my job. My own mother has this distorted idea that it's ghoulish. You could have felt the same way."

"Well, I certainly don't."

"I'm glad," Laurie said. "But you get my point. I don't think my mother would have married my father if he'd been a medical examiner, at least I don't think so."

"Are you trying to tell me that if my business is something you don't approve of, you won't marry me?"

"Paul, this is not an argument," Laurie said. "Now you are scaring me by making this discussion into something it needn't be. Please tell me what your business is."

"I'm in the defense business," Paul said with an edge to his voice.

"Okay, that's a start," Laurie said. She looked down into the swirled surface of her cappuccino. "Can you be a little more specific?"

"What is this, an inquisition?" Paul demanded.

"No, Paul, as I said, this is a discussion."

"And such an entertaining discussion!" Paul said sarcastically.

"Why are you being so defensive? This doesn't sound like you."

"I'm being defensive because too many people have the same prosaic response about the arms business."

"And you think I'm going to have the same response?"

"It's possible."

"What is it you sell?"

"I sell arms. Isn't that enough? Can't we talk about something else?"

"You mean like cannons, bombs, or guns."

"A little of all of them," Paul said. "Whatever is in demand."

"What about Bulgarian AK-47 assault rifles?" Laurie asked.

"Sure," Paul said, surprised at such a specific question. "It's one of my preferred products. It's a reliable, inexpensive, well-made weapon. Much better than the Chinese version."

Laurie closed her eyes. She could see a montage of images of Brad Cassidy's body and his grieving parents. She remembered how she'd felt when Shirley Cassidy said that her son was selling Bulgarian AK-47s to other skinheads. To think that Paul could be involved in such things was hard to comprehend, especially recalling the mayhem from guns she'd witnessed over the years in her professional position as a medical examiner.

Laurie took a deep breath. She was conscious her emotions were getting the best of her, and in such circumstances she knew she had a tendency toward tears. She didn't want to cry. Whenever she did, it irritated her to no end because it invariably precluded further discussion. She opened her eyes and looked at Paul. She read his expression as defensively arrogant.

"Do you ever think of the consequences of the guns you sell?" Laurie asked. She wanted to keep the conversation going.

"Of course," Paul said flippantly. "They provide people with the ability to defend themselves in a dangerous world."

"What about when the guns end up in the hands of violent, right-wing fringe groups?" Laurie asked. "Like skinheads?"

"They have a right to defend themselves just like anyone else."

"The problem is, with such bigoted hate groups, the guns tend to get used and they kill people."

"Guns don't kill people," Paul said cavalierly. "People kill people."

"Now you're sounding like a National Rifle Association spokesperson," Laurie said.

"The NRA has some very good points," Paul said. "Like the fact that the Constitution itself very specifically gives us the right to bear arms. When the government intervenes like it did with the Omnibus Crime Bill, it's acting blatantly unconstitutionally."

Laurie stared at her potential fiancé-to-be and shook her head. She couldn't believe they could be so far apart on such an important issue when they were so compatible in so many other ways.

Paul tossed his napkin onto the table. "I'm frankly disappointed that your response to my business has turned out to be exactly the hackneyed one I was worried about. Now you know why I didn't tell you sooner."

"I'm disappointed myself," Laurie said. "I don't like to think of you selling guns, particularly those Bulgarian assault rifles, wherever it is you sell them. I mean, you don't sell them in this country anymore, do you?"

"It's against the law, thanks to the unconstitutional Omnibus Crime Bill," Paul said.

"That's not what I asked," Laurie said. "I know they are banned. I asked you if you sold them."

Laurie stared at Paul. For a few moments he didn't respond. His only movement was the rise and fall of his chest with his respiration. Their eyes were locked in a kind of duel.

"Aren't you going to answer?" Laurie demanded incredulously.

"It's such a stupid question," Paul said haughtily, "I don't think it deserves an answer."

"But I'd like one," Laurie said defiantly.

Paul took a drink from his brandy snifter, held the liquor in his mouth for a moment, then swallowed. "No, I don't sell Bulgarian AK-47s in the United States. Are you satisfied?"

Laurie took a sip from her cappuccino. She didn't answer herself while she mulled over the conversation. She wasn't satisfied at all. In fact she was angry about the way Paul had responded to her reasonable questions. The good side was that the anger chased away her tendency toward tears. Inflaming her further, Paul was regarding her with an irritating superciliousness.

"Frankly I'm not pleased about any of this," Laurie said. "What prompted me to ask about the nature of your work was that I had been told you were in the arms business."

"By whom?" Paul demanded.

"I don't think that's relevant," Laurie said. "But from the same source, I was told that you were convicted of cocaine possession. Is there anything you'd like to say about that?"

Paul's eyes blazed in the reflected glow from the candle on the table. "This truly is an inquisition," he snapped.

"You can call it what you like," Laurie said. "From my perspective, it's clearing the air. These are issues that I should have heard from you, not someone else."

Without warning Paul stood up. His chair tipped over backward and crashed to the floor. Other diners looked up from their quiet meals. Several waiters rushed over to right the chair.

"I've had just about as much of this as I can take," Paul snarled. Angrily he reached into his pocket and yanked out his billfold. He took several hundred-dollar bills and tossed them contemptuously onto the table.

"This should cover the entertainment," he said. Then he walked out of the restaurant.

Laurie was mortified. She'd heard about such scenes occurring in public but certainly had never been involved in one herself. Timidly she picked up her cappuccino and took a few sips. Intellectually she knew it was silly for her to pretend that she wasn't bothered by what had transpired, but she couldn't help herself. She felt bound to maintain a charade of calm decorum. She even waited until she finished her coffee to request the check.

When she emerged from the restaurant fifteen minutes later, she was mildly concerned that Paul might be waiting for her. She was relieved when he wasn't because she didn't want to talk to him, at least not for a while. She stood at the curb to get her bearings. The restaurant was on Columbus Avenue on the Upper West Side. She was about to raise her hand to flag down a taxi to take her downtown when she realized she was only twenty or so blocks from Jack's. She decided to pay him a visit. More than anything else, she needed a friend.

When she got into a cab and gave Jack's address, the driver, who was a born and bred New Yorker, turned around and asked her to repeat it. After she had, he raised his eyebrows as if to say she was crazy, and they were off.

With little traffic, the ride went quickly. The driver turned left off Columbus as soon as he could and headed north on Central Park West. Laurie had to point out Jack's building because there was no number.

"You gonna be all right, miss?" the driver inquired after she'd paid. "This is a rough neighborhood."

Laurie assured the man she'd be fine and got out of the cab.

Reaching the sidewalk she looked up at the facade of Jack's building. It looked as sad as always with only a small piece of its decorative cornice still intact and two windows on the third floor boarded up.

Every time Laurie visited she couldn't help but marvel anew that Jack was still living there. She understood about the basketball, but she thought he could find a better maintained building even if he wanted to stay in the neighborhood.

The foyer was in worse shape than the facade. At one time it had been rather grand, with a mosaic floor and marble walls. Now it was only a shadow of its former self. The floor was missing more than half of its tesserae and the walls were stained and graffiti-filled. None of the mailboxes had functioning locks. Trash littered the corners.

Laurie didn't bother with the buzzer system. She knew it didn't work. Besides, the inner door had been broken into in the distant past and never repaired.

As Laurie climbed the stairs, her resolve waned. After all, it was late, and she'd not called and was coming uninvited. She also wasn't even sure how much she wanted to talk about her evening before she'd had time to mull it over herself.

On the second-floor landing she stopped. From behind the door of the front apartment she heard yelling and screaming. She remembered that Jack had said there was an interminable argument going on in there. It made her sad to think people had such trouble getting along with each other.

Laurie debated whether she should proceed. It wasn't until she thought about how she'd feel if the tables were turned—how she'd feel if Jack showed up suddenly at her apartment when he was needing a friend. Realizing she'd be flattered, she pushed on. When she got to his door, she knocked. There was no bell.

When the door was yanked open, Laurie had to suppress a smile. The look of surprise on Jack's stubbled face reminded her of the kind of exaggerated expression a pantomimist might employ. Jack was in his boxer shorts, a V-necked T-shirt, and backless slippers. A medical book was in his hand. He obviously hadn't expected company except, perhaps, for Warren or one of his other local basketball cronies.

"Laurie!" Jack said as if she were an apparition.

Laurie merely nodded.

For an extended moment they just looked at each other.

"Can I come in?" Laurie finally asked.

"Of course," Jack said, embarrassed that he'd not invited her in sooner. He stepped to the side. As he closed the door, he remembered his state of undress. Quickly he disappeared into the bedroom to find some shorts.

Laurie walked into the center of the room. There wasn't much furniture: a couch, a chair, a bookcase made out of cinderblocks and bare lumber, and a couple of small tables. There were no paintings or pictures on the walls. The only light came from a floor lamp next to the couch, where Jack had obviously been reading. The rest of the room was lost in shadow. An open bottle of beer was on a small side table. A medical dictionary was open on the floor.

Jack reappeared moments later tucking a shirt into khaki shorts. He looked apologetic.

"I hope I'm not bothering you," Laurie said. "I know it's late."

"You're not bothering me in the slightest," Jack said. "In fact, it's a nice surprise. Can I take your coat?"

"I suppose," Laurie said. She slipped out of it and handed it to him. He made a beeline for his closet.

"How about a beer?" Jack said as he searched for a hanger.

"No, thanks," Laurie said. She sat down in the frayed and tattered armchair. Her eyes roamed the room. She knew something about what motivated Jack's domestic asceticism, and it depressed her further. It had been eight years since Jack's family had been killed in the commuter plane crash, and Laurie wished he felt freer to enjoy his life.

"How about something else?" Jack asked as he came into the cone of light from the floor lamp. "Water, tea, or juice? I even have Gatorade."

"I'm fine, actually," Laurie said. "I just had a big dinner."

"Oh," Jack said simply. He sat down on the couch.

"I really do hope you don't mind me dropping in on you like this," Laurie said. "I was at a restaurant not too far away on Columbus Avenue near the Museum of Natural History."

"I'm pleased," Jack said. "I'm glad to see you."

"So I just thought I'd stop by," Laurie said. "Since I was so close."

"It's okay," Jack said. "Really. I don't mind at all. Honest."

"Thanks," Laurie said.

"Did something happen at dinner?" Jack questioned.

"Yes," Laurie said. "A bit of unpleasantness."

"I'm sorry," Jack said. "Was it because of what Lou and I told you this afternoon?"

"That had something to do with it," Laurie said.

"Do you want to talk about it?"

"Not really," Laurie said. "I suppose that sounds illogical, since I've come here to see you instead of going home to my apartment to be by myself."

"Hey, nobody's going to force you to talk about something you don't want to talk about."

Laurie nodded.

Jack couldn't tell if she was really okay or if she was on the verge of tears.

"Let's talk about you," Laurie said, breaking the silence.

"Me?" Jack questioned uneasily.

"I heard that Warren Wilson came by the office today," Laurie said. "What was that all about?"

Laurie was well acquainted with Warren and knew that he'd never visited the morgue. She and Jack had double-dated with Warren and his girlfriend, Natalie Adams, back when she and Jack had been seeing a lot of each other. They'd even gone on a wild trip to Equatorial Africa together.

"Did you ever meet Flash Thomas?" Jack asked.

Laurie shook her head. "Not that I recall."

"He's another one of the basketball regulars," Jack explained. "His sister suddenly and inexplicably died sometime last night."

"How awful," Laurie said. "Did they want you to look into it?"

Jack nodded. "It's quite a story. Do you want to hear it?"

"I'd love to," Laurie said. "But first maybe I'll take you up on the offer of something to drink. I'd love a glass of water."

While Jack went into the kitchen, he started telling the story of his afternoon. Laurie settled back and was instantly entertained. When she heard about Randolph Sanders's antics, she was indignant. "The nerve of sending the body out!" she said with emotion. "After you went to the effort of going all the way out there."

Jack shrugged. "To tell you the truth, I wasn't all that surprised. In my estimation, he's always had a chip on his shoulder towards us Manhattan MEs."

"I think he feels as if he's been unfairly passed over either as the Brooklyn chief or the deputy chief over here," Laurie said.

"He's been passed over, all right, but for good reason," Jack added.

When Jack got to the part about forcing his way into the funeral home to get the body fluid samples from Connie Davydov, Laurie found herself laughing so hard, she choked on her water.

Jack went on to tell Laurie about all the possible causes of death he'd come up with. He ended by admitting that Peter Letterman had found nothing; all the assays were negative, even the stomach contents.

"Interesting," Laurie said while she pondered all the points Jack had raised. "Too bad you couldn't have done a quick autopsy."

"I was lucky to get the skin sample," Jack said. "But what specifically would you have been looking for, other than the usual?"

"The EMTs specifically said she was cyanotic?" Laurie questioned.

"Yup," Jack said. "And they found low arterial oxygen when she got to the hospital to confirm it. That's why I thought the culprit was some drug that had depressed her respiration. I was so sure that when Peter reported he'd come up with zilch, I was stunned."

"I would have liked to make sure she didn't have a congenital right-to-left shunt that had reopened."

"I've never seen anything like that," Jack said.

"Well, it would explain the clinical situation."

"Any other ideas?" Jack asked. "Does any particular kind of poison or drug overdose come to mind?"

"If Peter didn't find anything in her stomach contents, I can't imagine what it could be," Laurie said. "But did you consider methemoglobinemia?"

"No, but isn't that rather rare?" Methemoglobinemia was a condition where the hemoglobin was rendered incapable of carrying oxygen.

"Well, you're asking me for something that causes cyanosis," Laurie said. "You should at least consider the nitrates and nitrites which can cause methemoglobinemia. Even the sulfonamides."

"But wouldn't that only be with someone who was congenitally susceptible?" Jack asked.

"Probably in relation to the sulfonamides," Laurie said. "But not necessarily with the nitrates and nitrites. Still, if you want to be complete, you have to consider it."

"Okay, you're right," Jack said. "I'll ask Peter to assay for them in the morning. Anything else?"

Laurie thought for a few more minutes, but then shook her head.

"There's one more twist to this story," Jack said. He then went on to tell Laurie about the rat die-off in the same Brooklyn neighborhood where Connie Davydov had lived.

"Do you think there's an association?"

Jack shrugged. "Your guess is as good as mine, but it is a curious coincidence." He told Laurie that Connie apparently lived in an old cottage in an enclave of similar buildings. He mentioned his idea about the plumbing being primitive.

"Seems like a far-fetched connection to me. If something deadly leaked up from the sewer, why would it only be in one house?"

"You got me," Jack admitted. "But let's go on to my other mystery." Next, Jack told Laurie about Ted's further analysis of the tiny glittering star. "It's as if the star were made of flypaper and dropped into a bowl of anthrax spores."

"Why is it that you get all the interesting cases?" Laurie teased.

"Come on!" Jack said. "I'm serious. Can you explain it?

Remember, I cultured all around the star, including the blotter it was sitting on and the desk itself. The PCR test is so sensitive it can detect as little as just a few spores. Everything was clean."

"You've stumped me again," Laurie said. She glanced at her watch. "Wow! It's after midnight, and I'm keeping us both up." She got to her feet.

"Are you going to be okay?" Jack asked. "You're welcome to stay here. You can have the bed. Half the time I fall asleep out here on the couch anyway."

"Thanks for the offer," Laurie said. "You've been very hospitable, but I really should go home. I don't have clothes for tomorrow or anything else."

"It's your call," Jack said. "You're more than welcome. But if you do go, at least promise me you'll give me a buzz when you get home. It's late to be wandering around even your neighborhood."

"Will do," Laurie said. She gave Jack a sustained hug.

Jack accompanied Laurie down the stairs and walked her to the corner. It was much easier to catch a cab on Central Park West.

As Laurie rode downtown she thought about the evening. She was thankful for Jack's hospitality and friendship. Talking with him—even just about work—had calmed her down considerably and provided her with some perspective. What had disturbed her most about the episode with Paul was her inability to have a dialogue with him. She didn't think of herself as being so rigid that she couldn't agree to disagree on certain points, although that didn't include his possibly selling illegal weapons. But if she and Paul couldn't communicate, then Laurie saw no future for the relationship irrespective of their apparent day-to-day compatibility.

By the time Laurie got to her own street, her thoughts had turned to the case Jack had told her about, and she smiled anew about his experience in the funeral home. She hoped he'd not get into trouble for it or for the visit to the Brooklyn ME's office. She was well aware that Harold Bingham and Calvin Washington had little patience for Jack's maverick methods despite their appreciation of his intelligence and competence.

As Laurie undid the myriad locks on her door, her neighbor's door creaked open. As per usual, Laurie caught a fleeting glimpse of Debra Engler's frizzy gray hair and bloodshot eye. Debra saw fit to remind Laurie of the lateness of the hour.

Laurie didn't respond. Her neighbor's nosiness at any hour of the day or night was the only thing Laurie couldn't stand about her living arrangement. She slammed her apartment door in protest and redid all the locks. She'd been directly rude to the woman on several occasions and had even told her to mind her own business, all without success.

Laurie petted Tom-2 and took off her coat in that order. Her affectionate Burmese was insistent and would have climbed up her leg if she'd tried to execute the two moves in reverse order. She even had to put the purring cat on her lap while she phoned Jack.

"Are you still awake?" Laurie questioned when Jack answered with a sleepy-sounding voice.

"Mostly," Jack answered.

"I'm checking in, as requested," Laurie said. "I'm home safe."

"I wish you'd stayed," Jack said.

Laurie wondered what he truly meant, but from previous experience, she knew better than to try to get him to explain. Besides, it was late. Instead she said, "I thought about Connie Davydov on the way home."

"Did you come up with any new ideas?"

"I did," Laurie said. "I thought of something else you could have Peter look for."

"Good. What is it?"

"Botulinum toxin," Laurie said. "It would have to be a high level, meaning she'd gotten a big dose."

There was a silence.

"Jack, are you still there?"

"Yeah, I'm here," Jack said. "Are you serious?"

"Of course I'm serious," Laurie said. "What do you think about botulism as the cause of death?"

"To use your words, it seems far-fetched," Jack said. "There were no cranial nerve or bulbar symptoms or, for that matter, any symptoms reported suggestive of botulism. Supposedly she walked into the bathroom and collapsed."

"But botulinum toxin certainly depresses respiration and would cause cyanosis," Laurie said.

"Yeah, but how many cases are there in a year?"

"More cases than of anthrax," Laurie said. "And you just had one of those."

"Okay, I get your point," Jack said. "I'll add it to the list along with the nitrates, nitrites, and sulfonamides that I'll give to Peter in the morning."

"Thanks for being there for me tonight," Laurie said. "It meant a lot to me."

"Hey, anytime!" Jack said.

Laurie hung up the phone and snuggled briefly with Tom-2. The thought went through her mind that Jack would be so wonderful if he . . . if he didn't act like Jack. Laurie laughed at the absurdity of the thought and got up to get ready for bed.

SIXTEEN

Jack could not remember a time in his life when he'd been more preoccupied by so many disparate problems. First, there was Laurie, who confused him both in her behavior and his own reaction to it. After she'd left early that morning, he'd had a devil of a time getting to sleep. He kept mulling over everything she'd said and done in the previous forty-eight hours. He'd still been feeling guilty about his jealous reaction to her engagement news and angry at her response to his attempt at apology, when she'd arrived on his doorstep unannounced. He didn't know what to make of it all.

And second, there were the two mysterious cases. Try as he might, he'd not been able to come up with an explanation for the grossly contaminated tiny star. As far as Connie Davydov was concerned, his strong suspicion that she'd been poisoned with a respiratory-depressant drug had been shot full of holes by the toxicology department, and despite several hours of reading and even more hours of thinking, he'd not been able to come up with a replacement theory. Laurie's suggestion of

methemoglobinemia was the only idea that he thought had
even a slight chance of being correct.

The last problem that was weighing on Jack was the need
to come up with some justification for his behavior at both the
Brooklyn ME's office and Strickland's Funeral Home. Bingham had just bawled him out the day before for something
that was tame by comparison. If and when Bingham got wind
of what had happened in Brooklyn, he'd be livid, and would
demand an explanation Jack was ill-prepared to give. For the
first time in his career at the Office of the Chief Medical Examiner, he truly thought that come evening, he might be on
forced administrative leave.

Not only did Jack have trouble getting to sleep, he also
woke up earlier than usual. Still trying to come to terms with
his various dilemmas, he bicycled to work just as dawn was
breaking. That gave him an hour to work in his office before
going down to the ID room.

When he arrived, Vinnie Amendola was in the process of
making coffee, and Dr. George Fontworth had just begun
looking over the cases that had come in during the night.

"Excuse me, George," Jack said. "What kind of day does it
look like autopsy-wise: heavy or light?"

George's sleepy eyes ran down his list.

"I'd say the light side of normal."

"Good," Jack said. "I'd like to take a paper day if you
wouldn't mind." A paper day was when one of the medical
examiners chose not to do any autopsies, but rather, took the
time to catch up on his never-ending paperwork. Normally
paper days were scheduled in advance.

"What's the matter?" George asked. "Are you ill?"

George wasn't being sarcastic. It was well known around
the office that Jack was a glutton for punishment when it came
to doing postmortems. He did more than anyone else, and by
choice. When anyone asked why, he said that keeping himself
busy kept him out of trouble.

"Health-wise, I'm fine," Jack said. "I've just got a lot of
things piling up."

"I don't see it being a problem," George said accommodatingly. "Of course, it might be a different story if someone calls in sick at the last moment."

"If that happens," Jack said, "just give a shout."

Jack walked over to the coffeepot.

"Are you finished yet, maestro?" Jack asked Vinnie.

"You can have a cup in two seconds," Vinnie said.

"Do you have any idea when Peter Letterman usually arrives?" Jack asked.

"The toxicology lab opens officially at nine," Vinnie said. "But I happen to know that Peter gets in early, usually before eight."

"Gosh, he spends a lot of time here," Jack commented.

"You should talk," Vinnie said.

With coffee in hand, Jack went back to the elevator to return to his office. He was surprised to run into Laurie, who was just arriving. Jack looked at his watch. He was amazed to see her.

"This is early for you, isn't it?" he asked.

"It is," Laurie admitted. "I'm turning over a new leaf. I'm going to concentrate on work for a while. It's something I always do when I'm upset about something."

"I see," Jack said. He wasn't sure if he should ask her what she was upset about or not.

"I want to thank you again for last night," Laurie said. "You really helped."

"But I didn't do anything," Jack said.

"You were there and you made me feel comfortable," Laurie said. "You acted like a friend, and that was what I needed."

They boarded the elevator. Jack pushed the button for the fifth floor.

"Do you want to tell me what happened at your dinner last night?" Jack asked hesitantly.

Laurie smiled. "Not yet. I've got to process it a bit more myself. But thanks for asking."

Jack smiled weakly He shifted his weight. It was amazing how easily Laurie could make him feel uncomfortably awkward.

"Are you going to work on your mystery cases today?" Laurie asked.

"I'm going to try," Jack said. "Any other ideas for me about Connie Davydov?"

"Only what I gave you last night," Laurie said.

"If you think of anything, don't hesitate to tell me," Jack said. "I might need it to keep the bounty hunters at bay."

Laurie nodded. She knew what Jack was referring to.

They walked down the corridor together. When they got to Jack's door they stopped.

"There is one thing I'd like to say," Laurie offered. "I want to apologize for the way I acted when you and Lou told me about Paul yesterday afternoon. I wasn't happy to hear it, but as you suggested, I was taking it out on the messengers. You two were right to tell me, although I'm not sure Lou was right to look it up in the first place."

"Jealousy makes people do strange things," Jack said. "And I'm speaking for myself."

"I'll take that as a compliment," Laurie said. "And good luck today."

"Thanks," Jack said. "I'll need it."

Jack went into his office and got back to work. He concentrated on the prisoner-in-custody case. If nothing else, he hoped to have that done by tomorrow to keep Calvin happy. While he worked, he glanced up at the wall clock repeatedly. When it got close to eight, he put down his pen and descended a floor to the toxicology lab.

As he approached the door, it didn't look promising. It was closed and the lab appeared dark through the frosted glass. Jack tried the door anyway. It was locked. As he turned around to head back to the stairs, he caught sight of Peter on his way along the corridor from the direction of the elevator. He'd just arrived, as evidenced by his coat over his arm.

"Did you think of something else to test for?" Peter asked as he arrived at the laboratory door. He had his key out.

"I did," Jack said. "Or actually, Dr. Laurie Montgomery did."

Jack explained about the methemoglobin idea as he followed the lab tech into the lab and his tiny windowless office. Peter nodded as he hung up his coat.

"That means I should look for things like amyl nitrite, sodium nitrite, and nitroprusside," Peter said as he donned his white coat. "Did this patient have a history of heart disease?"

"Not that I know of," Jack said.

"Then I can't imagine she'd be taking any of those drugs," Peter said. "But there's a handful of other substances that can cause methemoglobinemia. Do you want me to test for all of them, whether or not she'd be likely to be taking them as a medication?"

"Please!" Jack said. "I'm desperate."

"Okay," Peter said agreeably. He started out of his office. Jack trailed him like a puppy.

"When can you do it?" Jack asked.

"I'll set it up right away," Peter said. "It's better for me to get it going before Dr. DeVries gets here. Otherwise he'd start asking questions."

"I do appreciate your help, Peter," Jack said. "I hope I can reciprocate in some way. Speaking about your chief, do you happen to know about the status of David Jefferson's samples?"

"Is that the prisoner-in-custody case?" Peter asked.

"It sure is," Jack voiced.

"John was complaining about it yesterday," Peter said. "As far as I know it's done. Anyway it was positive for cocaine if that's what you wanted to know."

"Thank God for small favors," Jack said. "Calvin is going to be jubilant. Now if I can only be so lucky with Connie Davydov."

"I'll give it my best shot," Peter promised.

Jack started out of the lab but stopped when he remembered Laurie's final suggestion. "There's one other thing that Laurie suggested to test for," he called back to Peter. "Botulinum toxin."

Peter waved to indicate that he'd heard.

Jack climbed the stairs. With the Jefferson case sure to be completed by the Thursday deadline with what Calvin would consider a positive spin, there seemed to be a pinpoint of light at the end of Jack's current tunnel of problems.

Back in the office, Jack ran into Chet, who was brimming with news of his previous evening's experience at aerobics.

Not only had the girl with the curvaceous figure shown up, but she'd deigned to have a yogurt fruit drink with him after the class. Jack had to wait until he'd heard all about the woman before he could get a word in edgewise.

"Tell me, Casanova," Jack said. "Would you know how to get ahold of any of those vets who gave that seminar you went to yesterday?"

"I think so," Chet said. "Why?"

"I want to find out if and when they figure out what killed those rats. Also, whether any more of them had anthrax."

"I'll try to find out sometime today," Chet said.

"I'd appreciate it," Jack said, and quickly redirected his attention to his work spread out on his desk.

"Aren't you doing any posts today?" Chet asked.

"I've taken an unscheduled paper day," Jack said without looking up.

"Are you sick?"

Jack laughed. "That's what George asked. I wish I were. It would be a convenient excuse. I'm just trying to eliminate one of the reasons the front office is always on my case, namely, being perennially behind getting my cases signed out."

"One of the main reasons you're always behind is because you take on too many cases in the first place," Chet said.

"Whatever," Jack mumbled as he began scanning a section of David Jefferson's brain under his microscope.

After Chet left for the pit, Jack kicked the door shut to avoid the distraction of the casual visitor. Still, he found that he couldn't truly concentrate. As preoccupied as he was about everything, he was unable to keep himself from glancing up at the clock every so often. Particularly as the time approached ten, he started to worry about the phone ringing. He fully expected Cheryl to call with the standard message that the chief wanted to see him ASAP. After all, by that time in the morning both Dr. Jim Bennett and Gordon Strickland would have had more than enough opportunity to phone their complaints about Jack.

As if on cue, the phone did ring at ten sharp. Despite Jack's expecting it, its jangle unnerved him. For several rings he considered not answering. But recognizing the futility of putting

off the inevitable, he picked it up. To his surprise, it wasn't
Cheryl. It was Peter Letterman.

"I've got some surprising news for you," Peter said.

"Good or bad?" Jack questioned.

"I suppose you'll think it's good," Peter said. "Connie
Davydov did not have methemoglobinemia, but she does have
botulinum toxin in all the samples you gave me, including her
stomach contents."

"Good Lord!" Jack said. "This isn't some kind of sick joke,
is it?"

"Not at all," Peter said. "I ran several of the assays twice
just to be sure. The results were strongly positive, suggesting
the victim had a large dose. I can follow up with some quantitative tests, but that will take a while. I wanted you to know
the qualitative results right away."

"Thanks," Jack said. "I owe you."

"Glad to be of assistance," Peter said before ringing off.

Jack hung up the phone slowly. He felt a mix of emotions.
One was a kind of elation at the validation of his suspicions
about Connie Davydov having been poisoned. The other was
shock. Botulism probably was the last thing he expected.

Thrusting his chair back from his desk, Jack jumped up.
Throwing open his door, he ran down to Laurie's office. He
wanted her to be the first to know the news, since botulism
had been her suggestion. Unfortunately, her office was empty.
She was undoubtedly down in the autopsy room.

Back at his desk, Jack's mind churned over whom to call
first. With a delicious sense of reprisal, he settled on Randolph
Sanders. It took a few moments to get the doctor on the line.
He'd been in the middle of an autopsy. Jack had insisted to
the operator it was an emergency. When Randolph finally answered, his voice had an understandable urgency.

"Ah, hello, Randolph," Jack said buoyantly. "This is your
favorite colleague, Jack Stapleton."

"I was informed this was an emergency," Randolph
growled.

"And indeed it is," Jack said. "Just this moment I've been
informed that your case, Connie Davydov, which we had rea-

son to discuss yesterday, apparently succumbed to a rather large dose of botulinum toxin."

A pregnant pause ensued.

"How was this determined?" Randolph demanded.

"By my personal persistence," Jack said. "I went to the funeral home, where the director graciously allowed me to take some appropriate body fluid samples."

"I'd not heard that had occurred," Randolph said with a voice that had lost a good deal of its edge.

"Really?" Jack questioned. "I'd assumed you had. Nevertheless, as a favor to you, since we hold each other in such high esteem, I'm calling you rather than rushing down and informing Dr. Harold Bingham."

"I appreciate that," Randolph managed.

"Of course there is a practical aspect," Jack said. "Connie Davydov is a Brooklyn case. I would assume you'd like to get the body back as soon as possible. I'll also leave in your capable hands the chore of alerting the proper authorities."

"Of course," Randolph said. "Thank you."

"Not at all," Jack said, thoroughly enjoying himself. "It's nice to know we can help each other out on occasion."

Jack disconnected. He couldn't suppress a broad smile. Revenge had been sweet. It had been easy to tell just how much Randolph had been squirming.

Next, Jack put in a call to Warren. Jack briefly explained what he'd found concerning Connie and asked for Flash's work number. It took Warren a few minutes, but he found it and gave it to Jack.

Flash worked at a moving and storage company, and it took a few minutes for him to be located. When he finally came on the line he was out of breath. He'd been moving boxes around the storage facility.

"I got the answer about Connie," Jack said after he'd identified himself. "As Warren suggested yesterday, I think you're going to have to take your anger out on the basketball court and not Connie's husband."

"He didn't kill her?"

"It doesn't seem that way," Jack said. "She apparently died of botulism. Have you ever heard of that?"

"I think so," Flash said. "Isn't that some kind of food poisoning?"

"Generally, yes," Jack said. "It's caused by a toxin that a specific type of bacteria manufactures. What makes this bacteria particularly dangerous is that it can grow without oxygen. You used to hear about it mainly in connection with canned goods when the food wasn't heated enough during processing to kill the spores. But in your sister's case, the important thing for you to understand is that it appears that foul play wasn't involved."

"Are you sure?"

"I just got the report back from the laboratory," Jack said. "The technician assured me they checked the results. I'm personally confident she died of botulism, and except for a few apocryphal stories of the toxin being used to assassinate Reinhard Heyrich, one of Hitler's cronies, back in World War II, I've never heard of the agent being used in a deliberate poisoning. The stuff is not easy to come by. The idea of Connie's husband using it would be giving him more credit than he deserves."

"Damn!" Flash exclaimed.

"I tell you what," Jack said. "Warren and I will let you win at basketball the next time we're on opposing teams."

Flashed laughed halfheartedly. "You're too much, Doc! As competitive as you and Warren are, I can't see you guys throwing a game, no-how. Anyway, thanks for looking into this mess for me. I appreciate it."

"I'm glad to have been able to help," Jack said. "Now I have a question for you. What's Connie's husband's name?"

"Yuri," Flash said, practically spitting the name. "Why do you ask?"

"I'm afraid I have to call him up," Jack said. "With Connie passing away with botulism, Yuri is certainly at risk."

"I couldn't care less," Flash said.

"I can appreciate that," Jack said. "And as your friend, I couldn't care either. But as a doctor, I feel differently. Would you mind giving me his phone number?"

"Do I have to?" Flash asked.

"I suppose I could look it up," Jack said. "Or get it from

the Brooklyn office. But it would just be easier if you gave it to me."

"I feel like I'm doing the turd a favor," Flash complained before giving Jack the number.

Jack wrote it down. They talked for a few more minutes about possibly playing ball that evening before saying good-bye and hanging up.

Once they did, Jack immediately dialed the Brighton Beach number. As the call went through, he mentally outlined what he'd say. He wondered if Yuri Davydov would have an accent, and if he truly was the ogre that Flash believed he was. But Jack didn't get through. The line was occupied.

In a significantly more buoyant mood, Jack returned to his paperwork. With enhanced efficiency, he completed yet another of his cases. After placing it on top of the completed pile, he tried the Brighton Beach number again. He got the same busy signal.

Jack wasn't surprised. He imagined the man had a lot of calls to make in the aftermath of his wife's death. But as the morning wore on, and Jack continued to try to place the call with the same lack of success, he finally lost patience. He dialed the operator and asked for Yuri's telephone to be checked. A few minutes later the operator returned to say there was no conversation on the line.

"What does that mean?" Jack asked.

"It's either off the hook or out of order," the operator said. "I can connect you to repair if you'd like."

"Never mind," Jack said. He realized that Yuri was most likely at home but unwilling to talk to anybody. As understandable as it might be for the man to take his phone off the hook, it still frustrated Jack not to be able to get through; sometimes it seemed that nothing was easy. All he wanted to do was contact the man to warn him about possible botulism infection. Having put the case back in Randolph Sanders's lap, he expected the Brooklyn office to follow up with the case as they were legally bound to do. That meant alerting the Department of Health and ultimately Jack's nemesis, Dr. Clint Abelard, the city epidemiologist. As Jack had been duly informed on several occasions, it was Clint's job to do the follow-up, which, of course, included contacting Yuri Davy-dov. Yet, as a physician, Jack felt honor-bound to notify the widower himself.

Jack absently played with the telephone cord while ponder-ing the situation. There was always the chance that the Brook-lyn office could run into trouble by not getting the body back. After all, Jack reasoned, the body could have been cremated. If that was the case and no further samples were available to confirm the diagnosis, a delay would be inevitable. What it all boiled down to was that Yuri Davydov might not learn about his risk in time to make a difference.

Pulling open one of the drawers of his desk, Jack took out a map of New York City. He opened it to the Brooklyn section and searched for Brighton Beach. The assumption it was somewhere on the waterfront helped; he found it next to Coney Island, jutting out into the Atlantic Ocean.

Jack estimated that Brighton Beach was about fifteen miles away. He'd never ridden out to that area on his bike but he'd been as far as Brooklyn's Prospect Park on several weekend occasions and remembered how to get there. From the map he could see that Brighton Beach was a straight shot down Coney Island Avenue from the base of the park.

Checking his watch, Jack decided a bicycle jaunt to Brigh-ton Beach would be a nice way to spend his lunch hour, even if it turned out to be a two-hour-plus trip. Although Yuri Davydov's health was his main reason for wanting to go out there, he could also justify the outing as a reward for having made a significant dent in his paperwork and for coming up with a compelling alibi for the previous day's escapades. But what really clinched the decision was the knowledge that it happened to be a particularly gorgeous Indian summer day with strong sunshine, warm temperature, and gentle wind. As Jack explained it to himself, it might be the last great day weather-wise before winter's onslaught.

Before he left, Jack looked for Laurie again to tell her about the botulism, but he was told that she was still in the autopsy room. Jack decided he'd see her when he got back.

The trip was even better than Jack imagined it would be, especially going over the Brooklyn Bridge and riding through

Prospect Park. The Coney Island Avenue portion was less
stimulating but still enjoyable. As he passed Neptune Avenue,
he noticed something he'd not expected: all the business signs
were written in the Cyrillic alphabet.

As soon as Jack saw Oceanview Avenue, he pulled over
and asked directions to Oceanview Lane. It wasn't until he'd
asked three people that he found someone who could tell him
where to go.

Jack was surprised by the neighborhood. Just as Flash had
described it, there was a whole section of small wood-frame
houses jammed together in a cheek-by-jowl hodgepodge.
Some were reasonably maintained while others were dilapidated. Fences constructed of a mélange of materials separated
individual properties. Some yards were clean and planted with
fall flowers, while others served as junk heaps for doorless
refrigerators, TVs with their guts hanging out, broken toys,
and other discarded refuse. Roof lines angled off in bewildering juxtapositions, a testament to the uncoordinated way the
original structures had been enlarged. A forest of rusted TV
antennae sprouted like dead weeds from the ridgepoles.

Jack slowed and looked at individual buildings. Some still
had definite Victorian embellishments. Most were in sore need
of paint and repair. About half had freestanding garages. There
were a lot of dogs that barked and snarled as Jack rode past.
Very few people were in evidence and no children save for a
few infants in the care of their mothers. Jack remembered that
it was a school day.

The area had a grid of normal streets, but also numerous
lanes, some named, some not. The lanes were narrow, some
so narrow that they permitted only pedestrian traffic, and the
houses on them could only be reached by foot. Across all the
lanes stretched a spiderweb of telephone and electric wires.

Jack located Oceanview Lane with the help of a handpainted
sign precariously nailed to a telephone pole. He turned into
the lane and immediately had to pay attention to the large
cracks in the concrete pavement or his bike would have toppled over.

Few of the houses had numbers on them, although Jack did
see number thirteen written on a garbage can. Assuming the

next building was fifteen, he continued until he was abreast of it. The structure was similar to the others although it sat on a full foundation rather than the more typical cinderblock piers. It also had a two-car garage. The roof was asphalt shingle; a number of the shingles were missing. The screen door was torn. The downspout at the corner was broken, and the top part angled off precariously. The whole thing looked as though it might fall over if the front door was slammed hard enough.

A waist-high chain-link fence separated the tiny, overgrown front lawn from the concrete alleyway. Jack locked his bike to it. He opened the gate and approached the door. Venetian blinds in the windows on either side of the door were closed shut, so Jack couldn't peek in.

After vainly searching for a doorbell, Jack opened the torn screen door and knocked. When there was no response, he knocked harder. After one more attempt with sustained knocking, Jack gave up. He allowed the screen door to close with a thump. He was discouraged. After making such an effort to get there, he still was not going to be able to contact Yuri Davydov.

Jack was about to walk back to his bike when he became aware of a continuous, low-pitched hum. Turning back to the door, he listened. Now that he concentrated on the sound, he realized that it wasn't continuous but rather modulated, like a very distant helicopter or a fan with very large blades. Jack eyed the house warily. It didn't seem large enough for the size fan that would yield such a vibration.

Jack glanced around at the other houses in the immediate neighborhood. All seemed shuttered as if their owners were at work or at least not at home. The only person in sight was an elderly gentleman sitting in his yard who was totally unconcerned about Jack's presence.

Jack walked across the lawn to peer down between Yuri's house and his neighbor's. The separation was only about six feet, and it was bisected by the chain-link fence. After another glance at the elderly man, Jack walked between the buildings to emerge in Yuri's tiny backyard. There he found what looked like a metal furnace vent issuing forth from a recently patched hole in the house's foundation. The vent angled up-

ward to extend higher than Jack could reach. By touching the
vent and feeling the vibration Jack could tell he'd at least
found the exhaust for the fan. Considering the size of the
house, the kind of furnace the vent suggested seemed like
overkill.

Jack continued to circle the cottage. On the side facing the
garage was another door where Jack again knocked. Cupping
his hands around his face, he peered through one of the small
glass panels. He could see an L-shaped room that served as
both living room and kitchen.

Leaving the door, Jack walked along the garage toward the
front of the house. As he arrived at the patch of lawn, a
bearded man appeared walking along the alleyway carrying a
bag of groceries. Jack hadn't seen him until the last possible
moment because the garage had blocked his view.

This sudden appearance of the individual within arm's reach
made Jack start. He hadn't realized quite how uneasy his tres-
passing had made him. But as startled as Jack was, it was
apparently less than the stranger. The man dropped his groceries while trying vainly to get his right hand out of his
jacket.

"I beg your pardon," Jack intoned.

The man took a moment to recover. Jack used the time to
come out through the gate and help retrieve some of the man's
purchases, which had fallen out of the bag.

"I'm awfully sorry to have startled you," Jack said as he
picked up several boxes of cake flour, a frozen dinner, a tin
of cinnamon, and a bottle of vodka, which miraculously had
not broken.

"It's not your fault," the man said. He squatted down,
righted the bag, and began repacking his groceries. At the
same time his eyes kept nervously darting around as if he was
afraid someone else might startle him.

Jack handed over what he'd picked up. He couldn't help
but have noticed the man's strong Slavic accent. It seemed
appropriate given his dark beard and Russian-style hat.

"Are you a resident of this enclave?" Jack asked.

The man hesitated for a moment before answering. "I am,"
he said.

"Do you happen to know Yuri Davydov? He lives here in number fifteen."

The man made a point to look around Jack and study the building.

"Vaguely," he said. "Why do you ask?"

Jack struggled to get his wallet out of his back pocket. As he did so, he asked the man if he was Russian. The man said he was.

"I noticed all the signs up the street were in the Cyrillic alphabet," Jack said.

"There are a lot of Russians living in Brighton Beach."

Jack nodded. He opened his wallet and showed the man his shiny medical examiner's badge. Jack appreciated that the official emblem generally made people more cooperative and willing to answer questions.

"My name is Dr. Jack Stapleton."

"Mine is Yegor."

"Glad to meet you, Yegor," Jack said. "I'm a medical examiner from Manhattan. Would you by any chance know where Yuri Davydov is at the moment? I knocked on his door, but he's not at home."

"He's probably out driving his taxi," Yegor said.

"I see." To Jack, that meant that either Yuri was emotionally strong or there'd been the lack of domestic bliss Flash suggested. "When do you think he'll be getting home?"

"Not until late tonight," Yegor said.

"Like nine or ten?" Jack asked.

"Something like that," Yegor said. "Is there a problem?"

Jack nodded. "I need to talk with him. Do you know what taxi company he works for?"

"He just works for himself," Yegor said.

"That's too bad," Jack said.

"I'd heard that his wife just died," Yegor said. "Is that what you want to talk with him about?"

"It is," Jack said.

"Would you like to tell me what it is in case I see him?" Yegor said.

"Just tell him we know what killed his wife," Jack said. "But the important thing is that he call me because what killed his wife is very dangerous, and he could be at risk. Let me give you one of my cards, which you can give to him if you see him."

Jack took out a business card. "I'll even include my home number." Jack wrote on the back and handed the card to Yegor.

Yegor examined the front of the card. "Is this the address where you work?"

"That's it," Jack said. He tried to think if there were any other questions he could ask Yegor, but none came to mind. "Thank you for your help."

"It was my pleasure," Yegor said. "How late will you be at work?"

"Probably at least until six," Jack said.

"I'll tell Yuri if I see him," Yegor said. Then he nodded to Jack before continuing on his way.

Jack watched the receding Russian for a moment before looking back at Yuri Davydov's house. That was when he thought about leaving one of his cards under the door. The only potential downside was that when and if Clint Abelard came out and the card was brought to his attention, he'd have evidence of what he called Jack's interference. Then Jack would undoubtedly hear about it from Bingham.

"Ah, who the hell cares," Jack said out loud. He got out another card. On the back he wrote a message for Yuri to call him ASAP. He included his direct extension as well as his home number. Then he went back up the front walk and slipped the card under the door.

Jack unlocked his bicycle and pedaled away. He had it in his mind to take a quick loop around Brighton Beach before heading back to the office. He was mainly just curious about the area, but he thought that if he happened to see a veterinary office, he'd stop in to ask if they had information about the rat die-off.

SEVENTEEN

Yuri had never been more agitated in his entire life. The moment he'd come face-to-face with Jack Stapleton, it had felt as if his heart would leap from his chest. And to make matters worse, he hadn't been able to get the Glock out of his pocket, since it had gotten caught up in the lining of his jacket.

As it turned out, the vain struggle was for the best. If he had managed to get the gun out, his situation would be worse than it was. Jack Stapleton hadn't caused him to panic so much as the fear that Flash Thomas was there as well. Gordon Strickland had said they'd been together at the funeral home.

As soon as Yuri was sure that the medical examiner was by himself, he'd collected his thoughts enough to deal with him. He'd been stunned to learn that Jack Stapleton had somehow seemingly made the diagnosis of botulism.

After walking away from Jack, Yuri had not looked back. He'd gone directly to a local bar. Only then had he dared to glance behind him to see if Jack Stapleton had followed him.

Not seeing the doctor, Yuri had gone in, ordered a vodka, and slugged it down.

"You want another?" the bartender asked. Thankfully, it was someone Yuri didn't know. If he did, Yuri would have worried about his commenting about the beard. Yuri was afraid to take it off.

"A double," Yuri said. He was still trembling. The other issue that bothered him was that Jack Stapleton had obviously been walking around his property. That meant that he'd seen the laboratory vent in the backyard. Yuri had no idea what the doctor might have made of that.

The other thing Yuri worried about was whether Jack had looked through the back window of the garage. If he had, he might have seen the pest control truck. That could be as potentially damaging as seeing the laboratory vent.

Yuri glanced at his watch. He didn't know if he'd allowed enough time for Jack to leave, but he couldn't wait any longer. He paid his bar tab, polished off his drink, and picked up his groceries.

Walking back to the mouth of Oceanview Lane, he hesitated. He looked at his house and saw no one. Encouraged, Yuri started down the alley. He had his right hand in his pocket wrapped around the pistol butt, much as he had before. The difference this time was that he made sure the gun wouldn't be caught in the jacket lining. He was not about to be surprised again, particularly not by Flash.

The house appeared quiet. Yuri scanned the immediate neighborhood. With Jack nowhere in sight, he went through his front gate and rushed around to the side door. As quickly as he could manage, he got himself inside and locked the door behind him.

Leaning against the door he let out a deep breath of relief. A rapid glance around the interior suggested that no one had been inside. He set the groceries down and immediately descended the steps to the basement. He breathed another sigh of relief to see that the lock on the lab was undisturbed.

Back in the kitchen Yuri put the frozen dinner and vodka into the freezer. The rest of the boxes he left on the table. On his way to the bathroom he saw the business card on the floor by the front door. He picked it up. As he expected, it was another one of Jack's. Yuri added it to the one already in his pocket.

Yuri pulled off the fake beard. The adhesive was driving him crazy. When he looked into the mirror he saw that he had a minor rash where the beard had been. He washed his face. Unsure of how else to treat it, he put on some aftershave lotion. Unfortunately, it stung so much it brought tears to his eyes. When he looked in the mirror again, the rash was significantly redder. It looked much worse.

Back in the kitchen Yuri got his car keys out of the cabinet. Ever since he'd been in the bar he'd been agonizing over what to do about Jack Stapleton's appearance on the scene. Much as he hated to, he decided that it was serious enough to warrant alerting Curt and risking his wrath. But he would do it in person.

First, Yuri went to the front windows. He surveyed the alleyway through the slats of the venetian blind. Except for a young woman in a babushka pushing a child in a stroller, there was no one in sight. Nor were there any strange vehicles parked near his cottage. Walking to the kitchen door, Yuri looked out at the side door of the garage. It was only a few steps away. He debated putting the beard back on but decided against it for fear of aggravating the rash. Instead, he took the gun out of his jacket, held it in his left hand, and draped a towel over it. With his keys in his right hand, he opened the door.

After one last check to make sure there was no one about, Yuri went out the door. He locked it and opened the garage within seconds. Vigilant for any surprises and careful to keep the gun at the ready, Yuri made short work of getting his cab out of the garage and the overhead door closed. Accelerating down the alleyway, he began to relax. He turned out into Oceanview Avenue and headed for the Shore Parkway, the fastest route into Manhattan at that time of the day. As he motored up the entrance ramp, he bent over and stuck the Glock under the front seat.

Yuri knew that Curt would be furious at Yuri's upcoming visit to the firehouse, but Yuri was convinced he had no

choice. He could have called, but Curt would have been angry
at that as well, and Yuri was convinced it was far better to
talk to Curt face-to-face to emphasize the seriousness of the
situation. As he drove, Yuri got progressively more annoyed
that he even had to worry about Curt becoming irritated. It
was ridiculous for people working together for a common goal
to be so fearful of a partner's reaction. The only explanation
was that Curt was anti-Slavic like he was anti everything else.

The Brooklyn Battery Tunnel left Yuri in lower Manhattan.
Making sure his "off duty" sign was illuminated, he drove
north on West Street to Chambers before turning right and
working his way over to Duane Street.

Yuri slowed as he neared the firehouse. He didn't know
whether to park or not. Seeing a foursome of firemen playing
cards at a table on the sidewalk directly in front of the entrance
made him opt to stay in the car. The firehouse's huge overhead
doors had been thrown open to the glorious mid-fall day. Just
the shiny red fronts of the ladder truck and fire engine could
be seen.

Yuri pulled his cab up onto the ramp, then angled it off,
putting him parallel to the building. The men at the table
looked up from their game.

Yuri lowered his passenger-side window and leaned over.

"Excuse me!" he called. "I'm looking for Lieutenant Rogers."

"Hey, Lieutenant!" one of the men yelled over his shoulder.
"You got a visitor."

Curt emerged a few minutes later with a hand over his eyes
and squinting from the glare. Because of the bright sunshine,
the inside of the building was dark by comparison. His expression was one of curiosity until he caught sight of Yuri.
Then his countenance clouded with barely contained rage.

"What the hell are you doing here?" he snarled in a forced
whisper.

"We've got an emergency," Yuri snapped back. He reached
out with one of Jack Stapleton's business cards.

Curt took the card while casting a nervous glance over his
shoulder at his card-playing colleagues.

"What's this?" he demanded.

"Read it!" Yuri ordered. "It's what the emergency is about."

Curt looked at the card before raising his eyes back to Yuri's. Some of his irritation had metamorphosed to confusion.

"Operation Wolverine is in jeopardy," Yuri said. "We have to talk right now!"

Curt ran a worried hand through his short, blond hair. He looked around again at the card players. They were concentrating on their game.

"All right," Curt growled. "This better be important! There's a bar around the corner called Pete's. Steve and I will be there as soon as we can."

"I'll be waiting," Yuri said before accelerating down the street. He fumed about Curt's anger. In his rearview mirror he caught the firefighter studying the card briefly before turning back into the firehouse.

The bar was dark and smoky and smelled of old beer and rancid grease. There was a limited menu featuring hamburgers, fries, and soup of the day. Country music whined in the background at low volume. Every now and again, Yuri could make out a lyric about jilted love and lost opportunity. A number of men were having lunch and a brew. Yuri had to walk the entire length of the narrow tavern before finding an empty booth in the back next to the lavatory. He ordered a vodka and a hamburger and sat back. He didn't have long to wait. Curt and Steve arrived at the same time as the food.

The two firefighters slipped into the booth across from Yuri without bothering to greet him. Their vexation was palpable. They were silent while the waiter served the hamburger and placed a napkin next to it. The waiter looked at them inquiringly and they ordered a couple of drafts. When he'd left, Curt brazenly flicked Jack Stapleton's business card onto the table so that it skidded over to Yuri's side.

"Start talking!" Curt ordered. "And it better be good."

Yuri took a bite from his burger and chewed. He eyed his friends. He was being deliberately provocative by making them wait, but he didn't care. In fact, it gave him a bit of enjoyment.

"We don't have all day, for crissake," Curt snapped.

Yuri swallowed and chased his mouthful with a swig of vodka. Then, after running his tongue around the inside of his lips, he picked up the business card and tossed it back in the firefighter's direction.

"This Dr. Jack Stapleton is the medical examiner I told you about who I ran into at the Corinthian Rug Company Office."

"Big deal," Curt scoffed. "That was two days ago."

"Yesterday he showed up at the Strickland funeral home," Yuri said. "He was with Connie's brother."

"You didn't tell us that."

"I didn't think it was so important," Yuri said. "At least yesterday I didn't."

"But today you do?"

"Without doubt," Yuri said. He took another bite of his hamburger while Curt and Steve got their beers. Yuri paused until the waiter left. "Today Dr. Jack Stapleton showed up at my house."

"Why?" Curt demanded. His anger and arrogance had disappeared. Now he was concerned.

"He wanted to warn me that I was at risk for what Connie died of," Yuri said. "Apparently he's made the diagnosis she died of botulinum toxin."

"Oh, Christ!" Curt growled.

"How the hell did he do that?" Steve demanded. "You told us it wouldn't happen."

"I don't know what made him test for it," Yuri said. "But I do know he took samples from Connie's body."

"What did you say to him?" Curt asked.

"First of all, he didn't know he was talking to me," Yuri said. "When we ran into each other in the alley, I had the beard. I don't know if Stapleton would have recognized me without it, since I'd only spoken to him for a few minutes on Monday. But it was good I had it on just the same. Anyway, I told him my name was Yegor, and he believed it. I offered to convey a message to Yuri Davydov, but Stapleton wouldn't tell me what the message was, other than mentioning that Yuri Davydov might be in danger."

"But you believe he suspects botulism?" Curt asked.

"I do," Yuri replied.

"Do you think he'll be back?" Curt asked.

"Maybe not until tonight. I told him that Yuri Davydov was out driving his cab and wouldn't be home until sometime after nine or ten."

Curt looked at Steve. "I don't like this."

"Me neither," Steve said.

"I don't like it either," Yuri said. "He walked around my house. He undoubtedly saw the vent to the lab and heard the circulating fan. He might have even seen the pest control truck."

"Good God!" Curt mumbled.

"I think he's got to go, just like Connie," Yuri said. "The People's Aryan Army has to get rid of him fast, like this afternoon."

Curt nodded, then turned to Steve. "What do you think?"

"I think Yuri's right," Steve said. "If we don't act, this guy's going to single-handedly screw up Operation Wolverine."

"The trouble is, how do we get rid of him?" Curt said.

"The card has his work address," Yuri said. "He told Yegor that he'd be there until six. On the back of the card is his home telephone number. And I think he rode all the way out to Brighton Beach on a bike. Seems to me that should be enough information for the PAA."

"You're suggesting he rides his bike around the city?" Curt asked.

"That would be my guess," Yuri said.

"We could follow him when he comes out of work," Steve said. "Then hit him when he's vulnerable."

Curt nodded while he pondered. "How will we recognize him?"

Steve pointed to Yuri. "He'll have to come along to ID him."

"Can you be back here at five?" Curt asked.

"Where exactly?" Yuri demanded. "I know you don't want me at the firehouse."

"Right here in this bar," Curt said.

"I'll be here," Yuri said.

"All right, it's decided," Curt said. "The PAA will sanction Dr. Jack Stapleton. I'll make that an order." He looked at

Steve. "That means you'll have to get back to Bensonhurst right away to gather some of the troops. And for this kind of mission I think we should steal a van."

"No problem," Steve said.

"We'll need a lot of firepower," Curt said. "I want to make a fast, definitive strike. I mean, I don't want to shoot him just once and have him pull through."

"I agree, " Steve said.

"All right, that's it," Curt said. He polished off the dregs of his beer and started to slide out from the booth.

"We've got one more issue," Yuri said.

Curt held up.

"I want to move Operation Wolverine up to tomorrow, Thursday."

"Tomorrow!" Curt echoed with disbelief. "I thought you were going to have trouble meeting Friday's deadline with the anthrax powder."

"I worked most of the night and all morning," Yuri said. "With the second fermenter functioning as well as it is, we're in good shape. By tonight we'll have plenty for both lay-downs."

"I guess we could do that," Curt said. "Thursday or Friday, there's really no difference." He looked at Steve.

"No reason why not," Steve said. "The getaway is in place. That would be the critical issue."

"I think we have to do it Thursday," Yuri said. "As you mentioned last night, security is the issue. Even if we get rid of Jack Stapleton, we have no idea who he's talked to. To wait another twenty-four hours is taking a risk."

Curt gave a little chuckle. "You know, I think you're right."

"I know I'm right," Yuri said. "Provided we want to see Operation Wolverine succeed, which, of course, we all do."

"Absolutely," Curt said. "What time do you want us to come by tonight for the sausages?"

"Better make it late," Yuri said. "I'll need time to get them properly packaged. Let's say around eleven."

"Perfect," Curt said. "We'll be there." Curt slid out from the booth. Steve followed. Yuri stayed where he was.

"I want to finish my hamburger," Yuri explained.

"See you at five," Curt said. He gave a halfhearted salute before following Steve out of the bar.

Yuri watched them go. He thought their playacting at soldiering was pathetic, and he was embarrassed to be associated with them. Still, after their little meeting, he felt better than he had all day. It seemed that despite all the problems, everything was falling into place. As he chewed another mouthful of his burger he considered stopping at the travel agency on the way home to make his reservation to fly from Newark to Moscow Thursday evening. But then he thought maybe he should do it by phone, since he didn't want to take too much time. After all, he had a lot of work to do before eleven.

EIGHTEEN

Jack coasted to a stop at the OCME's loading dock and climbed off his bike. He was out of breath from the last frantic dash up First Avenue, when he'd kept up with the traffic. By doing so, he'd managed to keep the traffic lights in sync all the way from Houston Street and hadn't had to stop once.

Hoisting the bike onto his shoulder, he climbed up onto the platform and walked into the building. The jaunt to Brighton Beach had been wonderfully rewarding even if he'd failed to accomplish the original goal. Yet he'd done what he could in that regard. The rest was up to the phlegmatic bureaucracy of the Department of Health, or Yuri Davydov himself.

Jack stopped off in his office and hung his coat behind his office door. He noticed Chet's microscope was out on his desk with its light on and papers spread around it, suggesting he was in the middle of working on something, although at the moment he was nowhere to be seen. Jack guessed he'd ducked down to the vending machines on the second floor. Chet liked to snack in the afternoons.

Before sitting down at his own desk, Jack walked down the hall toward Laurie's office. He was still eager to give her the credit for the startling botulinum toxin diagnosis. Unfortunately, her door was closed, which was not normal. Jack could not remember another time when Laurie or her officemate had the door closed in the middle of the day. With a shrug Jack turned back to his office.

Jack had taken only a few steps when he heard a male voice raised in anger. He couldn't make out what had been said, but the disturbing part was that it seemed to have come from behind Laurie's closed door. Jack hesitated. A moment later he heard it again with a thump that sounded like a fist striking a metal desk or file cabinet.

Concerned, Jack returned to Laurie's door. He raised his hand to knock but wavered. Given the closed door, he worried about interfering, but then he heard a distinctive slew of swear words and another percussive thump. Then he heard Laurie's voice in a pleading tone say, "Please!"

Prompted by instinct more than thought, Jack knocked and opened the door at the same time. Laurie was backed up against the wall next to the file cabinet. She wasn't cowering, yet her face reflected a mixture of fear and indignation. Paul Sutherland stood in front of her, dressed in a dark business suit. His tanned face was flushed and his right index finger was no more than six inches from Laurie's nose. Jack's entrance had seemed to freeze him in place.

"I hope I'm not interfering," Jack said.

"But you are interfering!" Paul snapped, coming to life. "That's why the goddamn door was closed." He faced around toward Jack and challengingly perched his fists on his hips.

"I'm awfully sorry," Jack said. He bent slightly to the side to have a better look at Laurie around Paul's stocky silhouette. "Laurie, do you feel the same way?"

"Hardly," Laurie said. "I think this discussion, if you can call it that, was getting out of hand."

"Get out of here!" Paul snarled. "Laurie and I are going to have this out here and now."

"This is neither the time nor the place," Laurie said. "I already told you that."

"Well, it seems there's a disagreement here," Jack said lightly. "I don't mind offering my services as an arbitrator."

"I'm warning you!" Paul said. His eyes narrowed. He took a threatening step forward.

"Paul, please!" Laurie said angrily. "I think you should leave!"

Paul did not take his eyes off Jack. "Get the hell out of here!" he repeated.

"I heard you the first time," Jack said airily. "But this is Dr. Montgomery's office, and her wishes reign. I think it's time you left, unless you'd like to discuss the issue with Sergeant Murphy downstairs."

Paul lunged forward in an attempt to hit Jack with a round-house blow. Anticipating the punch, Jack leaned back out of reach. Then, taking advantage of Paul's momentary loss of balance, Jack grabbed a handful of his silk suit and yanked him out through the open door, into the hall. The maneuver was accompanied by a distinct ripping sound.

Paul quickly regained his footing and assumed a crouched position with his fists raised by his head, giving Jack the impression he knew how to box. Recognizing his own limited abilities in the sport, Jack debated whether to run or envelop the man in a protective bear hug. Luckily, Jack did not have to make a decision. A yell sounded from down the hall as Chet came running at them, an open bag of potato chips and a can of pop in hand.

Faced with overwhelming odds, Paul straightened up from his threatening stance. With angry gestures he examined his finely tailored jacket and found that it had been ripped.

"Sorry," Jack said, seeing the damage he'd caused. "Luckily, it looks like it was just a seam."

"What the hell is going on here?" Chet asked.

"Paul and I had a momentary disagreement," Jack said. "But thanks to you, I think it's ironed out, so to speak."

Paul wagged his finger at Jack's face the way he had with Laurie. "You're going to hear from me about this," he snarled. "Mark my words!"

"I'll look forward to it," Jack said.

"Paul, why don't you just leave?" Laurie said. "Unless you

want to be arrested, please go! I've called security."

Paul straightened his tie and tucked his matching pocket square back into his breast pocket. The whole time, he kept his eyes glued to Jack. "You've not seen the last of me," he spat. Then turning to Laurie he said with equivalent venom, "And I'll talk to you later." After squaring his shoulders he started down the hallway toward the elevator.

Jack, Laurie, and Chet watched him go.

"What was this all about?" Chet asked.

Neither Jack nor Laurie responded.

"Did you really call security?" Jack asked.

"No," Laurie said. "I was about to when I heard Chet's yell. It's better this way."

"Thanks for coming when you did, Chet," Jack said.

"Glad to help," Chet said. "Anybody want a potato chip?" He held the bag out for Jack and Laurie. Both shook their heads.

"Would you like to talk?" Jack asked Laurie.

Laurie nodded. "I would, actually."

"Chet, old sport," Jack said, giving Chet a pat on the back. "Thanks for being the cavalry, and I'll see you back at the orifice in a few minutes." "Orifice" was a comical malapropism for "office" that Jack and Chet frequently used when speaking with each other.

"I can sense when three's a crowd," Chet said. He set off, happily munching his snack.

Laurie led the way back into her office. She closed the door behind Jack. "I hope you don't mind me shutting you in here like this."

"I can think of worse fates," Jack said.

Laurie enveloped Jack in a sustained hug. Jack hugged her back.

"Thanks for being a friend once again," she said after a full minute of silence. She released her grip, gave Jack a crooked smile, and then sat down. She got a tissue out of one of her drawers and dabbed at her eyes. She shook her head. "I hate it when I cry," she said.

"It seems to me to be rather an appropriate response after having to put up with that kind of behavior."

Laurie shook her head in dismay. "I can't believe it. I'm flabbergasted. Just three days ago it was sheer bliss."

"What happened?" Jack asked. He leaned against Laurie's desk.

"Last night at dinner I tried to have a conversation with him about what you and Lou told me," Laurie said. "It didn't work. It immediately became confrontational."

"That's not a good sign," Jack said.

"Don't I know," Laurie said. She dabbed at her eyes again. "It made me feel he was hiding something, and that idea was bolstered by his behavior today. I shouldn't have let him in, but he called up from downstairs saying he wanted to apologize. Some apology!"

"What do you think he's hiding?" Jack asked.

"I'm not sure," Laurie admitted. "But I think he might be selling illegal Bulgarian AK-47 assault rifles."

Jack whistled. "That's bad news!"

"That's an understatement," Laurie said. She shook her head. "I suppose I could deal with his being an arms dealer if I understood it had some legitimate purpose for national defense. I certainly could forgive a past run-in with the law about cocaine possession, provided he wasn't still using the stuff. But I'd never tolerate his selling illegal assault rifles or guns of any sort to private people, particularly kids. It turns out that skinhead, Brad Cassidy, who I posted on Monday, had also been involved as some sort of middleman with those Bulgarian guns."

"My word, what a coincidence," Jack said.

"And you know my feelings about gun control," Laurie added.

"Indeed," Jack said. "So what does all this mean for Laurie Montgomery?"

"I don't know exactly," Laurie said with a sigh. "I suppose I'll let things slide with Paul and try to talk to him again in a week or so. Meanwhile, like I said this morning, I'll dive into my work. It'll take my mind off my disastrous personal life."

"I hope he leaves you alone," Jack said. "He strikes me as a rather persistent sort."

"I know what you mean," Laurie said. "Which brings me to the matter of asking you for a favor."

"Sure, what do you need?"

"I don't want to be sitting by the phone tonight, or tomorrow night for that matter. I'd like to be with friends. Do you think there's any chance you and I could go with Chet and Colleen to that Monet show Chet mentioned yesterday?"

"I'd have to check with Chet," Jack said. "But I'd be happy to go."

"Wonderful," Laurie said. "And as for tonight, what do you think about going out for a bite with me and Lou. I think I owe you guys something for my behavior last night, so it will be my treat."

"You don't owe anybody anything," Jack said. "I can't speak for Lou, but as for me, I'd be delighted to eat with you tonight. It will give me a chance to fill you in on what brought me here to your office a few minutes ago."

"And what was that?"

"Your suggestion about Connie Davydov was right on the money," Jack said. "She died of botulinum toxin."

"No kidding!" Laurie said. Her flushed face lit up with a smile.

"Scout's honor," Jack said. "Peter confirmed it this morning."

"Good grief!" Laurie exclaimed. "So what happened? Did you call Randolph Sanders?"

Jack pushed off from the desk. "I'll tell you all about it tonight. When and where shall it be for dinner?"

"Would eight be a good time?"

"Sounds fine," Jack said. "Where?"

"How about Lou's favorite restaurant in Little Italy?" Laurie said. "I haven't been there in ages."

"What's the name?"

"It doesn't have a name," Laurie explained.

"Okay, what's the address?"

"I can't remember."

"Wonderful!" Jack commented sarcastically.

"Pick me up on your way downtown," Laurie said. "I'll be

able to find it. It's on a little street off Mulberry. But come in a cab, not on your bike."

After a halfhearted promise not to bicycle to her apartment that evening, Jack went back to his office. As he walked in, Chet looked up from his microscope.

"So," Chet said. "What was that all about?"

"It's all very complicated," Jack replied, plopping himself down in his chair. Between the excitement with Paul and the long bike ride, he was suddenly feeling tired. "But one result is that Laurie has changed her mind about tomorrow night. So if you and Colleen still want some company, we're available."

"Great!" Chet said. He reached for his phone. "I'll give Colleen a call to see if she can get any more tickets."

"Wait a second," Jack said. "What about the veterinarian epidemiologists? Were you able to get ahold of any of them?"

"I did," Chet said. "I talked with a Dr. Clark Simsarian who chaired the seminar. I asked him if they'd come up with a diagnosis for the rats, but they haven't. They've also not come across any more anthrax ulcers."

"I've got a suggestion for them," Jack said. "Call Dr. Simsarian back and suggest they check for botulinum toxin."

"Botulinum toxin!" Chet said. "Is that what Connie Davydov died of?"

"Apparently," Jack said. "At least according to Peter Letterman."

"And you still think the rats and Connie might be related?" Chet questioned.

"It's a long shot," Jack agreed. "But since the vets haven't come up with anything else, they might as well give it a try. I stopped by a veterinarian's office out in Brighton Beach today. He said that even some local cats have been dying mysteriously."

"I'll pass the tip along," Chet said. "What about Randolph Sanders? Have you let him know about the botulinum toxin?"

"I did," Jack said. "And I'm embarrassed to say I enjoyed making him writhe."

"I'll be curious to hear the fallout," Chet said, shaking his head. "Deciding not to do an autopsy and then finding out the patient died of botulism is a medical examiner's worst nightmare."

"I'm curious, too," Jack said. "In fact, while you make your calls, I think I'll see what I can find out."

Jack phoned the Brooklyn office and asked for Dr. Sanders. Since the ME wasn't in his office, Jack had him paged. While he waited, Chet got through to Colleen and got a positive reaction. Chet gave Jack a thumbs-up sign just as Randolph Sanders came on the line.

"Sorry to bother you," Jack said into the phone with the same breezy style he'd used earlier when he'd spoken with the man. "Chet and I have been talking about the Davydov case. We're curious as to what's going on."

"It's a nightmare," Randolph said.

"That's just how Chet characterized it a moment ago," Jack said. He winked at Chet, who was waiting for Dr. Simsarian to pick up.

"I can't believe the luck," Randolph said. "Right after I spoke with you this morning, I called the Strickland funeral home, and they gave me a bit of bad news."

"I'm sorry to hear that," Jack said.

"The body has been cremated."

"Oh!" Jack moaned with feigned sympathy.

"There wasn't much I could do at that point other than turn the situation over to Jim Bennett."

"And what's he done?"

"Nothing yet," Randolph said. "But I know he has a call in to Bingham. This whole mess is gong to have to be handled by top brass, specifically Harold Bingham."

"I guess you must feel pretty bad," Jack said. In spite of his dislike for the man, he couldn't help but feel a tinge of true sympathy.

"Nothing like this has ever happened to me before," Randolph said.

"You'll get through this," Jack said. "In jobs like ours, it's impossible to catch everything. And you're doing the best you can at this point."

Jack and Chet hung up from their respective calls almost simultaneously. They turned and faced each other.

"You first," Chet said. "What did you learn?"

"There's no fallout," Jack said. "At least not yet. Bingham's in the loop but hasn't been told yet. The real problem is that the body's gone. It was cremated." Jack shook his head. "It's a mess. The only thing I know is that it's out of my hands."

"I couldn't agree more," Chet said. "And let it stay out of your hands! As far as Dr. Simsarian is concerned, he wasn't excited about your suggestion, but he said that he'd give it a try."

Jack threw up his hands. "Well, that's all we can do."

"Absolutely," Chet said.

Jack turned to his desk. In the center of his blotter was a slide tray with a Post-it attached. On it was a note from Maureen. The slides were the skin samples from Connie Davydov.

After getting his microscope out, Jack slipped one of the slides under the objective and took a look. Now that he had the diagnosis of botulism, the slides were superfluous. He'd taken the slice of skin to make sure the woman's swollen eye was from trauma and not infection, and that was what he saw.

Putting Connie's slides aside, he reached for David Jefferson's folder. He thought he'd polish off the case a day early and surprise Calvin. While he worked, he happily anticipated the thought of spending an evening with Laurie and Lou after an invigorating pre-dinner run on the B-ball court.

NINETEEN

"See you tomorrow!" Bob King called out as Curt emerged from the front of the firehouse.

Curt responded to the rookie with a wave that was more a wave of dismissal than acknowledgment. They were going in opposite directions on Duane Street after the shift change. "Come mid-morning tomorrow, I'll never have to see you again," Curt mumbled under his breath.

As the afternoon progressed, Curt had grown increasingly excited about Operation Wolverine. At last, all the planning and all the effort was about to pay off; the operation was now on the launch pad in the final countdown for a blastoff in less than twenty-four hours! The only remaining skirmish involved Jack Stapleton, and that snag was to be dealt with in the next hour or so.

Curt glanced at his watch. Since it was after five, he fully expected the mission operatives would all be at the rendezvous in Pete's bar. Steve had not called during the afternoon: a sure indication that everything had to have gone as planned.

As Curt rounded the corner he saw a plain, dark blue van parked in a loading zone close to the bar. On the driver's side door panel was stenciled the name of a Brooklyn plumber. Curt smiled. Undoubtedly it was the requisitioned vehicle.

The bar was practically empty. The whining country music that had provided the background earlier had been replaced with the harsh sounds of a group called Armageddon. Curt smiled again. It seemed so fitting.

The music was emanating from a boom box perched on a table in front of Carl Ryerson. In the smoky half-light of the bar, Carl's crooked grin and the swastika on his forehead gave him a particularly satanic aura.

"You like the sounds, Captain?" Carl asked. He'd caught Curt's smile.

Curt liked the troops to call him "captain"; it was appropriately respectful, and it promoted discipline. He squeezed into the booth and eyed his squadron. Carl was sitting directly opposite. Next to him was the redhead, Kevin Smith. Then there was the diminutive Clark Ebersol, followed by Mike Compisano. Steve was to Curt's immediate right. Everyone was in T-shirts with their tattoos visible, except for Curt, who was still in his class B fireman's uniform. The table was littered with a forest of beer bottles.

"Let's slow up on the drinking," Curt said.

"Hey, what else is there to do in a bar?" Kevin said. "We've been here for a good half hour."

"I didn't want to be late," Steve explained.

"Is that the van out front?" Curt asked.

"Yup," Steve said. "Thanks to Clark."

"What about the ordnance?" Curt questioned.

Steve leaned forward and lowered his voice. "There's three Kalashnikovs and two Glocks in the truck. I figured that would be more than enough. Hell, if the guy is on a bicycle, all we have to do is run over him."

"But then we shoot him just to be sure," Curt said.

"Well, we certainly have more than enough firepower," Steve said.

"Where's Yuri?" Curt asked. It was the first moment Curt realized the Russian wasn't there.

"I don't know," Steve said. "Maybe he got hung up in the traffic."

Curt looked at his watch. "We told the bastard to be here at five."

"Why don't we use the time to set up tomorrow morning?" Steve suggested. "I mentioned to Mike we might need him for a quick mission." Mike was the least enamored of the skinhead style and the most responsive to Curt's urging to tame its outlandishness. Now that his blond hair had begun to grow out, compared to his fellow militiamen he could almost pass for normal.

"Good idea," Curt said, but before he could elaborate the waiter appeared to take his order. Curt ordered a Bud Light.

"Listen up," Curt said to Mike after Curt's beer had arrived. He leaned forward. "We want you to put on business clothes in the morning: jacket, tie, the works. It's got to be early because we want you in front of the Jacob Javits Federal Building on Worth Street no later than nine-fifteen."

"I'll have to take off from work," Mike said.

Curt rolled his eyes. He reminded himself he needed patience when he talked to his troops. "Whatever," he said with a wave of his hands. "The important thing is that you are there at nine-fifteen. This operation has to go like clockwork."

"So what do I do, just stand there?" Mike questioned.

"No, you idiot," Curt said loudly. Then he lowered his voice. "We're going to give you a small smoke bomb that generates lots of smoke. It's about the size of a large firecracker, and you're to light it with a match. Most importantly it will not set off the metal detector when you go into the building."

"I have to go inside?" Mike questioned.

"That's right," Curt said.

"But won't they ask me why?"

"No! People are going in and out all day long."

Mike raised his eyebrows.

"I'm serious," Curt said. "You won't have a problem as long as you look halfway decent. Hell, it probably wouldn't matter even if you wore what you have on today."

"All right," Mike said. "So I'm inside. What do I do with the smoke bomb?"

"Get on the elevator and go up to the third floor," Curt said. "When you get off, go to your right. About thirty feet down the hall is a men's room. Got it?"

Mike nodded.

"Go inside the men's room and make sure no one else is in there."

Mike continued to nod.

"Actually, it probably doesn't matter even if someone is in there," Curt said. "Just get yourself in the last stall. There's a vent in there against the back wall. Unscrew the cover with a coin, light the bomb, toss it inside the duct, then put the cover back on."

"Is that all?" Mike asked.

"That's it," Jack said. "Then wander out of the building. The bomb's going to set off a smoke detector in the HVAC system so there'll be a fire alarm, but you just continue on your way. There also might be some confusion. After the alarm sounds, Steve and I will show up in minutes in our truck, and if you happen to see us, ignore us. That's all you have to do."

Mike gave a short laugh. He glanced around at the others. "That's a piece of cake."

"But it's an important piece of cake," Curt declared. "It's an important mission for the PAA."

At that moment Curt saw Yuri come in through the front door. Curt raised his hand to get Yuri's attention, and the Russian came over. "You're late!" Curt snapped.

"The traffic was bad getting into the Battery Tunnel," Yuri explained.

"Jack Stapleton better still be at his work," Curt warned. He stood up and went to the bar to pay the tab.

"All right, move out," Curt said a few minutes later when he'd returned to the table. He had to take bottles away from Kevin and Carl, who thought they'd carry out their unfinished beers.

Outside everyone piled into the van amid lots of excited laughter. With the promise of violence, the skinheads were

working themselves up to a fever pitch. Curt took the wheel
and had Yuri ride shotgun because the Russian could most
expediently identify the target. In the back there were some
arguments about who was going to sit where among all the
plumbing tools and lengths of pipe. Steve ended up having to
decide.

Curt made it a point to take Worth Street west in order to
pass the Jacob Javits Federal Building. He wanted to show
Mike where he was to enter the building in the morning. After
doing so, Curt turned north on the Bowery with the plan of
getting over to First Avenue via Houston Street.

"I don't want to take a lot of time," Yuri said nervously. "I
just want to point out Jack Stapleton, get out, and let you guys
do what you have to do."

Curt took his eyes off the traffic for a moment to cast a
questioning glance at Yuri. "We'll have to see how things
work out," he said. "We're kinda playing this operation by
ear."

"What does that mean?" Yuri asked. He was holding on
with both hands. Curt was driving aggressively in the traffic,
especially now that they'd turned north on First Avenue.

"It means we'll be making things up as we go along," Curt
said. "But why the rush? I thought you'd want to be along for
the whole mission."

"I have a lot of work to do to be ready for tomorrow," Yuri
explained.

"Oh, right," Curt said.

In the back of the van, new arguments erupted about who
was going to hold which weapon. Curt glanced in the rearview
mirror and was horrified to see his troops struggling over the
Kalashnikovs. "Get that ordnance out of sight," he yelled. "Jesus Christ! We'll have the cops pulling us over."

Amid grumbles, the weapons were placed on the floor.

Curt caught Yuri casting anxious glances back at the troops.
"They're a little excited," he explained. "They love this type
of operation."

"They seem more than a little excited," Yuri responded.

"What was that address again?" Curt called back to Steve.
Steve pulled Jack's card out of his pocket. "Five-twenty

First Avenue," Steve said. "I imagine it's up in the hospital neighborhood."

Curt began to slow down as they passed Bellevue Hospital on the right.

"There it is," Steve said while pointing to a glazed, blue brick building.

Curt pulled to the left side of the road just beyond Thirtieth Street, stopped, and put on his emergency blinkers. They were on the opposite side of the street and catty-corner from the morgue's First Avenue entrance. People were coming out of the building in clumps and either walking away or hailing taxis.

Steve came up between the front bucket seats. He, Curt, and Yuri stared at the front of the building and watched the people exit. "Looks like the employees are getting off work."

In the back of the van the troops reopened the argument about who was going to hold the Kalashnikovs. Curt had to yell at them to shut up.

"How are we going to know if he's not already left?" Steve asked. "We could be here for hours for nothing."

"He better not have gone," Curt said, glancing harshly at Yuri. "Let's try to give him a call. Give me that direct number he put on his card."

While Steve got the card from his pocket, Curt pulled out his cellular phone. As Steve read out the number, Curt punched it into his keypad. Then he lifted the phone to his ear.

It gave Jack a great sense of satisfaction to sign out yet another case. Marveling that he'd never been quite so caught up in his work since the day he'd been hired, he put the folder on top of the tottering completed pile. As he pulled his hand away, his phone rang.

"Jack Stapleton here," he said in his normal fashion. Instead of a voice, Jack heard a rushing noise, as if he was listening to a distant waterfall. Then there was the unmistakable honk of an automobile horn.

"Hello, hello!" Jack said into the mouthpiece all the more loudly.

Jack was treated to a click followed by a dial tone. He tossed the handset back into its craddle with a shrug.

"What happened?" Chet asked without looking up from his work.

"Who the hell knows?" Jack said. "I could hear traffic in the background but whoever called never said a word."

"Must have been an old girlfriend checking up on you," Chet said.

"Oh, yeah, right!" Jack said with as much sarcasm as he could manage. He looked at his diminutive stack of uncompleted files and debated whether to continue his marathon.

Then Chet's phone rang.

"She must have had the wrong number," Jack said with a laugh.

Chet picked up his phone. He sat up straighter when he heard who it was. "Yes, I'm still here, Dr. Simsarian," he said loud enough to be sure Jack could hear.

Jack turned around to look at his officemate, who'd also turned to face him. Their eyes met. Chet was wide-eyed with disbelief. "Really!" he said. "I'm amazed, too."

"Amazed about what?" Jack demanded.

Chet held up his hand toward Jack while continuing to talk into the phone: "Thanks for calling back, Dr. Simsarian. It's fascinating, and we'll be interested to hear the follow-up. I'll be sure to tell Dr. Stapleton about the results and convey your gratitude."

Chet hung up his phone.

"Don't tell me the rats were positive for botulinum toxin!" Jack said.

"You guessed it," Chet said. "He was flabbergasted. I am, too. What really made you even consider the idea in the first place?"

"Purely because it was the same neighborhood," Jack said.

"Connie Davydov must have eaten one of the rats," Chet said with a sinister chuckle.

Jack laughed, too, then commented that only two medical examiners could find such a concept laughable.

"I wonder if an infected rat would put out the toxin in its feces?" Chet asked.

"That's even a more disgusting idea," Jack said. "I suppose we could ask the veterinary epidemiologists. More realistically, I wonder if Connie Davydov put the rest of whatever it was she ate that was contaminated with the toxin down her disposal."

"Yeah, but enough to kill that many rats?" Chet questioned suspiciously.

"I know it sounds far-fetched," Jack admitted. "But you know how potent that stuff is supposed to be."

"Well, it will be interesting to hear if the vet epidemiologists can figure it out."

Jack got up and stretched. "I think I've had it for the night. I need the relaxation of a good hard game of B-ball."

"See you tomorrow," Chet said.

"Take care, sport," Jack said. He grabbed his bomber jacket from behind the door. He slipped into it as he walked down to the elevator. Remembering the fabulous weather from his afternoon jaunt to Brighton Beach, he was again looking forward to a relaxing bike ride.

"At least we know he's still in there," Steve said.

"True," Curt commented. "The question now is when is he going to come out? I don't know how long the troops will keep away from each other's throats." Just after Curt had hung up from calling Jack, Carl, Clark, Kevin, and Mike had gotten into another heated argument about the guns that had almost ended in fisticuffs. Curt had had to collect the weapons; they were now all on the floor at Yuri's feet.

"That's him on the bike!" Yuri shouted. He frantically pointed to Jack's figure as the medical examiner rounded the corner of Thirtieth Street and powered his way up First Avenue.

"Jesus, he's moving!" Curt said. He snapped off the emergency brake and accelerated out into the traffic. The driver of a taxi the maneuver had cut off leaned on his horn in frustration.

"Let me out!" Yuri urged.

"Not now!" Curt cried. "I don't want to lose the bastard."

Although the traffic was heavy, it was moving in sync and at a fairly rapid pace.

"The guy's a freaking dynamo," Curt complained. He drove aggressively, knowing it was the only way to close in on Jack. He was totally unconcerned about grazing other vehicles or having others run into his side or rear.

"Holy shit!" Steve swore as Curt cut off another taxi and there was a dull thump followed by the screech of metal against metal down the side of the truck. In the back of the van the loose pipe lengths were bouncing around, making a terrible racket. The troops were busy fending off not only the pipes but also a minor blizzard of nuts, bolts, and PCB pipe fittings that were raining down from where they were stored in shelves along both sides of the vehicle's interior. The inevitable New York City potholes were making the situation desperate.

"Yuri, get out of the goddamned seat and let Steve sit there," Curt yelled while fighting with the steering wheel.

"While we're moving?" Yuri questioned. He was holding on with white knuckles.

"Of course while we're moving," Curt yelled.

Yuri swallowed nervously and then tried to rotate off the seat. Steve had moved over to give him room. But at the same time, Curt saw the suggestion of an opening in the neighboring lane and swerved to take advantage of it. The movement threw Yuri into him. Curt responded by swearing and fending Yuri off with a forearm before struggling to retain control of the racing vehicle.

While Yuri clawed his way into the back of the truck, Steve swung into the seat. Just ahead he could see Jack's back. The medical examiner was pumping furiously. Jack was inching ahead between a speeding beer delivery truck and a Federal Express van.

"God damn it!" Curt yelled, as he could see Jack was about to slip in front of the vehicles. Curt was directly behind the beer truck. He leaned on his horn in frustration.

"Get a Glock!" Curt yelled to Steve. "I'm going to try to

come alongside the bastard so you can nail him. The trouble is, I'm going to have to find a way to get around this truck."

"What is this guy?" Steve questioned as he picked up one of the automatics and snapped off the safety. "A professional bicycle racer? He's going faster than the traffic!"

The United Nations building loomed up on the right.

Curt cut into the neighboring lane. There was another cacophony of horns and shouts from behind. Curt pressed the accelerator to the floor and the van gained on the beer truck. He had to let up on his speed as he came within a few feet of a taxi, but he'd moved ahead enough to spot Jack, who was now directly even with them.

Steve lowered his window.

"What do you think?" Curt yelled at Steve.

"I could shoot him, but I wouldn't be confident where I'd hit him," Steve shouted back. "We're bouncing around too much."

"I'd cut in front of the truck if this goddamn taxi in front of us would move his ass," Curt cried. As it was, they were slowly gaining on the beer delivery vehicle.

"Hold on!" Curt yelled when he decided he had the opportunity. He cut the wheel sharply to the right. The van skidded slightly before rocketing ahead of the truck and then swerving in the opposite direction. The driver of the truck slammed on his brakes, causing his tires to screech in protest. Curt fought to keep the van from fishtailing as Steve leaned the gun out the window. They'd come directly alongside of Jack.

Before Steve could draw a bead, Jack surprised them by braking suddenly himself and disappearing from view.

"What the hell?" Curt questioned. He eased up on the accelerator. The van slowed. "Where the hell did he go?"

"Behind us, I think," Steve said. He stuck his head out the window and looked back.

Seconds later Jack appeared right next to Curt's driver's side window. To Curt's astonishment the doctor flipped him the finger. Curt swore and struggled to get his window down while yelling for Steve to shoot the bastard.

Steve leaned across Curt's lap, but Jack had moved forward.

"Hold on," Curt yelled. He pressed on the accelerator and

the van leaped ahead. But just as they were coming abreast of Jack for the second time, Jack swung left into a clearer lane. Curt swore and moved left himself, but the lane was occupied. There was another thump as a taxi hit the side of the van. In the mirror Curt saw the taxi skid sideways to end up perpendicular to the oncoming traffic. Instantly there was a tremendous collision and a multi-vehicle pileup.

"Christ!" Steve exclaimed. He could see what had happened through the rear window of the van.

"Hold on, everybody, he's going left again," Curt yelled. No sooner had Curt changed lanes himself than Jack made a wide, arcing turn into Fifty-first Street heading west.

"God damn it!" Curt cried as he jammed on the brakes and threw the steering wheel to the left to try to follow. The van shuddered as it skidded sideways before the tires caught. Even so, it grazed a parked car on the right followed by one on the left before Curt regained complete control. In the distance they could see Jack methodically pumping.

"Doesn't he get tired?" Curt questioned. He pressed down on the gas and the van shot forward.

At Second Avenue they missed the traffic light. Undeterred, Curt inched out into the moving traffic amid horn honking and swearing. Steve hunkered down in his seat, since he was the one exposed to the oncoming vehicles.

"Up yours!" Curt yelled to a particularly irate driver. Despite moving against the light, Curt succeeded in making it across Second Avenue, and he accelerated again. Jack was already at Third Avenue waiting for the traffic signal there to change.

"We got him now," Curt snarled.

Ahead, the light changed to green. Jack started forward. Curt pressed the accelerator to the floor, jacking his speed up to over fifty miles per hour. He was determined to make the light. Curt's mouth went dry, since he knew it would be close. He prayed there would be no taxis jumping the light on their way north.

They streaked across Third Avenue without incident. Jack was only a half block away. But as they rapidly closed the distance, a car pulled out from a parking spot. Curt was forced

to brake rapidly. He came up to the very back of the vehicle
and leaned on his horn. The driver ignored him. Ahead Jack
was again leaving them behind by crossing Lexington Avenue.

"I don't believe this!" Curt yelled. He slammed on the
brakes and simultaneously hit the steering wheel with the heel
of his hand in frustration. The car in front had stopped at the
corner with a yellow light. "It's just our luck to get behind
the only driver in New York who stops on yellow lights." He
ran an anxious hand through his hair. "I suppose I could push
him out of the way."

"But look at the traffic," Steve said. It was bumper-to-
bumper and moving slowly on Lexington Avenue. "There's
no place for us to go, so don't bother. We'll catch him on the
next block."

Curt growled but didn't say anything.

"Let me out of here!" Yuri cried as soon as he was aware
they were stopped. He dragged himself forward between the
front seats.

Steve looked over at Curt, who shrugged his shoulders and
then nodded. Steve opened the door and climbed out. Yuri
scrambled out of the vehicle and stood on shaky legs while
Steve climbed back inside.

"We'll see you tonight," Curt yelled from the driver's seat.
"Sometime around eleven. You'll be ready, right?"

"I'll be ready," Yuri promised hoarsely.

The light turned green, and Curt honked his horn. The car
in front slowly made the turn to the left. Impatient, Curt
gunned the van before the car was completely out of the way.
They ricocheted off the car bumper, and the driver leaped out
to protest.

"Serves him right," Curt said with a malicious laugh as he
sped west.

In the distance Jack was crossing Park Avenue on a green
light. Steve braced. As Curt accelerated, Steve had no idea
what was going to happen at the intersection. He knew intu-
itively that they were not going to make the light. Fortunately
it ambered its way to red soon enough to force Curt to stop.
The traffic heading uptown was moving rapidly, and since it
was now coming on Curt's side of the van, he was instinc-

tively reluctant to try to cross against the light as he'd done on Second Avenue. While they were waiting, they could see Jack in the distance turn right on Madison Avenue.

"If we lose him, I'm going to be royally pissed," Curt groused.

"I bet he's heading for the park," Steve said. "He probably lives on the Upper West Side."

"You could be right," Curt said. "And what are we going to do if he does go into the park?"

"Follow him!" Steve said. "Provided we see where he goes in. We can always have one of the boys snatch someone's bicycle. The park is always filled with bikes." Steve swung around to look into the depths of the van. The wild ride had quieted the troops.

"Who's in the best shape to ride a bike?" Steve demanded.

The troops all pointed to Kevin.

"Is that right, Kevin?" Steve asked.

"I guess," Kevin said. "I'm in pretty good shape."

The light changed and Curt rocketed ahead. Steve turned forward and grabbed what he could to hold on.

At Madison the light was in their favor, and Curt made a rapid turn. The pipe lengths all rolled to one side amid swearing from the troops. Curt had to stop behind traffic waiting at the light at Fifty-second Street.

"I think I see him at the next light," Steve said.

"I believe you're right," Curt said. "Between the bus and the oil truck. Jeez, the guy's fearless."

The light changed and they were off.

"What should I do?" Curt said desperately. "We're not going to catch him with this kind of traffic on Madison Avenue."

"We do have his home number," Steve said. "Maybe we should wait and call him at home and try to get him to give us the address. One of us could say we were Yuri Davydov. Hell, maybe he'd come see us."

"That's an idea," Curt agreed. "But what do you think we should do now?"

"Let's head for the corner of Fifth Avenue and Central Park South," Steve suggested. "If he does go into the park, that's where it will be."

"Well, it's as good an idea as any other," Curt said. He wasn't happy.

They traveled north as fast as the traffic could allow. At least they were making the lights, but they knew Jack was as well. As they streaked across Fifty-seventh Street Steve happened to catch sight of Jack traveling west.

"Shit!" Curt exclaimed. The sighting had been too late to make the turn.

"I think it's okay," Steve said. "Keep going the way we are. Let's give Fifth and Central Park West a try."

The first street they could turn left on was Sixtieth, which was just as well. It led them to the northern part of Grand Army Plaza, where it joined the park. Curt crossed Fifth Avenue with the light and pulled over to the side of the road. He stopped by wooden police barricades blocking vehicular traffic from entering one of the park's drives.

"Well, there are certainly enough bikes available if we need one," Steve commented, trying to sound optimistic. Bicyclists were coming and going along with a host of in-line skaters and joggers. "Best of all, I don't see any cops."

Curt was looking back beyond the gilded equestrian statue of General Sherman to the area around the Pulitzer fountain in front of the Plaza Hotel. The area was jammed with a confusion of people, cars, buses, and hansom cabs.

"This is goddamned impossible," Curt complained. "I knew that once we lost sight of him it would be like finding the proverbial needle in the haystack."

"If I follow him on a bike, what do I do if I catch him?" Kevin asked.

"Lots of luck catching him!" Curt said. "The guy's a pro."

"He might stop," Steve said. "You never know."

"That's true," Curt admitted. "So give Kevin one of the Glocks. But more importantly, give him your phone so he can keep in touch with us."

Steve swung around and handed the gun and the phone to Kevin, who eagerly pocketed them. "You want me to go out and get a bike now?"

"No!" Curt said. "We're not doing anything unless we see the bastard. Actually I think we're going to have to fall back to plan B. The more I think of calling him and saying we're Yuri, the better it sounds."

"Holy shit, there he is!" Steve said, frantically pointing to a bicyclist who'd just swept past them no more than ten feet away.

"You're right!" Curt said. "Kevin, you're on!"

Kevin scrambled forward and climbed out of the door Steve had exited. Without a moment's hesitation he took off at a run. Steve climbed back into the van.

Curt and Steve watched as the husky Kevin vaulted over the police sawhorses, despite his heavy Doc Marten boots, and ran directly at a bicyclist who'd stopped at a water fountain. The man was still on his bike with one toe in its clip, but he was leaning over to drink. He was sporting all the proper cycling paraphernalia, including the helmet, tights, and padded gloves.

Kevin didn't hesitate. Without a word, he grabbed the bike and snatched it from under the man, upending him.

Kevin threw a leg over the bike and was about to take off when the bicyclist recovered enough to get a grip on one of the cycle's handlebars. Kevin responded by balling his big hand into a fist and laying the man out cold.

"Oh," Steve gushed. "Now that was a punch!"

Despite the crowd of people in the area, the incident happened so quickly that few individuals had actually witnessed it. Although several people went to the aid of the downed bicyclist, no one went after Kevin, who was pedaling furiously in pursuit of Jack. Since it was quite light despite the sun's having set, Jack could still be seen in the distance heading north.

"At least that went smoothly," Steve said. "Now what do you think we should do? Sit here?"

Curt scanned the area as if he expected the answer to be in the surroundings. After a moment's consideration, he shook his head. "No, I think we should head over to Central Park West. If Stapleton lives on the Upper West Side, that's where he'll come out."

Curt put the van in gear. At a comparatively leisurely pace he drove west on Central Park South. As he did so he pulled out his cellular phone, checked to make sure it was on, then put it on the dash.

TWENTY

Jack sat up and took his hands off his handlebars. With no
hands he coasted along the pathway strewn with dead leaves.
Just ahead was Central Park West and the exit across from
106th Street.

The ride home had been most enjoyable. The weather had
been as glorious as he'd anticipated. The ride up First Avenue
had had its normal share of aggravations, but it had been stimulating just the same. His nightly circuit around the Pulitzer
fountain had been so inspiring that he'd been moved to stop
to admire the resplendent nude statue of Abundance in the
fading daylight. But by far the best part of the trip, as usual,
had been the ride through the park. As soon as he'd broken
free from the clutch of people near the park's entrance he'd
poured on the speed. It had been as if he'd been flying in a
dream.

Jack waited for the traffic light to change before cycling
across the busy avenue and entering his street. He was now
in the cool-down stage of his ride and pedaled quickly in a

low gear with almost no resistance. He stopped at the fence at the basketball court. As he'd hoped and expected, a game was in progress. Once again Warren and Flash were on opposing teams.

"Hey, Doc, you going to run or what?" Warren called out. "Get yourself out here, man."

"You better be in good form," Jack called back. "'Cause I'm going to be trouble tonight!"

"Uh oh!" Spit yelled. He was one of the younger players but had become Warren's protégé. "Doc's threatening to make some house calls." The group teased Jack by calling any of his better moves "house calls."

"There's going to be plenty of house calls tonight," Jack shouted back. He pushed off and rode across the street. He was eager to get out on the court.

Jack hesitated on his stoop while debating whether he'd cab to Laurie's later or take his bike. He knew he'd prefer to bike, yet he wanted to humor Laurie. While he was arguing with himself over the issue he happened to notice another cyclist emerge from the darkening park. The only reason the man caught Jack's eye was that he seemed to be stumbling, as if exhausted or hurt.

Jack watched the man for a moment to make sure he didn't need assistance. But it was soon apparent he didn't. He took out a cell phone and made a call while pressing the button to make the traffic light change.

Having decided to cab to Laurie's, Jack hoisted his beloved bike to his shoulder and entered his building. In his haste he took the stairs two at a time. After keying open his apartment door, he rolled his bike inside and leaned it up against the wall. Without even taking the time to close the door to the hall, he rushed into his bedroom, removing his work clothes en route.

To his frustration, it took Jack a few minutes to locate his basketball gear. When he finally did, he dressed quickly. The finishing touches were a dark blue Nike headband and an old hooded sweatshirt. He then ran into the kitchen to grab a quick drink of water. Then the wall phone rang.

Jack debated whether to answer. His first thought was to let the answering machine get it, but then he remembered that he got few calls at home other than from Laurie. Thinking it might be her, he picked it up.

"Hello," he said briskly, but there was no response. He said hello several times. What he heard was just what he'd heard through the receiver at the office, down to the sound of rushing water and even a distant automobile horn. Disgusted, Jack hung up.

He got only a few steps out of the kitchen when the phone rang again. On the off chance there had been a mechanical problem, he went back and picked it up again. He was glad he did. It was Laurie.

"Did you just try to call me two seconds ago?" Jack asked.

"No," Laurie said. "Did your phone ring?"

"It's not important," Jack said. "What's up? I'm just on my way out to play B-ball."

"I know better than trying to keep you from that," Laurie teased. "I just wanted to let you know that it's going to be just you and me tonight. Lou can't make it."

"His loss, my gain," Jack said.

"You flatterer you!" Laurie joked. "Anyway, he did offer to call the restaurant where I wanted us to go. So I know we'll get good service. They love him there."

"Sounds good," Jack said. "Tell me, has Paul been pestering you?"

"Haven't heard from him since he left the office," Laurie said.

"Good."

"See you at eight," Laurie said.

"I might be a shade late," Jack said. "As I said, I'm only now just heading out. But I'll play only one game, and I'll call you before I leave."

"See you then," Laurie said. "Remember! No bike!"

"Aye, aye, sir!" Jack said. He hung up the phone.

Jack ran out to his closet and searched around the cluttered space for his "kicks," as Warren called sneakers. Impatient to get them on, Jack didn't even bother to lace them before rushing out his door. He was about to close and lock it when he heard his name called out loudly from down below. Not recognizing the voice, he leaned over the banister to take a look. Three men were looking up from the ground-floor hallway, and when they saw Jack, they immediately started up the stairs. They came at a run, their boots making a fierce clatter against the bare treads. The one in the lead was a blond fireman in a blue uniform.

Jack put his head back and sniffed for smoke. He sniffed again after turning his head in the direction of his apartment, but still couldn't smell any smoke. When he looked back down the stairs the lead man was already on the last flight leading up to Jack's level. But instead of carrying a fire axe or some other appropriate piece of firefighting equipment, he was clutching a gun.

Jack backed up into his doorway, totally confused. The other two men were in black leather jackets, not firemen's uniforms, and had shaved heads. Then Jack saw that the one bringing up the rear was carrying an assault rifle!

Curt stopped six feet away from Jack and knitted his brows. "You are Jack Stapleton, aren't you?" he asked, looking Jack up and down.

"No, he lives on the next level up," Jack stammered. He backed into his apartment and started to close the door.

Curt quickly stepped forward to get his foot inside. He pushed open the door and stepped in. Jack backed up. The two skinheads crowded in behind. The one with the rifle had a swastika tattooed on his forehead.

Curt's eyes quickly swept the spartan room. He glared back at Jack and studied him. Curt was clearly confused. "I think you're Jack Stapleton," he said.

"No, I'm Billy Rubin," Jack said, pulling the name out of nowhere. "Jack's directly above me." Jack lamely pointed at the ceiling.

"Captain, there's a bike leaning against the wall," Mike said.

"Yeah, I saw it," Curt said without taking his eyes off Jack. "But this doesn't look like a doctor's apartment, and I can't be a hundred percent sure with his guy's get-up. Take a quick look around for an envelope or something with this joker's name on it."

"I'll be happy to give Jack a message," Jack said. He eyed

the gun in Curt's hand as well as the rifle in Carl's.

"Thanks, wise guy," Curt snapped. "Just stand there and be patient for a sec."

Jack thought briefly about taking his chances by running into the bedroom and diving out the window, but he dismissed the idea as impractical, since he was on the fourth floor. He'd only get hung up on the fire escape.

"Why are you looking for him?" Jack asked.

"He has business with the People's Aryan Army," Curt said. "Serious business."

"I'm sure Jack isn't involved with any army," Jack said. "He's very much against war and violence."

"Shut up!" Curt said.

"I found something," Mike said near the bedroom door. He had picked up Jack's trousers and was struggling to get Jack's billfold out of the back pocket. He pulled it free and flipped it open. He whistled when he saw the medical examiner badge and held it up for Curt to see.

"Just check the name, for crissake," Curt snapped.

"Maybe we should discuss this business you were referring to," Jack said.

"There's nothing to discuss," Curt said.

"Ah, here's a driver's license," Mike announced. "And the name is Jack Stapleton all right."

"Jack frequently uses my apartment to change in," Jack offered.

Suddenly there was more clatter of heavy boots on the stairs out in the hallway. Steve's voice shouted up: "Hold up, Curt. There's been a misunderstanding!"

Curt's brow furrowed. He momentarily glanced in the direction of the open door but then immediately returned his gaze to Jack. Seconds later Steve, Kevin, and Clark stumbled into the room. Behind them were three other figures who leaped into the room, spread out, and shouted for everyone to freeze.

Curt spun around to find himself staring into the barrels of three Tec machine pistols.

"Don't even think about it," Warren warned as he zeroed in on Curt.

For a tense moment no one moved or breathed.

"Okay, Spit," Warren said, breaking the silence. "Get the pistol and the rifle."

Spit eased forward, holding his machine pistol in his right hand. He collected first the handgun, which he pocketed, and then the rifle. He stepped back.

"Now I want all you dudes to line up facing the wall," Warren commanded. He motioned with his gun.

There was a delay as a sneer spread cross Curt's face.

"Hey, man, you either do as I'm telling you or the story's over," Warren said. "You know what I'm saying?"

"Sorry, Captain," Steve said. "They came out of nowhere."

"Shut up," Warren yelled. "This ain't no rap session here."

With defiant arrogance, Curt stepped over to the wall, leaving his hands on his hips.

"Spit, pat 'em down," Warren commanded.

Spit put down the guns he was holding and went to each of the men facing the wall and searched for concealed weapons. He found nothing and stepped back.

"Okay, turn around," Warren ordered.

The men did as they were told. Except for Steve, who was clearly terrified, all the others had assumed brazenly bored expressions.

"I don't know where you white trash are from, and I don't give a shit," Warren said. "The point is, you don't belong in this here neighborhood. Now I'm going to keep all this firepower you brought here, but that's it. Nobody's icing nobody."

"Excuse me, Warren," Jack said. "I think we should call the police."

"Shut up!" Warren snapped with venom equal to that he'd directed a few moments earlier toward Steve.

Jack shrugged and took a step back. He knew Warren enough to know when he was pissed, and he was pissed now.

"Now I want you people to take your white asses down to your wheels and split," Warren said. "And believe me, if any one of you show up in this neighborhood again, that's the ball game. You'll be gone, no questions asked. And we'll be watching. You hear what I'm saying?"

"Warren," Jack said. "I . . ."

Warren spun around. He jammed a finger toward Jack's face. "I said for you to shut up," he snarled.

Jack took another step back. He'd never seen Warren show such rage.

"Flash," Warren said in a more normal voice. "You and Spit take these white honkies down and see that they leave the neighborhood. I've got to rap with the doc here for a few minutes."

As the group silently fled out, Warren turned to Jack and glared at him. Jack squirmed. He didn't know what Warren wanted him to say.

With the Tec pistol held in his left hand, Warren used his right to give Jack's shoulder a series of repeated angry shoves. Jack was forced progressively backwards until a final shove made him collapse onto his couch. Warren hovered over him.

"What's wrong with you, Doc?" Warren demanded. "You haven't caused this kind of trouble around here for two years. I thought you'd reformed. But now tonight this happens. I'm telling you, you're a drag on this neighborhood. You know what I'm saying?"

"I'm sorry," Jack said.

"A lot of good that will do if some kid gets shot because of you," Warren said. "What was this white trash after you for? I mean, these boys were serious bringing in Kalashnikov assault rifles. Shit! If they'd started spraying those around, a lot of people could have been hurt."

"Those were Kalashnikovs?" Jack asked.

"What do you think, I'm making this up?"

"Where were the Kalashnikovs made?"

"What kind of question is that, man? What difference does it make?"

"It might make a difference if they're Bulgarian," Jack said.

Warren glared at Jack for a beat before walking over to where Spit had put the Kalashnikov he'd taken from Carl. Warren picked the weapon up and carried it back to Jack. "Well, you're right," he said grudgingly. "They are Bulgarian. What does that mean?"

"I can't be positive," Jack said. "But I think it might have something to do with Laurie's new boyfriend."

"That doesn't sound good," Warren said. "Did you and Laurie split up?"

"Not exactly," Jack said. "And I think the new boyfriend is on his way out, but let me explain."

Jack told Warren about Paul Sutherland, and how Jack had probably humiliated the man that afternoon. He mentioned that Paul had threatened him indirectly. He also said that Laurie was concerned the man was dealing with the Bulgarian Kalashnikovs.

Warren's anger mellowed to a degree as he listened to the story. "I suppose there's no way you could have anticipated that these guys would have come over here."

"Of course not," Jack said. "I don't even know how they knew where I lived."

"That kind of white trash scares me," Warren admitted.

"They scare me, too," Jack agreed. "The blond guy in the fireman's uniform talked briefly about a militia called the People's Aryan Army. I'd heard that name on Monday from an FBI agent who's trying to learn about them. Have you ever heard the name?"

"Never," Warren said.

"Which leads me to ask why you let them go? I would have turned them over to the police in a heartbeat. The police and maybe even the FBI would have loved to get their hands on them."

"You're shocked because you really live in a different world, despite occupying this apartment," Warren said. "You don't understand about gangs. When I let them go, I was thinking of the neighborhood, not the police department's or the FBI's agenda. It's the same way I didn't want any of them to get hurt. It's not because I care about them! Shit, no! It's because it would start something. They'd be back. It's been my experience that this way they won't. Sorta live and let live."

"I'll have to kowtow to your experience on this one," Jack said.

"I'm afraid you didn't have any choice," Warren said. He took a deep breath and let it out slowly. "Now how about some hoops? You still want to run?"

"I think I need it more now than I did before," Jack said. He got up on wobbly legs. "I can't promise how effective I'll be. I feel shell-shocked even though no shells have gone off."

Warren preceded Jack out into the hall carrying the guns. Jack locked his door and caught up to him.

"Thanks for being there when I needed you," Jack said. "Since you've done it before, I think it's my turn next."

Warren laughed in spite of himself. "That'll be the day!"

Jack rang Laurie's bell and then turned to wave hello to Debra Engler. The nosy neighbor responded by slamming her door, which was a feat since it had only been open by slightly more than an inch. Jack turned back to Laurie's and heard the little click that sounded when Laurie opened her peephole. Jack waved. Then he heard all the locks being opened.

Laurie was in a buoyant mood despite the scene she'd had with Paul. She gave Jack an enthusiastic hug before disappearing into her bedroom for her watch and jewelry. Tom-2 rubbed affectionately against Jack's leg. Jack bent down to pet the cat.

"I trust you came in a cab like you promised," Laurie called out from the other room.

"No, I didn't," Jack answered.

Laurie's head appeared around the corner. She eyed Jack accusatively. "But you promised," she said.

"Warren brought me," Jack said. "And I hope you don't mind, I invited him to eat with us."

"Of course not," Laurie said. "Is Natalie coming, too?"

"No, just Warren," Jack said. "In fact, to be honest, he kinda invited himself. You see, I ran into a rather serious inconvenience this afternoon right after I spoke with you on the phone."

"What happened?" Laurie questioned. She came out from her bedroom. Her voice reflected her sudden concern. Knowing Jack as well as she did, she sensed that whatever happened was a lot more than an inconvenience.

"In Warren's vernacular, I was almost iced by the People's Aryan Army," Jack said.

Laurie's lower jaw dropped. "What on earth are you talking about?"

Jack gave Laurie a quick rundown of the events that took place in his apartment. When he described the guns, and Warren's timely arrival, she clamped a hand over her mouth.

"My God," she said. "What in heaven's name could have prompted such an ambush. I mean, I was the one who posted Brad Cassidy, if that was somehow involved. He's the only connection I know of with this People's Aryan Army."

"I don't think it had anything to do with Brad Cassidy," Jack said. "It couldn't have, because I had nothing to do with him. To tell you the truth, I think there's a slight chance it had something to do with Paul Sutherland."

Laurie's face blanched. She sucked in a lungful of air, and her hand returned to cover her mouth in horror.

"Hold on!" Jack warned. "There's no proof. It's just the only thing I could think of on the spur of the moment, and nothing else has occurred to me since. And believe me, I've been giving it a lot of thought since it happened. The only reason I'm willing to tell you is because you should know even if there's only a shred of possibility it is true."

"Tell me why it occurred to you!" Laurie said.

Jack described the three Bulgarian Kalashnikovs Warren confiscated from the men. Then he went on to remind her of Paul's implied threat that afternoon. When he finished, he shrugged. "I know it's extremely tenuous, but that's it."

Laurie sank into her art deco chair and lowered her head into her hands.

"Hey," Jack said, putting his hand on Laurie's shoulder. "You've got to keep in mind this is all conjecture."

"Maybe so," Laurie said. "But it makes a certain amount of sense." She shook her head. "How can someone's social life be so tumultuous?"

"Come on!" Jack urged. He gave her a series of reassuring pats on her back. "Let's not let this episode get us down. Let's go out and enjoy ourselves."

"Are you sure you still want to go after the experience you've had?"

"Absolutely!" Jack said. "Come on! We shouldn't keep Warren and Spit waiting."

"Where are they?"

"Down in their cars," Jack said. "Warren insisted on coming and bringing backup on the off chance members of the People's Aryan Army show up for an encore."

Laurie leaped to her feet. "You should have told me Warren was waiting." She rushed back into her bedroom.

"I told you he brought me," Jack called after her. He stooped down to return to petting the cat.

"Who is Spit?" Laurie yelled. "Or shouldn't I ask?"

"He's one of the basketball regulars," Jack explained. "Warren is his mentor and trusts him implicitly."

"How did he get such an awful nickname?"

"It comes from one of his less endearing character traits," Jack yelled.

When Laurie was completely ready, they took the elevator down to the ground floor and exited the building. They found Warren and Spit directly out front. Laurie and Warren enjoyed a sustained embrace, since they'd not seen each other in months.

"You're looking good, woman," Warren said, giving Laurie the once-over.

"You're not looking bad yourself, man," Laurie said, emphasizing the word "man."

Warren laughed and introduced Laurie to Spit. Spit acted embarrassed for the first time Jack had ever seen. He even turned his baseball hat around to face forward as a sign of respect, another first in Jack's experience.

"So where's this restaurant?" Warren said. "I'm ready to get stuffed."

"Come on," Laurie said. "I'll direct you."

The trip to the restaurant went quickly and without incident. On Warren's insistence both Jack and Laurie came with him while Spit brought up the rear in his car. Initially they talked about the disturbing incident in Jack's apartment, but by mutual consent that soon gave way to more enjoyable topics. Laurie was particularly eager to hear about Natalie Adams, Warren's "shortie," whom Laurie had not seen since the last time she'd seen Warren. Laurie was glad to hear that she and Warren were getting along fine.

Parking in Little Italy was always problematic, except for Warren. With his bottomless ash can, they took the spot in front of the hydrant closest to the restaurant. Spit was content to double-park because he wasn't coming inside. As Warren described it, he was just going to "hang out."

Jack was charmed the moment they entered. Not only was he attracted to the rich, herbed aroma of the spicy food, but he loved the kitschy decor with its black velvet paintings of Venice, the fake trellis with plastic vines and grapes, and the stereotypical red-and-white checkered tablecloths. He even liked the banal Chianti bottle with a candle stuck in the top that crowned each table.

"I hope we have a reservation," Warren said as he surveyed the crowded room. There were about thirty tables jammed into the space. All appeared occupied.

"Lou was supposed to call," Laurie said. She tried to get the attention of one of the harried waiters. She wanted to ask for Maria, the hostess. But Maria found her instead.

After having been enveloped by Maria in a bear hug, Laurie introduced Jack and Warren. Maria enthusiastically hugged them both.

"It's too bad Lou couldn't come," Maria said. "He works too much. The crooks don't deserve him."

To Jack and Warren's surprise an empty table seemed to appear miraculously. A few minutes later they were seated.

"Do you like the place?" Laurie asked Jack and Warren.

Both men nodded.

Laurie rubbed her hands eagerly. "Let's get some wine. I think I need it."

The dinner was a great success. The food was wonderful and the conversation captivating. Among other topics the three friends reminisced about their African trip two years previously. They even shared some of the stories with Maria, who joined them for a quarter of an hour.

By the time they were ready for dessert and coffee, Laurie asked Warren if he would mind if she and Jack talked shop for a few moments and discussed a case.

"Not at all," Warren said.

"It's one of Jack's who died of botulinum poisoning."

"It wasn't really my case," Jack interjected. "That's an important distinction. Besides, Warren is already intimately aware of it."

Laurie hit herself on the forehead with the heel of her hand. "Of course!" she exclaimed. "How could I forget?"

"She's talking about Connie Davydov," Jack said.

Warren nodded. "I guessed as much. Flash told me he was disappointed you think it was accidental."

"So you already knew about the botulism?" Laurie asked Warren.

Warren nodded.

Laurie let out an embarrassed laugh. "I guess I was the last to know."

"I called Warren this morning right after I found out about it," Jack explained. "I needed Flash's work number so I could call him."

"Whatever," Laurie said. "So what's the follow-up?"

"Not a whole heck of a lot," Jack said. "I'm afraid the case has gotten mired in bureaucratic red tape. By the time I called Sanders with the news about the botulism, the body had been cremated. That means there will be no autopsy, a fact that's going to be very embarrassing for the Brooklyn office to explain unless the information is not released. Anyway, it's going to be up to Bingham what to do."

"So that means the Department of Health has yet to be notified," Laurie said.

"I imagine that's true," Jack said.

"Well, that's terrible," Laurie said.

"Why is it so terrible?" Warren questioned. "Connie's already dead."

"But no one knows where the botulinum toxin came from," Laurie explained. "The real reason we medical examiners do what we do is to save lives. This situation with the botulism is a good example. There could be a source out there that's going to kill other people."

"Okay," Warren said. "I see what you mean."

"There's another part of this that neither one of you knows,"

Jack said. "In the same neighborhood where Connie lived there's been a major die-off of sewer rats."

"No kidding," Laurie said. "Are you implying they died of botulism, too?"

"Exactly," Jack said. "The cause was just confirmed a few hours ago."

"That means the source of the toxin that killed Connie went down the drain," Laurie said.

"Or somehow the rats infected Connie," Jack said. "Connie lived in an old, ramshackle cottage in a curious, anachronistic warren of others. You guys should see this little community. I have no idea of the adequacy of the plumbing, but judging from the exteriors and the haphazard way the cottages have been remodeled, I can't believe that the plumbing could be state-of-the-art."

Laurie shook her head. "I doubt that the plumbing had anything to do with this. It had to be the other way around. The toxin came from Connie's house. And it must have been a substantial amount of it to kill all those rats. I wonder if Connie did any home canning." Laurie looked to Warren.

Warren raised his hands. "Don't look at me. I never met the woman."

"Well," Laurie commented, "all this emphasizes that someone knowledgeable about epidemiology had better look around Connie's place for a source. At a minimum, her husband should be warned. If the source is still around, he's certainly at risk."

"I thought the same thing," Jack said. "In fact, I went out there today around noon to do just that."

"You talked to Yuri Davydov?" Warren questioned. "Does Flash know?"

"I didn't see the man," Jack said. "He wasn't home. I met a neighbor who said Yuri was out driving his taxi and wouldn't be home until nine or ten."

Laurie glanced at her watch. "That means he'd be home now."

"That's true," Jack said. "What are you suggesting?"

"Do you know the phone number?" Laurie asked.

"Yes, but it's no use," Jack said. "Mr. Davydov apparently has his phone off the hook."

"When was the last time you tried?"

"This morning," Jack admitted.

"I think it might be worth trying again," Laurie said. She picked up her purse and got out her cellular phone. "What's the number?"

"I don't have it here," Jack said. "It's in the office."

"I'll try information," Laurie said. "How do you spell Davydov?"

Laurie had no trouble getting the number. She checked with Jack concerning the address to be absolutely sure it was correct. When she dialed the number, she got a busy signal.

"So now you believe me?" Jack asked.

"I believed you before," Laurie said. "I just thought it reasonable to give it a try. So we can't call. That means we should run out there."

"Now?" Jack questioned.

"If we wait and the man dies, how would you feel then?" Laurie questioned.

"Guilty, I suppose," Jack said. "Okay, I'll go, but it's going to take some time. It's way out on the other side of Brooklyn."

"It shouldn't take that long now," Laurie said. "We can take the Brooklyn Battery Tunnel and the Shore Parkway. With no traffic, we'll be there before we know it."

"I'm not going," Warren said. "Flash told me the guy's a turd. I'll leave this up to you professionals. Spit and I will call it a night."

"That's fine," Laurie said. "We can take a cab."

"No need," Warren said. "You two take my wheels. I'll go home with Spit. Doc, you know where to park it."

"Are you sure?" Laurie asked.

"Of course I'm sure," Warren said. "You guys enjoy yourselves. And when you come back to the neighborhood, don't be concerned. There's going to be someone out there all night keeping an eye on things."

TWENTY-ONE

Yuri straightened up and stretched his back. He'd been busy reattaching the hopper to the Power Row Crop Duster out in the garage after having meticulously filled it with the anthrax powder. The whole procedure had taken almost two hours, including the time he'd had to spend in the lab inside the class A hazmat suit. But now it was done and the pest control truck was ready for its rendezvous with fate in the morning.

Yuri glanced at his watch and allowed himself to relax for the first time all evening. Ever since he'd managed to escape from crazy Curt and the others involved in the hair-raising pursuit of Jack Stapleton, Yuri had been in a minor panic. He'd been worried that he would not be able to complete everything he had to do by the eleven o'clock deadline he'd promised. But the worrying had been for naught. He was ready by ten-thirty, a half hour ahead of time. On the kitchen table were five one-pound plastic sausages stuffed with the light tan powder, waiting to be handed over to Curt and Steve. On top of them was the sealed envelope that Curt had requested. A heavy bath towel to pack them in was on the countertop.

After giving the side of the truck an appreciative pat for the role it was soon to play, Yuri glanced into the cab to make sure the keys were where he'd left them, hanging from the driver's side visor. He wanted no stupid mistakes in the morning like forgetting where the keys were. He planned to leave for Manhattan at eight o'clock sharp with his suitcase, fake passport, and airline ticket.

Yuri walked over to the side door. After one more admiring look at the truck, he flipped off the light. Before he opened the door, he stuck his right hand in his jacket pocket to grip the Glock pistol. He was still afraid Flash Thomas might show up, although at that time of night he considered the chances slim. At least he didn't have Jack Stapleton to worry about anymore.

As Yuri opened the door, he marveled that he'd not realized how truly crazy Curt was. Steve was weird, too, but not the way Curt was. Yuri knew he was no psychologist, but he imagined something terribly abnormal must have happened to Curt during his childhood to explain his personality. Yuri understood that Americans were covetous and violent and had little self-awareness, but Curt carried the traits to ridiculous extremes: his and only his view of the world was correct. But what really irritated Yuri was Curt's anti-Slavic bias, which had become progressively more apparent as time had gone on.

Holding his key at the kitchen door, Yuri hesitated. Musing about Curt's personality raised a worry that Yuri had not contemplated before. Considering Curt's selfishness, what was going to keep him from making arrangements so that his People's Aryan Army would get the credit for the whole bioweapon event even if Curt and the others had nothing to do with the Central Park laydown?

"Chert," Yuri murmured when he realized the validity of this new worry. Up until that moment the idea had not entered his mind.

"Mr. Davydov?" a feminine voice called out.

Shocked to hear his name, Yuri looked toward the alleyway. Despite the proximity of the houses in the area, Yuri had always made it a point to avoid socializing with his neighbors. His hand tightened around the automatic.

"Excuse me! Are you Mr. Davydov?"

Yuri had to squint in the darkness. With his carriage light off and no streetlights, all he could make out were two figures in the alley beyond his chain-link fence. He relaxed when he could tell they were both white. At least it wasn't Flash Thomas.

"Who wants to know?" Yuri asked.

"My name is Dr. Laurie Montgomery. If you are Mr. Davydov it is urgent I speak with you for just a few moments."

Yuri shrugged. Holding onto the pistol and being sure it was free if he wanted to pull it out, he advanced toward his fence. He could see that the second individual was male.

"Sorry to bother you so late," Laurie said. "I'm a medical examiner from Manhattan. Do you know what a medical examiner is?"

Yuri tried to speak but no words came out. Despite the darkness he recognized the other figure. It was Jack Stapleton!

Laurie took the silence for a negative response and went ahead and explained what medical examiners did.

Yuri swallowed with difficulty. He couldn't believe he was looking at Jack Stapleton. What possibly could have happened? Why hadn't he been informed? But then he remembered his phone was off the hook.

"And the reason we are here," Laurie continued, "is because your late wife, Connie, apparently died of botulinum poisoning. Do you know what that is?"

Yuri nodded. He could hear his heart beating and was afraid the two people he was confronting could hear it as well. He was at a loss as to what to do. Should he try to get rid of them? Should he try to get them inside and wait for Curt? He had no idea.

"We're very concerned that the source might still be in your home," Laurie said. "Did your wife do any home canning?"

"I don't know," Yuri stammered.

"Well, that would be key to review," Laurie persisted. "There are other possible culprits, like fresh garlic in oil. Frozen pot pies have been a source. By the way, are you Russian?"

"Yes," Yuri managed.

"I thought perhaps you were from your accent," Laurie said.

"Where in Russia are you from?" Jack asked, speaking for the first time.

"Ummm," Yuri voiced with hesitation. Then he said, "Saint Petersburg."

"I hear that's a beautiful city," Laurie said. "Anyway, there's a kind of whitefish favored by Russian immigrants that have been known to have carried the toxin. Is that something you eat often?"

"Not too often," Yuri said. He had no idea what Laurie was talking about.

"We'd very much like to come inside and take a look in your kitchen," Laurie said. "I cannot emphasize enough how potentially serious this could be."

"Well, I . . ." Yuri began.

"It will not take long," Laurie said. "We promise. You see, we've come all the way out here from Manhattan. Of course, we could call the Department of Health. Now, they would insist about coming in and would have legal authority to do so."

"I suppose it would be all right if it didn't take too long," Yuri said. He was beginning to recover from his initial shock. He certainly didn't want any public health authorities coming out during the night armed with a warrant. Besides, he was beginning to think of a way of turning this surprise visit to his favor.

"Thank you," Laurie said. She and Jack came through the gate.

Yuri preceded them back to the kitchen door. He opened it and stepped inside. Laurie and Jack followed.

Laurie's eyes swept the cramped L-shaped room. "This is . . ." she began. She hesitated trying to think of a word until finally saying: "Cute."

Jack nodded, but he was more interested in looking at Yuri. "That's quite a rash you have there."

Yuri touched his face with evident embarrassment. His other

hand was still in his pocket, holding onto the Glock. "It's some kind of allergic reaction."

Jack tilted his head to the side and looked at Yuri with narrowed eyes. "Have I met you someplace?"

"Surely not," Yuri said. He pointed to the kitchen. "All the food is right here."

Laurie immediately went to the refrigerator and pulled the door open. She bent over and looked at the contents. There was very little.

Jack followed but was curious about the objects on the table. "What are these?" he questioned while poking one of the clear plastic sausages with his finger.

Yuri leaped forward. "Careful!" he cried. He then calmed when Jack pulled his hand away. "I don't want those to break."

"Sorry," Jack said. "I didn't touch it very hard. Is this some kind of Russian delicacy?"

"In a way," Yuri said vaguely.

"Wait a second," Jack said suddenly. "I remember you. But aren't you from Sverdlovsk?"

"No, I'm from Saint Petersburg," Yuri said.

"Didn't I meet you in the Corinthian Rug Company office?" Jack asked. "I mean your neighbor, Yegor, told me you drove a taxi. Didn't you come to the rug company to pick up Mr. Papparis?"

"It must have been someone else," Yuri said uneasily.

"You're the spitting image of this guy," Jack said.

Laurie opened the freezer compartment of the refrigerator. All that was in it was a bottle of vodka and a tray of ice cubes.

"You don't have much food in here," Laurie commented.

"My wife ate fast food," Yuri said. "I ate on the road."

Laurie nodded. She opened the kitchen cabinets. Not finding anything suspicious, she stepped back and surveyed the tiny kitchen. "I don't see any home-canning implements."

"That's all downstairs," Yuri said.

Laurie turned to stare at the Russian. "So your wife did do some home food processing after all?"

"She used to," Yuri said. "Now that I think about it."

"Is there any of the food left?"

"I don't know," Yuri said. "I haven't looked for a long time. She used to go down there often."

"Could we see?" Laurie asked. She glanced at Jack, who made an expression of puzzled surprise.

"Why not?" Yuri said. He opened the door and descended.

Laurie and Jack exchanged confused glances and followed. By the time they got to the basement level, Yuri had the padlocked combination steel and heavy plywood door to the entry chamber open. He was inside unlocking the similarly stout door to the supply room.

Laurie and Jack stepped into the entry chamber. Their eyes took in the hazmat suit, the showerhead, and the plastic bottles of bleach. They smelled the distinct odor of chlorine in the air as well as the more subtle odor of fermentation. They heard the sound of the exhaust fan. They looked at each other in bewilderment.

Yuri was standing next to the door to the supply room. He pointed inside. "I think this is what you are looking for."

Laurie and Jack stepped over to peer gingerly into the supply room. As they did so Yuri slipped behind them. They saw the petri dishes, the agar, the jars of nutrients, and the spare HEPA filters.

"How about stepping inside," Yuri said.

Laurie and Jack turned to look at the Russian and gasped. Yuri had trained a gun on them.

"Please," Yuri said in an even voice. "Step inside!"

"We've seen as much as we'd like to see," Jack said airily, trying to sound unconcerned about the sudden appearance of the gun. He took a step forward, ahead of Laurie. "It's time for us to be on our way."

Yuri raised the gun and fired without hesitation. Upstairs, he'd been afraid to discharge the pistol for fear of disturbing the neighbors. But in the basement with the circulating fan going, he had no concern. Still, the noise had been deafening in the enclosed space. The bullet thudded into one of the floor joists. Dust rained down from the ancient floorboards above. Laurie screamed.

"The next time I aim," Yuri said.

"No need to shoot again," Jack said with a voice that had

lost all pretense of buoyancy. Raising his hands to chest
height, he backed up, forcing Laurie, who was between him
and Yuri, into the storeroom. Jack stepped in as well.

"Move back from the door," Yuri commanded.

Jack and Laurie did as they were told and pressed against
the concrete wall. The blood had drained from both their faces,
and they appeared as pale as the whitewash covering the cement.

Yuri came forward and closed the door. He fastened the
hasp and locked the padlock, then stepped back and looked at
the door. He'd designed it to keep people out, but he guessed
it would work just as well to keep people in.

"Shouldn't we discuss this?" Jack called through the door.

"Absolutely," Yuri said. "Otherwise you couldn't help me."

"You'll have to explain," Jack said. "But we're much better
listeners and far more helpful when we don't have to yell
through a door."

"You're not coming out, probably for several days," Yuri
said. "So make yourself comfortable. There's distilled water
on the shelf, and I apologize for the lack of a toilet."

"We appreciate your concern," Jack said. "But I can assure
you, we'd be far happier upstairs. We promise to behave ourselves."

"Be quiet and listen!" Yuri said. He looked at his watch. It
was going to eleven. "The first thing I want to say is that in
a few minutes the People's Aryan Army is going to be here.
Does that name mean anything to you?"

"Indeed," Jack said.

"Then I assume you know they want you dead," Yuri said.
"In fact, I'm surprised you are not dead, since I know they set
out to kill you this afternoon. If they find out you are here,
they will come down and shoot you for certain. I would prefer
you stay alive."

"Well, at least we agree on something," Jack said.

"They are very crazy and selfish people," Yuri said.

"I got that impression," Jack said.

"And they have a lot of guns and they like to use them."

"That was apparent as well."

"So my advice when you hear them is to be silent," Yuri said. "Does that make sense to you?"

"I suppose," Jack said. "But what was this talk about helping you?"

"Tomorrow morning the People's Aryan Army and myself are scheduled to release bioweapons in Manhattan," Yuri said. "This is not an idle threat. I have produced many pounds of potent, weaponized anthrax right here in this laboratory. I assume you doctors guessed that this was a laboratory."

"We had a sneaking suspicion," Jack admitted. "Especially since this looks like we're in a microbiological storeroom at the moment."

"That's exactly what it is," Yuri said. "Now, what I want you two to do to help is merely to make sure I get the credit for what's going to happen tomorrow."

Yuri waited for a response. Instead he heard Jack and Laurie whispering.

"Did you hear me?" Yuri asked.

"We were wondering if you produced botulinum toxin as well as anthrax?" Jack asked.

"I tried to," Yuri admitted. "But the culture grew too slowly to make enough toxin quickly enough for a bioweapon."

"What happened to the culture?" Jack asked. "Did it just go down the drain?"

"What happened to the clostridial culture is not important," Yuri said. "What is going to happen with the anthrax tomorrow is."

"We agree fully," Jack said. "And we'll make certain you get all the credit you deserve."

"Just to be absolutely sure, I want to tell you in detail what is planned for tomorrow," Yuri said. "That will make you extraordinarily credible witnesses for me."

"We're all ears," Jack said.

"If the People's Aryan Army arrives I will have to interrupt," Yuri said.

"We'll try to deal with the suspense," Jack said. "Let's hear it."

Yuri told Jack and Laurie the details of both laydowns, including the timing and the exact way Curt and Steve planned on getting the powder into the air-conditioning system of the Jacob Javits building. He told them how the firemen intended to shut down the annunciator panel for the entire building after they'd planted the material so that the powder would not set off the smoke detectors. He then went on to tell about how he was going to drive around Central Park at the same time in the stolen pest control truck. He finished by giving an estimate of the casualties from his plan, which he thought would be a million dead, give or take a couple hundred thousand. He said he expected the anthrax to spread out in an expanding arc at least fifty miles over Long Island. The only thing he didn't explain was his plans after the laydown.

"Where did you get this expertise?" Jack asked after a moment of awed silence.

"Are you really interested?" Yuri asked. He was flattered.

"As I said, we're all ears," Jack commented.

TWENTY-TWO

Curt nosed the Dodge Ram into Oceanview Lane and navigated past the inevitable trash barrels.

"Why the hell don't these people take these cans inside?" Curt complained.

"I wish I knew," Steve said. "Hell, I'm not going to miss coming over here. What a shithole."

Curt pulled to a stop in front of Yuri's garage, where he'd parked on the previous visits. He turned off the lights and the engine.

"He better have the stuff ready for us," Curt said. "Especially now that we have everything in place. We've lucked out having the captain on vacation. Your idea about us going in and telling him we were quitting after the event was the only part of the getaway I didn't like. I don't mind talking to the deputy. The guy's a nerd."

"Everything's falling into place," Steve agreed. "This time tomorrow we'll be watching chaos in New York City on television from western Pennsylvania."

"How many of those little timed detonators did you get?"

"A dozen," Steve said. "Just to be sure."

"You got your gun?"

"Of course."

"Let's go!" As Curt got out of the truck he grabbed the black rubberized canvas rabbit tool bag he'd brought from the firehouse. He'd checked its interior carefully for sharp edges or points. With the rabbit tool gone, there wasn't anything in the bag sharp enough to puncture the sausages.

They walked in silence. When they reached the front door, Curt knocked. While they waited they both did a little two-step against the cold. With the clear sky, the temperature had plummeted, yet both were in T-shirts. Their guns were in holsters tucked into the small of their backs.

"What the hell?" Curt questioned when Yuri failed to appear. He pulled open the broken screen door and pounded on the inner door with his free hand. He looked at Steve. "If he's not here I'm going . . ."

Yuri yanked open the door. "Sorry," he said out of breath. "I was downstairs."

Curt gave him a glare before stepping inside. Steve followed. Yuri closed and locked the door.

"Is it ready?" Curt demanded.

Yuri pointed toward the kitchen table. "It's waiting for you. But first how about a toast?"

"Why not?" Curt said.

Yuri eagerly went into the kitchen and got the vodka from the freezer. Curt followed and looked down at the plastic sausages.

"How much is here?" Curt asked.

"Five pounds," Yuri said while he got out three glasses.

"Are these the directions I asked for?" Curt questioned. He picked up the thick envelope and held it aloft.

"Yes," Yuri said as he walked out into the living room. "And I included some suggestions of what you might do after your laydown for your own protection. Just a few helpful pointers."

"Good," Curt responded. He put the envelope and the canvas rabbit tool bag on the table and joined the others.

Yuri poured out hefty dollops in each glass. He then handed them out and took one himself. He raised it toward the firemen. "To Operation Wolverine," he said.

Both Steve and Curt nodded. All three clicked glasses and then took swigs. Curt and Steve both sucked in some air after swallowing. As beer drinkers, they weren't accustomed to such strong liquor.

"How did the Jack Stapleton chase end up?" Yuri asked loudly. "I can tell you, the first part was exciting."

Curt and Steve exchanged glances. "Not so good," Curt admitted. "We lost him in the park. So it's a good thing that we've decided to move the operation up to tomorrow."

"You are all prepared?" Yuri asked.

"We're ready," Steve said. "We expect the false alarm to sound at about nine-twenty-five. That would mean we'd be going in on the target at just about nine-thirty."

"I'll be ready to start at nine-thirty as well," Yuri said. "Let's have another toast."

They touched glasses and drank again.

Curt wiped his mouth with the back of his hand. "We had a thought on the way over here," he said. "Maybe it would be best if we used all the anthrax for the federal building and just forget the park."

Yuri shook his head. "No, I want to do the park."

"What if we insisted," Curt said. He took a sip of his drink and eyed the Russian.

Yuri looked back and forth between the two firemen. "It would be too late to insist," he said. "The pest control truck is already loaded with the other five pounds."

"What about unloading it?" Curt asked.

"I can't do that," Yuri said. "The anthrax is loose in the hopper. I had to take the hopper off and load it down in the laboratory in the hazmat suit."

"It's not in plastic like ours?" Curt asked.

"No," Yuri said. "The agitator action wouldn't be strong enough to break the plastic."

Curt nodded. "Well, it was just an idea." He put his unfinished glass down on the coffee table. "Let's load up so we can be on our way. Tomorrow's going to be a big day."

The three men walked into the kitchen. While Yuri went over to the countertop to get the towel, Curt and Steve bent over the plastic sausages. Neither dared to touch them, knowing what was inside.

"You're sure these things are safe?" Curt questioned.

"As long as you don't break the seal," Yuri said. He reached over and picked one of them up.

Curt and Steve reflexively stepped back.

"The outside has been thoroughly decontaminated," Yuri assured them. "And it's been heat-sealed to be completely airtight." He extended the sausage toward Curt, but Curt pointed to Steve to take it.

Steve put out his hand. It was trembling slightly. Yuri laid the plastic sausage on his palm so that the ends hung down. It was about ten inches long.

"How many people could this amount of anthrax kill?" Steve asked. He hefted the object to appreciate its weight.

"A couple hundred thousand," Yuri said, "provided it was dispersed properly."

"The fed building's circulatory fans are going to disperse it fine," Curt said. He grabbed the canvas bag and opened the top. "Let's get the stuff packed up."

Yuri handed Curt the towel. He used it as a lining for the bag. Once it was in place he had Steve reach in with the sausage he had in his hand. Curt gingerly picked up another and carefully placed it next to the first.

"You don't have to be that careful," Yuri said. "The plastic is surprisingly tough. There's no way you could tear it with your hands."

Encouraged, Curt picked up the other three sausages in turn and put them in the bag. He put the envelope in on top. Then he handed the bag to Steve.

"I guess that's it," Curt said to Yuri.

"Good luck," Yuri said.

Curt started to turn, but as he did so, he drew his Glock from behind his back. In a quick smooth motion he whipped the gun around and pointed it at Yuri. Yuri's eyes opened wide and his mouth went slack.

Curt pulled the trigger. The bullet hit Yuri in the middle of the forehead just above the eyebrows. Blood and bits of gore sprayed back and splattered against the refrigerator. Yuri collapsed, as if his legs had been taken out from under him.

"Jesus Christ!" Steve shouted in consternation. "What the hell did you shoot him for?"

Curt thrust his gun back into his holster. He nudged Yuri with his foot. He was still technically alive, although barely. With the gurgling noises he was making, it was apparent to Curt that Yuri's end was near.

"I thought we were going to have the troops come back here later," Steve cried. "Why didn't you tell me you were going to shoot him."

"Are you going soft on me?" Curt demanded. He glared at Steve.

"Shit, no," Steve said. "But you could have let me know you were planning on doing something like this. It scared the hell out of me."

"I wasn't planning on it," Curt snarled. "But the bastard pissed me off with the way he was acting. Did you hear the way he said it was too late to insist when we were talking about taking the anthrax out of the duster? It was like he was giving us orders. The irony is that I was trying to give him a chance. Hell, if he'd thrown in with us on the proper target and not this stupid, senseless terrorist stuff, I wouldn't have done him in at all."

Steve put down the canvas bag and went back to the coffee table. He picked up his glass and took a generous swallow of the cold vodka. He shuddered. "I just wish you'd clue me in ahead of time about what you're thinking."

"Come on, you pansy!" Curt said. "Get the bag! Let's get out of here."

TWENTY-THREE

"Do you think they're gone?" Jack whispered.

"I think so," Laurie whispered in reply. "I believe I heard an outside screen door slam over the sound of the fan ten minutes or so ago."

Jack and Laurie were enveloped in utter darkness in the storeroom. When Yuri had gone upstairs he'd switched off the basement lights, which had also shut down the lights in the storeroom. For the entire time the People's Aryan Army had been there, the two imprisoned medical examiners had stayed frozen in their respective spots, afraid even to breathe. In the strained silence both had been violently startled by the sudden sound of the gunshot. Up until then they'd heard bits and pieces of the conversation through the thin floorboards and its linoleum covering.

"I'm afraid our favorite Russian got shot," Jack said in a more normal voice. He was still afraid to move or make much noise in case the People's Aryan Army's departure had been a ruse.

"I'm afraid so, too," Laurie said. "I could tell he didn't trust whoever it was who was coming to visit him."

"I think it was the same men who'd come after me," Jack said. "My apologies to Paul. This whole mess is a lot bigger than Paul's being angry at me. I'm afraid I was guilty of jumping to conclusions."

"Maybe so," Laurie said. "But for the moment it doesn't much matter. What are we going to do?"

"Try to get out, I guess," Jack said. "But I don't have a lot of confidence. Did you happen to notice the door? It's three-quarter-inch plywood reinforced with steel."

Laurie shuddered in the darkness. "I don't like being shut in here like this. It reminds me of all the terrible things that happened in connection with that series of drug overdoses I had to handle back in 1992."

"Come on, now!" Jack said. "I'm a bit claustrophobic myself, but this is nowhere near as bad as getting nailed into a coffin."

"It's a pretty close second," Laurie said. "And do you smell that fermentation odor along with the bleach?"

"I do," Jack said. "There must be a fermenter down here with a sizable, active culture of anthrax. Today when I walked around this house I saw a vent and heard a large circulating fan. I could kick myself for not guessing what it meant. I thought it was from a furnace, for crissake."

"This setup is the product of someone who knew what he was doing," Laurie said.

"Unfortunately, that's true," Jack said. "And that's what makes this threat tomorrow so very real. Bioterrorism briefly went through my mind with the Papparis case until a plausible source became evident. Even then it bothered me, because it was so convenient. I could kick myself again for having been so complacent and not more suspicious."

"You can't fault yourself," Laurie said. "After all, you did call the city epidemiologist. It was his job to do the follow-up."

"That's true, I guess," Jack said without much enthusiasm. "It's also true I called the director of the Mayor's Office of

Emergency Management, but it doesn't make me feel much better."

"What was his name?" Laurie asked. "He was the one who gave us the lecture on bioterrorism."

"Stan Thornton," Jack said.

"Right," Laurie said. "That was a disturbing lecture."

A short period of silence ensued. The two people felt confident enough to adjust their weight. They were both leaning against the concrete foundation wall and hadn't moved a muscle since the PAA's arrival.

"Oh, God!" Laurie exclaimed, breaking the lull. She shuddered again. "I can't believe we're having this relatively normal conversation locked in this dark, tiny dungeon knowing what's going to happen tomorrow in the Jacob Javits Federal Building. I wish to hell I'd brought my phone in here with us." Laurie had left her purse locked in the glove compartment of Warren's car, believing that carrying it would have made her appear unprofessional.

"That would have simplified things," Jack agreed. "But I think Yuri would have taken it away if you'd had it. He seemed to know what he was doing. I've got a tiny flashlight on my key chain. I'm going to turn it on."

"Please do," Laurie said.

The meager cone of light barely lit up a corner of the room. Laurie's troubled face came into view. She was hugging herself as if to ward off the cold.

"Are you all right?" Jack asked now that he could see her anguish.

"I'm hanging in," Laurie said.

Jack moved the small beam around the room. He stopped on the bottles of distilled water and moved them to a convenient location where they'd be able to find them easily later in the dark. "We might need these," Jack said. "I don't like to be pessimistic, but we could be in here for some time."

"That's a happy thought," Laurie said. She laughed mirthlessly.

The light played against the door. Since the door opened out, the hinges were on the other side. Jack felt around the door frame.

"Do you think it is okay for us to make noise?" Jack asked

"If the neighbors might hear, we should make as much nois as possible," Laurie said.

"I was thinking about the People's Aryan Army," Jack said

"I think they're long gone," Laurie said. "They got wha they came here for, and they're probably busy with tomor row's plans to assault lower Manhattan."

"You're probably right," Jack said. "There certainly was n reason for them to be suspicious we were here."

Using the heel of his hand Jack pounded the jamb aroun the door, probing for any sign of weakness. Unfortunately, i was all very solid. He put his shoulder to the door, backed u a pace, and then rammed it. He did it several times, each tim upping the force with which he hit. The door didn't budge.

"So much for the door," he said. He turned the light to shin against the whitewashed concrete walls. He tapped then lightly with his knuckles in various locations, searching fo evidence of deterioration. The walls were sound.

"I'm surprised this house has this kind of solid foundation," Jack said. "Looking at it from outside, it appears so flimsy."

"What about the ceiling?" Laurie asked.

Jack shined the light up between the joists. Almost imme diately the tiny flashlight began to dim.

"Uh oh," Jack said. "I'm afraid we're about to be plunged back into darkness."

No sooner had he said that than the light brightened for a moment and then rapidly dimmed again. A minute later it wen out altogether.

TWENTY-FOUR

Thursday, October 21
9:15 A.M.

Mike Compisano let his pale blue eyes rise up the face of the imposing forty-two-story Jacob Javits Federal Building. Its immensity intimidated him, as did the power of the authority it embodied. At the same time, its authority angered him.

Mike had become a skinhead because of the rage he felt as a member of a society that had left him behind like so much flotsam in the wake of a speeding ocean liner. From his perspective, the African-Americans, Hispanics, and Asians he'd been with in high school had more opportunity than he had as a true American thanks to affirmative action and a bunch of other screwy programs. And as Curt had pointed out to him, it was the government the federal building represented that made it all possible.

Unconsciously, Mike's hand slipped into the pocket of his baggy trousers. He fingered the smoke bomb he was to set off in the vent. He understood in a way he didn't completely comprehend that he was about to play a critical role in striking back at the people who had robbed him of a future.

Mike eyed the bureaucrats rushing past him to enter the building. They were the ones responsible for the mess the country was in. He would have preferred to stop one and smash his arrogant face had not Curt warned him not to make a scene.

Mike checked his watch. Finally it was nine-fifteen. He'd been standing in front of the building since eight-forty-five, trying to keep warm. He was dressed in the only suit and tie he had. He'd tried to brush his short blond hair to the side and make it lie flat, but it had refused to cooperate. It was standing up like a bristle brush.

Mike took a breath and started off. He was nervous and his heart was beating fast. He wanted so much to succeed, and was afraid something would go wrong.

The first challenge was security. Mike lined up and passed through the metal detector. To his chagrin it sounded.

"What'cha got, sonny?" one of the uniformed security men asked.

Mike nervously dug a hand in his pocket. He came up with a short, stubby screwdriver. He was worried a coin wouldn't work on the vent.

"So, you're planning on doing a little screwing today, huh," the man said with a chuckle.

Mike nodded. He was directed to come through the metal detector again without the screwdriver. There was no signal.

"Good luck," the security guard said. He handed the tool back to Mike.

Relieved at not being asked any questions about where he was going, Mike took the elevator to the third floor. As he disembarked he could hear the noise and feel the vibration of the machinery. He walked down the hall as Curt had directed, heading straight for a men's room. It was exactly where Curt had said it would be. Mike entered, according to plan.

Unfortunately, the last booth was occupied. Mike had to bide his time. He washed his hands for lack of anything else to do and waited. Finally the man came out. He eyed Mike briefly before washing his hands and exiting.

Mike went into the stall and closed and locked the door. The vent was just above his head. With the screwdriver he got the cover off without difficulty. Standing on the toilet he could look into the duct. It went straight in for about three feet and then angled off.

As instructed, Mike took out the smoke bomb. He lit a match and then touched it to the wick. It caught immediately. With a sideward flick of the wrist, he tossed the bomb into the vent. It ended up coming to rest at the point the duct angled off. Mike could see that it was already putting out smoke: a lot of smoke.

After replacing the vent, Mike left the stall and returned to the hallway. Back at the elevator he pushed the button and waited. It took only a moment to get down to the ground floor. Just as he was exiting the elevator, the building's fire alarm sounded along with a recorded announcement played over and over: everyone should leave the building via the nearest stairway.

Enjoying a sense of accomplishment, Mike went out the main entrance along with a handful of other people. Those trying to enter were told they'd have to wait until the alarm was investigated.

In the plaza directly in front of the building, a congregation began to form. Cigarettes were lit and strangers began to converse. As the minutes passed, the group grew in size as people continued to stream from the exit. Mike joined the burgeoning crowd but kept to the street-side periphery.

Within five minutes approaching sirens began to sound. A few moments later two fire trucks rounded the near corner and quickly pulled to the curb directly in front of the building. The first truck had "FDNY Engine 7" stenciled in gold letters on its side.

Mike looked at his watch. It was nine-twenty-nine. Glancing back at the lead fire truck, he saw Curt emerge from the passenger side of the front seat. He was dressed in full turn-out gear, which included his combination Nomex and Kevlar jacket, matching pants, leather helmet, and boots. Strapped to his back was his Scott pack in its harness with the face mask in easy reach. In his hand was a black rubberized canvas bag.

Steve got out from the back seat carrying a red high-rise

bag. Together they ran for the entrance ahead of all the othe
firefighters.

Mike turned and set out for the subway and the ride home
It made him feel proud to have been part of something tha
Curt had said might possibly save the country.

TWENTY-FIVE

"What time do you think it is?" Laurie asked.

"I haven't the faintest idea," Jack said. He stretched and groaned. "I know I slept for a while. Did you?"

"I think so," Laurie said. "It's amazing how difficult it is to judge the passage of time, especially when you can't see anything."

They had eventually sat down diagonally from each other on the concrete floor with their backs against the respective walls. There wasn't room to lie out straight.

"I can almost talk myself into seeing daylight when I stare up at the ceiling," Jack said.

"We've got to get out of here before nine-thirty if there's to be any chance of stopping the firemen before they get into the federal building and disperse the anthrax."

"I don't like to be pessimistic," Jack said. "But as Yuri said, we could be in here for several days, maybe even longer now that he's been shot. I think he planned to call and have us rescued so he could be sure he got the credit he coveted."

"Wait a second!" Laurie said.

"I've got all the time in the world," Jack answered.

"Shush," Laurie said. "I think I heard something."

They both held their breaths while they listened. They could just make out a distant yet distinct series of thuds coming from above.

"I think that's someone knocking on the door," Laurie blurted.

They both scrambled to their feet. In the utter darkness, they collided, then began shouting for help at the top of their lungs.

Simultaneously, they fell silent with their ears ringing from each other's shouts and their own echo. Once again they strained to listen.

"They had to have heard us," Laurie said.

"It probably depends on how much background noise there is outside," Jack said.

Next they heard the faint but definite sound of glass breaking. A moment later, there were faint sounds of footsteps across the floor above.

In a chorus Jack and Laurie again yelled for help. Jack groped for the door, then began pounding on it. Suddenly the light went on. Then they could hear muffled voices of people descending the stairs to the basement. A few minutes later there was the sound of splitting wood followed by a thump. The sound of the voices increased in volume. Whoever it was had gained access to the entry room to the lab.

Jack knocked against the door. "We're in here," he called.

No one answered, but there was a scraping sound as if a crowbar or some other implement was being forced behind the hasp. Again, there was the sound of wood splitting, only this time it was louder.

"I have no idea who this is," Jack whispered to Laurie.

"You don't think it's . . ."

Laurie didn't have time to complete her sentence. The harsh, creaking noise of the hasp being pried out of the door was followed by the door's being pulled open. Surprised but grateful, Jack and Laurie found themselves looking into the face of a not-so-happy Warren. Behind him was Flash.

"Oh, thank God!" Laurie said. She lunged forward and threw her arms around Warren.

Warren peeled Laurie's arms from around his neck while glaring at Jack. "Having to rescue you from weird situations, especially ones involving dead people, is starting to get to me."

Laurie pulled herself away while wiping tears of joy from the corner of her eyes.

"What time is it?" Jack demanded.

Warren looked at Flash and shrugged. "And this is the kind of thanks we get! The man wants to know the time."

"It's important!" Jack said urgently. "What time is it?"

Warren consulted his watch and told Jack it was quarter after ten.

"Oh, God!" Laurie said. She pushed Warren aside and headed for the door out of the entry room. Jack was right behind her.

"Watch out, up there," Warren shouted up the stairs. "It's not a pretty sight."

Laurie reached the top of the stairs and went directly to the kitchen phone. Jack came up behind her.

"Who should I call?" she demanded.

Jack thought for a moment. "Let me," he said. Laurie gave him the receiver. He punched in 911 and immediately asked for Stan Thornton, the director of the Mayor's Office of Emergency Management. He said it was a matter of extreme emergency. Knowing Stan Thornton's elaborate communication setup, Jack was confident he'd get him quickly.

Warren and Flash joined them in the kitchen. Yuri's body was half in the kitchen, half in the living room. The splatter against the refrigerator had coagulated and had turned brown.

"Are you guys going to give us an explanation or what?" Warren asked. He was still exasperated.

Both Jack and Laurie held up their hands for him to be quiet.

"Look at this," Warren said to Flash while throwing up his hands. "We come all the way out here, save their asses, and they treat us like this."

But Flash wasn't listening; he was preoccupied by his

brother-in-law's body. Yuri's face was frozen in an expression of perpetual surprise, with his eyes wide open, staring blankly at the ceiling. In the middle of his forehead was a perfectly round hole the size of a marble.

Meanwhile, Stan Thornton came on the line. Jack quickly identified himself and then cleared his throat before saying, "I think you might be facing your biggest challenge. Find out if there was a false alarm at the Jacob Javits Federal Building around nine-thirty!"

"Should I do it right now or you want me to call you back?" Stan questioned.

"Do it right this second!" Jack said. "I'll hold on." Jack held up crossed fingers. Laurie grasped them and closed her eyes in prayer.

Jack could hear Stan connecting himself with the Fire Commissioner. During the momentary delay, he told Jack that he believed there had been an alarm, and that he'd been told it was a false alarm caused by an apparent malfunctioning smoke detector. Seconds later, the Fire Commissioner confirmed it.

"Okay!" Jack said urgently, trying to organize his thoughts. "Call someone at the federal building! Anybody! Ask if the fire annunciator panel has been switched off and if there's been a sudden appearance of powder in the building."

"I don't like the sound of this," Stan admitted. He used another telephone line to connect himself with rapid dial to the building's security department. Moments later he was back on the phone with Jack.

"The answer to both questions is positive," Stan said. "Apparently there's fine powder everywhere. What is it?"

"Anthrax!" Jack blurted. "Weaponized anthrax!"

"Good God!" Stan exclaimed. "Where are you? How do you know about this?"

"I'm in a cottage at Fifteen Oceanview Lane in Brighton Beach," Jack said. "There's a dead Russian émigré on the floor. He was killed by a New York City fireman who's a member if not the leader of a militia called the People's Aryan Army. The Russian had built a lab here. In the garage is a pest control truck charged with more anthrax. There's a laboratory in the basement with, I believe, a fermenter filled with anthrax culture. We've been imprisoned in a basement store-room until just a few moments ago."

"Good Lord," Stan said. "Are you contaminated?"

"Most likely no," Jack said. "The Russian knew what he was doing, and he wanted us alive. Also the lab has a negative pressure ventilation system that must be properly filtered."

"All right, stay there!" Stan ordered. "Do not leave the house. We will come to you. Understand?"

"I suppose," Jack said. "I thought it best to get back to the morgue. I'm here with Dr. Laurie Montgomery. The morgue is going to need all the help it can get."

"After you've been deconned," Stan said. "For now stay put. We'll be there in minutes to secure the area."

The line went dead.

Jack shrugged his shoulders, hung up the phone, and sighed. "We missed it," he said with a voice that broke. Laurie put her arms around him and hugged him. He was choked up, and tears came to her eyes in sympathy.

"Hey, man," Warren said. "I think you better tell us what's happening here."

Jack nodded and took a deep breath. He started to speak but had to fight off more tears. After another sigh, he got ahold of himself. "Warren, I told you the next time someone had to be saved, it was my turn to save you."

"Yeah, well I'm not as stupid as you are, Doc."

"If you'd only gotten here an hour earlier."

"So now it's my bad," Warren commented.

"No, I don't mean to imply that," Jack said. "Believe me, I'm thankful you came at all."

"I had to wait to see if you two were going to show up at work," Warren said. "When you didn't, I thought maybe something strange had happened. I saw early this morning that my wheels weren't back, and I knew from Spit you hadn't come back to the neighborhood, but hell, I thought maybe you two shacked up at a hotel or something, making up."

"I wish that's what this evening had been about," Jack said. He looked at Laurie.

"Me, too," she added.

TWENTY-SIX

Stan Thornton had not been exaggerating when he said they'd be there in minutes. Jack, Laurie, Warren, and Flash had barely had time to sit themselves down on Yuri's couch and chairs when local firemen in class A hazmat suits showed up outside to cordon off the area and empty the neighboring houses of their occupants. It seemed surreal for those inside to watch all the activity because none of the firemen approached Yuri's house.

Sometime later, the percussive beat of helicopters hovering above filled the air before they slid off to land on the nearby boardwalk at the beach. A half hour after that, a group of men appeared in more serious-looking biological containment suits wielding HHAs, or hand-held assay instruments. This group split, with half going into the garage and the other half coming into the house. Several of those going into the garage were bomb experts checking to make sure there was no triggering device in the pest control truck.

Those that had come into the house briefly introduced them-

selves before spreading out to the various rooms and going
down to the basement laboratory. They ignored Yuri's body.
Ten minutes later the leader of the house group met in Yuri's
kitchen with his counterpart from the garage. They conferred
briefly before the leader of the house group used a hand-held
radio device to communicate with a distant command post,
presumably in Manhattan.

"We've got two hot areas," the man said. "The agent in the
pest control truck is definitely weapon-grade anthrax. That is
confirmed. There is no triggering device. The lab has two active fermenters with anthrax cultures. There's a jury-rigged
pulverizer contaminated with anthrax powder. There's also a
hood similarly contaminated. There's an active negative pressure ventilation system with HEPA filters in place. There's no
contamination in the rest of the house. Over."

Jack and the others couldn't hear the response because the
man held the radio up to his ear. They saw him nod a few
times, then verbally agree before signing off with the typical
"over and out."

He came directly over to the group. His face was mostly
hidden by the glare of the clear plastic face mask.

"All of you are to leave the house," he said. "In the alleyway, turn to the left. Pass under the caution tape. That divides
this hot area from the warm area beyond. Where the alley joins
Oceanview Avenue you will see a decon tent. It's red; you
can't miss it. They will be waiting for you."

The group got to their feet and started toward the front door.

"Thank you," Laurie said to the man, but he didn't respond.
He was already on his way back through the kitchen on his
way to the basement.

"Man, they are serious," Warren commented as they walked
down the front walk.

"For good reason," Jack said. "This is the real thing. New
York could be seeing casualties in the tens of thousands, if
not more."

"Shit, man," Flash complained. "I told you guys this Yuri
was a bad mother. You should have let me come out here and
taken care of him."

"He had a gun," Jack said. "And he didn't seem too reluctant to use it."

"Yeah, well, I wouldn't have come out here empty-handed neither."

As the group walked they couldn't help notice that the whole area was deserted. They saw no one, not even any dogs.

"This is kinda weird," Warren said. "Like we're all alone."

Just as the group had been advised, they found a red tent in the middle of a completely deserted avenue.

"Where did everybody go so fast?" Warren questioned.

"I don't think they had any trouble getting people to leave," Jack said. "People are terrified of contagion. I shudder to think of the panic in lower Manhattan right now."

"It reminds me of an old science fiction movie," Flash said. "I think it was called *The Day the Earth Stood Still.*"

The group was greeted by a small team of people in lower-level biocontainment dress than those in Yuri's house. The person in charge was a woman who introduced herself as Carolyn Jacobs. She had the group strip and stand under makeshift showers of weak bleach solution where they were forced to scrub themselves. Then, after dressing in government-issue coveralls, they were immunized against anthrax and started on a course of ciprofloxacin.

"Man, I never expected all this," Warren complained.

"You should feel thankful for the vaccine," Jack said. "They don't have a lot of it, and I'm sure they are going to run out in Manhattan. There's no way there's enough for everyone."

The flap covering the entrance to the decon tent was suddenly pulled aside. In walked a lean, clean-cut, martial-appearing African-American man in his thirties. He was dressed in an orange jumpsuit with the acronym CIRG on his left upper arm. Sewn above a zippered breast pocket was a name tag: Agent Marcus Williams.

"I'm looking for Dr. Stapleton and Dr. Montgomery," he said crisply.

Jack raised his hand. "I'm Stapleton."

"I'm Dr. Montgomery," Laurie said.

"Excellent," Marcus said. "Would you come with me?"

Jack and Laurie immediately got to their feet.

"What about us?" Warren questioned.

Jack looked at Marcus and raised his eyebrows.

"Your name, sir?" Marcus asked Warren.

"Warren Wilson, and this is Frank Thomas." Warren pointed at Flash. Flash raised his hand.

"Sorry, I have no orders for you people," Marcus said. "I would assume you should remain here."

"Damn," Warren said. "Doc, make sure they don't forget us."

"Don't worry," Jack said.

Jack and Laurie emerged back out in the daylight. They had to hustle to catch up with Marcus, who'd strode off toward the waterfront.

"Where are we going?" Jack asked.

"I'm to escort you back to the temporary command center," Marcus said.

"Where is that?" Jack asked.

"Lower Manhattan," Marcus said. "In a trailer in front of City Hall."

"Can we slow down a little?" Laurie questioned. She was having to run every couple of steps.

"I was to get you back there ASAP," Marcus said.

"What's happening in the city?" Jack asked.

"I'm not privy to the latest developments," Marcus said. "There is a lot of chaos."

"I can imagine," Jack said.

"Are you FBI?" Laurie asked.

"I am," Marcus said.

"What does CIRG stand for?" Laurie asked.

"Critical Incident Response Group," Marcus said. "We're specially trained to handle NBC incidents."

Laurie looked at Jack. She hated acronyms, especially when the definition of one led to yet another.

"That's nuclear, biological, and chemical," Jack explained.

Laurie nodded.

They crossed a mostly deserted Brighton Beach Avenue and passed under the el, which was part of the New York City subway system. A spiderweb of yellow caution tape blocked one of the entrances. Jack suspected that the transit system had been shut down.

After another block they came to the waterfront. Setting on the beach and boardwalk were a number of helicopters with various markings. Marcus headed for one of the smaller ones. It was an FBI Bell Jet Ranger.

He opened the door and motioned for Jack and Laurie to climb into the back. The pilot was already starting the rotors. Marcus made sure the doctors donned headsets to permit conversation.

After they'd gotten airborne, the trip to Manhattan was shockingly short, particularly for Jack, who was aware how long it had taken him on his bike the day before. The pilot landed on the green in front of City Hall. The makeshift helipad was cordoned off by firemen in hazmat suits. As the aircraft descended, the chaos that Marcus had mentioned was painfully apparent to both Jack and Laurie. In contrast to the deserted calm of Brighton Beach, there were crowds of panicky people streaming west, heading into the wind. Parked along Broadway were a number of National Guard trucks. The soldiers in protective gear had disembarked, but they were aimlessly milling about with their rifles in their hands, apparently unsure of their role.

"When the initial announcement was made, there was mass panic," Marcus explained. "The police thought they'd be able to control it, but they couldn't."

Jack shook his head. Pandemonium was only going to make the situation that much worse, with contaminated people mixing with those initially uncontaminated.

Marcus didn't wait for the rotors to stop. He opened the door and motioned for Jack and Laurie to disembark. He set off at the same rapid pace that had left Laurie behind in Brighton Beach. Jack and Laurie ran to catch up.

The construction trailer that was serving as the field command post had been placed in the plaza in front of City Hall, about six city blocks directly south of the Jacob Javits Federal Building. In that location it was safe from contamination since the day's moderate wind was blowing from the southwest, vectoring to the northeast.

Marcus opened the door. Emanating from the interior was a loud babble of voices coming from a milling confusion of Department of Health officials, police, FBI agents, firemen, and Department of Defense officers. The Department of Defense personnel were from the army's USAMRIID, the Marines' CBIRF, and an interservice unit designated as CBQRF. Laurie knew that USAMRIID stood for the United States Army Medical Research Institute of Infectious Disease, but she had no idea what the other two abbreviations stood for.

"Please," Marcus yelled over the noise. "If you wouldn't mind." He pointed through the throng and led Jack and Laurie to an interior door. He knocked, stuck his head in, then gestured for Jack and Laurie to enter.

As the door closed behind the two medical examiners, relative peace descended. They were in an office about eight by twelve with three other men. Dozens of temporary phone lines had been brought in. Phones littered the desk running the length of the right side of the room. In contrast to the confusion in the outer office and the pandemonium outside in the streets, the three men were seemingly calm. All were sitting down. Jack recognized only one. It was Stan Thornton, the director of the Mayor's Office of Emergency Management.

"Sit down," Stan suggested. He pointed to two empty desk chairs. Jack and Laurie sat down as requested.

Stan's height was apparent even while sitting. The tall man was dressed casually in a tweedy jacket. With his tousled hair, rumpled clothes, and intellectual mien, he looked more like a college professor than a high-level civil servant.

Stan introduced Jack and Laurie to the other two men: Robert Sorenson, an FBI Supervisory Special Agent, and Kenneth Alden, an officer of FEMA, the Federal Emergency Management Agency.

"Would you like some coffee?" Stan asked. "You must be famished after your ordeal."

Jack and Laurie declined but were surprised to be offered coffee so casually during such a crisis.

"Can I ask how things are going?" Jack questioned.

"Certainly," Stan said. "With as critical a role you two have played in this event, you are more than entitled to know. As you can see from outside, we've done a poor job maintaining any semblance of order. There was widespread panic that frankly overwhelmed us and proved beyond a shadow of doubt that a real event is far different from an exercise. We couldn't keep the people in the building. And because a plume developed from the building's vent, the whole section of Manhattan west of here became contaminated with the powder."

Stan paused. Jack and Laurie looked from one face to another. What Stan had just related was terrible news, yet the men seemed curiously unconcerned.

"But there has been one significant development that is undoubtedly in our favor," Stan said. "Would either of you have any idea of what that might be?"

Jack and Laurie looked at each other quizzically, then shook their heads.

"At first we thought that this was too good to be true," Stan continued. "Our HHAs or hand-held assay instruments were not giving us a positive reading for anthrax," he said. "Certainly not like we got out in Brighton Beach where you were. Now, of course these hand-held units only test for the four most commonly expected bioweapons. So we had to wait for more comprehensive backup technical support before we could be sure. Just a few minutes ago we got final confirmation. The powder is not anthrax. In fact, it is not a biological at all. It is merely very finely milled flour—cake flour—colored with cinnamon."

Jack's and Laurie's mouths dropped open in disbelief.

"Now, it is our general consensus that this was not meant as an elaborate practical joke, especially given the pest control truck in Brighton Beach filled with weapon-grade anthrax and a dead body in the house. Therefore, the FBI is extremely interested in apprehending the perpetrators, and any information you can give us about these individuals and the People's Aryan Army will be enormously appreciated."

Jack and Laurie looked at each other and shook their heads in shocked surprise.

"That crazy Russian!" Jack said.

"It's fantastic!" Laurie marveled. "He double-crossed the People's Aryan Army and inadvertently saved the day."

"What exactly do you mean?" Robert Sorenson asked.

"There was apparently some disagreement about the target or targets," Jack said. "Yuri Davydov wanted to drive the pest control truck around Central Park . . ."

"Good Lord!" Stan said with a shake of his head. "That could have caused a million casualties."

"But the People's Aryan Army wanted to do the federal building," Laurie said. "And apparently there wasn't enough bioweapon for both, so Yuri Davydov must have improvised with cake flour and cinnamon."

"He knew what he was doing," Stan said. "Some people think weaponized anthrax is white, but it isn't. It's a light tan or amber color."

"Obviously what Yuri Davydov did not expect was to be killed by his co-conspirators," Laurie added. "I guess the People's Aryan Army considered him disposable after they'd taken what they thought was their share of the anthrax. Actually, from what we overheard, the People's Aryan Army wanted it all, but Yuri Davydov had put it into the pest control truck so they wouldn't be able to get it out."

The three men looked at each other and nodded.

"That seems to fit the facts as we now know them," Ken Alden said.

"We lucked out with this one," Robert Sorenson said while stretching. "That's all I can say, and that said, it doesn't speak well for all our planning and exercises to date regarding bioterrorism. Our counterintelligence didn't block it, and our response system didn't contain it."

Jack and Laurie looked at each other. Spontaneously they leaped to their feet and threw their arms around each other. After the tension and fear engendered by their incarceration, the good news filled them with joy. They hugged and laughed, unable to contain their relief.

"Whenever you're ready, we'd like to debrief you immediately about the People's Aryan Army and their alleged fireman leaders," Robert Sorenson said. "The bureau is going to put the highest priority on their apprehension and prosecution."

EPILOGUE

Thursday, October 21
1:30 P.M.

"Try another station!" Curt said.

Steve leaned over and twirled the dial until the radio came in reasonably clearly.

They were in an old Ford pickup truck that Steve had bought for five hundred dollars under an assumed name. They were about fifty miles from New York City, and the radio signals were getting progressively weaker. They'd heard one news flash soon after getting into the truck a half hour earlier, just when they were starting westward on Interstate 80. The news flash had been brief. It had only said that there had been a major bioweapon event in lower Manhattan, resulting—so far—in general panic.

At the time, Curt and Steve had cheered wildly and high-fived in a delirium of excitement. "We did it!" they'd shouted in unison. But now they wanted more details, but they were having trouble finding any follow-up reports.

"There's probably a government-sponsored media black-out," Curt said. "They never want the public to know the truth about anything: Waco, Ruby Ridge, even who shot JFK."

"I'm sure that's it," Steve said. "The government is afraid to let the public know."

"God, it went perfect," Curt commented. "A goddamn perfect military operation!"

"It could not have been any better," Steve agreed.

Curt looked out at the rolling countryside, resplendent in fall colors. They were in western New Jersey approaching the Pennsylvania border. "Jeez, what a beautiful country," he said. He gripped the steering wheel harder. He laughed. He felt great. In fact, he felt as if he'd had ten cups of coffee.

"Do you want to stop for lunch in Jersey or wait until Pennsylvania?" Steve asked.

"I don't care," Curt said. "As excited as I am, I'm not hungry."

"I'm not hungry either," Steve said. "But I sure wouldn't mind washing my hands. I know Yuri said it was safe touching those plastic sausage things, but it still bothers me knowing what was inside."

"Hey, where's that envelope?" Curt asked.

"You mean Yuri's?" Steve asked.

"Yeah, the one with the directions on making the bio-weapon," Curt said. "He told us he also wrote some pointers of what we should do after the laydown."

"I got it with all the maps and shit to get us to the various safe houses," Steve said. "You want me to get it out?"

Curt shrugged. "Why not. Let's see what we should do for our protection." Curt laughed again. "As if we need that little prick's help at this point."

Steve reached back behind his seat and pulled out a folder closed with an elastic cord. He opened it, shuffled through the contents, and pulled out Yuri's envelope.

"Whoa! This thing is thick," Steve said. "What'd he do? Write a book?" He extended it toward Curt so he could take a look.

"Open it, for crissake," Curt said.

Steve got his index finger under the sealed flap and tore it open. From inside the envelope, he pulled out a thick card sealed with another flap.

"What the hell?" Steve said.

Curt took his eyes off the road long enough to take a gander. "What does it say on the front?"

"To Curt and Steve from Rossiya-matoshka," Steve said. "Whatever the hell that means."

"Open it up!" Curt said.

Steve tore through the tab and as soon as he had the card leaped in his hands and snapped open. At the same time a coiled spring mechanism propelled a sizable puff of powder into the air along with a handful of tiny glittering stars.

"Shit!" Steve yelled, startled by the small explosive device.

Curt had started as well, mainly because Steve had. He had to fight to keep control of the truck.

Both men sneezed violently and their eyes watered briefly.

Curt brought the truck to a stop by the side of the road. Both men were coughing, the powder tickled their throats. Curt grabbed the card away from Steve, who then got out of the pickup to whisk the glittering stars off his lap.

Curt examined the card. There was nothing written inside. He looked in the envelope. There was nothing there either. Then, all of a sudden, he had a terrible premonition.

AUTHOR'S NOTE

Unfortunately, much of what the characters in *Vector* say about bioweapons and bioterrorism is true. This holds most notably for Detective Lou Soldano's comment concerning the potential for a major bioterrorism attack in the United States or Europe: *it is not a question of whether one will occur, but rather, when.* Indeed, there have already been several minor bioterrorist events in the United States.

In 1984, there was an intentional contamination of restaurant salad bars in Oregon, causing an outbreak of salmonellosis in 751 people. In 1996, there was an intentional contamination of muffins and donuts in a hospital laboratory in Texas, causing an outbreak of *Shigella dysenteriae* in forty-five people.

The threat of bioterrorism has risen progressively in the world, particularly over the last decade. Consider the example of Aum Shinrikyo, the apocalyptic sect that released sarin gas in the Tokyo subway in March 1995. At the same time the cult unleashed its chemical attack, it was engaged in an active bioweapons program involving both anthrax and botulinum toxin, just like Yuri Davydov was in the novel. They'd even gone so far as to send a delegation to Zaire to explore the possibility of obtaining the Ebola virus for weaponization.

The Soviet Union had maintained an enormous covert bio-weapons program prior to its dissolution in 1989, despite being a signatory to the 1972 Biological and Toxin Weapons Convention (BWC) strictly forbidding such activity. At its height, the program employed more than fifty thousand scientists and technicians in research and production facilities. It was administered under the aegis of Biopreparat, which was under the Ministry of Defense. The program purportedly has been dismantled by the Yeltsin government (although many experts fear not completely), resulting in a diaspora of tens of thousands of highly trained bioweapon personnel. Considering Russia's current economic dislocations, the question invariably arises: where are these people now and what are they doing? Some, perhaps, are driving taxis in New York City like Yuri Davydov, the disaffected émigré in *Vector,* and meeting up with equally disaffected members of the violent far right.

Rogue nations like Iraq, Iran, Libya, and North Korea have added to the rising threat of bioweapons. In the aftermath of the Gulf War, the United States and its allies were shocked to learn the size of Iraq's stockpile of bioweapons and production facilities, whose existence had entirely eluded intelligence operations. This revelation served as a sharp wake-up call to the various allied governments. Regrettably, at the same time, the discovery captured the attention of terrorist groups and individuals worldwide who suddenly became intensely interested in bioweapons. The attraction is simple: bioweapons are inexpensive to make; require materials, equipment, and expertise that are easy to procure (some of the information is even on the Internet); and, for the most part, involve biological agents that are readily available. As an added feature, bioweapons are the best weapons of mass destruction for covert use. The effects of their release take many hours or even days to materialize, giving the perpetrators time to escape.

Adding to this unfortunate circumstance of the rising threat of bioweapons is the current social, economic, and political reality of the world. With mounting religious fundamentalism in some countries, thwarted nationalistic goals in others, economic deprivation in many, and, in the industrialized west, the increased desperation of violent far-right groups whose agenda has stalled in an era of increased globalization, there has been a worldwide rise of terrorism in general. The combination of this increase with a heightened appreciation of the evil attractiveness of bioweapons is what makes the current situation so critical.

In *Vector*, medical examiners were the first to confront an occurrence of bioterrorism in the form of a single case of anthrax. Lamentably, since there was a simple but unverified explanation for the case in the story, the doctors' index of suspicion of bioterrorism was not adequate for them to insist on proper follow-up. If they had, the event as it unfolded could possibly have been prevented. This is an important lesson. Leaving fiction for the real world, there is a high probability that the medical profession would be the first group of professionals to interface with a bioterrorism event, and that distinct possibility must be part of medical thinking these days. This is particularly true for illnesses caused by agents known to have bioweapon potential.

Yet the medical profession's responsibility with regard to bioterrorism goes beyond detecting an episode and treating its victims. The medical profession has an ethical duty to continue to institutionalize the opprobrium currently associated with the use of bioweapons. Members of the medical profession of all countries must insist on investigating any suspicious disease incidents within their borders and report such circumstances to the world forum. If that had happened in Sverdlovsk in 1979 following the anthrax leak from a Biopreparat bioweapon facility, the Soviet medical profession would have done the world a service. It would have exposed the illegal Soviet offensive bioweapon program. Instead, the world was treated to elaborate KGB disinformation, and Biopreparat continued its illegal and ethically repulsive secret work for another ten years.

Another reason the medical profession has an ethical role to play in relation to bioweapons is that this technology represents the ultimate perversion of biomedical research. Indeed, with the help of the burgeoning field of bioengineering, the possibility exists of constructing new doomsday organisms. Experts shudder at the thought of combining the contagiousness of the common cold or even smallpox with the pathogenicity of Ebola.

As is the case with the nuclear threat, the public feels it can do little to thwart the development or deployment of bioweapons. But that is not entirely true. The public can play a role in this worsening biological nightmare by being cognizant of the threat bioweapons pose. Counterintelligence is the only way to actually prevent occurrences, and the public should be suspicious and vigilant. Since it is true that small labs and production facilities can be made in private locations like basements or spare rooms, it is important to be on the alert for tip-offs, like fermenting odors or the sound of constant, circulating fans. These should be reported to the authorities. Any unexpected traffic or theft involving microorganisms, microbiological equipment, microbrewery fermenters, biocontainment gear, or pest control spraying devices should also be brought to the attention of law enforcement.

With everything else there is to worry about these days between AIDS, famine, economic woes, civil war, ethnic cleansing, and global warming, it seems there is hardly room for the specter of bioterrorism. Yet few threats have the capability of killing so many so fast. For years we lived under the fear of nuclear winter annihilating the human race. Now there is a similar threat from biology.

Finally, on a more positive note, governments and local authorities, particularly in the United States, have started to consider seriously the menace of bioterrorism and have begun to act. Money has been appropriated. The Department of Defense and the FBI have formed specialized response units. Major cities like New York have tasked their emergency management organizations with the problem. There have been efforts at training on the local level and exercises to mimic real events. Still, the results to date are equivocal. It may take an actual bioterrorist strike to harden government initiative, but by then, for many, it will be too late.

Much needs to be done, and we all have to contribute. Let's not wait for an incident like the planned one in *Vector* to solidify our resolve.

Robin Cook, M.D.
Naples, Florida
December 1998

SELECTED BIBLIOGRAPHY

1. Davis, Lorraine, et al., editors, *Medical Aspects of Chemical and Biological Warfare*. Washington, D.C., Office of the Surgeon General, 1997.

    This is a thoroughgoing, textbook treatise.
2. Falkenrath, Newman, and Thayer, *America's Achilles' Heel: Nuclear, Biological, and Chemical Terrorism and Covert Attack*. Cambridge, MA, M.I.T. Press, 1998.

    This is the best general book on the subject that I found. It focuses directly on policy implications.
3. Hamm, Mark, *American Skinheads: The Criminology and Control of Hate Crime*. Westport, CT, Praeger, 1993.

    I didn't know the difference between skinheads, punks, and rockers until I read this book. I found it fascinating, particularly in relating these movements to rock music.
4. Laqueur, Walter, *Fascism: Past, Present, Future*. New York, Oxford University Press, 1996.

    This is an extraordinarily readable book about a movement that most of us thought had been defeated in World War II. I found it inordinately stimulating, particularly in relation to the current economic and social turmoil in Russia.

5. Lundberg, George, *Journal of the American Medical Association* (JAMA). Chicago, Vol. 278, No. 5 (August 6, 1997).

   This entire issue of *JAMA* was devoted to the issues of bioweapons, biowarfare, and bioterrorism. It is written from the point of view of the health-care provider.

6. Preston, Richard, "Annals of Warfare: The Bioweaponeers." *The New Yorker,* Vol. 74, No. 3 (March 9, 1998).

   This is a wonderfully written article that is bound to disturb any reader.

7. Remnick, David, *Resurrection: The Struggle for a New Russia.* New York, Random House, 1997.

   This is another enormously readable, enlightening, and ultimately disturbing book. It is a must for anyone interested in the current chaotic situation in Russia.

GLOSSARY

ANTHRAX: An infectious and usually fatal disease of warm-blooded animals, particularly sheep, goats, and other ruminants, that can, on occasion, be transmitted to humans. Human-to-human spread generally does not occur. By common usage, *anthrax* also refers to the causative agent, *Bacillus anthracis*. This bacteria is present in soil worldwide. Anthrax is well suited as a bioweapon because it is capable of forming hardy spores that can remain stable for decades. The deadliest form of this disease occurs when the spores are inhaled and germinate in the lungs. Death can be rapid.

BIOTERRORISM: The threat or actual use of a bioweapon to cause widespread terror and/or mayhem, often deployed to exact revenge or promote an ideological agenda.

BIOWEAPON: A biological weapon of mass destruction composed of living organisms (e.g., bacteria, viruses, fungi) or the products of such organisms.

BOTULINUM TOXIN: A toxin produced by the bacteria *Clostridium botulinum.* Botulinum toxin is a neurotoxin, exerting its effect by interrupting nerve cell function. Clostridial neurotoxins have the dubious distinction of being the most poisonous substances known to science. These toxins can be ingested, inhaled, or injected to exert their deadly effect. It is estimated that less than a pound (or less than a half kilogram) would be enough to kill every man, woman, and child on earth.

TOXIN: A poisonous substance produced by a living organism.

WEAPON OF MASS DESTRUCTION (WMD): A nuclear, chemical, or biological weapon capable of killing or incapacitating tens of thousands or even millions of people and/or destroying vast areas.

From "the man who invented high-tech horror."
—USA Weekend

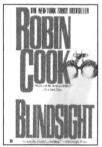

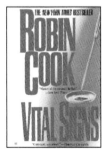

"THERE'S A FRIGHTENING LOGIC IN THE IDEA
THAT YOUR NEXT BREATH MIGHT KILL YOU."
—*Publishers Weekly*

A disgruntled Russian émigré is poised to lash out at the
adoptive nation he believes has denied him the American
dream. A former technician in the Soviet biological weapons
system, he possesses the knowledge to unleash into the
streets of New York City the ultimate terror: a modern
bioweapon. But before he executes his final act of vengeance,
he must first experiment on a few unsuspecting victims...
With signature skill, Robin Cook has crafted a page-turning
thriller rooted in up-to-the-minute biotechnology. *Vector* is
all-too-plausible fiction at its terrifying best...

"[The] King of the Mind-bending Medical Thriller
returns with a...killer-poison more dangerous than
any before it." —*Kirkus Reviews* (starred review)

DR. ROBIN COOK,
a graduate of
Columbia Medical
School, finished his
postgraduate medical
training at Harvard.
He is the author of
*Toxin, Chromosome 6,
Contagion*, and
numerous other
bestselling novels.

Photograph of the author © 1992 by John Earle

17299

UPC

0 71831 00799 5

ISBN 0-425-17299-6

$7.99 U.S.
$10.99 CAN